Kathryn started her working life as a retail pharmacist but soon realised trying to decipher doctors' handwriting wasn't for her. In 2011, backed by her family, she left the world of pharmaceutical science to begin life as a self-employed writer.

She lives with two teenage boys and a husband who asks every Valentine's Day whether he has to bother buying a card again this year (yes, he does) so the romance in her life is all in her head.

kathrynfreeman.co.uk

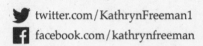

twitter.com/KathrynFreeman1
facebook.com/kathrynfreeman

Also by Kathryn Freeman

The New Guy

Up Close and Personal

Strictly Come Dating

Mr Right Across the Street

The Beach Reads Book Club

THE ITALIAN JOB

KATHRYN FREEMAN

One More Chapter
a division of HarperCollins*Publishers*
1 London Bridge Street
London SE1 9GF
www.harpercollins.co.uk
HarperCollins*Publishers*

A catalogue ... ...ibrary

ISBN: 978-0-00-853533-9

This novel is entirely a work of fiction. The names, characters and incidents portrayed in it are the work of the author's imagination. Any resemblance to actual persons, living or dead, events or localities is entirely coincidental.

Printed and bound in the UK using 100% Renewable Electricity
by CPI Group (UK) Ltd

Chapter One

Anna sat in her dad's kitchen and watched the rain pour down. She was miserable; the day was miserable. Her life was miserable. Three days ago, it hadn't been. Then she'd had a place to call home, a job, and a loving boyfriend. Only it turned out the loving boyfriend was in fact a cheating bastard, and now she'd lost the lot.

'He's not worth it.'

Her dad, sipping at a gloopy green smoothie – one of his morning rituals – gave her his steely police stare. He might have retired from the force last year, but in his own home he was still very much the Chief Superintendent.

'I know.' In her heart, she did. Any guy who could sleep with another woman behind his partner's back wasn't worth getting upset over. Angry, yes. That was how she wanted to feel. Not this pathetic sadness. This feeling that somehow it had been inevitable. 'I didn't just lose him though, did I?'

'That place you lived in was never yours – it was his. And you'll find another job.'

Both were true statements, but surely only an ex-policeman could see her situation with such a clinical eye. She'd loved Miles Rutherford, or at least she'd thought she had. She'd certainly loved her times with him. Charming, dashing, he'd given her previously dull life some real gloss. And God, how he'd dazzled her as they'd worked together in his restaurant. She'd been in awe of his calm when the rest of them had been running around like headless chickens, his flair when he'd put together the menus. His skill. Despite the pressure they'd been under, working with him had been an unexpected joy. It was no wonder she'd fallen for him.

Tears crept down her face and her dad let out a deep sigh. 'He was never right for you. I always figured you'd come to your senses and realise that.'

'How can you say that? We were good together.'

'In a restaurant, maybe.' He put down his newspaper – another of his morning rituals – and gave her another of his no-nonsense looks. 'I know you don't want to hear this, but you were turning thirty, your friends were all getting married...' He shrugged, not finishing the sentence.

'You actually think I was so desperate to settle down that I lived with the first guy who asked me?'

'Of course not.' Another sigh, only this time there was an edge of frustration to it. 'I'm no good at this kind of talk, you know that. Always shove my foot in it.' He paused, looking out of the window briefly before settling his gaze back on her. 'But I know my daughter deserves more than a man who can't keep his trousers zipped. She should be with a guy who loves and appreciates her for the amazing woman she is.'

A lump lodged in her throat and Anna slipped off the bar-stool to throw her arms around his neck. 'Thanks, Dad.' She sniffed. 'And now you're making me cry again.'

'You don't have to thank me for speaking the truth.' He squeezed her back and Anna absorbed the love behind the gesture. Since her mum had left – make that since her mum had *abandoned* them – to return to Italy when Anna was ten, it had just been her and her dad. Hard times, during which Anna had both hated and missed her in equal measure. She'd felt betrayed, hurt and confused, but one thing her dad had made sure she'd never felt was unloved.

As she unwound her arms from his neck and stood up, she caught sight of movement out of the kitchen window.

Her dad saw the direction of her gaze. 'Sheila's got a visitor.'

They both watched as a guy in black leathers climbed off a motorbike outside the neighbour's house. When he pulled off his helmet and shook his shaggy blond hair, the penny dropped. 'Is that Jake?'

'Yep. Visits her every Saturday on that death trap.'

Anna hadn't seen their neighbour's son for several years. She'd heard a lot about him though – ever since the family had moved into their street the infamous Jake Tucker had been the favourite subject of gossip for neighbours with nothing better to do. Of course he didn't help himself, or his mum, by giving them so much to gossip about. *Always in trouble, that one. His poor mum – the shame he brings to the family! What do you expect from a lad who was brought up on that estate?*

She'd also heard about his exploits from Miles, who'd ended up on the wrong end of one of Jake's fists. 'How long has he been out of prison?'

Her dad wrinkled his brow. 'Must be coming up two years. Poor Sheila's worried about him.' He grimaced. 'Can't be easy, readjusting once you've been inside, even if it was only for six months. Sheila said the fire station wouldn't give Jake his old

3

job back because of his record so he's been drifting, picking up casual jobs here and there.' He patted Anna's hand. 'At least I don't have to worry about you. I'm sure you'll find it easy getting another job with your experience.'

Anna wasn't so sure. Miles, or at least the Rutherford name, carried a lot of influence in the town and especially in the restaurant business. And it wasn't like they'd parted as friends. Hard to, when she'd found him having sex with Tilly, one of the waitresses, in their bed. The visual of the blonde on her hands and knees, Miles behind her... Nausea crept up Anna's throat, leaving a bitter taste in her mouth.

And all on the sheets she'd flipping well changed that morning.

She shook off the image and stared at Jake as he ambled up Sheila's drive, long legs encased in black leather. Looked like a stint in prison hadn't rid him of that irritating swagger, though his boyishly good-looking face had a harder edge to it now, accentuated by the dark-blond stubble on his chin. As he shifted his helmet under his arm, a piece of paper fell out of his jacket and fluttered onto the driveway. She waited for him to notice, but he carried on walking.

'Damn it.' Her dad glanced questioningly at her. 'Jake's dropped something. Guess I should tell him. Might be important.'

Reluctantly she grabbed a coat, opened the kitchen door, and jogged over to pick up the now soggy paper. 'Hey, Jake.' He halted and turned. Damn, he was tall. She'd forgotten that. Also how intimidating he was, she remembered belatedly as a pair of bold blue eyes locked onto hers. Most people would smile at this point, maybe say hello, but Jake was clearly way too cool for that because he just quirked an eyebrow. 'You

4

dropped this.' She glanced down at the paper and noticed a phone number with a girl's name scrawled next to it. Typical. 'You wouldn't want to disappoint Tracey.'

His lips tilted in a smirk. 'Trust me, I never disappoint.'

God, he was annoying. Always had been, as far as she could remember. Jake had been twelve when the Tucker family had moved in next door and though he was two years her junior, he'd acted like the big man even then. By the time he'd turned sixteen... She cringed as she remembered that day.

As if he knew where her thoughts had headed, he winked. 'Don't need to tell you that though, do I? As I recall, you once heard me definitely not disappointing.'

Irritated, both at him and at herself for allowing him to rattle her, she shoved the paper into his hand and started to walk away. She was getting wet, and for what? All so he could stand there and throw snide remarks at her? He unbalanced her, and she hated it. If it was another few years before she saw him again, it would be too soon.

'Visiting your dad?'

Jake wasn't sure why he'd decided to carry on the conversation. Probably something mean in him that liked seeing Anna flustered. And getting wet. Seemed he'd not grown up.

Anna slowed her stride and swivelled round, her body language stiff as a board. That summed her up, really. Stiff and starchy. He guessed that was what happened when you were brought up by a cop. He'd had a bollocking from the Chief Super a time or two. *I'll have to tell your mum. She'll be disappointed in you.* Yeah, he'd never admit it, but the guy had made him feel two feet tall. Thank God their paths rarely crossed now, beyond a cursory nod.

Anna's striking green eyes stared back at him. He'd never really understood how a woman who was half-Italian could be so *rigid*. He'd never met her mum – apparently she'd walked out on them when Anna was a kid – but his own mum had told him the woman was a dark beauty with a fiery temper. He saw the looks: glossy brown hair (when it wasn't wet), striking eyes, olive skin, and curves he could appreciate when she wasn't throwing mental daggers at him like she was now. He'd like to bet she never lost her temper though, never let go of that cool control.

'Actually, I'm staying with Dad for… a few days.'

The hesitation made him pause and he studied her. How many years since he'd seen her? Before his stint inside, that was for certain. He wasn't sure what normal looked like on her, but he doubted it was this washed-out. He also knew enough about the guy Anna had been shacking up with to guess what might have happened. 'All not well in paradise?'

If eyes could spit, hers would be doing exactly that. 'None of your business.'

Clearly he'd touched a nerve and he immediately regretted his words. He wasn't usually such a git, but she rubbed him up the wrong way. Had done ever since she'd looked down her nose at him the first day they'd moved in next door. To be fair, he'd been in a bad place, just turned twelve and still grieving the loss of his dad from a heart attack earlier that year. He'd not wanted to move from the estate he'd grown up on, and where his mates still lived. Plus, he'd hated that it was the money from his dad's life insurance that had paid for the new house in the so called 'better' area – a place his dad had always dreamt of living.

'Seems to me you've stuck your nose in my business a few times,' he retorted.

She gave a dramatic eyeroll. 'Don't tell me you're still bearing a grudge for what happened that night.'

'Actually, I was remembering the day we moved in.'

She narrowed her gaze. 'What, when I caught you smoking?'

He could still remember the look she'd given him. Only fourteen yet bristling with a holier-than-thou attitude. *You shouldn't be doing that. Didn't anybody tell you it's bad for you?* She'd had it in for him from day one. Not surprising that several years later she'd told her daddy when she'd found out he'd invited his mates over for a party the first time his mum had left him overnight.

'I don't regret telling you off.' She flicked her hair back over her shoulder – a pure *fuck-you* gesture. 'You were way below the legal age and besides, smoking is bad for your health.'

'How about the night you called your daddy to break up my party? Do you regret that?'

Finally, his words did the trick and she looked uneasy, her eyes not quite meeting his. 'You were only sixteen. I heard a scream. What was I supposed to do, ignore it? I was worried for your sister.'

It might have been twelve years ago but he felt the insult like a slap round the face. 'Yeah, so you said. As if I'd ever let any harm come to Daisy.' He loved his baby sister – hell, he loved both his sisters. No way would he ever let anything happen to them.

'Your mum asked us to keep an eye on you as it was the first time she'd left you in charge of Daisy overnight. I heard lots of male laughter, drunken voices.' She angled her chin. 'I did the right thing. The *responsible* thing.'

And now *he* couldn't meet her eyes. Having his mates over and drinking when he'd been in charge of Daisy hadn't been responsible. It had been frigging stupid. Then again, that was him all over. Doing stupid things without thinking first. 'Yeah, and what did your dad find when he came dashing over,' he taunted, 'blue flashing lights an' all?'

He couldn't tell if she was blushing but he reckoned he'd at least equalled the score.

'Are we really talking about some night that happened *twelve* years ago?'

He shrugged. 'We can talk about why you're living back with your dad if you like.'

Her eyes flashed. 'Or we can discuss what's happened to you in the last three or so years since I last saw you.'

The superior look on her face told him she knew exactly what had happened to him. Of course she did. The whole town knew he'd been banged up in prison for six months for punching Miles Rutherford. 'Strikes me you might want to hit him yourself right now.'

He must have guessed right because she tore her gaze from his and sucked in a deep breath, clearly clutching hard at that icy control. Finally, she glanced back at him. 'Say hi to your mum from me.'

With those quietly spoken words she turned her back on him and walked off. It made him feel mean, dirty. She'd only come over to do him a favour. If she'd not spotted that he'd dropped Tracey's number, he'd have missed out on a couple of days' work next week, laying a new patio. 'Hey,' he called out just as Anna reached her dad's front door. When she looked back, he held up the note. 'Thanks, you know, for picking this up.'

He'd obviously pissed her off because she didn't even give him the polite smile. Just ignored him, stepped inside, and shut the door behind her.

He sighed and headed back up the drive, finding his mum frowning at him from her doorstep. 'I hope you've not been rude to Anna.'

Because seeing his mum always brightened his day, no matter how shitty – and recently there had been a lot of shitty – he bounded up to her and lifted her off her feet.

'Put me down, you daft boy! You're all wet,' she complained, but the twinkle in her eyes took the heat out of her words, as did the beam of pleasure that crossed her face.

'How long have you been standing there?'

'Long enough to hear you wind the poor girl up.'

He snorted. 'Nothing poor about her.' And her curves were all woman, he added silently.

She gave him a stern look. 'You of all people should be more sympathetic.'

'Me, why?'

'Because you know what Miles is like. He screwed you over, and from what I hear he's now screwed Anna, too.'

He started to laugh. 'Whoa, enough of the bad language.' He pointed to his chest. 'Sensitive ears here. Besides, I thought *screwing* was what you were supposed to do when you live with someone.'

She gave him a none too gentle slap at the back of his head. 'You know what I mean. Now come and say hi to your sister before she heads off to work.'

He ducked his head as he manoeuvred out of the way of the damn chandelier she'd insisted he hang for her in the hallway, bought because she wanted a bit of fancy. When he'd complained it was too low she'd smiled. 'I don't care. You're the only visitor we get over six foot and you'll just have to learn to dodge it.' And he had, in the main.

After hanging his sodden leather jacket on the peg and yanking off his boots – his mum was watching – he pushed open the door to the living room. Daisy jumped to her feet when she saw him and he bent to hug her. Twenty-one now, he found it hard to accept she was a grown woman and not the kid sister he'd spent years looking after while his mum had been at work. 'How are you doing, Buttercup?'

She prodded him in the ribs. 'I told you a million times, stop with the dumb nicknames, Jakey.'

'Oh wait, you prefer Cowslip? Bluebell?'

She huffed, prodding him in the ribs again. 'Mum, tell him to stop being annoying.'

'I'm not getting involved.' Their mum put her hands on her hips. 'You two are as bad as each other. Now, I'm going to put the kettle on while you pretend to be normal, civilised children.'

He and Daisy grinned at each other. 'So, what's new?' he asked as he sat down next to her on the sofa.

'Miles came into the pub the other night.'

That made him sit up. 'He didn't—'

'Chill. He makes sure never to come up to the bar when I'm serving.'

Relief flowed through him. 'Okay, good.'

'Wasn't so good for Anna next door, though. Heard him mouthing off about how he'd kicked her out of his house and the restaurant.' She screwed up her face. 'He said some nasty stuff about her. He's such a bastard. And she doesn't have a big brother to defend her.' Daisy kissed his cheek. 'She's not lucky like me.'

He smiled. 'It's part of the job description. Annoy your sisters, take the piss out of them, but protect them, always.'

She looked at him sadly. 'Yeah, but it shouldn't have to land you in prison. I know you don't like talking about it but—'

'Stop. It's two years' worth of water under the bridge.' He kissed her forehead. 'Are you happy?'

'Well, yeah, of course. I mean, one day I'll be a nurse and have my own place, but the pub earns me good money while I'm doing my studies.' She nudged him. 'And living with Mum's pretty cushy.'

He laughed. 'Then that's all that matters.'

She frowned and worried at her lower lip. 'Mum says the fire station still won't take you back, even though your sentence is spent now.'

The shock of it still hadn't sunk in. For two years he'd held on to the hope that he'd get his old job back. Now that hope had been yanked from under him. He didn't know how much of their decision was down to Rutherford influence, how much down to his previous brushes with the law, and how much down to the fact his old boss, the guy who would have vouched for him, had retired to Spain. He did know he felt at a loss now, unsure what the hell to do. As a firefighter he'd been someone, a guy his dad would have been proud of. A guy *he'd* been proud of. Now, what was he? An ex-con who did casual work. The odd jobs he'd once done around his shifts – labouring, gardening, hell, he'd even learned plumbing – now they were *all* he did. And he could only see more of the same yawning in front of him.

But Daisy was looking at him with big, worried eyes, and he couldn't, wouldn't, have her feeling guilty. 'Hey, you know me. I'm smart as shit. I'll find something else. Something better.'

And in case someone up there was listening, and in case they could see that he wasn't a bad person, just a guy who'd made bad decisions, he crossed his fingers and sent up a silent prayer.

Chapter Two

R eeling from her encounter with Jake, Anna retreated into the sanctuary of her bedroom. Her dad's eyes had been full of questions – apparently she looked as unhinged as she felt – but she'd stalled them.

'I'm going to my room to check out jobs online.'

It was true enough, but first she needed a minute to recover her composure.

She couldn't believe he'd raised that bloody night again. How typical that he'd managed to twist things so that she was the one feeling embarrassed. She *had* heard a scream, and she had been worried about Daisy.

As an eighteen-year-old virgin, how was she to know the scream had come from one of the girls who'd been – very happily – having sex with Jake outside on the decking? Or that Daisy had been safely asleep in her bed?

Even now, she felt her cheeks burn. The whole situation had been made worse by the fact that Jake's then-girlfriend had been in Anna's class at school, and had gleefully told the entire class what had happened.

Annoyed with herself, she dug out her laptop. No more moping, crying, or letting Jake get under her skin. She needed to find a job and somewhere to live. It didn't help that the Rutherfords owned the three best restaurants in the area. If she was going to work as a chef, she thought glumly, it wasn't going to be here.

Her dad tapped on the door and pushed it open, his expression full of concern. 'Are you okay?'

'You mean aside from being homeless and jobless?' She groaned. 'Ignore me. I'll pull myself together soon.'

'I know you will.' He perched on the end of her bed, as he had done countless times while she'd been growing up. 'Meanwhile, you know you can stay here for as long as you need.' He gave her one of his sheepish smiles, so at odds with his gruff appearance. 'I happen to like having my daughter around.'

'You mean your stomach enjoys it.'

'Can't deny that's one of the perks. Still'—he made a huffing noise—'you know what I mean.'

'I do, and you know I like being here too, it's just…' She didn't know how to phrase it. 'I'm thirty, Dad.'

'And you don't want to be living with your old dad – I get it.' He paused, eyes searching hers. 'You know you don't have to look for a job round here, don't you? I'd hate you to feel tied to this place because of me. The world's your oyster. Maybe this is a chance to explore it.'

Her smile felt wobbly. 'And now you're trying to get rid of me.'

'Wherever you go, I will hound you with visits and definitely outstay my welcome.' He nodded towards the computer. 'Promise me you won't just find another job, Anna. Take your time and find your dream job.'

'Dream job.' She had to swallow to loosen her throat. 'That's a lovely idea but how on earth do I search for that?' Idly, she typed *dream job* into the search engine and ran her eyes down the hits. 'Dream jobs that don't feel like jobs. Eleven dream jobs that really exist.' She clicked on the second link and read out the list. 'Penguinologist, tea taster, fortune-cookie writer. *Panda* nanny?'

He chuckled. 'Maybe you need to refine the search a little.'

'Wait, this one is for an island caretaker. Comes with a beach hut.' She paused, thinking. 'You know what? You might be onto something, Dad. Not sure I fancy a tropical island but what if I can find a job that comes with accommodation?' She quickly refined the search and scanned the hits. 'Wow, there are actually jobs that involve living in a castle.'

'That sounds more fitting for my princess than living back with her dad.'

'Very funny. But seriously, this does actually sound do-able. I've managed a restaurant; I reckon I could manage a castle and its estate.' She clicked on the next post. 'This one needs someone who can also cook for the owners and their guests when they come to stay.' She felt a bubble of excitement as she scrolled down the job description. 'Oh my God, the castle is on Lake Como. The contract is for a year and it comes with a two-bed apartment in the castle itself...' Her breath caught. 'Wow, look at the views, Dad. It's stunning.'

Her dad rose from the bed and glanced over her shoulder. 'Your mum loved the Italian lakes.'

Her eyes darted to his and she saw the flicker of sadness before he had a chance to hide it. 'I've changed my mind. I don't want to go to Italy.'

He placed a hand on her shoulder and squeezed. 'Don't be

daft. Italy is in your blood. You even speak the language. That job looks perfect for you.'

She had tingles, she realised as she stared back at the photo. Honest-to-God tingles racing down her spine. 'It does… Damn it. They're looking for a couple.'

He shrugged. 'I doubt that's set in stone. I'm sure you can convince them to hire you as the manager and bring on contract workers for the jobs you can't do.'

'Maybe. They do sound desperate because they want the couple to start straight away.' She tried not to get her hopes up, but it was hard when there was nothing else in her life to grasp hold of. 'I'll give them a call.'

But half an hour later, all the energy, the fizz, had drained out of her.

Her dad looked up from his newspaper when he heard her walk in to the living room. 'I phoned the number and spoke to the recruitment people. They said the owners were very clear they're looking for a couple to manage the Lake Como property. They tried a formal management team once and didn't like it. Said it felt like going to a hotel rather than their Italian home. For the last ten years a married couple have been managing the place and it's worked so well the couple have become firm friends of the family. Sadly the wife's been diagnosed with cancer so they've been forced to retire. The owners are looking for another couple to replace them with the hope they can build a similar rapport. Bugger, bugger, bugger.'

'Hey.' He stood and gave her one of his hugs. The ones that had got her through the devastation of her mum walking out on her and the trauma of being dumped by her first boyfriend. 'There'll be other similar jobs out there looking for a smart, hard-working, talented chef-cum-manager-cum-brilliantly-resourceful-woman.' He smiled. 'It's just a question of finding it.'

Their conversation was interrupted by a knock on the front door. Her dad went to answer it and Anna had to resist the urge to run back upstairs when she saw who it was.

'Anna, Jake wants a word.'

Seriously, she'd managed to avoid the man for three years and now, when she was feeling at her lowest, she had to endure his company twice in one day?

Drawing in a breath, she straightened her shoulders. He wasn't going to rattle her a second time.

Jake had actually walked past the Chief Super's front door, but his conscience had started to prick the nearer he'd got to his bike, Daisy's words running through his head. He might not be a fan of Anna's, might even believe that if you went to bed with a rattlesnake, you shouldn't be surprised to get bitten. Still, it didn't seem right that the rattlesnake was mouthing off behind Anna's back. Miles had once done the same to Daisy and while he wasn't about to risk prison again fighting for Anna's reputation, he did reckon he should at least warn her about what was being said.

So he'd manned up, knocked on the door, and forced himself to look the Chief Super in the eye as a twenty-eight-year-old man might, and not a sixteen-year-old kid.

Whatever the guy thought about Jake's stint in prison, he'd given no hint of it when he'd answered the door. Just nodded at Jake's request and disappeared back into the house.

Anna looked wary as she walked over to him. 'Yes?'

Now she was in front of him, he realised he should have left Daisy to talk to her. Or his mum. Anyone with more tact than he had.

'Look, I'm not sure how to say this.' Yeah, great start. He shoved his hand in the pocket of his leathers and tried again. 'You probably think I'm shoving my nose in your business again, but Daisy overheard some stuff in the pub and, well, I thought you should know.'

Her face paled, her expression tightening. 'What stuff?'

And shit, he really wasn't equipped to tell her, not without seriously upsetting her more than he already had. 'Stuff that Miles was saying to his mates about you. How he'd kicked you out… that sort of thing.' He was way out of his comfort zone here. He enjoyed getting one over her, but not like this. 'If you want the details you need to talk to my sister. I just figured—'

'You'd come and rub my nose in it.'

'Whoa.' He took a step back, stung as much by the icy glare as the words. 'You reckon *that* was my motivation for knocking on your door?'

'Wasn't it? The chance to show me my *paradise* is anything but?'

Okay, maybe he'd used the term glibly earlier but hell, it wasn't like he'd come to crow. 'Think whatever you want. I'm done here.'

Thoroughly pissed off, he started to stalk off but her voice stopped him in his tracks.

'Wait, Jake.'

He wanted to keep his anger, but when he turned to look at her, he saw her eyes glisten. Damn it, he never could stand seeing a woman cry.

'Sorry.' She gave him a wan smile. 'I was taking my anger out on the wrong guy.'

He nodded, accepting the apology. 'If you plan to take it out on the right guy, be careful.' He was a glaring example of what could happen if you weren't careful around Miles Rutherford.

'Careful is my middle name.'

He should have figured that. She wouldn't lose her head, like he had. For the first time, he felt a smidgen of grudging respect for her, though for anyone having to live or work with all that careful control, that prissy attitude, it must be a bloody nightmare.

With another incline of his head, he ambled down the drive to his bike. There wasn't much he looked forward to these days, but sitting on the bike was one of them, even when it was drizzling, as it was now. Whether he was weaving through heavy traffic or zipping down the dual carriageway, it was the only time he felt really free. Sometimes he dreamt of just climbing on the back of it and heading off, no plan, no destination in mind, just seeing where the road took him. Starting again somewhere nobody knew him.

Maybe he would. But first he had a bathroom to tile, the job courtesy of his mum.

Sighing heavily, he shoved his helmet back on. Freda, the woman his mum had put him in touch with, was a right battleaxe, but she was also tight enough to get the job done the cheapest way possible, which was him.

———

Two hours later, surrounded by dust and broken tiles, he was being scowled at by Freda, who stood in the bathroom doorway with her arms crossed over her ample chest.

'Do you have to make so much mess?'

Give me a break. He tried his best smile. 'We talked about this. Before I put the new tiles on, I have to take these old ones off.'

'Maud said when she had her bathroom done, they just tiled over the old ones.'

Bully for Maud. He'd like to bet her old bathroom hadn't been as minging as Freda's. 'That only works if the original tiles are in good shape.' See, he could be tactful.

'Well, I'll be expecting you to clean it all up. I've only got you to do the job as a favour to your mum. Otherwise I'd have brought in a professional . Someone I didn't have to keep an eye on.'

He jerked his head up to look at her. 'Sorry?'

'Don't act all coy with me, young man. I know you've been inside.' She sniffed. 'I'm taking a big risk having you in my house, so you'd better do a proper job.'

With that she waddled off, probably to phone his mum and complain.

With a curse of frustration he slumped to the floor, broken tiles crunching beneath his boots. Was this going to be his life from now on? Treated like a criminal, left to do crappy jobs for small-minded people because he'd made some stupid decisions? He wasn't going to say *mistakes* because if he had his time again, he'd still do everything he could to protect his sister.

Wretchedly, Jake stared at the mess of a bathroom. He couldn't even walk out. Not only would that be grossly unfair to his mum, he needed the blasted money Freda might, if he was lucky, pay him. Rent was due next week and his funds were scarily low. He'd lost enough of his pride and he didn't think he could handle having to move back in with his mum.

Especially with the Chief Super and Christ, maybe even Saint Anna, living next door. It would feel like being back in flaming prison.

That bike ride sounded more and more appealing.

Chapter Three

A nna checked her face in the mirror. If she was going to face Miles, she wanted to look her best. Her shoulders slumped. Fine, her best was too much of a stretch. Taking hold of the *miracle* concealer, she dabbed a bit more under her eyes. Sod it, why was she bothering? Maybe he should see what his actions had done to her. It was his fault she looked like crap. The sooner she got her stuff out of his house, the sooner she could start moving forward.

As she opened the front door, she spotted Sheila next door hauling shopping bags out of her car boot. Jake must have got his height from his dad because his mum was short. His eyes were like Sheila's though, but in Jake's case the blue was even more vivid.

'Hey, let me help you with that.'

Sheila smiled. 'Don't you worry – I'm used to it.'

Anna ignored the older woman and took hold of a couple of the bags, following her up the drive to her front door. 'You should get Jake to help you.'

Sheila laughed as she unlocked the door. 'I usually do, but

23

this afternoon he's busy on a job.' She leaned closer to Anna. 'Poor boy will be wishing he was here, helping me with the shopping. The woman he's working for can be really difficult. When she asked me if I knew anyone who could update her bathroom on the cheap, I wasn't sure whether to give her his number or not.' A small sigh left her lips as she plonked the bags on the kitchen table. 'He's found work hard to come by though, so I figured he could put up with holding his tongue for a few days.'

Anna wasn't sure how to reply to that. Her own experience suggested Jake didn't hold back on what he thought.

'I saw the pair of you having words this morning. I hope he didn't upset you.' Sheila glanced at her as she started unpacking and putting things in the fridge. 'When it comes to that Miles, our Jake seems to lose his head.'

From what she remembered, Jake lost his head quickly and easily over most things. 'I suppose you heard what happened with Miles and me?'

Sheila stopped unpacking and gave Anna's arm a pat. 'I did, love. I'm really sorry that man hurt you.' She nodded towards the kettle. 'I'm about to make myself a brew. Be lovely to chat if you're not in a hurry to get off.'

'I'm not.' Seeing Miles could wait. As she helped put the rest of the shopping away, Anna realised how much she wanted to talk to another woman about what had happened. It had been a long time since she'd last had a proper heart-to-heart with Sheila but back when she'd lived with her dad before, she and Sheila had been close. 'You know, I can remember sitting in this kitchen pouring my seventeen-year-old heart out when Paul dumped me.'

Sheila chuckled. 'And then Jake wandered in and overheard us. You were mortified, but he was oblivious to it.'

Shaking her head, she went to fill up the kettle. 'What did he say? Something about—'

'"Don't know why you're moping. The guy's a dick."' She remembered it vividly. Distraught at being told by Paul he didn't want to see her anymore and that he'd never really fancied her anyway, her humiliation had been complete when Jake had basically implied she was stupid for going out with Paul in the first place.

'That's right. He never was one for tact, but Jake's heart's always been in the right place.' Sheila held up the mugs. 'Let's sit down and drink these. I'll put the rest of it away later.'

As she followed Sheila into the little conservatory – she'd had it put on the back of the house because she liked to look out onto her garden – Anna thought about Sheila's words. Had Jake genuinely had her interests at heart when he'd knocked on her dad's door earlier to tell her about what Miles had been saying?

Or had he wanted to create problems for Miles? The man had helped put him inside, after all.

'So, how are you coping, love?' Sheila asked when they'd both sat down. 'Your dad says you've given up your job.'

'I couldn't face the restaurant. Seeing Miles and Tilly together, knowing that everyone knew what had gone on...' She shuddered. 'I know I should have put my big-girl pants on and brazened it out but my heart wasn't in it. I realised I didn't want the damn job anymore, not if I had to work for him. I want a fresh start away from it all.'

Sheila smiled sadly. 'I can totally understand, and I bet my Jake can, too. He's finding it hard to get a decent job since he came out of prison. Folk aren't prepared to give him a chance. Seems to me you've both ended up paying the price for knowing that Rutherford.'

How bizarre that for once, she and Jake had something in common.

She'd never really got to the bottom of why Jake had punched Miles – it had happened before they'd starting dating – but she'd not been surprised to hear he'd ended up in prison over it. There was a reason her dad had had dealings with him over the years. Even though Jake had ended up being a firefighter, his bad-boy rep had followed him.

'Well, I hope Jake finds something soon.' Anna drank back the rest of her tea and stood up. 'I'd better get going. I'm off to pick up the rest of my stuff from our— from Miles's house.'

Sheila's face softened at her slip. 'You'll find a place of your own soon, love.'

'I hope so. I've got a bit saved up but really I need to find a job first. Or, if I'm lucky, a job that comes with its own accommodation a long way from here.'

'That sounds like a plan, but do jobs like that actually exist?' Sheila asked as she followed Anna to the front door. 'I'm thinking Jake could do with something similar. Get him away from this town.'

'Tell him to google *dream job*. He'll be amazed what comes up.'

As she waved goodbye to Sheila and walked down the drive to her car, Anna wondered what Jake would think if he came across the castle job on Lake Como. Knowing him, he'd rope a woman in to pretend to be his wife.

Anna scowled as she climbed into her car. She'd be bloody annoyed if she found out Jake had conned his way into *her* job. Then she laughed at herself. As if a castle on Lake Como was ever really on the cards for someone like her. What did her dad call her? Grounded. Yep, a polite term for boring, sensible, careful. She was hardly going to up sticks and move to Italy. No matter how perfect it sounded.

An hour later, as she stood in what had once been her bedroom and zipped up a suitcase containing the rest of her clothes, a move to Italy – or frankly anywhere away from Miles – didn't just feel do-able, it felt essential.

'Come on, Anna, don't be like this.'

Miles stood in the doorway, hands on his hips, brown eyes pleading with her. She loved his eyes – at times they could be so soft. *Had* loved, she corrected herself. 'Don't be like what? A woman betrayed? A woman you've been talking about behind her back?'

He snapped his head back. 'What do you mean?'

'Stop it.' She turned to face him, the anger she'd wanted to find at last burning through her. 'I think you've lied to me enough, don't you? If you're going to slag me off, at least have the decency to admit it.'

'I haven't.' His eyes wouldn't meet hers.

'I know you have.'

A flush crept up his neck. 'Okay, I might have said some stuff about being glad to get rid of you, but I was angry and lashing out.' This time when he looked at her, she finally saw some regret. 'I was angry at myself, Anna, for being so stupid. I don't mean to get caught,' he added hastily, clearly seeing her reaction. 'I mean to have slept with Tilly in the first place.'

'You did though.' Her voice caught and she had to swallow several times before she felt she could speak again. 'So clearly I can't trust you anymore.'

'That's ridiculous.' He threw his hands up in the air. 'You're going to chuck what we had away for one dumb mistake?'

'What we had?' Flashes of the angry words he'd thrown at her that night came crashing back. 'You said I drove you mad. That I was... what was it? All meticulous and squeaky clean and sometimes a man wanted dirty?'

'You'd just caught me with my blasted pants down. I was mouthing off to cover up how humiliated I felt. I didn't mean any of it.'

It had hurt more than she'd ever admit. Was she lacking in bed? Was she too staid, too missionary? 'And what about my lack of flair in the kitchen? Did you mean that?' She felt her hands start to shake and hurriedly picked up the case. 'Forget it. I can't tell what's lies and what's not anymore.' She glanced around the room. 'If you find anything else of mine, you can bin it. I don't want to see you again.'

As she struggled down the stairs, she heard him curse. 'That's it? You're just buggering off?'

She almost laughed. As if it was that easy.

When she reached the front door, he was behind her. 'Please, don't leave. Not like this.' His voice softened to the one that had persuaded her into his bed in the first place. 'We were good together.'

'Were we?' She felt traitorous tears well up. 'If we had been, we wouldn't be in this situation.'

You wouldn't have gone off and had sex with someone else in our bed.

He huffed out a breath. 'I guess it's goodbye then. Good luck finding another job in a restaurant round here.'

Bastard. She glared at him. 'If you deny me a decent reference, I'll get the lawyers on you.'

She heaved the case into the boot of her car but as she

jumped into the driver's seat her bravado crumpled and tears streamed down her face. Why did people who were supposed to care for her end up kicking her in the teeth? First her mum, then Paul, now Miles. Was she that hard to live with? To love? Inhaling a shaky breath, she slumped forward and rested her head on the steering wheel.

Stop feeling sorry for yourself. Dad loves you. He never left you.

Yes, that was better. Sitting back up, she wiped away her tears, drew in a deep breath, and headed back to the one constant in her life.

Later that evening as she sat on her old bed with her laptop in front of her, she typed *dream job* and *Lake Como* into the search bar. The photo of the castle stared back at her – the calm of the lake, shimmering in the sun, reflecting the green of the trees. The glorious backdrop of the mountains. A job she could start straight away, where she could still cook. They even needed a fluent Italian speaker.

Never mind the job being perfect for her, *she* was perfect for it.

If only she had a partner. One who could supply what she couldn't: gardening and handyman skills.

Unconsciously her mind wandered back to Jake. A man not afraid to break the rules.

Her heart gave a little jump, nudging against her ribs. Before she had time to question it, she'd phoned Sheila for Jake's mobile number.

Then, heart in her mouth, she dialled his phone and waited for him to answer.

'Who is this?'

Typical Jake. 'It's me. Anna.'

Silence. Her pulse began to race. Weird how intimate it felt, talking to him on her phone, while sitting on her bed. Thank God he couldn't see her.

'Yeah?'

She shook her head at his unpromising response. What had she expected? *Great to hear from you*? 'I wondered if we could meet up tonight. I've got a proposal for you.'

More silence. When he finally spoke, she could hear the mockery in his voice. 'Is there a ring involved? Only, I've got to warn you, I'm not sure we're at that stage just yet.'

You want him onside, she reminded herself. So she clamped down on the terse reply – *you and I will never be at that bloody stage* – and forced a smile into her voice. 'No ring, but I will buy you a beer.'

'Is the offer dependent on me saying yes to whatever favour you need?'

Play nice. 'I didn't say it was a favour I wanted.'

'You didn't have to. No way are you offering to buy me a beer from the goodness of your heart.'

She was starting to wonder if this was worth it. Even if he was agreeable, and even if they pulled it off, could she really put up with him for a whole year?

And the alternative is?

Besides, she was only sounding him out. It was surely worth the price of a beer, and an hour spent biting her tongue. 'You're right, it's not from the goodness of my heart. I want to discuss something that could be advantageous for both of us.'

Another pause. She could almost imagine him rubbing at the stubble on his chin. 'Okay, I'll bite. See you at the King's Arms. Eight o'clock. Mine is a pint of whatever beer is the most expensive.'

With a shake of her head, and a silent question to herself as to what on earth she was doing, she ended the call. Yet as she opened her wardrobe and fished around for something to wear – so she felt good for her benefit, not his – her heart lifted, ever so slightly. The evening was bound to come to nothing, but even putting up with Jake for a few hours was better than moping.

Chapter Four

J ake ambled into the King's Arms, eyes searching for a dark-haired, olive-skinned woman with flashing green eyes and killer curves. He smiled to himself. Put like that, it sounded like a dream date. Shame the woman in question had Anna's annoying personality. She wanted to buy him a beer yet didn't need a favour? Yeah, right, pull the other one. It wasn't the first time since he'd been out of prison that someone had invited him for a drink on the pretext of getting some plumbing/DIY/car-repair job done on the cheap. Apparently that was what ex-cons were good at: cheap manual work. He was just surprised Anna had stooped that low, though he guessed she was unemployed now.

He caught sight of her in one of the booths in the corner. She had a pint of something brown waiting for him, and a glass of red wine for herself.

'It's a dodgy craft beer,' she said in lieu of a greeting. 'The most expensive, as per your instructions.'

Raising an eyebrow, he shrugged off his jacket and draped

it round the back of the seat before plonking himself down opposite her. 'This non-favour must be pretty huge.'

'What do you mean?'

Reaching out, he took a swig. Too hoppy, too poncy. Served him right for trying to be clever. 'You, doing as I'—he mimed quotation marks—'instructed.'

She inhaled, shaking her head, glossy brown hair sliding over her shoulders. 'Are we going to sit here and have a civilised conversation, or are you just going to make snide remarks?'

He smirked. Probably something was seriously wrong with him because he really got a kick out of winding her up. 'Can't I do both?'

'I know you can do the snide,' she muttered, then seemed to catch herself and gave him an overly polite smile. 'I'll get straight to the point. Save us both the torture of sitting here discussing the weather.' Pulling out her phone, she tapped on the screen a few times and then placed it in front of him. 'Take a read of that and tell me what you think.'

He stared down at it, frowning. 'You're asking my opinion on a job vacancy?'

'Sort of, yes.'

He rubbed at his chin. 'Got to say, you've got me stumped. Figured you were going to give me some sob story about how your car's knackered and you can't afford to get a garage to look at it now you're out of a job.' Dazed, he shook his head. 'Never thought you'd be asking me for career advice.'

'I'm not.'

Of course she wasn't. Acutely embarrassed, he took another swig of the pretentious beer. 'So why am I looking at this?'

Now it seemed it was her turn to look away and reach for her drink. 'Read it first and then I'll tell you.'

He glanced over the advert. Looking after some fancy castle in Italy for a year. Sounded like a doss of a job, frankly. A bit of gardening, he suspected, some maintenance. Taking care of guests now and then. 'You and Miles made up and moving out to Italy then?'

'What?' He watched as she swallowed the sip of wine she'd just taken. 'You think I'd take him back after what he did? What he said?'

Jake shifted on the chair. 'You asked Daisy, huh?'

'No.' She glanced away sharply. 'I didn't need to. I can guess.'

He didn't mind winding her up, seeing the prissy formality get flustered. He didn't like seeing her upset. 'If it helps, I figure he wouldn't have you work in his restaurant if you were a shit chef. And as for you being shit in bed...' He winced as her face paled and then went scarlet. Yep, tact still wasn't part of his skillset. 'I figure he's got a small dick.' He threw her a grin, hoping to ease the awkward factor. 'Must have been tough to get excited over it.'

She raised her eyes to the ceiling, her face losing some of its heat. 'I'm not here to discuss Miles's anatomy.'

'Right, then tell me what you are here for, instead of leaving me to play guessing games.' Sitting in his dive of a flat watching re-runs of whatever was on Dave had to be better than dealing with the prickly Anna.

Again, she looked uncomfortable. He kind of liked it, but he also wanted her to spit out whatever it was she wanted to get off her chest – her voluptuous, had to be a D-cup at least, chest, not that he'd looked, much – so he could finish his beer and go.

Finally, her eyes met his. 'I want to apply for that job.'

'Good on you. Sounds great.' He took a healthy swig of his drink. 'Can I go now?'

She let out a hiss of frustration. 'Why are you always so antagonistic?'

'Why don't you just tell me what the hell we're doing here?'

Briefly she closed her eyes. When she opened them again, she aimed them straight at him. 'It needs a couple.'

'I can see that. Good luck finding someone to be your other half... Whoa.' He reared back, stunned. 'Wait a minute. You're not suggesting *we* hook up?'

'God no.'

And yeah, he was relieved, but she didn't need to be so snotty about it. 'Thought of being with a real man too scary for you, huh?'

She gave him a look loaded with sharp mental daggers. 'Right now, the thought of being with any man makes me queasy.'

Frustrated, he leaned forward across the table. 'Then what the blazes are you suggesting?'

Again her eyes found his, and this time there was a spark of challenge. 'I'm suggesting we pretend to be a couple.'

He liked to think he wasn't stupid, but his brain seemed to take an age to process what she'd said. 'You want me to pretend to be your husband if you get an interview?'

'It doesn't say we have to be married.'

He let out a bark of laughter. 'Oh well, that's okay then. Just a plain old living-together couple, eh? I mean, we can't spend more than five minutes in each other's company without arguing but sure, that's entirely do-able.' He had a vision of him putting his arm around her, and started to laugh harder.

'Christ, this business with Miles must have totally fried your brain. You realise if I so much as touched you, you'd slap me round the face?'

The green eyes flashed. 'I think I can manage to refrain from slapping you for the length of an interview.'

'You think?' Amused, he leaned back on his chair. 'And you really believe these people will be convinced that you'—he waved at her, only now taking in the expensive-looking green jumper—'and the dude with the tattoos are a couple?'

'You could wear a long-sleeved shirt.'

Annoyance pricked. 'I could, huh?'

She had the grace to look embarrassed. 'Sorry.' Her shoulders lifted in a shrug. 'Maybe I like tattoos. Lots of women do.'

He had an image of Miles in his head. Clean-shaven, neatly styled dark hair. Expensive tailored shirts, chinos. Fancy leather brogues. No way did the guy have any ink. 'And do you?'

'It doesn't matter, does it? We just need to convince them we can do the job and that we... love each other.'

The whole concept set him off again and he started to laugh, which in turn made her cross, which only made him laugh harder. 'Jesus.' Shaking his head, he thrust a hand through his hair. Unlike her ex, his was overly long. Since coming out of prison he'd not wanted to cut it. A reminder to himself he was free to do what the hell he liked. 'And what happens if by some miracle we pull that off? Do I come down with some mystery illness for a year?'

'We go to Italy.'

He stared at her, stunned. She wasn't seriously considering... 'You and me, living and working together.

37

Pretending to be a couple. For a whole fucking year?' He laughed so loudly the people around them started to stare. 'You really have lost the plot.'

Anna watched Jake crack up with increasing levels of annoyance – and, she had to admit, curiosity. She'd never actually seen him laugh, only his smug smile. He had dimples, she realised with a start. Though maybe she should call them grooves as they lined either side of his mouth, the effect shockingly attractive.

Or it would be, if the laughter hadn't been aimed at her.

'I don't see what's so funny. Your mum said you've found it tough getting a decent job since you, well, you—'

'Came out of prison?' he interrupted. His laughter had vanished and his voice carried a sharp edge.

'Yes.' Determined not to be intimidated by him, she raised her chin. 'And she said you could do with getting away from the area.'

'She did, did she?' His expression hardened and suddenly it was easy to see the ex-prisoner. The guy who wasn't afraid to throw a punch. 'Quite the chat you two have been having about me.'

A worm of guilt wriggled through her. 'It wasn't like that.' God, this was so bloody hard. Maybe she *had* lost the plot. They couldn't have a civilised conversation even before Miles had decided to be an absolute prick. Now Jake knew what her ex had been saying about her, and if that wasn't mortifying enough, he also knew she was so hurt by it, so desperate to get away from it, that she was prepared to contemplate not just pretending to like Jake, but to be in love with him.

'Then enlighten me. What was it like?'

The tight words, the uncompromising blue stare, brought her attention back to the man sitting opposite her. As usual, he wore a T-shirt, even though it was March and still chilly outside. It had probably once been black but had faded to dark grey, and clung to the defined muscles of his chest. He was attractive – she couldn't deny it. Handsome, even, despite the scar that bisected his right eyebrow, making him look like he was permanently smirking. He probably was, at least when he was talking to her.

'We were talking about me. How I need to find a job and a new place to live. I told your mum I was looking for a fresh start, somewhere different.' She paused, hating to drop Sheila in it, but aware that if she had any chance of getting Jake on side, she had to tell the truth. 'She said she thought that would be good for you, too. Get you away from this town.' Anna risked looking at him. 'You know your mum and I have always got on. She was being empathetic – her way of trying to encourage me.'

He stared back at her, his striking blue eyes unafraid not just to look at you, but right through you. 'You ever hear from your own mum?'

The question threw her. 'Not often, no.'

He nodded. 'Hard to be mad at mine then. She's always been here for me.'

Encouraged by his rare show of reasonableness, she pushed the conversation back where she wanted it. 'So, what do you think about pretending to be a couple and applying for the job? I mean, you can do most of what they're looking for, yes? Not the cooking, obviously, but the maintenance part.'

His expression tightened. 'I can *do* maintenance, yeah.'

Wow, he was touchy. A thought occurred to her. 'You are

single? From the way your mum was talking, it sounded like you were.'

'Then I guess I am.'

He was deliberately making this difficult but if he thought that would deter her, he was wrong. 'So there's nothing to stop you, is there? I mean, I know it's a long shot but it has to be worth a try. Yes?'

He scratched at the stubble on his chin and shifted to his default position: arm stretched languidly along the back of the chair, legs crossed at the ankles. 'What happened to the Anna who does no wrong?'

'Just because I called you out for smoking and was worried about Daisy doesn't mean I'm some sort of goody-two-shoes.'

He let out a low laugh, heavily laden with sarcasm. 'Sure you're not.' His eyes searched hers. 'Your dad's okay with this?'

'I'm not a child. I don't need his approval.'

He inclined his head, though the way he continued to stare at her made it clear he knew that despite her words, she wouldn't be doing this unless her dad was okay with it. 'You're sure it's a good idea to do this with me? Big if, I know, but *if* Miles ever got to hear you were in Italy with the guy he hates, he'd be hopping mad.'

'So?'

'So, the Rutherford influence spreads far and wide.'

'I doubt he'll care but if he does,' she grinned, 'upsetting him is an added benefit.'

Jake clearly didn't believe her because his eyes narrowed on hers, daring her to look away. Pretty eyes, she thought distractedly, if they weren't in such a powerfully male face. Eventually, he must have seen she was telling the truth because he smirked. 'Okay.'

Her heart jumped. 'Okay... what?'

'Okay, apply for it.' He gave a lazy shrug of his shoulders. 'Why not?'

'Really?' She cringed, aware she sounded too squeaky, too excited, but after the last few days of misery, this felt like a chance of something different, a new chapter. Who knows, maybe even a whole new book and God, she needed that. Needed her life to take a totally different path from the one it kept repeating.

His gaze skimmed over her. 'You know the chances of us being able to pull this off are about the same as us being crushed by a meteor, while being struck by lightning?'

'No.' He raised his eyebrows at her response. 'It's higher than that.' Not much though, now she thought about it. She'd come here thinking all she had to do was convince Jake to give it a go, but really that was the easy part. 'It's all in the preparation. I'll take another look at the advert and make a list of all the things they're looking for. Then we can match it with our skillset for the application. If we get an interview, we'll need to memorise important details about each other that a partner would know, like family history, birthdays, favourite foods, places, that sort of thing, so we sound convincing as a couple. I'll pull together some likely questions and we can practise answering them. Maybe we can get Dad to pretend to be the owner—'

'Whoa, hang on a minute.' Jake sat bolt upright, all laziness gone from his body. 'I'm good with giving this a go – nothing to lose as far as I can see – but no way are we involving your dad.'

Finally, she felt the power shift between them. 'Why not?' She smiled sweetly. 'Don't tell me you're still afraid of him.'

He huffed out a laugh. 'Only person I'm afraid of is my mum.'

She knew for a fact that was a lie. For all his faults, Jake doted on his mum, on his whole family as far as she could see. And they doted on him. 'You definitely used to be scared of Dad. When I was round your place talking to your mum you'd strut about, all sure of yourself. Then my dad would knock on the door and you'd leg it upstairs.'

He shook his head, for once looking embarrassed. 'I was *twelve*.'

'Bet you were more scared of my dad than you were of your own.' A shadow crossed his face and immediately she regretted the mention. 'You must miss him,' she said awkwardly, belatedly remembering his dad had died of a heart attack before they'd moved next door.

For a brief moment she thought Jake was going to open up a little, answer her properly. But then his mouth curved in that annoying crooked smile. 'Is this the getting-to-know-each-other part of the schedule? 'Cos it seems we're jumping the gun. Need to get the interview first.'

'Fine.' She was more comfortable keeping to the impersonal details with him anyway. 'I'll take a look at the application and be in touch with what you can add from your side.' A thought occurred, one she'd totally overlooked in her desperation to get a job and get away.

'Wondering what to put about my record?' He raised his brow, or was it the scar causing that knowing smirk?

Seems he had a really irritating ability to read her. 'No.' If she was going to start lying, now was as good a time as any to practise. 'As you said, no point jumping the gun. We can discuss that when we get an interview.'

'When?'

'I back myself to put together a persuasive application.'

'Okay then.' He rose to his feet with the casual ease of a man comfortable in his body. Because she hated the way he now towered over her, she jumped up, too, though she still had to angle her neck to look at him. 'Guess I'll see you around.'

'Guess you will.' Instinctively she held out her hand.

He stared down at it, then laughed softly as he reached to shake it. 'Is this some sort of gentleman's handshake? Because I'm no gentleman.'

For a second she missed what he said, caught in the warmth of his clasp, the rubbing of his callouses against her palm. 'I know.' She swallowed, finding her throat suddenly dry. 'I don't need a gentleman. Just a guy willing to be my fake partner.'

'Fair enough.' He grinned. 'You realise fake partners have to kiss each other at some point, not just shake hands.'

Heat crept up her neck and she jerked her hand away. 'I'll worry about that if and when we get to it.'

Laughter crossed his face. She wondered if she'd ever see him laugh *with* her, rather than *at* her. 'You heading back to your dad's now?' His eyes teased. 'I can try that gentleman thing and walk you back.'

'Thanks, but no. I'm… seeing a friend.'

Another nod, another knowing smile. 'Sure you are.'

He picked his black leather jacket off the back of the chair, eased it over his powerful shoulders, and ambled out of the pub the same way he'd ambled in – with long, lazy strides.

When she was sure he was out of view, she slumped down on the seat, wondering why she'd lied so she didn't have to walk back with him.

The embarrassment of having to ask for his help? The usual uneasiness of their conversation? It had to be that, surely, and not the confusing reaction to shaking his hand. Whatever it was, she had to sort herself out because if they were going to pull this off, she'd have to spend a lot more time in his company.

Chapter Five

He had to be out of his ever-loving mind, Jake thought as he stared down at the stack of cards, tied together with a black ribbon – yes, a bloody *ribbon* – that had landed though his letterbox while he'd been finishing off Freda's bathroom.

On each notecard was written a heading and beneath it, in the neatest, fanciest handwriting he'd ever seen, was information relating to the heading. He picked up one at random.

> *FAVOURITES*
> *Colour = crimson red*
> *Film = Notting Hill*
> *Book = Me Before You*
> *Drink = champagne*
> *Food = pizza*
> *Perfume = Jo Malone*

With increasing levels of disbelief, he flicked through the others. Cards headed: birth details, likes and dislikes, education, domestic... He took a second look at that. For Christ's sake, she'd actually written down what side of the bed she slept on and the brand of toothpaste she used.

With an exasperated huff, he dived onto the sofa and picked up his phone.

'You got the cards then?' Anna said in greeting.

'You are one crazy woman. You know that, right?'

He imagined her giving him one of her looks. The one where her eyes turned the colour of a forest and a frown line appeared between them. 'The interview is tomorrow. We need to know everything about each other by then.' He heard a rustling and imagined her holding the single sheet of paper he'd scrawled a few basic facts on. 'Clearly I'm going to have to quiz you further on the journey, but at least if you read my cards *you'll* be prepared.'

'Because they're really going to ask me why you use Sensodyne and I use Colgate.'

A sharp exhale. 'The more we know about each other, the more comfortable we'll be acting like a couple. You think real actors just speak a part, without getting to know the person they're pretending to be?'

She was nuts. 'We're not acting, we're bullshitting. Bluffing.' And he'd been doing that all his life.

There was a pause, and he suspected she was carefully tempering what she wanted to say because, for once, she needed his help. 'Fine. Call it whatever you want. It's already clear from how fast they've arranged the interview that they're desperate. We might really have a chance if we put some effort into it.'

He guessed he couldn't argue with that. Especially as the effort she'd been applying had got them the interview in the first place. It made him realise that while he'd been treating it as a bit of a game, it wasn't that to her. 'You really want this job, huh.'

It wasn't a question, but she answered him anyway. 'Of course.' Another hesitation. 'Don't you?'

'Honestly? I don't know.' He dragged a hand through his hair, trying to work out his feelings. A year in Lake Como doing very little sounded frigging fantastic, which was why he'd agreed to the charade in the first place. But that had been like agreeing to go to the moon with a mate if he could build a rocket – great idea, never going to happen. Now he was part interested, part terrified that Anna's sheer bloody determination was going to get them both to the moon. 'Can you really see you and me working together?' He shook his head and got to the crux of the matter. 'Us living in the same space and not wanting to kill each other?'

A beat of silence. 'If we're lucky enough to get this, we can manage things so we keep out of each other's way.' He heard her clear her throat. 'Look, if you've changed your mind—'

'I haven't.'

'Okay.' He waited, certain her desire for structure, her need to pin down details, would mean she couldn't leave it there. And he was right. 'This is really important to me. I don't want to go through all the hassle, the stress, only to find you decide to pull out, so if you're not sure—'

'I said I'll do this,' he interrupted, annoyance pricking. 'I keep my word.'

'I didn't imply otherwise.' Her clipped retort told him he wasn't the only one getting wound up. 'I just need to know if you're fully committed because if you're not…'

He waited for her to continue. When she didn't, he let out a soft laugh. 'If I'm not?'

'I'll find someone who is,' she countered, but her voice lacked conviction.

'Sure. I bet you know hundreds of guys desperate enough, and mad enough, to go through with this.'

The pause on the other end was so long he wondered if the connection had failed, but then he finally heard her cool tone again. 'I'd rather duck out now than get my hopes up only to find them crushed.'

Her voice caught on the last few words. The rare moment of weakness was enough to remind him why this meant so much to her. 'I can't promise we'll smash the interview, but I can promise I won't pull out.' Because he couldn't help winding her up, he added. 'Usually I make the promise the other way round.'

It took a second for her to get his meaning. 'That's an image I don't want in my head, thanks very much.'

'Hey, if we're going to be a couple tomorrow, you're going to have to pretend that's exactly what you want. Me pulling out. And thrusting back in. Again, and again, and—'

'I believe they're more likely to ask about our toothpaste preferences than our preferred sexual positions.'

God, she was so cool. Unflappable almost. It impressed him and brought out the worst in him in equal measures. 'Well, just in case, I like it most ways: corkscrew, wheelbarrow, doggy style—'

'Thank you. I get the drift. Perhaps if you put the same amount of effort into listing your other likes and dislikes, we might stand a chance of getting the job.'

There she went again. 'Ever thought of being a school teacher?'

The question seemed to surprise her. 'Why?'

'Thought those caustic putdowns might be more effective in the classroom than the kitchen.'

He heard her draw in a breath. Imagined her face tightening with all that frightening control. 'All I'm asking is that you please read and revise the cards I sent you.'

'Is there going to be a test?'

'Yes. It's called an interview. I'll pick you up tomorrow at nine o'clock.'

She ended the call before he could offer to put her on the back of his bike instead. He grinned as he imagined her sitting all stiff-backed, interview suit screwed up around her thighs. A helmet covering her carefully styled hair.

That desire to mess her up a bit, to find out what was beneath the gloss, niggled again, surprising him. It had been a while since he'd spent so much time thinking of a woman, even if most of the thoughts were along the lines of: *she annoys the fuck out of me.*

With a sigh, he picked up the damn cards and started reading them.

Wednesday morning, and the clock on her dashboard said 8.55am. Anna considered knocking on Jake's door but figured she didn't need to give him another excuse to mock her. Last night had been hard enough, what with his sarcastic teacher joke and his crude sex talk. She winced at the memory. She wasn't a prude – she could usually talk sex without getting embarrassed – but talking about it with Jake had made her flush hot and cold. Suddenly she'd felt like that eighteen-year-old virgin again, mortified at calling her dad for what had actually just been Jake and his girlfriend having sex.

She shook herself. She was a different person now. One quite capable of dealing with men, even those as frustrating, and as intimidatingly sexual, as Jake.

Easing out of the car, she straightened her suit skirt, checking it for wrinkles. Thankfully none. The last time she'd worn it had been at a friend's wedding. The colour was one of her favourites – a deep red – and though it was probably a bit over the top for an interview she figured it didn't hurt to look smart.

'Whoa.'

She turned to find Jake ambling down the steps from his flat.

His eyes swept up and down her and he grinned, revealing those attractive grooves and giving his face a boyish look. 'Nice legs.'

Sarcasm she could handle, but his compliment took her off guard. 'Thanks,' she mumbled, turning and opening the car door again to hide the fact that she might, possibly, be flustered. By the time he lowered himself into the passenger seat, she had herself back under sufficient control to give him the same once over he'd given her. Fair hair – no, that was wrong. Fair hair belonged to guys who looked neat, guys a girl could take home to meet her parents. Jake's hair was dirty-blond; it was too long to be neat, though at least it looked clean, and he'd shaved, which was a plus. He had on faded jeans that showcased a pair of muscular thighs. Above that was a black leather jacket, stretched over his wide shoulders, and beneath it a black T-shirt that fitted tautly over the hard lines of his chest.

Sexy. She couldn't deny it. But... 'This is your interview outfit?'

He glanced down at his jeans, as if he'd forgotten what he was wearing. 'Hey, I chose the non-ripped pair.'

She tried to swallow her irritation but she was too tense, and the interview meant too much to her. 'This is just one big joke to you, isn't it?' When he just stared back at her, she found she couldn't keep it all bottled up any longer. 'Why are you doing this? You've already admitted you don't think we can work together, so why didn't you duck out when I gave you the chance?'

He shrugged, huge shoulders seeming wider in the confines of her car. 'Maybe I fancy the idea of a year bumming around in a castle on Lake Como.'

Frustration bubbled over and she hit the steering wheel. 'God, Jake, this is serious for me. A chance to get away from the mess of my life here. To manage a castle, live in Italy, cook food for guests that I've created, not that someone has told me to make. I want this.' *I need this.* She swallowed as emotion reared like a giant wave, threatening to crash over her. Desperately she turned away, biting into her cheek. She couldn't, wouldn't, cry in front of him.

'I want it too.' His quietly spoken words made her jerk her head round to stare at him.

'Do you, really? Because that's not the impression I get. Your lack of preparation.' She waved in the direction of his clothes. 'The casual get-up. It seems to me you're trying to sabotage it.'

His jaw tightened. 'I don't have a suit. Never had any need to wear one and I'm too skint to buy one right now.'

Damn it. She should have thought of that. Some of the anger fizzled away. 'Sorry.' She tried to smile. 'I'm wound a bit tight.'

No change there. She was sure he muttered the words under

his breath, but she didn't get a chance to grill him because he spoke again. 'You chose that natty suit because it's your favourite colour. Crimson. This car is a hybrid because you're passionate about the environment, though that passion doesn't extend to not eating meat because you love all food, especially pizza, which is your favourite. That probably comes from your Italian mum, who left you and your dad when you were ten and gets in touch once a year when she sends you a birthday card. 20th August.' He glanced at her. 'That's a shit deal.'

'Yes.' But it wasn't the offer of sympathy that surprised her most. 'You memorised the cards.'

He dug into his jacket pocket, took out the cards, now without their tidy ribbon, and waved them at her. 'You told me to.'

'Since when did you ever do what you were told?'

'Don't worry, I won't make a habit of it.'

His eyes glinted with amusement, like the sun reflecting off the Caribbean Sea, and her breath caught in her throat. When he wasn't glowering at her, he was ridiculously attractive. To take her mind off the fact, she busied herself putting the postcode into the sat nav. 'As you clearly know a fair bit about me,' she said once she'd finished, 'why don't you use the headings on my cards and tell me about yourself.'

He smirked, suddenly looking too big in the small confines of her Mini Countryman. 'You want to get to know me, huh?'

'For the purposes of getting a job that comes with accommodation in a castle on Lake Como. Yes.'

His soft laughter filled the car. 'Gotcha.' He looked down and pulled up the first card. Then shook his head and shuffled it to the back of the pack. 'Okay then, dislikes.'

'What about the first card?'

Another grin, this one with a hint of devil about it. 'I like a woman to get to know me before I tell her which side of the bed I sleep on.'

Part exasperated, part amused, she pulled out into the traffic. 'Fine. I don't care what order you do them in, as long as you get through them all by the time we arrive in Dorset.'

She didn't need to look at him to know he was smirking again. 'Dislikes. People telling me what to do.'

She rolled her eyes, aware it was going to be a very long journey.

Chapter Six

Jake glanced over at the sat nav. Thank fuck – only a few more miles to go. It meant they'd be crazy early for the interview but no surprise there given Obsessively Organised Anna was in charge. More importantly, it would mean an end to this mind-numbing getting-to-know-each-other crap. Okay, that wasn't fair, he'd kind of enjoyed learning about her and her foibles from the cards last night, but now the focus was on him, he'd had enough.

'Did we cover what sports you did at school?'

'Football. Good enough to play for the county—'

'Not good enough to play for your country. I remember.' She bit into her bottom lip. 'What about allergies? We didn't cover that, or if you have any health issues?'

He glanced sideways at her. 'No allergies. And the chlamydia's healed up a treat, thanks for asking.'

She clenched her jaw, which of course made him snigger. He stopped abruptly when he saw an imposing white mansion looming up in front of them. 'Shit, is that where we're headed?'

'Looks like it.' It was her turn to grin. 'Not feeling so cocky now, huh?'

He tried to give a casual shrug. 'It's not me who's desperate to impress them.' Though the more he thought about escaping to Lake Como for a year, the more the idea was growing on him. Even the knowledge that he'd have to work with Anna didn't seem as awful as it had at first. He kind of enjoyed sparring with her. When she wasn't bossing him around. Or making him feel stupid. Or irritating him with her apparent inability to chill the hell out.

Silence descended for a few blessed seconds as she eased the car through the open gates and onto the sweeping driveway.

'Your stint in prison.'

He sighed. 'What about it.'

'What are we going to say about it?'

'The conviction is spent; I don't have to declare it.' He'd thought long and hard about it. 'If I do, they won't hire us, that's for certain.' His experience with the fire service had shown him that.

Her eyes darted briefly to his. 'I know you hit him, but getting a prison sentence for it seems a steep price to pay.'

'Yeah, well it didn't help that he hit his head on a rock when he fell. Or that I have a fearsome right hook. Also didn't help that I've had a few brushes with the law prior to it.'

'Brushes?'

He quirked his lips. 'I'm practising being polite.'

'Will you tell me *why* you hit him?'

He studied her side profile. 'Suddenly worried I'm dangerous?'

'I wouldn't be doing this if I were.' While he tried to work out why her words mattered so much to him, she groaned. 'Oh God, we didn't discuss how we met.'

'We were neighbours.'

'I don't mean in real life, I mean...' She glanced at him. 'Oh, you think we should stick as close to the truth as possible.'

'That's the art of a good lie.'

'Yes, that sounds sensible.' He thought he'd got away without any further discussion but a beat later she was firing more questions at him. 'How long have we been a couple? What first attracted us to each other? Who moved in with whom? Why have we decided to apply for this job?' He could see her body becoming more and more tense as the car scrunched up the driveway. 'I've been so focused on details I've forgotten the important stuff. Damn it, we need more time. This isn't going to work.'

He waited for her to park before turning to face her. 'Will you chill the hell out? As long as we don't answer at the same time, we've got this. Whoever takes the lead can make up the details; the other person just has to go with the flow.'

She stared at him wide-eyed. 'But I can't operate like that. I need to be prepared.' Breaking the gaze, she looked down at her hands, which were gripped tightly in her lap. 'That's how we coped when Mum left. Dad said everything is easier if you're organised and he was right.'

Interesting. He had a feeling he'd just got a glimpse into why she was so uptight. 'Everything is also easier if you keep things simple.' He tapped her on the shoulder so she'd focus back on him. 'Just look at me when you want me to answer and I will.' He grinned, trying to calm her down. 'I've got GCSEs in bullshitting.'

'Okay, okay.' She breathed in and out a few times. 'But—'

'We've been going out two years. I was first attracted to

your impressive tits and curvy arse. I moved in with you because you refused to live in my dump. We're applying for the job because we fancy living abroad for a while.'

'My…' She briefly shut her eyes, as if trying to blot out what he'd said. Then she inhaled a deep breath and opened them again. 'We're applying for the job because it sounds like the opportunity of a lifetime. We're considering running a B&B or maybe a boutique hotel in the future so this seems like a perfect chance to gain some experience and we can't wait to make them and their guests feel at home.'

He smothered his grin. 'That works too. What about my arse? Is that what attracted you? Or was it my big—'

'Ego?'

He laughed. 'And she's back.'

For a moment she held his gaze and he felt a weird sensation in his chest. A kick of his heart. An awareness of her he'd not felt before. On one level he'd always known she was a looker, but it was like suddenly his body was reminded of that, too. 'We should kiss.'

She reared back, looking shocked – or was it disgusted? As if he'd suggested they climb into the back and have sex. 'Is that some sort of joke?'

And this was why his head needed to remind his body he didn't like her. 'I'll tell you what's a joke. Us trying to pull off being a couple when we can't even touch each other.'

Anger shot through him and he shoved the door open and jumped out. Was the thought of kissing him *that* repulsive?

'We can't look like we're rowing.' She eyed him warily over the roof of the car before glancing behind her at the house. 'They might be watching.'

He shrugged, hands in his pockets. 'So, give them something else to see.'

'Don't be like this,' she hissed.

'Like what?' He glared back at her. 'You asked me to pretend. I told you what I think will help.'

Anna knew she was having a mini meltdown. What she didn't know was how to get out of it. Suddenly this all felt too much. A charade she couldn't possibly pull off. She'd never been any good at lying so trying to pretend to be in love when she wasn't, especially with someone as… as… she couldn't even describe to herself how she felt about Jake. He irritated her, confused her, unsettled her. Yet sometimes it felt like he understood her a bit, too.

Kissing him though? It was way too much. Even the thought of putting her arms around him felt impossibly intimate.

'We could hold hands.' She swallowed, feeling her palms begin to sweat at the thought. 'That seems more professional.'

He exhaled heavily, clearly unhappy. And sure, kissing probably wasn't a big deal for him; he treated intimacy with the same casual nonchalance he did everything else. But she didn't do casual, didn't do carefree or laid-back. She wanted to, but it was like her body was hard-wired to be stiff. Miles's cutting comments, which Jake had neatly summarised as her being shit in bed, didn't help.

Slowly he walked round the car. When he reached her side, he stared down at her, expression inscrutable, eyes burning into hers, daring her to glance away again. 'Okay, Ms Roberts.' They were so close she felt the warm flutter of his breath against her face, the fresh, woody smell of whatever he'd showered with. 'Are we doing this?'

'Yes.' It came out like a squeak and she had to clear her throat and try again. 'I'm ready if you are.'

He gave her that part smirk, part cocky grin. 'I'm always ready.'

His big, warm hand grasped hers and as she felt the roughness of his palm, the strength of his grip, her body did a strange thing. It began to lose some of its tension.

'Two years,' she mumbled. 'We've been together two years and—'

'I like your curvy arse and big tits.'

This time when he said it, she was prepared. Or at least she thought she was, but when she saw the amusement brighten the blue of his eyes, the grin split his face, and the grooves flash by the side of his mouth, her pulse sped up. 'I see I'm living with a Neanderthal.'

He laughed, that low, soft chuckle that seemed incongruous on a man who could violently punch another in the face. It made her wonder again why he'd done it. She knew Miles's version – that Jake had taken exception to something he'd said – was likely a very whitewashed version of the truth.

She had no time to ponder it any further because the door opened, and they were ushered inside.

Henry and Penelope Harper seemed nice. Their son Nigel, not so much. For the first ten minutes of the interview the couple had talked about the castle. Their love for it had shone on their faces and in the animated way they'd spoken. It seemed Henry's grandfather had bought it for his wife when she'd spotted it from across the lake one holiday and fallen in love with it. Henry's father had married his own wife there and Henry and Penny had followed suit forty years later.

'I know it sounds daft, it would be easy to get a management company in to run it, but it's important to us that the people who take care of our castle love it like we do. That we feel they're part of our family and not just there to do a job.' Penelope – *please, dear, call me Penny* – smiled. There was a touch of the regal about it. Pleasant, yet not quite reaching her eyes. 'Without that we might as well do as Nigel would like and sell up to a hotel chain.'

Nigel looked stony-faced. 'I'm only thinking of what's best for you both. Now Steve and June have had to step down, it would save you a lot of hassle.'

'But that's what this lovely couple could do. Take away the hassle.'

'Maybe.' Nigel rested his gaze first on Jake and then on her. There was something cold about the grey eyes that raked over her, as if searching for a weak point. 'Or maybe they'll not be up to the job, which means more hassle for you. Maybe they'll take advantage of you, sneaking their mates in, having parties there, causing damage to the furnishings you've carefully, lovingly chosen. Then you'll have to sack them and go through the pain of more interviews, more stress, wondering if every couple you talk to are going to take advantage of you, and of the castle.'

Wow. Anna glanced at Jake, who gave her a blunt, this-was-your-idea-you-sort-it look. As the tension became palpable, she cleared her throat. 'Why would we abuse our position when taking care of the castle is something we're so excited about doing? As you can see from our application, we've got everything covered so you can be hassle-free. Maintaining the building, getting it ready for you and any guests, chauffeuring, cooking for you. I've worked in one of the best restaurants in the county so I know how to cater for fine dining. I also speak Italian so we can easily work with the local community if needed.' She looked pointedly at Nigel. 'We're most definitely up to the job.'

Henry made a humming noise which could have been agreement, or boredom, or disbelief. 'I see Jake can put out a fire if it's needed too, eh?'

He looked over at Jake who'd been quiet up to now. Anna wasn't sure if he was deliberately leaving her to talk, or if for once he'd lost some of his breezy confidence.

'I could.' Jake shifted on his chair, big arms hanging loosely by his side – arms, she noted, whose tattoos were covered by his long-sleeved Henley T-shirt. He gave the impression of being relaxed, yet she could see the tension in his jawline.

'Why did you give it up?'

Oh shit. It was an obvious question. Why hadn't she thought of it?

Anna watched as Jake stiffened. 'I'd rather not say.'

Henry looked taken aback by the blunt statement. 'Well, that is your prerogative, young man, but I have to say, I find it an odd attitude to have at an interview.'

Anna held her breath as Jake leaned forward, arms resting on his thighs. He glanced first at Henry, then at Penny.

'All you need to know is it has no bearing on my ability to take care of your castle. Or your guests.' He flicked a look at Anna. 'This woman has been looking after herself and her dad since she was ten, and working in a restaurant since she was eighteen. She's half-Italian, so food's in her blood, but she's got a cooking diploma to back that up. Plus, she did an accountancy course so she can manage the books.' With a brief smile, he sat back. 'I just do as she tells me.'

Wow. Not only had he remembered details from the cards, he'd strung them together like he really believed what he was saying. Like he believed in her. Anna had to remind herself he was only doing what he'd bragged he could do: bullshitting.

'Well, yes.' Penny smiled politely again at Anna. 'You do seem perfect for the role.'

'We both are,' Anna corrected. 'I couldn't fix a leaking tap, wouldn't know where to start if the power went out and I've never repaired a roof or cut back a hedge.' She turned to Jake, who quirked an eyebrow, clearly wondering if she wanted him to take over now. With a small shake of her head, she reached to squeeze his hand in a gesture she hoped would look like affection. 'And though this guy actually never does what I tell him, he can be relied on to do what is needed.'

Her joke seemed to amuse Henry, thank God, and he roared with laughter. Penny let out a graceful chuckle beside him. Nigel remained unsmiling

'Well, young man'—Henry gave Jake a considering look—'could you undertake a powerboat course in the next few days? That is, if you don't already have a licence.'

'No boat licence,' Jake batted back coolly, as if he was asked that question most days. 'But I could make time to get one.'

Henry glanced at Penny, communicating silently. Then he cleared his throat. 'I have to be honest, we were looking for an older couple because that worked well for us before, and because we're old.' He chuckled at his own joke. 'But your application stood out from the rest as being the best fit to our requirements, so we decided to speed the process along and meet you for ourselves without involving the agency first. Currently nobody is living in the castle and though we have two good friends keeping an eye on it, we really want it lived in again as soon as possible.' He looked at Jake before resting his eyes on her. 'Would you be able to fly out next week?'

Her heart leapt. 'To visit, or…?' She hardly dared to hope.

'To take care of it for a year. Maybe longer, if both parties are agreeable.'

For a few seconds she was so shocked, she didn't know how to react. 'I… I mean, we…' She felt Jake's hand clasp hers.

'What Anna's trying to say is yes, we definitely could.'

'Oh God, yes, of course we could. That's…' She drew in a breath, trying to calm herself when what she really wanted to do was jump up and down. Then she felt the squeeze of Jake's hand. A reminder that this wasn't just her job, it was *their* job. She might be going to live in a castle on Lake Como, but she couldn't do it without Jake. It was enough to temper her excitement. 'Thank you. We won't let you down.'

She risked a look at her 'partner'. He winked, a slow smile spreading across his face. How ironic that she was now the one unsure if this was the right move, and he was the one looking as if he couldn't wait to get there.

Chapter Seven

J ake hauled the second of Anna's cases off the carousel and onto the baggage trolley. Considering they were going to be in Italy for a year, he was secretly impressed she only had two. His sisters needed a huge case when they went away for a week.

Still, he wasn't going to resist a little dig. Especially as the woman was wound as tight as a duck's arse.

'Sure you brought enough clothes?'

She didn't acknowledge him, too focused on looking through the weighty folder she'd clung tightly to all day, as if it contained the keys to the castle. He guessed on one level it did, but...

'You know you didn't have to print all that crap out, right?' He pointed to his phone. 'It's all on here.'

Finally, she glanced up at him. 'Which is fine until the battery dies. Or you lose it.' Another rifle through the folder. 'Here it is. We're to be picked up by Marco. I think he was the neighbour they talked about who was keeping an eye on the place for them. Marco and Sara.' She scanned the note again.

'They'll pick us up from the short-stay carpark so we need to head there now. It will be quicker if you push the trolley.'

It was like having his very own travel guide, he thought as she marched off, her bum, encased in tight denim, swaying invitingly. But God, she was already driving him nuts and they'd not even arrived at the castle yet. Ever since Penny and Henry had – unbelievably – offered them the job, Anna had been like a woman possessed. He wasn't sure she'd even given herself time to be *happy* about it. She'd gone straight into monster organisation mode, flinging out instructions like a bloody drill sergeant.

He'd not been kidding when he'd told her one of his major dislikes was being told what to do.

'Hey.' She stopped marching to turn and look at him. 'Who put you in charge?'

She looked nonplussed. 'Someone has to get us where we need to be. You don't seem to be rushing to help.'

'No point when you've taken over.'

She looked down at her watch. 'We can stand here and bicker, or we can go and meet Marco and Sara and get to the castle.'

Reluctantly, he pushed the trolley forward. The airport was teeming with people: kids chasing each other, couples holding hands, men and women in suits striding towards the exit, briefcases in hand, designer cases trailing behind them like some sort of badge of honour. *Look at me, I'm so sophisticated I do business in Milan.* Well, for once he had something to crow about. He, Jake Tucker, was going to live in a sodding castle.

Which was why he didn't get Anna's angst. He'd figured she'd be excited too, but it was like this was all a chore now. 'Having second thoughts?'

'Of course not.'

'Could have fooled me. I've seen more enthusiasm in a school maths class.'

She swung round to face him. 'Can we not do this now?'

'Seems to be a perfect time. In about five minutes we've got to pretend to be in love and excited about this new adventure.' He could see the moment it dawned on her that Marco and Sara weren't just a taxi service. They were friends of their employers. People who would report back immediately if they sensed anything suspicious.

'Yes.' She seemed to shake herself. 'It's possible I've been so focused on the logistics I've blocked out what it is we're about to do.'

'You mean the bit about managing a stonking castle on a cool lake in Northern Italy. Or the bit about living together.'

She bit into her lower lip. 'The second one.'

And now he got it. A grin split his face. 'You're scared shitless of sharing this apartment with me.'

She glanced away briefly, then snapped her head back. 'I wouldn't put it that crudely but yes, fine, I am worried how we'll get on.' Her chin lifted in a defensive gesture. 'You can't tell me you've not had a few wobbles too since the interview.'

'Honestly?' He rubbed at his chin, glad to feel the stubble back. 'No. I'll miss Mum and my sisters but they'll come out and visit. Other than that, poncing about in a castle here versus retiling Freda's bathroom? No contest where I'd rather be.'

'And you're not worried about, you know, *us*?'

'You planning on poisoning my food?'

Her dark brows shot up. 'Not unless you really piss me off.'

'I'll bear that in mind.' An alarming thought occurred to him. 'Are you worried I'll jump you?'

'Jump me?'

'You know, bash down the door to your room, strip off

my clothes – though maybe I could do the stripping thing first. Anyway, somehow I'd end up naked in your room and—'

'I can work out the rest.'

She looked appalled – at the thought of seeing him naked? Him barging into her room? Both? He tried to see the situation from her side. 'Look, I get why you might be nervous. I'm an ex-con.' As always, the words tasted bitter on his tongue, as did the memory of what he'd had to endure to earn the label. 'You're wondering if you can trust me.'

'I'm not.'

Her response was fast and firm but he'd had two years of people reassuring him that of course he was still the guy they knew, before going on to blank him or, in the case of his old fire station, refusing to re-employ him. 'Wouldn't be human if you weren't.'

She blew out a frustrated breath. 'I'm worried we won't be able to keep up this cover of being a couple, that I'll not come up to scratch in the kitchen, that we won't work well together, that we'll spend so much time arguing we'll end up doing a poor job of taking care of the place and disappointing the Harpers.' She inhaled, her green eyes zeroing in on his. 'I'm not worried you'll jump me. Or punch me. Or run off with the silver.'

She looked so much like an annoyed school teacher that he started to chuckle. 'Fair enough.' There was a big gap between trusting someone and getting on with them, but at least one of the hurdles was out of the way. 'Is now a good time to suggest we try kissing?' Her face went so red he thought she was going to blow a gasket. 'Chill, I'm pulling your leg.' He started to push the trolley forwards again but as they headed towards the carpark, the devil on his shoulder couldn't resist adding.

'Our first time should be special. Not some hurried affair in a busy airport.'

He thought he'd got the last word in, but just before they stepped into the carpark lift, she muttered under her breath. 'Poisoning is sounding more and more tempting.'

Sitting in the back of Marco's car with Jake, Anna felt her shoulders and back begin to relax, the closer they came to their destination.

The last few days had been a blur of activity and stress. Heaps of stress. Would Miles provide a decent reference? Would the fire station? When those had thankfully come through, there had been the contract paperwork, sorting the travel, tying up loose ends. Packing. Jake was no help, though to be fair he'd been busy getting his powerboat licence. Besides, though she trusted he wouldn't hurt her – or jump her, as he'd so elegantly put it – she wasn't sure she could trust him with organising the most spontaneous, daring – and, she sensed, *important* – thing she'd ever done.

But now they were here, the towns flashing past, glimpses of the lake tempting her from between the houses and trees. She was in Italy, on the way to live in a castle.

'*È la prima volta che visiti il Lago di Como?*' Sara asked from the passenger seat.

Sara wasn't Marco's wife, Anna had quickly come to realise; she was his daughter. Apparently Rosa, the wife, had suggested Sara come along as she spoke better English. But as soon as Sara had realised Anna spoke Italian, she'd stuck mainly to her local tongue and while Anna had welcomed the chance to practise, Jake looked uncomfortable.

Anna replied, confirming yes, it was their first time visiting Lake Como. She glanced sideways at Jake and saw he was still staring out of the window.

Finally taking the hint, Sara switched to English. 'The castle is just up here. About five minutes' drive from Bellagio. You must visit the town when you, how do you say it? Settle in? It's very beautiful.' She glanced over her shoulder at them and winked. 'Romantic.'

Oh help. For a while there she'd forgotten she was supposed to be one half of a couple.

As if he'd forgotten too, Jake immediately flung his arm around her, pulling her against his side. 'Sounds good, but Anna doesn't lack romance.' He smirked down at her. 'Do you, babe?'

Her smile froze on her face. *Relax, woman.* But that was way too difficult when she could feel his warmth through her jacket, the coiled strength in the arm wrapped around her. He felt so different to Miles, bulkier, more muscular. He smelt different, too. Where Miles always wore expensive cologne, Jake smelt of the outdoors – fresh, rugged.

They rounded a corner and suddenly she forgot all about who was holding her as the castle came into view. 'Oh my God.' She sat bolt upright, heart hammering so fast she could barely breathe.

'Impressive, isn't it?'

Anna shook her head. Impressive was the manor house in Dorset where they'd had the interview. 'It's magnificent. Majestic. Like something from a fairy tale.' Red tiles on grey brick, it had a main tower with arched windows and turrets. Honest to God turrets. The small two-dimensional images on the job advert had done it a serious injustice.

Beside her, Jake cleared his throat. It was the only hint that he was as moved as she was. 'How many rooms does it have?'

Sara laughed. 'I have no idea. Mum might know. Enough that a hotel chain thinks they can turn it into a luxury boutique hotel.' She paused, eyes on the castle as Marco steered the car through the front gates. 'It's been in Henry's family for three generations, so it's very special to them. It's why they don't want to sell.'

'The son wants them to though,' Jake pointed out, his comment far more direct than Anna would have been.

Sara made a dismissive sound. 'He can do what he likes when he inherits but until then it's not his decision.'

'At the interview he said he was thinking of his parents.' Jake managed not to sound contemptuous. Just. 'Something about making life easier for them.'

Sara snorted. 'He thinks of the big bag of money he'd get from the hotel company.' Then she clamped a hand over her mouth. '*Merda!* I should not be saying this to you.'

Jake grinned. 'Hey, you can trust us. We're not going to snitch. We sensed he didn't want us to get the job.'

Uncomfortable with how Jake seemed to be intent on digging dirt, Anna shoved her elbow into his side in warning. Ignoring his startled look, she turned back to Sara.

'We're so grateful they gave us this chance to take care of their beautiful castle. I can't believe how lucky we are.'

'We're all here to help. I live with Mum and Dad in the villa next door. Not so big, but living by the lake, it is special – you will see. It's why I still live with my parents at the age of twenty-four,' she said on a laugh. As Marco pulled up outside the front entrance, she glanced at them both. 'You will make special memories while you are here.'

Jake started to laugh, but thankfully he turned it into a cough before it became obvious. 'That's what we're all about,' he managed, grasping her hand and bringing it to his lips. 'Making special memories.'

The gesture was ridiculous, but when Anna glared at him his eyes danced back at her and something weird happened to her pulse.

Hastily, she grabbed the door handle and jumped out of the car. Her heart lifted as she turned around, drinking it all in. The castle... a bloody castle, imposing yet so, so pretty set against the backdrop of the lake, surrounded by trees, snow-capped mountains in the background. 'I'm in love.'

Jake slid an arm around her waist. 'Sure you are, babe.' He waggled his eyebrows. 'But maybe we should wait until we're alone before you show me how much, huh?'

Couldn't he see his act was too much? Then the penny dropped. Of course he could; he was just winding her up, as always. She glared silently at him and he looked blankly back at her.

Sara translated Jake's words to the bemused Marco, who chuckled. 'We go soon.'

Marco began to haul the cases out of the boot and Sara walked up the steps to unlock the front door.

Suddenly Anna felt a hand under her legs and before she knew it she'd been lifted into Jake's arms. 'What the—? Put me down!'

Sara whipped her head round to look at them and Anna realised belatedly that she should be laughing, not glowering.

'Babe.' Jake stared down at her with stormy blue eyes, as if he really had been trying to be romantic and her rebuff had hurt. 'I just want to carry you over the threshold.'

Gritting her teeth, she threw her arms around his neck and slapped on a sweet smile. 'Sorry, darling. I forgot what a romantic you are.'

And if he'd been her real lover, if this hadn't just been a ploy to annoy her, she might have appreciated the charm of the gesture and the strength of the man who carried her effortlessly up the steps.

Once inside he let her down carefully, his body coiled tight. Why did he suddenly look like the injured party?

But then she glanced around her and their petty niggle was forgotten. It was... Words almost failed her. 'It's... sumptuous. Like a stately home, only cosier. Like I could live in it, rather than just stare in awe at it.'

'You *will* be living in it.' Sara started speaking Italian to her again, waving her arms, signalling for her to follow. 'Leave the men to sort the luggage. Come with me and see your new apartment. Then Marco and I will give you the grand tour and leave you to settle.' She winked. 'Maybe make use of the big bed.'

They climbed three flights of stairs. 'You live in the top of the tower,' Sara declared as she pushed open the huge wooden door and walked down a small hallway into what was clearly the living area. 'The views are magnificent, yes?'

Anna knew her jaw had fallen open. While the décor in the apartment was more comfortable than grand, it was the view from the windows overlooking the lake that made her gasp. 'Why don't Penny and Henry use these rooms?'

'You wait till you see theirs. They are lower, so the view is less dramatic, but they have so much space.' Sara's deep brown eyes were full of warmth. 'I think you will be happy here.'

Anna could only nod. There would be difficulties ahead, not least the small matter of living with Jake and not wanting to throttle him, but it was surely a small price to pay.

Chapter Eight

Jake stood next to Anna on the doorstep and watched as Marco and Sara climbed into their car.

'Don't forget, welcoming dinner at ours next week. Mum will make you a real Italian pizza,' Sara shouted as Marco ducked into the passenger seat.

'Can't wait,' Jake muttered under his breath as the car engine started. Marco and his daughter seemed okay, and maybe if it was just him going along, and they spoke English instead of Italian, he'd be looking forward to it. The thought of more tortuous hours pretending to be in love with Anna the Untouchable though... yeah, he could do without that.

'They're only being friendly.' Anna's smile slipped the moment Marco and Sara disappeared out of view. 'They seem nice.'

'Maybe. Or maybe Penny and Henry have asked them to spy on us.'

Her eyes narrowed. 'Are you always this suspicious of people?'

'Prison tends to have that effect.' He glanced sideways at

75

her. 'Thought you'd be suspicious too, considering what Miles did to you.'

A cloud crossed her face. 'Thanks for the reminder.' Her bearing stiffened. 'Anyway, if you do suspect they're spying on us, it was hardly a good idea to grill Sara for dirt on Nigel.'

The irritation that had started when she'd begun jabbering away in Italian in the car, increased when she'd dug him in the ribs like he was some unruly sidekick, and spiked when she'd glared and glowered every time he'd touched her, now boiled over. 'I was finding out how the land lies,' he replied tightly. 'Considering the guy doesn't want us in the job, I thought it would be useful information.'

'What about all that kissing my hand and carrying me over the threshold?' Her eyes shot arrows at him. 'You do realise how laughably over the top that looked?'

'Well, sorry for failing to act the part to your required standards. Maybe if you'd written some instructions on one of your blasted cards, I'd know what I'm supposed to do.' It was his turn to glare. 'And maybe if you stop acting like a nervous virgin every time I so much as touch you, we might have half a chance of convincing Marco and Sara we're a real couple come to take care of their mates' castle. And not a couple of poor con artists.'

Christ. He dragged a hand through his hair and stalked out. Turning right, he headed down to the calm of the lake, walking past the swimming pool, which was currently covered over. He guessed he'd be learning a lot about pool maintenance. And making fancy shapes out of trees, he mentally added as he carried on past the ornate gardens before reaching a boathouse and a wooden jetty that stretched out into the glistening green water. Walking to the end of the jetty, he hunkered down, crossed his legs in front of him, and inhaled a deep lungful of

Italian air before finally taking a moment to savour his surroundings.

'It's amazing, isn't it?' He'd been so engrossed he hadn't realised Anna had stepped onto the jetty. He watched her warily as she came to sit next to him. 'And the water looks inviting too, but I bet it's freezing.'

Fearing he was about to get pushed in, Jake steeled himself. If he was going in, she was coming with him.

'Much as I love a swim though,' she added, thankfully keeping her hands resting on the jetty, 'I'll wait and go in the pool.'

Unsure if that was a subtle hint to put *sorting pool out* at the top of his to-do list, he took the path least likely to rock the nervous truce she could be offering – and least likely to result in a lake dunking – and kept quiet.

'Have you been to Lake Como before?' She gave him a small smile. 'I told Sara we hadn't been, so I guess that might be one more lie we have to watch out for if you have.'

And that, he supposed, was her version of an olive branch. As he was going to have to live with her, he'd be stupid to turn it down. 'I've been abroad three times before now. Paris with a girlfriend for a long weekend. A mad week in Ibiza with a bunch of the guys from the fire station when I turned twenty-one. Another mad week with the same guys in Croatia two years later.' He screwed up his face as he tried to remember. 'I have a hazy recollection of clubs, dancing, and too much booze in the sun.'

She wrapped an arm around her legs, hugging them. 'Sounds… like the sort of holiday I can imagine you having.'

'Yeah?' He'd bet she had him pigeonholed as unsophisticated. 'No doubt you check out the art galleries and museums.'

She rolled her eyes. 'Hardly.' Her gaze shifted to the lake. 'For me it's always been about the food. Checking out the supermarkets, the local restaurants. I remember going with a guy to Paris and he was horrified when all I wanted to do was enrol us on a two-day cookery course. We broke up pretty soon afterwards.'

For the first time since he'd left his house this morning, Jake let out a genuine laugh. 'Poor bloke. At least when I went, the girl I was with didn't make me cook.'

Her attention turned back to him, and he couldn't help but think her eyes looked like the lake, green and shady. 'What happened to her?'

'Turns out Paris was okay, but she had her heart set on more glamorous destinations.' And what a kick in the teeth that had been to see a photo of her a few weeks later cuddling up to some floppy-haired guy in a swanky resort in Barbados. Apparently, Jake had been good enough to have sex with for ten months, good enough to go to Paris with for a dirty weekend that had cost him his entire savings, but not good enough to hold onto her the moment she'd found out he might end up in prison.

'You mean she ditched you for a better holiday?'

She'd ditched him for *a guy who's going places that don't include prison*. But he wasn't going to admit that to Anna. 'Had to be that. Can't see any other reason for dumping me.'

Anna rolled her eyes again but she didn't reply and for a few moments all he could hear was the gentle lap of water against the jetty and the swish of the trees.

'I thought you were only doing it to wind me up.' Her words punctured the quiet and when he turned to face her, she wore a wry smile. 'I didn't think you were the type to go for the hand-kissing and threshold-carrying.'

He huffed out a laugh. 'I'm not.'

'Then you *were* trying to annoy me.'

'Not at first.' He stared down at the water, wondering if Anna was right and he'd find his balls freezing off and floating next to him if he went for a swim in it. 'I guess I felt pissed off when you were all speaking Italian. Then when I tried to put my arm round you, you went stiff as a board, which hacked me off even more. I mean, we are supposed to be a couple. At least I'm trying to act like part of one.' It niggled him, the way she reacted to his touch. Sure, they were pretending, but he didn't mind putting his arm around her. Even reckoned he could enjoy kissing her.

'You're right. I'll be better.' She paused again and when she spoke this time, her voice was quieter, less sure. 'It felt strange, having your arm round me.'

He tried not to feel offended. 'I don't usually get that complaint.'

She let out a soft laugh. 'I bet.' Another pause, as if she was carefully planning what to say. 'I dated Miles for eighteen months, and lived with him for six of those.'

And now he understood. He shifted closer to her, smiling to himself as she eyed him warily. 'Chill. I'm just going to put my arm round you. Get you used to me.'

She fitted easily against him. Felt good too. Kind of soft and curvy which he was a fan of. Plus, he liked the smell of her hair.

'What do you reckon?' he asked after a while, surprised how content he felt right now. The tranquil setting, the quiet, his arm round an attractive woman. 'Think you can manage not to wince next time I do this?'

Anna drew in a breath, and tried to get her body and her mind to calm. Not easy when she was around Jake.

Even less easy when he had his arm round her.

'I think I can manage that.' Her brain scrambled to work out how she felt. When she'd first seen him on the end of the jetty she'd wanted to shove him in, but now she realised that was unfair. It wasn't his fault she didn't feel easy or comfortable being so close to him. He was at least trying to make this work.

'What about this?'

He dropped his arm from around her shoulders and reached for her hand. He'd held it before, as they'd headed into the interview, so it felt more familiar. Also more intimate, she thought with a jolt as she stared down at the long male fingers wrapped around hers.

She jerked her hand away from his grasp. 'I've got the message. When we see Sara and Marco I'll be fine.'

He nodded, a lazy smile playing round his mouth. 'Do we need to practise the kiss yet?'

And this was why she found it almost impossible to relax around him. 'I'm certain we can manage to act like a couple in front of others without needing to kiss.'

The left corner of his mouth lifted. 'Scared you'll enjoy it?'

There was some truth in his statement. She and Jake were worse than chalk and cheese; at least they both began with c. They wound each other up, irritated each other. Like two boxers in a ring, they both came out swinging, wanting to land a punch. Yet she'd reacted oddly to his touch. How much more confused would she be if he kissed her? 'I'm scared that even with a lot of practice, I won't enjoy it enough to be convincing.' Quickly, she jumped to her feet. 'We need to unpack and sort out what needs doing. Penny said the people who managed the place previously have left a file in the study so we should go through that and make a list.'

Jake eyed her from his sitting position, legs crossed, arms resting loosely on his thighs. He wore his black leather biker jacket paired with ripped jeans this time, and another black T-shirt. He dressed like he didn't give a damn what people thought. Probably he didn't. 'Do whatever you need to do. I'm staying here for a bit.'

'Fine. When do you want to meet to go through the file?'

He shrugged his big shoulders. 'Later.'

You knew he'd be hard to work with when you suggested this idea. 'How about six o'clock?'

'What's the rush?'

She drew in a breath, working hard to keep her voice even tempered. 'We have responsibilities. Don't you think it's important to at least familiarise yourself with the place tonight in case anything goes wrong?'

'It's survived the last week with nobody in it. I'm pretty certain it can survive another night without me rushing to find out where the stopcock is.'

Anna had a sudden flash of harsh reality. Take away the beauty of the setting, the joy of leaving the fallout of her split with Miles, and she was left having to live and work with a man who would drive her crazy. 'Well, I'm going to unpack and get organised.'

'Of course you are.'

God, she hated those little digs of his. 'What do you mean by that?'

He waved his hand at the lake. 'Why take a moment to sit and enjoy when you can sit and start making lists instead?'

'This isn't a holiday,' she pointed out, annoyed. 'We're *both* here to do a job.' Maybe she shouldn't have emphasised the *both*, because his eyebrows shot up.

'Worried I'm not going to pull my weight?'

She sighed, the early morning start catching up with her. 'I don't want another row. All I'm saying is I'd feel more reassured if we went through the file together so we can list out our respective responsibilities.'

'I didn't say I wouldn't do that.' He rose fluidly to his feet, his movements surprisingly nimble for such a big guy. 'But right now, I'm more interested in wandering down to that local bar we passed and having a beer.'

She waited for him to ask her to join him but he didn't. Instead he loped off towards the castle. The fact he'd turn up alone at the bar was hardly a glowing endorsement of their happy-couple status and flew in the face of everything he'd just said about putting on a good act. She was alarmed to realise she also felt hurt that he clearly preferred to be by himself rather than with her.

Make that hurt and lonely, she thought a short while later as she wandered through the castle, familiarising herself with the rooms. Each was so different. The rooms at the front were in the old part with high, ornate ceilings and stone floors. The walls were painted in muted colours which made the original features like the architraves and fireplaces really stand out. The kitchen, where she'd headed first – no surprise there – was about three times the size of the one she was used to cooking in at Miles's restaurant. It had a huge range cooker which was going to take some getting used to, but from the array of gleaming copper pots and pans hanging on the wall above it, she wasn't going to be short of things to put on it. The granite worktop gleamed, and the island in the middle looked perfect for food preparation.

But as beautiful as it all was, as unbelievable that she was here, the place felt eerie, the walls echoing as she made her way through, making her very aware that she was the only person there.

Thankfully, the solitary moment was broken as her phone started to ring. When she saw who it was, some of the loneliness lifted.

'Hey, Dad, I was about to call you. We're here!'

'And?'

She turned and headed towards the stairs and her – she winced, *their* – apartment. 'It's crazy beautiful. Like a film set. I'm not sure how I'm going to cope with taking care of it all or cooking in the largest kitchen I've ever worked in, but…' Her voice caught and she paused, trying to keep a handle on her emotions. She should be happy. This was what she wanted, wasn't it?

'Don't go getting the wobbles now.' Her dad's voice was firm yet achingly familiar. 'You've coped with running our house since your mother left. If you can do that at ten, you can manage a castle at thirty.'

She smiled through the tears. 'But I had you to help me.'

He huffed out a breath. 'I wasn't much help, if I recall. And anyway, you've got Jake.'

Did she have him, she wondered? Or now that he was here, was he going to repeat what he'd done tonight and run off and do his own thing, leaving her to manage the place alone?

'Anna?'

'Yes, sorry.' She couldn't worry her dad, so she forced a cheery tone. 'I'll be fine and you're right, I've got Jake.'

There was a pause on the end of the line and when her dad spoke again, she knew he'd seen right through her. 'Do you want me to have a word with Sheila? The lad doesn't listen to many people, but he listens to her.'

She groaned. 'I can just imagine how well that would go down. No thanks. I was the one who wanted this. He's doing me a favour. I'll work it out.'

'He's not doing it from the goodness of his heart. He's with you because he needed the break, too. Don't let him shirk his responsibilities.' He paused. 'Despite the troubles he's had, he's not a bad lad. I wouldn't have let you go with him if I thought he was.'

Anna laughed. 'Let me? Have you forgotten I've grown up?'

'You'll always be my little girl. And I'll always look out for you whether you want me to or not.'

Her heart squeezed and in that moment, she wanted to be back home receiving one of her dad's hugs, him telling her everything would be all right. Just as he had in those dark days when her mum had left.

But then she glanced out of the window at the view and shook herself. This was going to work. It had to. She'd make sure of it.

Chapter Nine

Jake stood at the bar, bottle of Peroni in hand – when in Italy – and looked around him. Not exactly humming. Then again, it was mid-week and off-season, so maybe it wasn't surprising.

He took a slow sip of the lager and smiled at the blonde barmaid who, thank God, was from London.

'We've not seen you here before.' She gave him a coy look from beneath her eyelashes. 'I'd have remembered.'

'Just moved here.'

'Oh.' In what looked like a calculated move, she nibbled at her bottom lip. 'We'll hopefully be seeing a lot of you then.' Another smile. 'I'm Phoebe.'

'Jake.' He took another swig. 'Good to meet someone who speaks English.'

'You'll be okay here. Will, who owns the place, is from Blackpool originally.'

He gave a silent cheer. He'd have people to talk to besides Anna. The thought of her sitting alone in the castle sent a dart of guilt through him.

Her choice, he reminded himself.

You didn't ask her if she wanted to come, his better half retorted.

'So, what brings you to Lake Como?'

Phoebe's question was accompanied by another admiring look from her big blue eyes. He wasn't unused to female attention. It seemed some women went for tattooed guys with a bad-boy rep and hair in need of a good cut. But unlike at home, where he'd been happy to take up some of the offers, out here he wasn't free and single. Even if he had been, he wasn't sure he'd have flirted with Phoebe. He preferred a bit of a challenge.

It had to be why he kept asking Anna to practise kissing. He wasn't sure he really wanted to kiss her – strike that. He was very sure kissing her wasn't a good idea. If it sucked, it would be embarrassing and make it even harder to live with her. If it didn't suck… yeah, it would also be hard to live with her because then he'd want to do it again. Still, he was pretty certain she'd never agree, so he couldn't see the harm in sparring with her, getting a rise out of her. Not when he enjoyed it so much.

Aware he'd not answered Phoebe's question, he placed the bottle on the bar and looked her straight in the eye. 'We're here to manage Castello sul Lago.'

Her blonde eyebrows bounced. 'We?'

'I'm here with my… Anna.' Crap, he didn't know how they were supposed to refer to each other. Partner? Girlfriend? Girl? Lady/woman? Other half?

Phoebe looked confused and the guilt that had slithered into his gut began to feel heavier. Why would a guy abandon his girl on the first night of their new adventure?

Because the girl in question wanted to make blasted lists.

But he'd known what Anna was like when he agreed to this. She'd been the teacher's pet at school – so his ex, the one who'd been in the same class as Anna, had gleefully informed him. The one with the neatest homework that everyone wanted to copy, the one who always had the right textbooks with her, who turned up on time.

And if it hadn't been for her diligence, her organisation, he'd be slumped in front of his crappy TV in his dive of a rental right now.

Guilt won and he downed the rest of the bottle. Just as he turned to go, a dark-haired guy came out from the back and greeted him with a '*Buonasera.*'

Taking a punt, Jake nodded. 'And to you, mate.'

The man laughed. 'A fellow Brit.' He stuck out a hand. 'I'm Will.'

Jake grasped it. 'Jake. Just moved into Castello sul Lago which is about the only Italian I know.'

'I've lived here for two years and still find it hard so you're doing me a favour by sticking to the mother tongue.' He cocked his head. 'Are you one half of the couple who've come to take care of the place for Penny and Henry?'

'Yep. Me and Anna.' Will glanced around and Jake felt that damn guilt prick again. 'I'm the less conscientious half. She's back at the castle, making lists, so I snuck out for a bit.'

'Lists?' Will gave him a sympathetic look. 'Good luck with that, mate. I reckon you'll get an earbashing when you get back.'

'Nothing I'm not used to.' He was more bothered that she might not talk to him at all.

'Well, Steve and June, the people before you, came here a

lot so I hope you guys will do the same.' He laughed. 'The bar takings will sure miss Steve.'

Jake grinned. 'I'll do my best to make up for it.'

'You do that. And if you need any help finding local suppliers or tradesmen, Steve constantly used to bend my ear back about issues he had so I've probably got a fair amount of useless-but-might-possibly-become-useful info stored here.' He tapped his head.

'Sounds good to me.'

'And tell your wife the same if she wants local food suppliers.'

'Anna's not my wife.' Christ, there couldn't possibly be two people less suited to marrying each other. Will was still looking at him, so he forced a smile. 'Still practising, you know?'

Will laughed. 'Well, working and living at the castle is about as good a warm-up as you're going to get.'

Jake was just starting to realise it. Except he wouldn't even be getting any sex out of it. He shook Will's hand again. 'See you around.'

'Bye, Jake.' Phoebe caught his eye as he turned to leave. 'Don't be a stranger.'

He smiled back but his mind was already back at the castle. And how much trouble he'd be in.

He found the door locked, and made a mental note to make sure he had a set of keys with him next time he decided to have a fit of pique.

'Hey.' He tried a smile when she finally answered his bell-ringing, her expression closed off.

She glanced at her watch, and then at him. 'Got bored, did you?'

Funny how she knew exactly how to rub him up the wrong way. 'Hardly. The barmaid was blonde and from London.'

Her expression tightened. 'I realise this was my idea, but when you agreed to it, I thought there was an understanding between us that you'd play your part.'

'I am doing.' Frustrated, yet also aware he wasn't blameless, Jake stepped inside. 'Look, I had one beer, introduced myself to the barmaid and the owner, Will, who's also from England. Told them *we*'—he emphasised the word—'were here to manage this place. Then I came back.'

She nodded and turned to walk through the entrance hall and over to the archway that led to the tower staircase. He followed her, eyes on her backside – a view he was really starting to enjoy. He imagined it would be firm to the touch, but not bony. A bum to really clutch onto, to squeeze and fill his hands with…

Shit. He was getting hard.

Think of the lists she's been making. Yep, that did the trick.

'You could have come with me,' he said as she went to sit down on the red velvet corner sofa in their small but fancier-than-anything-he'd-ever-lived-in-before sitting room.

Anna swallowed the retort she wanted to make: *you didn't ask.* It sounded too needy. Of course she hadn't needed his permission to go with him. And the fact she was put out he'd not offered was on her.

'I wanted to get a feel for this place. And to read the file Steve and June left us.' She nodded down to where she'd left it on the large dark-wood coffee table.

He bent to pick it up, idly flicking through it. 'Did you learn anything useful?'

'You need to read it. It contains all the information on what needs doing when, where to find equipment and tools, instructions for how to use them. Did you realise there's a—'

'Swimming pool that will need maintaining? Fountain that doesn't work? Boat that will require servicing?' he asked sardonically.

Okay, so he'd taken notice while he'd been wandering outside. He didn't have to be so smug about it. Despite her annoyance, she felt a twinge of relief. 'I've written down what I think are my responsibilities and what I think are yours. If you want to take a look, we can discuss them.'

He barely glanced at the sheet of paper. 'Fine.'

'You're not going to read it?'

He wandered over to the fridge in the open-plan kitchen and poked his head inside. 'You're on inside duty, I'm on outside. Unless something needs fixing inside.'

She supposed that was a pretty good summary of what she'd taken the last hour to compile. But still. 'There's more to it than that. Penny and Henry want regular updates and we need to plan what we're going to do when we have guests. Obviously I'll be in charge of the meals, but there will be other things like shopping for the food and collecting guests from the airport.'

He shut the fridge door and cast his eyes over the worktop. Spotting a bottle of red wine they'd been left, he waved it at her. 'Fancy a glass? I was hoping for a beer but there's nothing in the fridge.'

'I'm fine, thanks.' She watched with interest as he dug about in the drawers for a corkscrew and struggled to uncork the bottle. After pouring himself a glass he sauntered over to the sofa in that loose-limbed way he had, eased himself down, and placed his feet up on the coffee table. 'The list?' she reminded him.

He stared blankly at her. 'What about it?'

'Do you agree to it?'

He sipped at his drink, wincing. 'Never been a fan of wine.'

'Maybe you've been drinking the wrong wine.'

He gave her a lazy smile. 'Then it's lucky I've got an expert with me to show me the error of my ways.' Raising his glass, he looked over at her. 'What do you think? Colour okay? Looks pretty red to me.' He took a sniff. 'Smells grapey enough.'

With a huff she went to the bottle and poured herself a glass, then took a moment to savour the aroma before taking a sip. 'It's a Barolo from the Piedmont region, which isn't far from here. Made from the Nebbiolo grape, it's rich and full-bodied with aromas of cherries and fruitcake. It happens to be one of my favourites.' It was her turn to smirk at him. 'Maybe it's too refined for your taste buds.'

'Probably.' He took another sip. 'Guess I can get used to it. I've got used to worse things, that's for sure.'

A shadow crossed his face and it didn't take a genius to work out what he was thinking. 'How bad was it?' she asked quietly, unable to imagine how awful it must have been to be locked away for six months.

'How bad was what?'

He had to know what she meant, but she clarified anyway. 'Prison.'

For a second he just stared at her, those bold eyes searching hers, looking for God knows what. 'You want the dirt on how many times I got rogered or shanked?'

Stung, she glared back at him. 'You're such a jerk. Why do you always have to twist everything I say?'

'I'm just clarifying what you want to know.'

'You're not. You're mocking me, like you always do.' She rose to her feet. 'I'm off to bed. I guess I'll see you around. If you have an issue with anything on the list, you can take it up with me tomorrow.'

He remained irritatingly silent, just sitting there, drinking the wine he didn't even like.

'Happy first day,' she muttered under her breath as she turned to leave, taking the wine with her. At least she could enjoy that in the privacy of her room. Better alone than with Jake's smug, mocking presence.

She'd reached the door when he spoke again. 'Which bedroom have you picked?'

Coming to a halt, she turned to face him. 'I haven't yet. I was waiting for you, but now I'm going to put my stuff in the one with the en suite that also happens to have the best view and the biggest bed.'

'Fair enough.' His mouth curled up at one side. 'For the record, I'd have let you have it anyway. When you've slept on a single bed in a six-by-nine cell, anything else feels like luxury.'

She supposed it was an apology of sorts, but it was too little too late. 'You know this was supposed to have been a night of celebration.'

'You're the one walking away.'

Exasperated with him, she raised her eyes to the ceiling. 'Thanks, blame it all on me. In fact, you can keep blaming me for the next twelve months. I was stupid to think you and I could possibly live and work together but now we're stuck with it.' Her voice caught on the last few words. Determined not to cry, she swallowed and raised her chin. 'I suggest we keep out of each other's way while it's just the two of us here.

At least that way we might both make it through the year without committing murder.'

Holding tight to her emotions, she walked out, taking care to shut the door as calmly as she could behind her.

A dream job in a dream location, but sadly with the wrong person by her side.

You don't need him to make this a success, she reminded herself as she sat on the bed a short while later, watching the lights of the villages and towns around Lake Como reflect off the water. Lifting her wine glass, she raised a toast in the empty room. 'Here's to the next twelve months.' Crossing her fingers, she added, 'Whatever it brings, please God I'm ready for it.'

When she woke the following morning and glanced out of the window, the sight that greeted her was one she really *wasn't* ready for.

Jake, wearing only a pair of black trunks, was walking back from what had clearly been an early swim in the lake. Unable to help herself, she pressed her nose further against the window, staring down at him as he strode across the lawn.

Her heart quickened, and between her legs she felt an embarrassing flush of arousal. The man was maddening, infuriating, but he was also, honest to God, the sexiest sight she'd ever seen. Wide shoulders, sculptured muscles, a well-defined six-pack. Thighs that looked carved out of stone. Oh and tattoos: one she'd not seen before on the top of his right arm, another that ran up his left arm and then across the upper part of his chest, ending in a blaze across the left pec. From here it looked like it was a big cat of some sort.

She'd never thought tattoos particularly sexy. Until now.

Shaking herself, she stepped away from the window and into the shower. There she turned the dial to cold and tried to rid the images from her mind. She could not afford a crush on Jake Tucker. It would make life unbearable.

Chapter Ten

Jake briefly patted his groin as he set off to the pool-house. Yep, his balls were still intact. Fuck, the lake had been cold though.

Anna had been right. Then again, she'd probably been right about a lot of things last night. It was just that he hadn't been in the mood to hear them. He was going to have to get used to her ways and stop being so damn touchy around her.

She was an organiser. He needed to embrace it, be *grateful* for it, because one of them needed to be.

She was also going to ask him personal questions. Unless he wanted to be permanently at loggerheads with her, he had to suck it up and answer. Maybe she wasn't asking so she could needle him. Maybe she was asking because she was *interested*.

He knew he'd been a dick about the prison question. And the list. And if he was honest, waltzing off to the bar without her, too.

Clutching the pool manual, he opened up the fancy timber pool-house and made his way to the service room. She wanted to swim in a pool; he could make that happen. Though apparently first he had to clean the filters, vacuum the floor, brush the walls, check the pH and chemical levels, and top up the water.

Whatever she'd put on her list for him this morning, it would have to wait.

Several hours later he sauntered back up to the castle – yep, that giant Disney building in front of him was his frigging home for the next twelve months. He couldn't resist a smirk to himself: from prison cell to Italian castle.

All thanks to Anna.

Some of the spring left his step. Time to eat humble pie.

The castle had more rooms than he'd been prepared to count – he'd got bored after twenty – but it wasn't difficult to find her. He just had to head to the kitchen. Not the small one they had in their tower flat, but the huge one with the monster island and a lorry load of pots and pans hanging on the wall.

She was crouching down, searching through one of the cupboards, her dark hair tied back. When he coughed, she looked up with a start. He watched as her expression went from surprised to cool. 'Yes?'

Okay, so now he wished he'd taken a moment to actually think about what he was going to say.

'I've fixed the pool. It's ready to use.'

'Oh.'

Clearly, she was still mad at him. 'Is that all you have to say?'

Slowly she rose to her full five-and-a-half-foot height. 'Sorry, did you want congratulations? A *jolly well done*?'

Jesus, she wound him up. 'Wouldn't harm.'

'Then consider them bestowed upon you.' A stray strand of hair came loose from its elastic and as she tucked it behind her ear he had an urge to go up and pull the damn band off. To ruffle her hair with his hands until it cascaded around her face. 'Have you read the list of responsibilities I put together yet?'

He sighed, shoving his hands in his pockets. 'Give me a break. I've been working on the damn pool all morning.'

'Well, if you'd bothered to read it, you'd have seen there are more important jobs. We don't actually need the pool to be operational until we get the first of the guests.' Her and her sodding lists. As he quietly seethed, she gave him a perplexed look. 'Oh, I guess *you* wanted to use it. It must be a lot warmer than the lake.'

'*I'm* happy with the ball-freezing lake.'

She gave him a blank look. 'Right.'

You came here to apologise. Tell her you did it for her. He opened his mouth, but the words wouldn't come out. He felt as if he'd been slapped. The kid who'd brought his parents a cup of tea, only to be told they didn't want it because it was cold. And the stupid thing was, his parents had never been like that. It was only Anna who'd ever managed to make him feel small. Scratch that, Anna and her dad. Clearly, it was a Roberts superpower.

'What do you want me to start on then?' And yes, now he sounded surly which would only get her back up even more, leading to another blasted argument.

'God, Jake, I'm not your boss.'

He sighed, wondering if there would ever come a time when he and Anna could actually talk to each other without griping. 'You wrote down a list of my responsibilities. Sounds pretty bosslike to me.' And yep, he wasn't helping the situation.

'If I were your boss, I'd have sacked you by now,' she

muttered, turning away from him and walking towards a large cupboard.

'On what grounds?'

She tugged out what looked like several giant carrier bags. 'Being a jerk.'

He had to fight not to smile. 'At least you've only got another 364 days to put up with me.'

'Thank God it's not a leap year.'

This time he saw her lips twitch, too. Feeling like they'd navigated onto calmer waters, he nodded to the bags. 'What am I filling them with?'

'Food.' She gave him a wide, overly bright smile. 'We're going shopping.'

He groaned, wondering how long those waters were going to remain calm with him trailing round the supermarket after her. 'Told you I hate being told what to do.'

'True, but then you did ask, so...' She pushed the bags into his hands.

'And how are we getting to these shops?' Please God she wasn't going to drag him on a bus.

She plucked a key out of her jeans pocket and dangled it in front of him. 'If you'd read the file, you'd know there's a car for us to use in the garage. They've already put us on the insurance.'

He snatched the key from her hands. 'Fine. I'll drive.'

Quick as a flash, before he had time to work out what she was doing, she grabbed it from him. 'It's got four wheels, not two.'

'Funny.' He looked down at her – physically. Mentally he knew she was way above him. 'I have a licence for two and four wheels.'

She looked smug. 'And how many times have you driven on the right side of the road?'

She had him there. He knew it, and she knew it. But he'd never backed down in his life. Even though it had once put him in jail. 'I'm sure I can manage.' He raised an eyebrow. 'Unless you want to do all the guest pick-ups?'

That had evened the score. No way would Miss Organised want to slog off to the airport when she could waft through the castle making sure everything was ready.

'Fine. I just need to—'

'Make a list?'

He watched amusement vie with annoyance as she held his stare. 'Check what we need.' Her lips curved. It was only a fraction, but his heart made a funny jump in his chest. 'And then make a list.'

As she marched off to the large walk-in pantry he tried to work out why seeing her smile was so important.

Same reason you fixed the pool, dumb arse. He wanted to say it was his way of apologising, but deep down he knew there was another reason. He was starting to like her.

If there was one task that almost beat cooking food, it was shopping for it. Especially when the shops were in a different country. And even better when you had a guy to haul the shopping into the car.

Anna glanced sideways at Jake as he drove them back to the castle. Apparently it didn't matter that he was driving on the right for the first time. He drove with the same laconic ease with which he did most things. The sure touch of his hands on the steering wheel had her wondering if he made love the same way: fluidly, confidently. His powerful tattooed body moving rhythmically...

Groaning inwardly, she dragged her gaze away and told herself to remember what a jerk he had been yesterday. And how he'd spent this morning sorting out the pool instead of the more urgent tasks Steve and June had set out, like getting the trees pruned, the grass mowed. Fixing the shower in one of the bedrooms.

I'm happy with the ball-freezing lake. She still couldn't work out why he'd started on the pool first if he didn't want to swim in it. Had he done it because he'd not given any thought to which jobs were most urgent? Or simply because he knew she didn't want him to do it? She wouldn't put that past him, and yet... for all her gripes, she didn't think he was that contrary. Plus, he hadn't read her list, so he didn't know it wasn't on there for this week.

'Wondering how it's possible for a guy to be so good-looking?' He caught her eye and gave her his trademark crooked grin.

Damn it. Mortified to be caught staring, she averted her gaze and stared out of the front windscreen. 'Humble, too. How refreshing.'

'Ah, so you admit I'm good-looking then?'

This time when she looked at him she gave him a deliberate scrutiny. 'I suppose you must be. I have standards, even in fake partners.'

He gave her a brief, sardonic look. 'If Miles made the bar, anyone can.'

'Thanks for the reminder.' Embarrassed, she turned away. It was one thing to feel stupid at not seeing Miles for the lying cheat that he was, and another for Jake to rub her nose in it.

'What do you women see in him?'

The question was asked so quietly Anna wasn't sure it was one. And when she risked a furtive glance at him he was looking straight ahead.

'He can be charming.'

'Yeah?' His expression tightened. 'But mostly he's a monumental arsehole.'

'You're not going to find me disagreeing with that.' When Jake didn't reply, she glanced at him, and was surprised to find a grin playing around his mouth. His very attractive mouth. 'What are you smiling at?'

He shrugged, lips still curved upwards, grooves peeping. 'You agreed with me.'

She had to fight not to smile back. 'Well, there's a first time for everything.'

The rest of the journey took place in silence, but for once it wasn't strained. Anna watched the scenery flash past and felt a small lift of her heart. Last night had been a low point but maybe things would get better from now on.

As Jake drove through the castle gates though, her phone pinged with an email. When she tapped to read it, her heart sank again.

'Damn it. Nigel's coming to stay next week.'

'Speaking of arseholes,' Jake muttered as he parked up outside the front door.

'We don't know him so we shouldn't judge.'

Jake shook his head as he eased out of the car. 'I know the type.'

'Takes one to know one?' she queried sweetly as she reached into the boot to help him take in the shopping bags.

His jaw clenched. 'If you think I'm an arsehole, why did you ask me to come here?'

'It was a joke. Since when have you become so sensitive?'

He stared at her a moment, eyes as bright as the blue sky behind him. As they locked on hers, she felt another flutter of attraction. Shit. Ever since she'd seen him in his trunks, her body had started a *whoa, this guy is really hot* vibe. She needed to squash it, fast. Having a crush on him might help their pretending, but it would make living with him hell. He was cocky enough as it was.

With another shake of his head he broke his gaze and started to haul the bags out. The veins popped on his forearms, visible where he'd pushed up the sleeves. *Stop looking*. Dragging her gaze away, she hurried up the steps ahead of him.

'Right,' he said as he dumped the last of the bags onto the island. 'Where's this blasted list of jobs that's so important?'

When she told him it was up in their apartment, he nodded and stalked off, hands in his pockets. *Normal service has been resumed*, she thought grimly as she forced her gaze away from his retreating back – and tight, neat backside – and focused on putting away the food. But as she worked, the niggle from earlier returned. Why had he fixed the pool? She had a suspicion that she knew, and if she was right, it made her reactions to him earlier feel churlish. He'd been a jerk last night, no question. But she had an awful feeling she'd been the jerk this afternoon.

It was after seven when he finally appeared in their living area. His hair was even shaggier than usual, his hands dirty and his now damp T-shirt clung to his chest.

'Don't say anything,' he muttered darkly when she raised an eyebrow. Grabbing a glass out of the cupboard, he filled it with water and proceeded to drink it all without pausing for breath.

'Thirsty work?' She tried not to smile, but it was hard when he looked so disgruntled.

'You can cross fixing the first-floor shower off your list.'

'Great.' Her lips twitched. 'Looks like the shower fought back.'

Shoving the glass onto the worktop, he glowered at her. 'I won.'

Oh God, he was too funny when he was annoyed. 'That's why you've got the bad-ass rep.'

Another glower. 'Anything else you need me to do before I clean up?'

And that's why she was starting to like him, she realised. He might rebel against her lists, but already he was proving he wasn't afraid of hard work. 'Nope. Just, you know, maybe take this shower with your clothes off?'

His eyes found hers, his expression daring her to laugh, and it was hard, so hard, to keep a straight face. But then suddenly his face broke into that trademark cocky grin. 'Want to come and watch, eh?'

Thankfully, he turned away before he could see how flustered he'd made her. Why was it as soon as she thought she had the upper hand, he pinched it away from her?

When he came back out, wet hair slicked back, dressed in jogging bottoms and a T-shirt, she'd managed to collect herself.

He dived straight for the fridge, then frowned. 'Why did you move the beer?'

'Bottom shelves are for raw meat and fish because that's where the fridge is coldest. Middle shelves for dairy, top one is warmest so that's where we keep stuff that doesn't need cooking. Like beer.'

He stared at her as if she had a screw loose. 'What if I like my beer really cold?'

'I'd rather you had warm beer than I get food poisoning.'

He muttered under his breath as he dragged out a bottle and unscrewed the cap.

'There's chilli in the pot if you want it. Rice is in the pan next to it.'

Bottle poised in front of his mouth, he froze before lowering it down again. 'You cooked for me?'

'I cooked for me,' she lied. 'You can have the leftovers.'

He eyed her like he didn't believe her, then lifted the lid of the pot simmering on the hob and inhaled. 'Hell, that smells good.' His brow quirked. 'You know it's my favourite?'

From her seat on the sofa she tried a casual shrug. 'We're fake partners. I've put a great deal of effort into knowing such details about you.'

He frowned, clearly struggling with the mixed messages. 'Any reason you made chilli?'

'Any reason you fixed the pool this morning?'

Understanding dawned and he smirked. 'Touché.' She watched as he shovelled some rice into a bowl and topped it with an eyewatering amount of chilli. Then, after picking up his beer and a large serving spoon from the drawer he sat on the sofa next to her. As he began to dig in, he nodded his approval. 'Tastes as good as it looks.' There was silence for a minute as he continued to devour it. 'Sorry I was a dick yesterday,' he said after a while.

He didn't look at her and she sensed apologising wasn't something he did very often.

'Sorry I snapped this morning. Though in my defence, I only did it because you were such a dick yesterday.'

'Yeah, yeah.' Another pause while he spooned more chilli into his mouth. She tried to imagine Miles, or any of her boyfriends, eating chilli with a serving spoon, and couldn't. 'For the record, prison is a hot button for me.'

She could understand that. 'Mine is Miles.'

Finally, he looked at her. 'Is that all? Pretty sure I've pressed more than one.'

Amusement made his eyes glitter and once again she felt the power of his attraction. 'Pretty sure you'll keep pressing them, too,' she retorted, mainly to remind herself that no matter how sexy she was starting to find him, he was still the same guy who took great delight in butting heads with her.

Chapter Eleven

He'd thought they were going round for a casual get-to-know-you pizza, but when he walked up Marco and Rosa's drive with Anna, Jake could hear music. And when they followed it round the back and looked in through the big patio windows, they saw the house buzzing with people.

His heart sank. He wasn't antisocial, but not speaking the language was a bit of a handicap to meeting locals. As was putting on an act. He glanced at Anna, whose expression looked as wary as his.

'Two years,' he reminded her.

'What?'

'That's how long we've been together. I was attracted to your—'

'I remember.'

'And you were attracted to my huge—'

'Ego.' She bit into her lip. 'I know it sounds stupid, but I'd forgotten about this part.'

'You mean how you're supposed to be madly in love with me?'

'Yes.'

Irrationally annoyed that she seemed so upset at the thought of having to act as if she at least liked him, he grasped her hand. 'We don't have to be one of those couples who sticks to each other like glue, you know.' Though if she wandered off, he'd be stuck if they all spoke Italian.

She slid him a sideways glance. 'I'm getting used to that. It's not like I've seen you much these last few days.'

'Is that a dig?'

She exhaled. 'I guess it's more of a question. Where have you been?'

'Exploring. Not much point coming out here and not making the most of it. You should do the same.'

'Maybe I will, when I've got time.'

'Maybe if you weren't so obsessed with your lists, you'd have time.'

'Maybe if I didn't have so much to do, I wouldn't need to be so obsessed with lists.' She glanced down at their clasped hands, grimaced, then squared her shoulders. 'Let's do this.'

The way she treated pretending to like him as if it was one of the nasty chores on her to-do list pissed him off. He knew women who actually *wanted* to be all over him.

Pulling her towards him, he stared down at her. 'Let's do *this*.' As her big green eyes widened in surprise, he bent and kissed her. It was brief, just a press of his lips against hers, but shit, he felt the tingle from it race through him, touching parts he really didn't want reacting just as he was about to walk into a crowd of people.

She gasped, pupils so dilated her eyes looked black. 'What was that for?'

Because I wanted to. The realisation sat uneasily with him. How long since he'd been with a woman who'd actually wanted his mouth on her? Apparently too long. 'Now if I kiss you in there,' he nodded to the party, 'you won't act like a startled deer.'

She didn't get a chance to reply because the doors opened and Marco appeared, a broad grin on his face. 'Ciao! Welcome, welcome.' He waved his hands, gesturing them to come in, a string of Italian words tripping off his tongue that sailed over Jake's head. Anna replied though, the mouth he'd just kissed now forming a warm smile.

As he watched Marco introduce Anna to an older Italian woman, it struck him how bloody gorgeous she was. Not just attractive, he was starting to realise. There was more to her than that. She had a luminous quality, something that set her apart from all the women he'd ever met. Maybe it was the Italian part of her, maybe the fact that her dark good looks hid an impressive inner steel. Something he'd not appreciated until now. How else had she picked herself up from being kicked in the teeth by Miles and, just two weeks later, ended up managing a castle on Lake Como?

He felt a tug on his hand. 'This is Rosa, Marco's wife.' Anna's smile was too wide, too false. 'Apparently they mentioned they were having us over tonight and the rest of the village decided to turn up and greet us, too. Isn't that amazing?'

The evening was going from bad to worse. The language barrier was tough enough, but he was also uncomfortably aware of how he looked next to Anna. It didn't matter when he was her neighbour, winding her up, but now that he was supposed to be her partner, he felt the gulf between them. She was a professional chef, a dark-haired, classy beauty. He'd been chatted up enough to know he was good-looking, but suddenly the ridiculousness of him and Anna as a couple hit him. He was the scrappy tomcat next to her sleek pedigree. Their relationship might not be real, but he didn't like the idea of these people whispering behind his back. *'Surely she could do so much better than him?'*

Her elbow contacted with his side and he found her glaring up at him.

'Sorry.' He forced a smile. 'That's… great.'

Thankfully Rosa wasn't put off by his pathetic response. She clapped her hands, said something in Italian, and gave him an enthusiastic kiss on each cheek. Before he knew it, she'd propelled him into the house and he was being introduced to people whose names he had no hope of remembering: Giuseppe, Maria, Franco, Sofia… The faces blurred and the smile froze on his face.

Half an hour later, he was so happy to see Anna again that his greeting – wrapping an arm round her waist and planting a kiss on the top of her head – was entirely genuine.

Anna, who'd been chatting away in Italian to Sara, gave him a bemused look. 'Everything okay?'

'Sure.' He turned on his full smile. 'Just pleased to see you, babe.'

Sara looked sympathetic. 'Mum is… what do you call it? I think… a social animal? She forgets not everyone else is.'

'It's not that, at least not so much.' He found it hard to concentrate when he could feel the heat of Anna's body against his side, the soft curve of her waist against his palm. 'I don't speak any Italian.'

Anna shifted sufficiently away that he was forced to drop his hand from her waist. Then she smiled overly brightly at him. 'I'll have to teach you, darling.'

The move away felt like a slight, and the offer to teach him made him feel even less her equal: the scrappy, *uneducated* tomcat.

'You should do that,' Sara said, looking at Anna with something like awe. 'You are so fluent. You speak like a local.'

'Thanks, but your English is pretty great.' As Sara shrugged off the compliment, Anna added, 'I had a head start. My mum was… is Italian.' She stumbled over the words and Jake forgot his prickly annoyance long enough to feel a dart of sympathy for the daughter abandoned by her mother. 'I did brush up a bit before I came here though.' Of course she did. Anna the girlie swot, ever prepared. She glanced up at him. 'I should have given you some lessons, too.'

Oh yeah, he could just imagine how much she'd enjoy listening to him mangle the language she spoke so fluently. It probably explained why, when he spotted a blonde head across the room, he decided to excuse himself. 'I'll catch you later. I've just seen someone I know.' *And who I can actually speak to without needing bloody lessons*, he added silently.

———

Anna watched with mounting embarrassment as Jake sloped over to talk to the pretty blonde with the spectacular cleavage, who'd just given him a wide, familiar smile.

Sara clearly saw the direction of her gaze. 'Have you met Phoebe yet?'

'No.' Yet it was more than obvious Jake had. Maybe during one of his many excursions, while she'd been left changing sheets and cleaning. If she'd realised how many rooms there were in the castle, she might have split their responsibilities differently.

'She works at the local bar.'

Anna remembered the conversation that first night. *The barmaid was blonde and from London.* 'This is the same bar run by an English guy called Will?'

'Yes.' Sara eyed her questioningly. 'You don't go there yet?'

'No. Jake popped in there the first night we arrived while I unpacked.' Because she was aware how bad it looked, she smiled. 'He travelled lighter than I did.'

'Ah yes, I understand. I find it hard packing for a two-week holiday. A whole year.' She grinned. 'That would be very difficult.'

Anna tried to focus on Sara and not on Jake, who was laughing at something Phoebe said, his face as relaxed as she'd ever seen it. It made her realise he never looked so at ease with her.

'I wonder if we will see Will later.'

Anna dragged her gaze from Jake. 'Are he and Phoebe an item?'

'Oh no. At least, I don't think so.' There was hesitation in Sara's voice.

'This Will, is he good-looking?' She waggled her eyebrows. 'Single?'

Sara covered her face with her hands and started to giggle nervously. 'Maybe.'

Anna found she was really warming to the younger woman. She seemed so open and easy to talk to.

'He doesn't notice me though.' Sara sighed. 'It is why I keep practising English. So I can talk to him like Phoebe can.'

Anna wasn't so sure it was Phoebe's conversational skills that Will was after. Or Jake, she thought, not liking the knotty feeling in her stomach when she looked at them. Not jealousy, she told herself. She was tense because he was embarrassing her, paying attention to Phoebe when he was supposed to be in love with her.

Anna forced her attention back to Sara. Better to focus on her new friend's love life rather than her own fake one. After quizzing Sara on past boyfriends, she asked how long she'd had a crush on Will – apparently since she'd moved back home after taking a job in Bellagio working as a teacher.

'I like the job, but living at home again is difficult.' Suddenly Sara groaned. '*Oddio!* What is Mum doing? She is so embarrassing. I hope your Jake likes to dance.'

He's not mine. Thankfully, she swallowed the words. 'Er, well, actually I don't think…' She tailed off as her eyes landed on him. 'Apparently he does.'

'You did not know?'

What had Jake said? The art of a good lie was to stick as close to the truth as possible. 'We've not had the chance to dance together very often.'

Sara started to giggle. '*Mamma mia*, why not? He's hot.'

Anna watched in disbelief as Jake began a series of increasingly sexy moves, thrusting his hips, his body twisting sensuously to the beat. There was dancing, and there was dirty dancing. Dear God, this was most definitely the latter. Heat spread through her, pooling between her legs and before she did something stupid like salivate, or spontaneously combust, Anna swung her attention onto his dancing partner.

Rosa whooped and giggled like a woman half her age as Jake played up to her, encouraging her.

Behind her she heard a male chuckle and turned to see Marco watching, his face alive with humour. 'Your Jake, he make my Rosa very happy.' He continued in Italian, describing how he found dancing hard now because of arthritis in his hip. 'My Rosa, she's not danced for years.'

Anna gave him a distracted smile, too caught up in Jake. Others had joined in now, but it was Jake who stood out. *He's not just attractive*, she realised. *He oozes sex*. On one level she'd always known it – since the family had moved next door she'd watched him coming and going with a steady procession of girls. But he'd always been in a box titled 'jerk' so it had been easy to ignore him as she'd got older. Now she wondered if the title was fair. She'd seen glimpses of a nicer side to him: the way he cared for his mum, the fact he'd fixed the swimming pool for her. And a guy who could make a woman like Rosa so happy couldn't be all bad.

At the end of the next song Rosa tapped Jake on the shoulder, said something to him, and pointed over to Anna. He nodded and started walking over to her. Anna's heart started to bounce as she caught the gleam in his eye. It rattled against her ribs when his hand captured hers.

'Rosa says I should dance with you.'

'Oh no, I'm good, thanks.'

His eyes narrowed, and some of the joy she'd observed while he'd been dancing left his face. 'I know you're *good*,' he whispered under his breath, emphasising the word. 'But are you willing to dance with someone *bad*?'

Around her, Marco and Sara were pushing her onto the floor, encouraging her. Across the room, Phoebe was watching intently.

Rosa crossed over, her rather large chest heaving. 'Rosa tired.' She pretended to fan herself. 'Your boy, he is *molto* sexy dancer, yes? But he wore me out.' She beamed as she patted Jake's cheek. 'Now he wear you out.'

She had no choice, she realised, darting another look at Phoebe. Not if she wanted to convince everyone she really was

114

Jake's adoring partner. So she allowed Jake to tug her onto the floor.

'Jesus, Anna,' he muttered as he turned to her. 'At least try and look like you're enjoying this.'

'I've never been any good at dancing,' she hissed, acutely embarrassed. 'And you'd know that if you really were my partner.' She tried to move as the music started, but she felt awkward, her legs like they were made of raw spaghetti instead of the soft noodles of Jake's limbs. 'I'm going to look stupid.'

'You will if keep looking like you want to kill me.' His hands slid down her arms before shifting to her hips, holding her in place. 'Remember, this was Rosa's idea, not mine.'

Of course he hadn't wanted to dance with her. His words didn't help. They made her feel even less sexy.

He sighed. 'Turn your brain off, for God's sake. Clear your mind of everything but the beat.' She felt one broad palm slide over her lower back, drawing her against his powerful frame. Then he dipped his head, his breath fluttering against her ear. 'Relax and move with me.'

'"Relax," he says. How can I bloody relax when your fan club are watching me?'

He drew back a fraction, blue eyes glittering with humour. 'I've got a fan club?'

'Shut up. I'm not here to massage your ego.'

He chuckled and she hated how her body reacted to the sound, as if it was the sexiest noise it had ever heard. 'We'll treat it as a slow dance. Like we just want to wrap our arms around each other. Think you can do that?'

She nodded and as his arms tightened around her, her body adjusted to his, moulding against the hard lines. It was physical attraction, nothing more, but her lids fluttered closed when his hands slid lower, over the curve of her bum.

'Where…' She sounded hoarse and had to clear her throat. 'Where are you going with those hands?'

Another low rumble of laughter. 'I'm copping a feel.' When she tried to shift he simply pressed his hand against her, anchoring her in place. 'I'm a guy who wears jeans to interviews, who doesn't shave that often, has tattoos, and hasn't been to a barber in a long time. You really think I'm going to dance with my woman and not have my hands all over her?'

'Okay.' She swallowed, unwillingly coming alive as his hands continued to smooth over the lower part of her body. Soon it became clear she wasn't the only one getting turned on.

'Yeah, sorry. Curvy bodies do that to me.'

She glanced over her shoulder and saw where his gaze was directed. 'Bodies like Phoebe's?'

He huffed out a laugh. 'Sure. Like Phoebe.'

She hadn't liked her question, yet she found she liked his answer even less. Taking care to smile in case they were still being watched, she slid out from his arms. 'I think we've put on enough of a show tonight. I'd like to go home now. With Nigel and his friends coming on Friday, I've a lot to do tomorrow.'

'Fine.'

After saying their goodbyes, they walked back in silence, a growing tension between them she didn't think was entirely emanating from her. 'Are you annoyed with me?' she asked when they reached the castle.

He stared down at her, his handsome face shadowed by the moonlight. 'Why would I be?'

'No reason I can think of.' She hadn't been the one flirting with another guy, embarrassing him.

'Then I can't be, can I?'

She wasn't convinced by his response and as she lay in bed a short while later, her body still humming from the evening, she wondered if maybe he was finding this weird sexual energy between them as difficult to handle as she was.

Chapter Twelve

He'd slept badly, so for once Jake was grateful for the biting cold of the lake as he powered up and down between the buoys.

Anna had felt like a live wire in his hands. Curves, warmth, the press of her heat against his groin. His body had reacted as if he'd put his finger in a damn socket.

For a moment he'd thought she'd felt it too. Then she'd spoken about putting on a show, when he'd totally forgotten anyone might have been watching.

As he waded out and grabbed at the towel, he reassured himself it was just the combination of a physically attractive woman in his arms and too long since he'd had sex.

After drying off he headed back to the castle, but as his gaze fell on the swimming pool, he froze. Anna. He watched, spellbound, as she shrugged off a robe. She was wearing a bright red – she'd say crimson – one-piece, the curves he'd felt last night now gloriously on display beneath the Lycra.

Immediately his groin reminded him it was still alive, despite the cold it had been subjected to.

Taking care not to be seen, he took a different path back to the front door, making a mental note to give her a wide berth today. Let his libido calm the hell down.

As luck would have it, she spent most of the day tucked away in the kitchen. It meant that while he mowed the lawn he was able to practise some Italian from the podcasts he'd downloaded, without fear of her seeing and taking the piss.

When he tapped on the kitchen door just after six, she was still there. And looking frazzled, he noted, taking in the flush on her cheeks and the strands of hair escaped from the ponytail.

'Everything okay?'

'No, everything is definitely not okay. I messaged Nigel to find out if he or his guests had any meal requests. He messaged back saying *surprise us*. What am I supposed to do with that?' She practically spat the words out and he was relieved that for once, her irritation wasn't directed at him.

'Surprise him with chilli.'

'Chilli?' She looked at him in horror. 'I can't serve chilli to Penny and Henry's son. It's too ordinary.'

Yeah, that told you, Tucker. 'I liked it.'

'Of course you liked it. You're…' She stalled, biting into her lip.

'Don't stop there. I'm intrigued to find out what I am. Rough? Common?'

Her eyes flashed at him. 'Now you're putting words into my mouth.' She waved at the plates neatly set out on the island. 'I'm too busy to soothe your ego right now. I have to come up with some menus by tomorrow evening and nothing I've made so far seems to work.'

She was always so in control; it was quite an eye-opener

seeing her like this. 'Make what you used to make in the restaurant.'

'You think I haven't thought of that?'

'You've cooked meals for dozens of people in a night. This is just four. What's the problem?'

Her eyes avoided his. 'The problem is, he's Penny and Henry's son. I need it to be perfect.' Finally, she looked at him. 'What did you want, anyway?'

'I'm off to the bar. As you gave me stick for not asking you last time, thought I'd better check if you wanted to come.'

'The bar?' Her expression turned incredulous. 'We've got four guests coming tomorrow and you're swanning off?'

Christ. Dragging a hand through his hair, he tried to rein in his temper. 'I'm not *swanning* anywhere. I'm walking to the bar for a bit of downtime.' His eyes scanned her face. 'From the look of you, it would do you good, too.'

'Thanks,' she muttered and yet again he knew he'd said the wrong thing.

'I just meant you look hassled.'

'I am. I told Penny and Henry I could cook.'

'You can.'

'But can I? I mean, can I really cook like they're expecting me to?' He had another flash of those eloquent green eyes. 'How about things your end? Is the car washed, grass mowed, leaves swept, hot tub ready, boat serviced in case they decide they want to use it?' She rattled the items off from memory without taking a breath. 'We promised them we could do this.'

Okay, he knew he still had to do the boat, but he'd clean forgotten about the hot tub. 'Will you chill? I've got tomorrow to finish everything off.'

Her eyes became even wider. 'But you're picking them up from the airport. You'll need to leave by twelve.'

And now she was pissing him off. 'I know when I need to leave.'

She closed her eyes and inhaled a deep breath. When she opened them again, she gave him a tired smile. 'Sorry, ignore me. I'm frazzled. Enjoy your evening.'

The apology, the show of vulnerability... He had a sudden desire to wrap his arms around her and reassure her everything would be okay. But then she turned her attention back to the stove and the moment was gone.

So too was his evening, he thought sourly a little while later, as he stood at the bar, beer in hand. Instead of savouring it, and enjoying the banter with Will, he couldn't stop thinking of Anna – and boy, had he tried. When he'd left she'd looked upset, despite being in a kitchen, a room he knew from her dumb cards that she thought of as her special place, where she went to *de*-stress. Tonight, it had been giving her stress.

And you didn't help. He wasn't proud of the way he'd behaved. Instead of listening to her, he'd been too busy taking offence at perceived slights – and hell, he *was* common – and he hadn't taken enough time to think about what needed to be done before Nigel came.

His phone pinged and he stared down at it, his mood lightening when he saw a string of messages on the family WhatsApp group.

DAISY: *Bro, how is the Italian adventure? Anna throttled you in your sleep yet? Love your fav sis x*

MUM: *I'll ask her to throttle you soon if you don't phone home. Love, the mother you seem to have forgotten. Xx*

He sniggered before moving to his elder sister's comment.

EMMA: *Speaking of forgetting, remember you promised your niece and nephew they would get to stay in a castle and they don't get to go without me. Love, the big sis who mopped up your pee so you owe her. x*

God, his family, they cracked him up. He also missed them, he realised. Missed being with people who knew exactly who he was and loved him anyway.

He quickly typed out a reply.

Castle banging, Italy cool. I'm still alive. Just. Will work on castle promise if Em promises to shut up about pee. I was three and she was hogging the loo.

As he slipped the phone into his back pocket he realised he'd have to broach the subject of his family coming over with Anna. It was part of the contract that they could have guests as long as it was the off-season and nobody else was staying.

'I hear Rosa had you dancing the other night.'

He looked up to find Will had returned from serving another customer. 'Yep. She's a wild one, all right.'

'I was bummed I missed it, but someone had to tend bar and I gave Phoebe the night off as she seemed to want to go.' Will looked over his shoulder to where the woman in question was clearing tables. Sure enough, when she caught Jake's eye, she gave him a flirty wave.

'Seems she's got a crush on you,' Will remarked dryly. 'Better warn Anna.'

'Anna's not worried.' She'd not batted an eyelid when she'd assumed his hard-on had been for the blonde, when in fact it had been the voluptuous brunette in his arms that had ignited his libido.

'Did you see Sara?'

'Yeah, she was there.' He eyed Will curiously. 'Why the question? Are you and she…?'

'No.' Will didn't meet his eyes. Instead he started to carefully wipe down the top of the bar.

Jake started to laugh. 'Got you. You're not, but you want to be, though you're too… what, shy? Nah.' He scratched his head. 'Too crap at Italian to ask her out?'

Will shook the cloth at him. 'I realise this is too subtle for you, but the bulldozer approach isn't always the right one. Sometimes a man has to go in gently, work up to it. Sara's only recently moved back here to live with her parents. I'm giving her time to readjust.'

Jake wondered how the guy had sussed him out so fast. He'd never been subtle in his life.

'Anyway, enough about me. As a barman I'm meant to listen, not talk, so what's up with you?' Will pinned him with a look. 'Any reason you're propping up my bar by yourself again?'

Jake picked guiltily at the label on the beer bottle. He needed to be more careful. People noticed when he was by himself. 'It's a big day for us tomorrow. Got our first guests – Nigel and his fiancée plus two of her mates.'

Will grimaced. 'I don't envy you.'

'You know Nigel?'

'Not really. He usually prefers the bars in Bellagio to here. I just meant it must be hard, having the bosses' son as a guest.'

'Anna's getting pretty worked up over it.'

Comprehension dawned across Will's rugged face. 'And now we've found the reason you're seeking refuge here. June used to get stressed, too. She reckoned Nigel was waiting for them to slip up so he could tell his parents he was right all along and they should sell up. Rumour has it he's in cahoots with a hotel chain and gets a huge backhander if a deal goes through.'

It confirmed what Sara had let slip when they'd first met her and didn't help ease Jake's conscience. Drinking back the last of the bottle, he set it down on the bar. 'I'd best go back and help her.'

Will grinned. 'And I thought you were a tough guy. Willing to stand up to his missus.'

'Yeah, I'm tough. But not stupid.'

Will laughed, and Jake waved goodbye with a pang of sadness. He'd once had mates he could make laugh like that, and he missed it. When he'd hit Miles, it hadn't just done for his career, it had broken up his childhood gang. The mates he'd been to school with, hung around with, got into trouble with, had apparently been too scared of the Rutherford influence to want to see him when he'd come out. It made him think of the conversation he'd had with Anna in the pub when he'd warned her that pretending to date him would make Miles cross. She'd not been worried. Instead she'd laughed and said it was an added benefit.

But she was worried now.

His stride lengthened.

Anna felt like weeping, only she didn't have time. She was, of course, being utterly ridiculous. As Jake had correctly pointed out, this was just four people. And as for the meals she'd once served up in the restaurant, she could cook them with her eyes closed.

But she hadn't wanted to serve Nigel menus Miles had devised. She'd wanted to create her own.

Her heart jumped as she heard a tap on the door.

'Jake.' She put a hand to her chest. 'God, you scared me. I wasn't expecting you back yet.' She wanted to ask if Phoebe had been there, but thankfully her pride stopped her.

His eyes skimmed over the dirty pans that had piled up, the messy work surface and the plated meals lined up on the island which were now cold. 'You're supposed to be the tidy one.'

'I've not got round to clearing it up yet.' To her surprise he pushed up the sleeves of his black Henley and rounded the island. 'What are you doing?'

He gave her a bland look. 'What does it look like?'

She didn't need to answer because when he shoved the plug into the sink and turned on the taps, it was obvious. 'I don't need you rescuing me. I can manage.'

'Sure you can.' But he squirted washing-up liquid into the sink and began to scrub the first pan as if she'd not said anything. 'So, what are you making them?'

'I...' She felt the prick of unshed tears sting her eyes. 'I've not decided.'

He glanced at the food on the island but didn't say anything. For the next ten minutes he scrubbed pans and cleaned worktops with an efficiency that surprised her while she pretended to trawl through her folder of menu ideas – the one she'd religiously collated over the years, hoping one day, when she opened her own restaurant, it would inspire her.

A scrape of metal over tile alerted her to the fact that he'd pulled out a stool. When she looked up she found him sitting opposite, elbows on the island, eyes on her.

'Here's what we're going to do,' he announced. 'We're

going to warm up these dishes in the microwave, then take a few mouthfuls each. We vote yes or no, and move on to the next one.'

She shook her head. 'I've already tasted them. None of them were good enough.'

'Yeah, well, now it's my go.' He flashed her a grin that caused a squirmy feeling in her stomach. 'If it's shit, you know I'll tell you.'

He would, too. There was no softly, softly with Jake; he said it how it was. Yet after Miles, who'd told her he adored her then cheated on her, and after her mum, who'd said she loved her in one breath then disappeared out of her life in the next, his honesty was starting to feel refreshing. 'Okay.'

They made their way through the dishes methodically. One time Jake screwed up his face; another time he winced. Yet when he grinned and gave her a thumbs-up it felt big, important. Like maybe she could create dishes from scratch.

'Are you going to tell me why you've had a meltdown over this?' he asked as they moved onto the last plate – fresh tonnarelli pasta with crab and *cacio e pepe*.

Embarrassment scalded her cheeks. 'I want to prove I can do it.'

'Of course you can. You've been doing it for years.'

His blithe retort rankled. 'I've been cooking for years. Miles was the one who devised the menus.'

'So this is all about you creating a menu for the first time?' He shook his head. 'I don't buy that. You must have played around with menus while you were working for him. Made suggestions.'

'I did.'

Those intense blue eyes trapped hers and she found she couldn't hold his gaze. But he'd clearly seen all he needed to see, because he swore. 'You've got to be kidding me. You've let the crap Miles spouted get to you?'

She wanted to deny it, because the dismissive way he said it made her feel stupid, but he stared at her with such a knowing expression on his face, the lie died on her lips. Instead she looked away. 'What do you think of the crab?'

He exhaled sharply, his frustration clear, but thankfully he let the matter drop. 'What's the sauce?'

'*Cacio e pepe*. Basically, cheese and pepper.'

He smirked. 'But that doesn't sound fancy enough.'

For the first time that evening, she felt her mouth wanting to smile. 'No.'

'Okay then.' He took a mouthful, chewed, and swallowed. She tried not to look at his Adam's apple as it bobbed up and down in his throat. 'I still prefer the chilli but yeah, we can put that on the yes list.'

She scanned what she'd written. 'You realise there are only two rejects.'

He shrugged. 'Guess what, maybe Miles was talking out of his arse. Maybe he made shit up about you because he didn't like the idea of people knowing he'd been dumped. Maybe he's a lying tosser who should never be listened to or believed again, ever.'

A bubble of laughter left her and the weight she'd felt on her shoulders eased a little. 'You never did say why you hit him.'

Jake shifted on his stool. 'What did he say?'

'That you're a hothead and took exception to something he said about your sister.'

'True enough.'

She watched his expression tighten, his face close off. 'There's more to it than that.'

'It's Daisy's business, nobody else's.'

As frustrated as she was at his tight-lipped response, she couldn't help but admire his loyalty to his sister. Slipping off the stool, she collected up the plates and stacked them in the dishwasher. 'I've made sure there's fresh sheets on the beds and given the whole place a vacuum and dust. Now I've got the menu ideas, all I need to do tomorrow is shop for the ingredients, prep for the dinner, and put fresh flowers in the rooms.' She turned to face him. 'What do you have left to do?'

He shook his head. 'You know, we'd get on a lot better if you loosened up.'

It was hard to take offence when his eyes were bright with amusement. And when he'd just dragged her out of the hell of self-doubt and put her back on a path towards self-belief. 'We'd also get on a lot better if you removed the giant chip you've got on your shoulder.'

His eyebrows shot up to his hairline. 'What chip?'

'The one that assumes I don't like you, that I don't trust you. That I think you're... what did you say earlier? Common? When actually I'd been about to say you like chilli because you're straightforward, unpretentious. It's a good thing,' she added, because he was still staring at her.

A slow smile spread across his face. 'Well, who'd have thought after all these years Anna Roberts sees some good in me.'

Had she really been that judgemental? The thought brought a sting of shame to her cheeks but before she could explore his comment any further, he'd eased off the stool and was sauntering out of the kitchen. 'Jake.' He halted in the doorway and turned, hands resting on the top of the door frame, sleeves still rolled up, revealing part of the tattoo on his left arm. Even his forearms, with their ropes of veins over muscle, oozed sex appeal, she thought distractedly. 'Thanks for your help tonight.' She could leave it at that, but if she wanted to try and connect with him more, she had to open up. 'You were right. I did let what Miles said get to me. I... I started to panic that I couldn't do this.'

He nodded. 'But now you remember he's a tosser.'

Her lips twitched. 'Now I remember.' But because she was still her, and he was still him, she had to ask. 'You will check the hot tub tomorrow, and make sure the car's clean inside and out before—'

'What part of loosen up did you not understand?' he interrupted, but the accompanying roll of his eyes suggested tolerance rather than annoyance.

Not waiting for her to answer he turned and strode off, leaving her with the impressive sight of his broad back and a feeling that maybe, just maybe, they'd moved from sniping ex-neighbours to tentative friends.

Chapter Thirteen

Jake had revised his opinion of Nigel. He wasn't so much an arsehole – Jake reserved that term for people who were really nasty, like Miles. Nigel was more of a first-class prick. Maybe that was what having too much money did for you.

Ever since he'd picked the guy up from the airport he'd been demanding: bags to the room; remove the flowers as his fiancée had hay fever; set up a TV in their bedroom. He seemed intent on driving Jake up the wall. As for his three female companions, Jake had never seen so much flesh on display considering it was April and wasn't *that* hot. He wondered what they'd wear if they came back in the summer.

'Ooh, we should take the boat out,' Clarissa, Nigel's fiancée, announced, bouncing up and down like a three-year-old. 'It's like, so cool, zipping around the lake on a speedboat.'

The party made their way out onto the rear patio where they sat on the fancy wicker furniture Jake had spent yesterday washing down. A job, just like making sure the gas for the outdoor heaters was full, that Anna hadn't reminded him about but he'd done anyway because, guess what, he wasn't totally clueless. He didn't need lists and constant reminders.

He carefully placed the four cocktails they'd ordered onto the table in front of them – yep, apparently they thought they were in a hotel and he and Anna were their private servants. They also had the sense of humour of a bunch of school kids because, though Jake had once definitely laughed at the idea of ordering drinks called Sex on the Beach, a Screaming Orgasm, Blow Job, and The Slippery Nipple, he had been thirteen at the time.

Venetia batted her eyelashes at him. 'Look, Jake's just given me a Screaming Orgasm.'

While the rest of them hooted with laughter, Jake fixed a smile on his face. He bloody loved flirting with women, but Venetia and Tatiana only saw him as a bit of rough. They didn't see *him*. His mind flashed back to Anna in the kitchen, dark hair tied back, surrounded by plates of neatly chopped… *stuff*, mixing the cocktails with a professional ease before going back to turn the *stuff* into canapés for the evening meal.

If he was going to flirt with anyone, he realised with a start, he wanted it to be with the focused, obsessively organised, outwardly ball-bustingly confident yet inwardly surprisingly insecure woman currently slaying her inner dragons in the kitchen.

'Jake?'

He snapped his attention back to Nigel, who looked annoyed.

'I asked what the situation was with the boat.'

'It's good to go. I checked it over yesterday.'

'And you know about boats?'

I know more than you. He kept his thoughts to himself and the smile on his face. 'I know my way around a car engine. Boats aren't very different.'

Tatiana crossed her long, shapely legs and darted him a look under her heavily made-up lashes. 'I do love a guy who doesn't mind getting his hands dirty.'

'Liar, Tat.' Venetia smirked. 'You love a guy who doesn't mind getting dirty, full stop.'

As he could see Nigel getting more and more frustrated, Jake threw Long Legs a cocky smile. 'I spend a lot of my time getting dirty.'

She giggled, then took a provocative sip of her cocktail. 'What do you think of sex on the beach?'

Behind him, he heard the sound of a throat being cleared. He turned to find Anna with a pinched expression on her face. Ignoring him, she slid the plate of olives and some fancy, swirly pastry things onto the table. 'I thought you might enjoy these with the cocktails.'

After giving the seated group a bright smile, she turned and strode back into the castle, not once looking in his direction.

Nigel barked out a laugh. 'Looks like she's got the hump with you.'

Jake flicked a glance at Anna's retreating figure – he was a fan of the dress, even more a fan of the toned legs it revealed. 'I'm sure it's only temporary.' He nodded towards the lake. 'I'll go and get the boat onto the water. Leave you to drink your cocktails in peace.'

'Come back and join us,' he heard Venetia say – or was it Tatiana? It was hard enough remembering their names, never mind which belonged to the blue-eyed blonde with the very busty figure, or which belonged to the redhead with the legs that went up to her armpits. He liked simpler names. *Like Anna.* Crap, he had to stop thinking of her as anything other than the occasionally annoying woman he was pretending to be in a relationship with. If he started to fancy her – or worse, to think of her as actually accessible – he'd spend the rest of the year with a bad case of blue balls and raging disappointment.

Half an hour later, having seen them all safely into the boat, he headed back to the kitchen. *Safely* was a relative term. He wouldn't want to take three giggling women wearing sky-high heels, and one guy who thought he knew it all but clearly didn't, onto the water. Not sober, and certainly not after they'd had a strong cocktail. He'd offered the life jackets hanging in the boat house but they'd all refused and, frankly, he wasn't their minder so he'd untied the boat from the mooring and waved them off. He figured they all had phones if someone ended up overboard. And to salve his conscience, he'd give Nigel a call once he'd found out why Anna seemed to have forgotten they were supposed to be a loving couple.

'Hey.'

She glanced up and gave him a cool look which actually made his blood heat. The difference between the Anna of yesterday and today was remarkable. Yesterday she'd been a bag of nerves; today she had poise and a steel backbone.

'Why did you blank me? Did you forget we're meant to like each other?'

She arched a dark brow and he felt another pulse of arousal. He was definitely going crazy if he'd started to find her standoffish attitude sexy. *But you've seen the other side.*

'I think it was you who forgot.' She returned her attention to the chopping board and began to slice the potato with clinical efficiency.

'What do you mean?'

'I realise you didn't sign up for a year of celibacy but please be discreet.'

He stared back at her. 'What the hell?'

'*I spend a lot of my days getting dirty.*' Fluttering her eyelashes and putting on a dodgy accent, Anna repeated back the words he'd said to Venetia/Tatiana.

'That's a piss-poor imitation of me.'

'Sorry, my voice doesn't go low enough to get the sexy husk.'

Despite his annoyance, he felt a dart of satisfaction. 'Sexy husk, huh?'

She shot him a venomous look. 'What you should be focusing on is the part where you agreed not to humiliate me.'

Anna knew she was out of line, but God, when she'd heard them flirt with him, when she'd heard him flirt back, she'd seen red.

'Humiliate you?' Jake's expression turned from smug to disgusted. 'How the hell am I doing that? For the last few days you've banged on about how important good old Nigel and his party are, how everything has to be perfect for them, how we have to make sure they feel welcome.' Hands on his hips, he gave a disparaging shake of his head. 'What was I supposed to do? Blank them like you blanked me? Tell them to stop flirting because my partner doesn't like it?'

'And if I really were your partner, that's how you'd behave? Cosy up to any woman who showed you attention?'

He stilled, his body wound tight. 'I don't cheat.'

She snorted, wounds from a month ago still painfully raw. 'So say all men, until the opportunity presents itself.'

Blue eyes raked over her face and she knew they saw more than she wanted him to when he sighed. 'Seems I've touched a nerve.' He pulled up a stool and eased onto it with the masculine grace that was part of his make-up. 'Truth is, their flirting was pissing Nigel off.' Jake gave her a sheepish smile, dimples out in force. 'So I kind of encouraged it.'

Damn, he was a hard man to stay cross with. 'I want to say you're being juvenile.'

'Can't deny that.'

'But inside I'm quietly fist-bumping you. The man is driving me up the wall.'

They shared a grin and the combination of the glint in his eyes and the curve of his sexy lips woke a swarm of butterflies in her stomach. *Stop being distracted. Get back to the point.* She cleared her throat and forced her gaze away. 'So anyway, if you want to have sex, please make sure it doesn't get back to the people who know us here. One humiliation a year is enough for me.'

The moment was well and truly broken. His stool scraped across the flagstones as he rose to his feet. 'Same applies to you.'

'Oh trust me, I won't be having a clandestine affair with anyone.'

'Miles put you off sex, has he?'

He's crushed my confidence and made me doubt my sexuality to an extent I'm terrified at the thought of being with someone else. Feeling bitter tears prick her lids, Anna turned and pretended to wash something in the sink.

The sound of a ringtone was a welcome distraction. And

was that a Beatles song? Jake groaned as he dug it out of his jeans pocket. 'What's bloody Nigel want now?'

'You gave him a ringtone?'

He smirked. '"The Fool on the Hill" by the Beatles. Figured if I gave him a ringtone I'd know whether to bother taking the phone out of my pocket.'

Walking away from her, he answered the call, leaving Anna fighting not to smile. So many of their interactions had been barbed that she'd not fully appreciated Jake had a sense of humour until now.

When he came back in, he was shaking his head. 'Looks like our fool has gone and got himself stuck on a sandbank. Guess I'd better go and rescue them.'

'I'll come with you.'

'Don't trust me not to push him in?'

This time she couldn't stop the smile. 'More like I want to see him stranded and helpless.'

As it turned out, she didn't just get the treat of seeing Nigel looking helpless about fifty metres out. She had the treat of Jake stripping off his shirt and jeans.

She knew she'd been caught gawping when she heard a low chuckle. 'What's caught your interest?'

You. The powerful chest, rippling with taut, hard muscles. Strong thighs, defined calves, dusted with a fine layer of fair hair. An impressive bulge between his legs that, God help her, she wanted to stare at, to cup, and feel its weight.

He didn't just ooze sex, it dripped from him.

Flustered, she dragged her gaze back to his highly amused face. 'I was looking at your tattoos.' And it wasn't a lie. On the shoulder she could see an emblem that she recognised as being that of the local fire and rescue service. But it was the bold art that swept across his left pec that really drew the eye, emphasising the muscled power behind the ink. 'Nice lion.'

He smirked, twitching his pecs, his expression telling her he knew damn well it was his chest she was ogling, not his ink.

With quick, efficient movements he strode into the water and swam out to the boat. She watched as he pushed it off the sandbank, much to the clear enjoyment of the female occupants. She could just imagine the scene when they got back to shore. *Ooh Jakey, you're so strong. Did I mention I like a strong man, as well as a dirty man?* Anna shuddered. Nope, she wasn't going to hang around for that, though in truth she wasn't much better, standing there ogling the man silently.

As she made it back to the castle her phone beeped with a message. When she saw who it was from, her jaw automatically clenched. Why hadn't she deleted his damn number?

MILES: *Is it true? Are you really holed up in Italy with Tucker?*

Her instinct was to delete both the message and the contact, but she wasn't sure where Miles's head was. Was he peeved because she was getting on with her life? Because it was Jake she was with? Or was he humiliated because he thought she'd run off with Jake? She didn't care which it was, but she needed to make sure he wouldn't make trouble for them in Italy. Thinking carefully, she messaged back.

Not that it's any of your business but I'm working in Italy with Jake.

Hoping that would give him sufficient information to

soothe his ego, she walked back to the kitchen. Tonight would be a big test. If Nigel and his female companions ate what she served without complaint, she might forgive him for being annoying, and them for flirting with her man.

The thought rolled so easily through her it took a moment to realise her mistake.

Her pretend man.

Chapter Fourteen

Back in the kitchen following his sandbank rescue mission, Jake parked his bum against the wall, folded his arms and watched silently as Anna served out the starters.

She looked hot. And it had damn all to do with the temperature of the kitchen. The way she moved between the hob and the sink, the fridge and the island, was like a dance. If he'd realised how sexy women looked in the kitchen he'd have dated a chef, though there was a chance the sexy was down to Anna and not her job title. Hair tied back again, black apron over a neat short-sleeved white shirt. It shouldn't be a turn-on, yet the fire in her eyes, the glow to her olive cheeks... His groin tightened. Shit, he was in a world of trouble if he kept having this reaction to her. Yet had she had a similar reaction to him earlier when he'd taken off his shirt by the lake? Muscles and tattoos did it for some women, but her track record suggested she was into pretty boys like Miles: well-dressed, charming, professional.

'Are you really not going to change?' she asked, for once her focus in his direction.

He looked down at his jeans. 'What does it look like?'

'It looks like you can't be bothered, when I thought we were aiming for professional.'

'*We* didn't decide that. I wanted to tell them to come to the kitchen to get their meal. Nowhere in the job description did it say I had to be a bloody waiter.'

'It didn't say you had to flirt with the guests, either, but apparently you can manage that.'

He liked that it annoyed her. 'Some jobs are easier than others.'

In a blur of activity she nudged white round things from a pan and onto white plates, spooned black bits on top of it and then drizzled some concoction around it in swirls.

'What is it?'

She stood back, surveyed her work, and clearly considered herself satisfied because she picked two plates up and motioned for him to do the same. 'Roasted scallops with caviar and a black garlic and parsley sauce.'

He inhaled. 'Smells good. Can't say I've had a scallop. Or caviar. Or black garlic.'

She nodded over to a plate resting by the sink. 'Tonight's your chance.'

For some strange reason his heart skipped a beat. 'You saved one for me?'

'Of course. But you get the practice version. After we've delivered these to our guests.'

She whipped off her apron and walked ahead of him, all professional in her blouse and black skirt. Yet beneath the veneer he knew there was a sinfully gorgeous body – one he had a feeling she'd forgotten she had, thanks to Miles's betrayal.

As he followed her out, his mind skipped back to their

argument earlier. The thought of her condoning him having discreet affairs left a bad taste in his mouth. Despite her insinuation, he wasn't driven by his dick. Prison had taught him he could do without. Since he'd come out though, he'd only seemed to attract women interested in the ex-con. He wanted to believe he was worth more than that.

The redhead at the table gave him a slow wink when he settled the plate in front of her. 'Thanks, handsome.'

Aware of Anna watching, he smiled politely. 'Enjoy.'

Nigel tapped at his glass. 'We need another bottle. Actually, make it two. The Châteauneuf-du-Pape 2016. I'm sure there's some in the cellar.'

Jake knew there was a tonne of wine in the cellar. How the hell he was supposed to find that one? 'Give me a clue. Is it red or white?'

Nigel looked appalled. 'Good God, is that some sort of joke?'

'Hey, I'm funnier than that.' Jake knew, without looking, that his female fan club had just lost some of their interest. Yeah, they liked the idea of the rough, but when it came down to it they wanted a guy who could tell his Chateau Nines from his Tesco bargain bucket.

Anna cleared her throat. When he glanced over at her, he found she was fighting not to laugh. 'It's a French red.'

'There.' Nigel flapped his hands in Anna's direction. 'Thank God one of you has a discerning palate.'

Jake shrugged. 'But if your bog gets blocked, you'll be thanking God one of us knows how to unblock it.'

Struggling to keep a straight face, Anna started to back out of the room. 'We'll, um, go and get the wine. Enjoy your scallops.'

Once she'd made it into the kitchen, the laughter burst out

of her. 'You've traumatised him. I doubt he's ever met a guy who doesn't know his wine.'

'Yeah, well, I've never met a guy who maroons himself on a sandbank and expects someone else to push him off.'

Her smile faded a little, though her expression softened. 'I don't suppose you have.'

An hour later their guests had decamped to the main lounge, Nigel declaring they'd take coffee and whisky – a single malt Macallan. Oh, and a bottle of vintage Dom Pérignon for the ladies. Jake had been half tempted to ask what brand of blasted coffee beans he wanted. There had been no show of gratitude for the food Anna had toiled over.

'Their plates were empty. That's enough,' Anna declared as they stacked the dishwasher but he knew their lack of praise was gnawing away at her.

'Well, they should learn some manners. The meal was fucking awesome.' At her start of surprise, he shook his head. 'Just because I don't know my Château Wotsits doesn't mean I don't know great food when I eat it.'

'Thank you.'

Her smile wobbled slightly, causing a funny feeling in his chest.

She settled a coffee pot and cups and saucers on a tray, along with some fancy chocolates. He snagged a bottle of champagne from the fridge – apparently she'd already found out the Dom stuff was Nigel's preferred tipple. Hooking that under his arm, he grabbed glasses and the whisky he'd fetched from the cellar.

'Why don't you both join us?' Nigel declared as she placed the tray on the table, alcohol clearly making him lose sight of the fact that since he'd arrived, he'd treated them like lackeys. After giving Jake a short study, his focus turned to Anna.

'Unless of course you've still got the hump with him for flirting with these lovely ladies?'

Anna stilled, her gaze flying over to Jake's. She really was a piss-poor actor. Luckily one of them had bullshitting down to a fine art. Plonking the whisky bottle and glasses next to the coffee, Jake turned to Anna and cupped her face. 'You were never worried, were you, babe?' He smiled into her shocked eyes. 'You know I only have eyes for you.'

She drew in a breath – surprise, gearing to say something, he didn't know – and then bit down on her plump lower lip, the action causing an unfortunate, and surprising, bolt of arousal.

'You know, I can't figure you two out.' Nigel's voice sounded behind him. 'You seem awkward around each other. She doesn't seem to like you much.'

Tell me something I don't know. As Jake struggled with how to reply, he became aware of the soft feel of her skin against his palm. Of the floral tones of whatever the hell she washed her hair with. Of the swirling emotion in her green eyes that was slowly sucking him under.

'Then there's how you look, your wildly different personalities.' Nigel's voice kept buzzing, like an annoying wasp. 'You don't seem to fit.'

Jake's gaze dipped to Anna's mouth and he tuned the noise out. She had one gorgeous pair of lips. Soft, parted slightly, as if inviting him in.

He dipped his head, nipped gently, experimentally, at that plump bottom lip.

Immediately lust crashed through him and he pressed his mouth more firmly against hers, heat arrowing through him as he tasted her sweetness. Needing more of her, more taste, more connection, his tongue sought entry, flicking, tangling with hers, sending his groin rearing into life. Instinctively his other hand smoothed down her spine, stopping at the lush curve of her bum – a part he'd wanted to revisit ever since that slow dance. Somewhere in the back of his mind he knew this was supposed to be an act, but in that moment it felt vividly, wildly, real.

What are you doing?

The silent question in her eyes slammed through the fog of his arousal and he dragged his mouth away, his hand slipping from her cheek.

Anna's heart was racing, her breathing too shallow, her body too hot, too tight. There was putting on a show and there was... oh boy, there was *that*. She could still feel the heat of his palm searing through her skirt. The soft tickle of his stubble.

She could still taste him on her lips.

'Trying to prove something?'

Nigel's unamused voice broke into the moment. Feeling unbalanced, she tried to move away but Jake's hand shifted from her bum to her waist, holding her firmly in place.

'Just showing you we fit where it counts.' His eyes, now a midnight blue, briefly locked onto hers before he turned to Nigel. 'Thanks for the offer to join you – we'll share a glass of whisky.' He glanced back at her. 'Okay with you, babe?'

No, she wanted to scream. Stuff the whisky, she needed to race back to the privacy of her bedroom and analyse what on earth had just happened. Jake had kissed her. Not a peck, a glancing press of lips against lips, but really *kissed* her. As if he'd wanted to. And her reaction had been so intense, her knees were still shaking.

But four pairs of interested eyes were watching her. 'Yes, fine.'

Her voice had a husk to it that caused Jake's eyes to darken another shade before he let her go and reached for the champagne, handing it to her with a dry smile. 'Anna's our wine pro. My skills stop at taking a cap off a beer bottle.'

There was no defensive tone to his voice. As with the wine earlier, he was unapologetic. It made her wonder about the chip she'd accused him of having on his shoulder. Did it only appear when he was with her?

After serving the drinks, Jake sat on the one free armchair and patted his knee.

Oh God no. He couldn't mean… His mouth quirked, and when he nodded her pulse rocketed. Wasn't this going too far? *She doesn't seem to like you.* With a prick of shame, she realised she was letting the side down.

Feeling horribly awkward, she walked over to him, heart hammering. He must have sensed her hesitation because his hands slid to her waist and he pulled her confidently onto his lap. Rock-hard thighs hit her backside and immediately she was enveloped by warmth and that unique Jake Tucker smell.

Just act natural, she tried to tell herself. *Like you do this every evening.* But it was so hard when her senses were surrounded by him and her every movement was being watched and analysed.

'Relax.' The whispered command fluttered against her ear, sending a shiver of awareness through her.

With a casual ease she could only envy, Jake shifted her more snugly against his chest. Then, resting one hand on her thigh, he picked up his whisky with the other and offered it to her. She clutched at the glass as if it were a life raft, then took such a big gulp it caused her to cough.

'Careful, babe.' Amusement glittered in his eyes before her turned his focus onto Nigel. 'What are your plans for tomorrow?'

It was hard to follow the conversation; she was far too conscious of the man whose lap she was sitting on. She felt a dizzying combination of warmth, protection, and hyper acute awareness. Her skin tingled, reacting to every brush against his, every movement. It was a huge relief when Nigel's fiancée announced she wanted to use the hot tub.

Or it was, until Jake let out a quiet groan. 'You'll have to give me a few minutes to check the chemical levels are okay.'

Nigel narrowed his eyes, red spots appearing on his cheeks. 'That should've been done before we came. It's a pretty basic requirement, like having the pool and the boat ready.'

Silently, Anna slipped off Jake's lap, watching as he rose slowly to his feet. '*Basic* requirements,' Jake stated mildly, 'are a roof over your head and food to eat.'

Nigel's flushed deepened. It could have been caused by anger or alcohol because he was obviously drunk. 'You know what I mean. I was referring to the fact that a clear part of your role is to get everything ready for us. Just as it would be if it were a hotel.'

Ignoring Nigel, Jake turned to Clarissa. 'I'll be back shortly.'

As tension pinged around the room, Anna followed Jake out and onto the back patio.

'You reminded me to do it and I forgot,' he stated tightly as he hauled the covers off the hot tub situated at the far side. 'That's on me. Him being an arse about it? That's on him and I won't apologise for it.'

'I wasn't asking you to.' She watched as he checked the pH levels, his movements quick and efficient. 'They've all had a lot to drink. I'm not sure getting in a hot tub is a good idea.'

Jake snorted. 'I'm sure it's not. Nor was taking the boat out earlier. But while making sure these *basic* requirements are ready for him is part of my responsibilities, babysitting isn't.'

After a few minutes Jake declared it okay for use. As they walked back to the sitting room together, she was so acutely conscious of him her heart fluttered when his arm accidentally brushed hers.

'I know why you kissed me. It was quite...' *Devastating. Mind blowing.* 'Convincing.'

Jake halted, eyes darting to her mouth before giving a brief shake of his head. 'It was way more than that.'

Before she could ask him what he meant, he was walking ahead of her.

'Hot tub is good to go,' Jake announced as they joined the others. 'If this were a hotel,' he added, looking pointedly at Nigel, 'there would be warnings about not using it if you've drunk alcohol. As it's a private residence you're responsible for yourselves.' He slid his arm around her waist and winked down at her. 'Anna and I are off to bed.'

God, flirty Jake – even if it was pretend flirty Jake – was devastatingly attractive.

As butterflies flapped in her belly she became aware of Venetia and Tatiana looking enviously at her. Feeling a smidgen of the old confidence Miles's words and actions had managed to shatter, she looked them both in the eye, raised her chin, and smiled.

I'm the one who gets to go to bed with him, she wanted to crow.

Even if the beds were in separate rooms.

Later, when she was lying alone in her room, she found herself wondering what it would be like to really go to bed with Jake Tucker. Would he grip his T-shirt by the hem and shrug it off over his head in that sexy way men had? Would his tattoos flash, his muscles ripple as they slid over each other? When he flipped open the button of his jeans and slowly dragged the zip down over that perfect bulge, would…

With a deep sigh, she turned over and forced her mind to think of all the jobs she had to do tomorrow.

Chapter Fifteen

Twenty minutes after he'd said goodnight to her, Jake tapped lightly on Anna's door. He didn't know whether she was one of those people who crashed out when they went to bed. If she was, he'd have to handle this alone.

And actually, maybe that would be a good idea because shit, his body was still humming from their kiss. Too late, he remembered why kissing her – *really* kissing her – was a bad idea. The good news was that it hadn't sucked, so he didn't have to live with the embarrassment of her smirking at him, forever holding it over him that he was a bad kisser. The bad news? He now had to live with the alternative, potentially nuclear, non-sucking option.

He desperately wanted to kiss her again. And again. And on way more than her mouth would be pretty bloody fantastic, thank you very much.

'Jake?'

Her sleepy answer crashed through his wayward thoughts. 'Who else are you expecting?'

He heard a huff, and a moment later the door opened and she appeared in a pair of shortie pyjamas.

Holy shit. He now had a new favourite look on her. Who'd have thought someone so prickly could look so cute?

'I've had a call from Nigel.' He coughed to clear the scratch from his throat. 'Apparently he's been sick. Before you have a meltdown, cleaning it up isn't an issue – I've dealt with worse.' He could thank prison for that. 'But I can't do sympathy. Not when it's self-induced. And not when the guy's a first-class prat.'

She looked as exasperated as he felt. 'And you think I can?'

'You're a w—'

'If you say *woman*, I'm going to throttle you. Being female doesn't automatically mean we have to play nursemaid.'

He gave her his extra-sweet smile. 'I was going to say you're a warm-hearted person.'

She let out a long-drawn-out sigh. 'Neat catch. Wait while I get some clothes on.'

His eyes slid down her shapely legs. 'I'm sure Nigel will feel better if you turn up like that.'

She raised her eyes to the ceiling. 'Not happening.'

When they made it to the patio, they found Nigel in his trunks sitting on one of the wicker armchairs, face looking as pale as his scrawny chest. Clarissa was perched on the side of the hot tub, looking at her fiancé with a cross between horror and disgust. Figuring she must have seen Nigel's body before, Jake guessed the disgust was from... yep, there it was, splattered in technicolour glory all over the paving slabs.

'This is your fault.' Nigel skewered Anna with a look. 'I've clearly got food poisoning.'

Anna blanched and Jake felt an unexpected tug of

protectiveness. 'Come on, this has nothing to do with what you've eaten. You've been frolicking in a hot tub, drunk. What did you expect to happen?'

Nigel's face went from pasty white with a hint of green to heated pink. 'I don't like your tone.'

Anna's hand grasped Jake's and gave it a warning squeeze, but it didn't matter who he was talking to, biting his tongue wasn't going to happen. 'And I don't like your accusation that Anna's given you food poisoning. Especially when it's very clear you're the only one feeling ill.'

'I don't know about Venetia and Tatiana; they've gone to bed already. As for Clarissa...' Nigel turned to his fiancée, who looked ready to bolt from both the vomit and the man who'd produced it. She was going to struggle with the *in sickness* part of her wedding vows. 'You said you were feeling nauseous, didn't you?'

'Er, yes.' She clutched at her stomach before darting inside.

Jake figured she was about as good an actor as Anna was.

'Funny, I ate the same meal as you did, mate, and I feel absolutely fine.' Jake gave Nigel a hard look. 'So don't think you're going to pin this one on Anna.'

The pink flush on Nigel's face turned to a deep red, and Anna's hand wriggled from his. 'I'm sorry you feel it was the food that made you sick. We'll clear up here while you go and dry off.' She paused. 'Can I get you anything? Peppermint tea? Water?'

'Water.' Nigel rose to his feet. 'If you can manage that without cocking it up.'

Jake saw red. Fuck this prat. Striding over to Nigel he blocked his path and stared down at him. Funny how mouthy guys turned quiet when faced with someone taller and bulkier.

'Anna isn't your servant. She's not even your employee. Treat her with respect or get your own damn water.'

Nigel's eyes bulged with anger. 'I'll be telling my parents of your behaviour.'

'Is that supposed to scare me?'

Nigel bristled. 'Get out of my way.'

'Jake.'

Anna's voice floated across to him and when he glanced over at her, her face was pinched tight, her eyes begging him to stop. Reluctantly, he moved to the side.

'You'd better make a good job of cleaning it up,' Nigel said as he stepped inside, the big man again now Jake wasn't in his face. 'I don't want the place smelling of sick tomorrow.'

'Prick,' Jake muttered under his breath as the guy disappeared inside.

'I agree, but he's also Penny and Henry's son.' Anna dropped down onto the wicker sofa. 'And we've just made him really angry.'

Jake gaped at her. 'He's just accused you of giving him food poisoning. You're the one who should be angry.'

Her eyes looked impossibly large in her face yet her voice, when she spoke, was so small he had to strain to hear it. 'Maybe I did.'

'Bollocks. I've watched you in the kitchen; you're borderline obsessive. Everything is neatly ordered, surfaces meticulously wiped clean. Christ, you even moved the beer in our fridge because it was apparently in the wrong place. No way did you cause this.'

She rocked forward, briefly burying her face in her hands before looking up at him. 'Mistakes can still happen. Maybe I didn't cook his scallop for long enough, or his chicken.' She waved a hand in his direction. 'And maybe it would have helped if you hadn't wound him up.'

He couldn't believe it. 'I was defending you.'

'I'm perfectly capable of defending myself.' With a sigh, she stood up. 'I'd better get him his water and try and smooth his ruffled feathers.'

'Sod his ruffled feathers. He shouldn't go around making false accusations.'

'We don't know it's false. We do know he can make our life really difficult. Maybe even get us fired,' she added quietly before heading inside.

Annoyance hummed through him as Jake stared down at the vomit. Why was it rich, entitled people thought they could say what they liked?

Because they hold the power. The reminder was a nasty dose of reality and he felt his shoulders slump. Maybe he should have kept his big mouth shut. He'd tangled with the rich and entitled before, and ended up with a criminal record for his efforts. Yet the thought of letting Anna believe this was somehow her fault... no. Call him hot-headed, quick-tempered – and sure, he was both of those things – but he'd witnessed her vulnerability in the kitchen a few days ago. No way could he stand by and let another creep squash her confidence.

———————————

Anna's heart contracted as she stood by the patio door and watched Jake on his hands and knees, biceps bunching as he scrubbed at the paving slabs. When he'd loomed over Nigel, stubbled jaw set tight, big body pulsing with power, scar on his eyebrow giving his face a mean look, for the first time she'd seen the dangerous side of him.

The hard man capable of punching someone. The tough man who'd endured prison.

But here was the other side. The man on his knees cleaning up sick had not just stood up for her. He'd believed in her.

Tears pricked and she had to swallow the urge to cry. Not that long ago she'd believed in herself, too. Somehow she'd let Miles shatter that confidence.

Now Jake of all people, a man she'd been at loggerheads with since she was fourteen, was helping her put herself back together.

As if he sensed her, he looked up. 'How's Mr Puke-a-lot?'

She let out a choked laugh. 'It's a good job their rooms are on the other side so he can't hear.'

Jake shifted to his feet. 'That's the kindest name I've got for him.'

He was annoyed with her. She could feel it in the set of his shoulders, the way he didn't meet her eyes. 'Nigel accepted his glass of water, told me they would have croissants tomorrow morning, and in the evening they'd dine out.' That had hurt, especially considering all the effort she'd gone to, trying to perfect the menu.

'Good.' He emptied the bucket he'd been using onto one of the flower beds. 'Means we get a night off.'

If only that was how she saw it, and not as evidence of her failure. 'Have you finished here?'

'Yep. It's officially a vomit-free zone.'

'You said you'd cleaned up worse.'

His eyebrow quirked – or maybe it was that scar again. 'Imagining blood and guts?'

'No.' She gave him a small smile. 'Okay, maybe a bit.'

He avoided her eyes. 'Prison toilets are far worse, trust me.'

'You really don't like talking about it, do you?'

'It depends who's asking.' Finally, his gaze found hers. 'I don't like talking about it with you, no.'

That stung a bit. 'You think I judge you for it?'

'I think that's a natural human reaction, yes.'

She still wasn't sure she liked the answer, but in all honesty she had judged him in the past, put him in a box labelled *trouble*. 'Is there anyone you have talked to about it?'

He gave her his trademark smirk. 'Worried for my mental health?'

'It's important to talk things through,' she stressed, not deterred by his attempt at fobbing her off. 'If you keep them bottled up, they fester.' She'd learned that from her dad, who'd always encouraged her to talk about her mum.

'I've talked some to Mum, some to my sisters and a couple of mates.' A shadow fell across his face. 'Before Rutherford scared them off.'

'Girlfriends?'

He let out a low laugh. 'Fishing for info on my sex life now?'

She had to admit she was curious. 'You know all about mine. It's only fair.'

With a shake of his head, he gazed down at the floor. 'Funny thing. Once you've been inside, you're either a magnet for bored, rich housewives who want the thrill of sex with an ex-con, or you're to be avoided at all costs.' The vivid blue of his gaze snared hers. 'I don't mind being a dirty fantasy but I won't be a dirty secret.'

So many emotions crossed his face: irritation, frustration, anger. What shone through them all though was his clear sense of self-worth. It explained why he wouldn't be told what to do by her, or by Nigel. Why he wore jeans to an interview. Why he spoke his mind and damn the consequences. This was a man unbowed by his experience in prison, or the way he'd been treated afterwards by his supposed mates, by the fire station. By women.

He stood strong and proud in the face of it all.

It made her ashamed that she'd allowed Miles, his words and his actions, to diminish her.

Jake nodded down to the bucket and brush. 'I need to put these in the shed. Then I'm going to grab a beer and head down to the jetty to decompress. Want to join me?'

She opened her mouth to say no, it was late and she was headed back to bed. But then she paused. Was that who she'd become? The person who always said no? Who put work, chores, duties... anything, before pleasure? Yet thanks to Nigel's fit of pique, she didn't need to spend tomorrow in the kitchen. She had a day off. 'Thanks. I'd like that.' She wasn't sure why her chest felt so tight. 'Why don't I get the drinks and meet you there?'

She found him a few minutes later sitting in the same place as on that first day. He faced the lake, arms wrapped around his crossed legs, T-shirt taut across the muscles of his broad back. It was hard to ignore the way her stomach swooped at the sight, or the way her heart beat that little bit faster. Last time she'd met him here she'd been able to admire his looks objectively, very aware he wasn't her type.

Now her body was sending her confusing signals.

He must have heard her approach because he turned and patted the place next to him, accepting the beer she proffered with a brief smile. 'Cheers.' She settled down next to him and he clinked the bottle against her glass of wine.

Silence fell between them. So many things she needed to say, but as she stared out across the dark lake, the words died on her tongue. Suddenly it seemed safer to keep a barrier between them, to remain sparring partners.

Beside her, he cleared his throat. 'I'm not good at keeping my mouth shut. I know pissing off Nigel wasn't cool, but when people badmouth those I care about, I can't keep quiet.'

It was a lot of words, yet her mind fixated on just one. 'You care about me?'

He rubbed at the back of his neck and as his arm touched hers, tingles raced across her skin. 'Sure.'

Her heart bounced against her ribs. Part of her wanted to push, to ask what he meant by *care*, yet it scared her to realise how much his answer mattered. What if he was just being flippant? If he was still in pretend mode? *Sure I care – we're supposed to be an item, aren't we?*

But he had opened up, and it was wrong of her not to do the same. 'Thank you for sticking up for me.' She swallowed a mouthful of wine while she ordered her thoughts. 'I should have said that straight away, but somehow with you I snipe first, think later. It's like you bring out the worst in me.'

'Ditto.' He glanced sideways at her. 'I used to call you Saint Anna.'

She groaned, believing it. 'Compared to you, I was.' Aware how that sounded, she cringed. 'I didn't mean—'

'You did, and why not?' He took a swig of her beer. 'I've done lots of shit I'm not proud of.'

She was dying to ask what – and, more importantly, *why* – but they'd reached a rare moment of comradeship so instead she sipped at her wine and enjoyed the peace. And the pricks of awareness every time her body touched his.

Eventually he drained his beer and, noting her empty glass, jumped to his feet. 'Time to hit the sack.'

He stretched out a hand for her to take and as she grasped

it, he pulled her easily to her feet, their bodies bumping as she found her balance.

Still holding her hand, he stared down at her, the moonlight reflecting in his eyes, making them seem luminous. Suddenly the air around them felt charged, crackling and sizzling as his gaze roamed her face.

Was he going to kiss her again? Anticipating it, her heart let out a huge thump. A real kiss from Jake Tucker. Not for an audience, not because he was playing a part, but because he *wanted* to kiss her.

But then he dropped her hand and took a step back.

Disappointment settled like a heavy stone in her belly. Of course he wasn't going to kiss her, not if he didn't have to, and she needed to be thankful for it. Going outside the pretence was a very dangerous line to cross.

They walked back to the castle in silence but it had lost some of the ease from earlier, at least for her. She felt on edge, needing to escape his presence and her muddled thoughts.

'Well. Interesting day,' he remarked as they climbed the stairs to their apartment. 'I started it serving Screaming Orgasms and ended it mopping up sick.'

Despite her mixed mood, she smiled as he held the door open for her. 'Let's hope tomorrow is less eventful.'

'I'm supposed to be ferrying our guests to Bellagio in the morning if their delicate stomachs are sufficiently recovered. Do you want to come?'

He was busy shutting the door behind them, so he missed her look of surprise. 'Need me to act as a buffer to Nigel?'

The corners of his mouth curved in amusement, though his eyes glittered with an emotion she couldn't identify. 'Something like that.'

Why did her stomach feel so squishy? 'Then count me in. As it happens, I now have the day off.'

'Good.' Then, in a gesture so unexpected it caused her to inhale sharply, he bent and kissed her cheek.

She was still frozen in shock outside her room, hand on the place he'd kissed, long after he'd shut the door of his bedroom.

Chapter Sixteen

Jake woke the next morning feeling... There was no other word for it. He was horny.

Sitting next to Anna on the jetty last night. The crush of her big, bouncy breasts as she'd bumped into him when he'd helped her stand. His body flooded with arousal at the memory. He'd so very nearly kissed her after that. No excuse of keeping up the pretence that people were watching. She'd have known, without doubt, that he wanted her. Him, the ex-con. Her, the uptight daughter of a cop.

Jesus, he couldn't make it up.

The big... the frigging *huge* question was: did he just want to have sex, or did he want to have sex with Anna?

Prissy Anna, Saint Anna, he reminded himself.

She was nowhere to be seen as he padded into their kitchen. No doubt she'd been up an hour ago, baking bloody croissants rather than getting them from a shop like a normal person.

Idly he scrolled through his phone while he waited for the kettle to brew.

A predictable message from his mum.

Phone me. If I don't hear from you soon I'll imagine you at the bottom of the lake.

He was twenty-eight and his mum still worried if he didn't check in every few days. Then again, when he considered what he'd put her through, he was bloody lucky she still wanted anything to do with him. He tapped out a quick reply.

If you read this you'll know I'm not at the bottom of the lake. Will phone soon.

And then, because he remembered how religiously she'd visited him in prison, the stoic look on her face when people had stared and whispered when they'd seen them together in the months after he'd been released, he added:

Love you x

Half an hour later, the guests plus Anna were settled in the boat. He'd tried not to look at Anna's cleavage as he helped her in. And almost succeeded.

Nigel had given him a frosty greeting, but as he'd wished Anna a civil good morning, Jake had smiled back at him. He could be the bigger man.

'Shouldn't take us long,' he announced as he eased the boat from the jetty. 'About fifteen minutes, barring any mishaps with sandbanks.' Okay, so it looked like he was just bigger in size but hey, any man who puked up after getting into a hot tub drunk and then blamed someone else for it deserved taking down a peg or twenty.

Thankfully, as the boat chugged merrily towards Bellagio, the orange and yellow colours of the old buildings creeping closer, his passengers seemed more interested in looking around them than making polite, or even impolite, conversation. Jake didn't miss the way Venetia and Tatiana's gazes kept drifting in his direction. Nor did he miss the invitation in their eyes.

If he just wanted sex, there it was, almost on a plate.

The fact he wasn't interested sent alarm bells clanging in his head. Fuck. Maybe he didn't just want sex. Maybe he wanted sex with the olive-skinned, dark-haired beauty sitting on her own at the front of the boat.

'We'll need picking up this afternoon,' Nigel announced as Jake tried to push thoughts of sex from his mind and guided the boat onto a vacant mooring. 'After last night's fiasco, tonight we'll go to the Mistral for dinner.' Nigel continued to whine on with his instructions. 'Make the reservation for 8pm. They know us so it won't be a problem.'

'Decent of you to give us the night off,' Jake deadpanned. 'Thank you.'

He caught Anna hiding a smile.

Nigel pursed his lips, clearly unsure whether Jake was finally being the subservient puppet he wanted, or if he was being sarcastic.

As soon as the group were safely on dry land and out of earshot, Anna burst into laughter. 'Oh God, I shouldn't.' She bit into her cheek. 'But you thanking him for the night off... it was too funny.'

For once, he lacked a witty comeback. He was too busy taking in this relaxed version of her – the animated face, the dancing green eyes, dark-brown hair flowing in waves over her shoulders.

'Wow, this place is to die for,' she gasped as he helped her off the boat, her gaze sweeping across the old town. 'Look at those cobbled streets, the pretty pastel colours. It's unbelievably elegant.'

He stared down at his jeans, his faded grey Henley, then back at her cream linen jacket and pink cut-off jeans. 'Elegant is a good word.' Something he'd never be accused of being.

'Come on, let's explore.' She frowned, some of the joy on her face fading a little. 'Oh, you've been here already, haven't you?'

Of course he had. Those first few days when she'd been buried knee-deep in lists, he'd been out enjoying himself. Feeling free, for the first time since prison. 'I only came to suss out the mooring,' he lied, tying up the boat and helping her out.

He led her through the cobbled streets and up narrow winding steps to take in the amazing views of the town. Then he took her to Punta Spartivento at the tip of the town where the three branches of Lake Como met. A place that had stunned him on his previous trip.

'It's like the Alps are actually touching the lake.' Her tone was awed as they rested against the long wall, staring out at the reflections of the mountains on the calm water.

'Glad you came, huh? Left those lists behind for a few hours?'

'The lists are important,' she countered defiantly, her chin jutting forward in the confrontational way he was well used to. 'Without them we wouldn't have been ready for Nigel and would likely be in even more trouble than we are.'

It was an unwelcome reminder of what had happened last night. Frustrated at himself for upsetting the mood, he shoved his hands into his pockets. 'We're scheduled to catch up with Penny and Henry today anyway. When we explain what happened, I'm sure they'll be okay.'

Tension once again tightened Anna's shoulders. 'They're not likely to believe us over their own son.'

She had a point, but... 'Fact is, Nigel was sick after going into a hot tub after drinking all day. And despite Clarissa's little act, we know he was the only one out of the six of us who was.' Because he didn't want her stewing over it anymore, he pointed to the café ahead. 'Why don't we have lunch there? You can get food made by someone else for a change.'

She slanted a glance in his direction. 'Did you eat there when you came here last week?'

'No, I...' He caught her smug look and knew he'd been rumbled.

'Why pretend you've not been here before?' She angled her head, her confusion clear. 'I would have been fine checking the place out by myself. You could have sat in one of those bars by the dock and flirted with the women who eyed you up when we arrived.'

He didn't know where to start with that verbal volley. 'What women?'

She scoffed. 'Come on, you must have seen them. I told you, just be discreet, that's all I ask.'

'You really wouldn't care?'

Her eyes darted back to scanning the lake. 'We're in a fake relationship. I care that nobody rumbles that. And that I'm not taken for a fool again.'

The raw hurt Miles had inflicted showed in her strained expression. She looked so vulnerable that he ignored who he was, who she was, and gave in to his need to touch her. After tracing a line down her cheek with his index finger, he cupped her chin, forcing her wary green eyes to meet his. 'Miles lost you. He's the fool.'

She blinked, the green of her irises glistening. 'Thank you.'

The gratitude in her expression, the unguarded way she looked at him, made him want to give her more. 'I pretended I hadn't been here because I wanted to spend the morning with you.' Her eyes widened and he felt a big tug in his chest. 'As for our relationship, it doesn't feel entirely fake right now.'

As Jake's dazzling blue eyes crashed into hers, Anna's knees began to tremble. Had he really just admitted he felt this pull, this attraction, too? Or, wait, she was getting ahead of herself.

'You mean you don't find me quite as annoying?'

A smile tilted his lips. 'Yes, Anna. I don't find you quite as annoying as I used to.'

Maybe that wasn't as much as she'd hoped for, but combined with his teasing expression it sent warmth spreading through her chest. 'I don't think you're such a jerk, either.'

He laughed softly and her stomach did a sort of whoosh. 'We should celebrate this major achievement before we start banging heads again.'

They found an outside table and chose quickly – panini for him, a smoked chicken salad for her. As she took a sip of her mineral water and glanced over his shoulders at the dramatic backdrop, and then at him, she knew in later years she would remember this as the day she had lunch with Jake. Not with the cocksure bad-boy neighbour who enjoyed embarrassing her, but the guy who'd stuck up for her when she'd doubted herself. Who was surprisingly entertaining when he dropped the defensive guard he wore around her. Incredibly *sweet* when he wanted to be. And devastatingly attractive without even trying.

This man intrigued her.

'I feel I know bits and pieces about you,' she mused after the waiter had gone. 'But I don't know the real stories behind them.'

He took a swallow of his Coke. 'If this is your way of asking me again why I hit Miles, my answer remains the same.'

'It's not.' She sighed inwardly. The guard was back. 'I meant... let's take your family. I know you were a tearaway as a kid, but when I look at your mum and sisters, it's hard to understand why.'

'That's because you grew up at the posh end of town. Graffiti, drinking stuff you pinched from your dad or from an offie, smoking – usually weed if you could get it... it's just things the kids in our estate did when we hung out.' He caught her eye. 'Rearranging the gnomes in old Sedgwick's garden was a highlight. That never got old.'

'Yet when you moved to live next door you still got in trouble. I know because Dad used to stress out about having to tell your mum.'

'Not as much as I did.' He gave her a grin that she imagined he'd tried on the teachers at school. 'She might be a short arse but Mum scared the crap out of me.'

'Then why?'

'Trying to psychoanalyse me?'

'An impossible task. I'm just trying to understand you.'

His gaze drifted down to his glass. 'I guess when Dad died

I lost my way for a bit. I hated that we'd moved from the estate. Mum thought of it as a fresh start but the new place wasn't us, wasn't me. Wasn't him either, even though he'd always wanted to move there.'

'What was he like?' she asked softly, moved by the sadness in his expression.

He looked back over at her, eyes bright with emotion. 'He was the best guy I know. Family was everything to him. He taught me to stand up for myself, be proud of who I am and where I came from. And to take care of the people who matter.'

It was clear Jake took after his dad. 'I'm sorry I never met him.'

His eyes held hers and the vivid blue softened. 'Thanks.'

All too soon Nigel phoned to say they wanted to be taken back.

As the castle came into view, Anna felt a sense of looming dread at the phone call they were about to have with Penny and Henry.

'Let's get this over and done with,' she muttered as they closed the door on their apartment and walked into the open-plan living area.

Jake leaned back against the kitchen worktop and let out a huff of laughter. 'Yeah, that's not usually what women say to me.'

She groaned. 'God, you're so...' The eyebrow with the scar lifted and together with the crooked grin and laid-back stance, the word that sprang to mind was *sexy*. 'Sex-obsessed.' That was better.

His other eyebrow shot up to join the one with scar. 'If I was sex-obsessed,' he said finally, eyes raking hers, his voice so low she felt the vibrations shiver through her, 'you wouldn't be sleeping in that big master bedroom alone.'

An image flashed through her mind of him lying across her bed, hands behind his head, big, muscular body stretched cockily out before her, naked, and her heart jumped into her throat.

As if he sensed the direction of her thoughts he smirked before plonking himself down on the sofa and reaching for the phone lying on the coffee table.

Penny and Henry. The stark dose of reality cooled her blood. 'Okay.' She squared her shoulders as she went to sit next to him and his lips twitched. 'What?'

'We're not going into battle.'

'Aren't we?' His easy-going attitude annoyed her. 'What if Nigel's already told them I gave him food poisoning? They could fire us over it. Then what do we do? We're back in the UK. I'm back living with Dad, no home, no job…'

A pair of big, warm hands clasped hers. 'Take a breath, Anna.'

She was ashamed to find she was shaking. 'Sorry.' Feeling unbalanced, too aware of his touch, she tugged her hands away. 'I've got this.'

He leaned back, crossed his legs at his ankles, and stretched his arms out along the sofa. The king of chill. 'I don't doubt it.'

'It would help if you were a tiny bit nervous, too,' she muttered as she searched through her contacts.

'What's to be nervous about? They believe us or they don't. They fire us or they don't. We'll deal with it.'

'That's where we differ. I like to control the situation, not let it control me.' That was how she'd managed her life ever since her mum had left. Control as much as she could so she wasn't taken by surprise again. It was also why Miles's betrayal had come as such a body blow. Once again, she'd had the rug pulled out from under her.

'Yeah, well, some things in life you can't control.'

His expression had gone from laid-back to harsh but there was no time to explore why because it was showtime.

Taking a deep breath, she called their employers and put the phone on speaker.

'Nigel tells us he got food poisoning last night.'

Penny's bald statement sent Anna's pulse into overdrive. But just as she prepared to reply, Jake cut in.

'He can spin that yarn all he likes but it wasn't food poisoning. He was sick because he'd been drinking heavily all day and then decided to use the hot tub.'

Penny coughed and Anna knew she hadn't taken kindly to Jake's *I don't care who you are, I'll say it as it is* approach.

'What Jake's trying to say,' Anna interrupted, 'is that we think Nigel's sickness could have been down to other reasons.'

'I see.'

'It's possible the combination of alcohol and heat from the hot tub made him dehydrated, causing him to feel dizzy and nauseous. We all ate the same food but only Nigel was sick, which isn't what we'd expect if it was food poisoning.'

'No, I don't suppose it is.'

Having got over that bump, the rest of the call went smoothly, Henry ending it by announcing they were planning to visit next month.

Anna exhaled in relief when they signed off. 'Well, we've got another visit to prepare for but at least we didn't get fired, though it looked a bit shaky at first.'

Jake jumped to his feet, surprising her. 'I'm not going to apologise for saying my piece, or for sticking up for you.'

Irritation positively bounced off him. 'I'm heading out for a bit before I have to take Nigel and his harem out to dinner.'

With that he strode off, leaving Anna to wonder what on earth had happened to the warm, witty guy she'd spent the morning with.

Chapter Seventeen

He'd trounced off like a hormonal teenager. As Jake sat at the bar nursing his Coke – thanks to Nigel and his *you need to drive me to a restaurant tonight because I'm an arse* – he'd calmed down enough to realise he'd reacted badly.

He wasn't usually weighed down by such a giant chip on his shoulder. What had his dad always said? *Doesn't matter where you're from, son, you're as good as the next man.*

And better than the one standing next to him, he'd always tagged on with a wink.

But after ending up in prison, being shunned by so-called mates once he'd come out, rejected by the fire station... it was hard to keep believing that. Hard not to think he was somehow *less* than he had been. Especially when he was around Anna. Composed, professional, smart, she was everything he wasn't. He was glaringly aware it was only thanks to her that he wasn't now facing the prospect of returning to a life of tiling bathrooms for battle-axes like Freda.

Yet again she'd had to use her tact and diplomacy to

smooth things over with their employers. *I like to control the situation, not let it control me.*

He knew a dig when he heard it. Did he wish he was more like that? Did he think if he'd controlled the situation with Miles better three years ago he wouldn't have ended up in prison? Hell, yes. But if he was put in the same situation again, would he be able to? It was like asking a lion not to roar, not to protect his family.

'Anna not with you?'

He was jerked out of his introspection by Phoebe, who strode up to him, breasts clearly visible in her tight, low-cut top. Why didn't he react to them? Why was his stubborn body attracted to Anna's unattainable curves instead?

'Nah. She's busy taking care of our guests.'

Phoebe regarded him quizzically. 'Doesn't she mind you leaving her to come here?'

And now his pathetic storming off was doing the one thing Anna didn't want: embarrassing her. As he struggled with a reply, Phoebe considered him. 'You know, I watched you two at Marco and Rosa's the other week. You don't look like a couple.'

First Nigel, now Phoebe. Either they were both really shit actors, or it was laughable that someone like him could possibly attract someone like Anna. 'Yeah, well, opposites attract.'

She held his gaze. 'I reckon you and I aren't that opposite. And for the record, I'm definitely attracted, if you're ever interested.'

It had been a while since he'd been hit on so blatantly. 'Thanks, but me and Anna, we're solid.'

Solid? Was that really the best he could come up with? It had to have been bad because Phoebe now looked smug, as if she knew something he didn't. Like the fact his non-existent relationship was on the way out.

'Ciao, Jake.'

He breathed a sigh of relief at the arrival of Sara, though he didn't miss the way her eyes scanned the bar as she walked over to him. 'Hey, Sara.'

'Anna not with you?'

The second time he'd been asked tonight. Next time he felt like storming out, he needed to go to a different bar. Or hey, maybe he could actually swallow his pride, acknowledge his poor behaviour like a mature adult, and ask Anna to join him. 'No. She's phoning her dad.' *Liar, she's probably sitting by herself, wondering what on earth she said.*

'You should tell her to come over when she's finished.'

The thought made him pause. 'That's a good idea.' Waving his phone at Sara, he nodded to the door. 'I'll just be a minute.' As he headed out, he caught Sara having another furtive glance round the room, and the penny dropped. 'Will's round the back sorting out an order. He won't be long.'

Sara put a hand to her face and blushed. 'Am I that obvious?'

He winked. 'Not to him.'

Anna answered on the fourth ring. 'Jake?'

Okay, time to be the man your dad thought you were. 'I'm still not going to apologise for sticking up for you. But I am sorry about, you know, disappearing on you afterwards.'

'You mean flouncing off?'

He leaned against the outside wall of the bar and scuffed at the stones with his boot. 'That wasn't a flounce. More a... stride. I strode off.'

'We can agree to differ.' She paused. 'Do I get to know why?'

How to reply without coming across as even more of a dick than he already had? 'I handled the call badly. I know it, you know it. I guess I didn't need you pointing it out.'

There was a long pause. 'When did I do that?'

'Come on. All that bit about controlling the situation rather than letting it control you? Then ending with your relief that we'd not got fired – insert, thanks to *you*. Though it looked shaky at first – insert, thanks to me?'

'Sorry?'

'Look, forget it. It wasn't my finest hour. Why don't you come over here and I'll buy you a drink to apologise?' When she didn't reply, he added. 'Sara's here and asking after you.'

'Is that why you need me to come over? Does it look like we've had a row?'

His let his head fall back against the wall and exhaled a deep breath. 'Yes, I'd like you to come over because if I'm always here by myself it looks bad for both of us. But also because it's our local bar and you've not been to it yet.' He hesitated, then added. 'And because, weird though it sounds, I actually like talking to you. When we're not arguing.'

He heard her huff of laughter. 'Weird though it sounds, an invitation like that is hard to turn down.'

His face cracked into a grin. 'Get your curvy arse over here then.'

Anna's heart picked up pace as she entered the bar. She could pretend it was because she knew eyes would be watching her and Jake together, but the words *I like talking to you* and, yes, *curvy arse* kept playing through her head.

Automatically her eyes zeroed in on him, as if they were

trained to find their target. Leaning against the bar with a lazy grace, his hair rumpled, a sexy smile playing at the edges of his sensual mouth as he talked to Sara, he didn't just draw her eyes. Other women were giving him surreptitious glances as they chatted to their companions.

And then there was Phoebe, who stood behind the bar and was practically pushing her breasts under his nose.

Anna mentally scolded herself for being a bitch. Still, if Jake *was* hers, she'd be making it very clear to Phoebe, to every female here, that he was taken.

'Hello, darling.' She walked straight up to him, pressed a hand on either side of his ridiculously sexy face, and kissed him.

Clearly taken by surprise, it took him half a second to recover his composure. Another half a second to put his hands over hers and, mischief dancing in his dazzling blue eyes, to kiss her back. Thoroughly. Until her heart was racing, her knees buckling, and every part of her ached and wanted.

Slowly, he drew back. 'Hey, babe.'

And yes the *babe* was put on, the kiss just an act, but it was hard not to wonder how it would feel to have all that masculine sexiness directed at her for real.

His hand slipped around her waist and rested in the hollow of her back. It felt warm, protective. Arousing.

Sara greeted Anna with a kiss on each cheek. 'I told you.'

'Told me what?'

'This place, it is very romantic.' She eyed her thoughtfully. 'You seem happier than when you arrive.'

She was, Anna realised with a start. Miles and what he'd put her through was now more of a dull ache than a sharp pain. An ache she could ignore most of the time.

'Maybe the romance will work for you, too.' She smiled,

looking pointedly at Will, who was now talking to Jake but whose eyes kept glancing in their direction.

The sound of screeching brakes outside made everyone jump.

'What on earth was that?' Shaken, Anna looked around her, only to find everyone else looking as startled.

Everyone but Jake, who slammed his glass onto the bar and raced out without saying a word.

'Sounds like a car going too fast.'

A split second after Will's pronouncement, there was the awful sound of metal scraping, followed by an almighty crash.

For a few moments there was a shocked silence. Then everyone started talking at once.

'We should call the emergency services.' Anna's heart was racing like she'd run a marathon. 'That sounded awful.'

And where the hell was Jake?

Sara moved round the bar. 'I'll phone them.'

Wordlessly, Anna and Will dashed outside where a small crowd had collected, all staring down the road. About fifty metres ahead, on the apex of the bend, steam – or was it smoke? – was billowing into the air from the remains of a crumpled car. The driver must have misjudged the corner and smacked straight into a tree.

That's when she saw him.

'Jake's there.' Heart in her mouth, she began to run towards the accident.

'It looks like he's helping someone out of the wreckage,' Will panted, jogging along next to her. 'He needs to be careful. That could go up in flames any moment.'

'He used to be a fireman.'

'No shit?'

Will no doubt had a tonne of questions about how a fireman had ended up managing a castle in Italy.

As they got closer she saw Jake bend and ease the person he'd helped onto the ground before turning and heading back to the car.

'Jake!' she called out as she rushed towards the woman on the floor. Clearly dazed, she was sitting up, blood seeping from a gash on her forehead.

Jake's head popped out from the mangled metal. 'Stay back.'

What about you? she wanted to scream, but he disappeared again.

Heart racing frantically, she knelt next to the woman and gave her a smile she hoped looked confident and reassuring – nothing like the twisted bundle of fear and panic she felt inside. The woman reassured Anna she was okay, just bruised and shaken. She was more worried for her husband, who was still in the car.

'I'm terrified it will burst into flames,' she whispered in Italian.

You and me both, Anna thought silently, but she squeezed her hand and started to ask her about where they'd been heading, whether they had any children. Anything to take their minds off the sight in front of them.

A few minutes later two things happened to soothe her panic. She saw Jake emerge with his arms around a man. And she heard the sound of sirens.

'Your husband is out.' She pointed to where Jake was now raising the man onto his shoulders in the traditional fireman's lift. 'Everything will be okay.'

'Watch out!'

A second after Will's warning, there was a booming noise and the remains of the car burst into flames.

'Jesus, that was a close call.' Will was staring at the fireball, looking as stunned as Anna felt. A few seconds earlier... Her stomach lurched as she thought of Jake being swallowed by the flames.

'Are the sirens for us?' Jake asked as he carefully eased the man onto the ground beside his wife.

Anna nodded; speech was beyond her.

He heaved out a sigh, face lined with sweat. 'Thank God someone thought to phone them.'

'Sara did it.'

'Only after you prompted me.' Sara came up from behind them, her face betraying her shock.

Jake's gaze raked hers. 'Thanks.'

She saw something in his expression that made her feel taller, her back straighter. Respect. She wanted to tell him she wasn't the one who'd heard the screech of brakes and immediately raced towards it. She wasn't the one who'd pulled the driver and passenger out of the wreckage with no thought of his own safety.

But she couldn't say any of it because Jake had turned his attention to the man on the floor, feeling his pulse, checking for wounds, listening to his breathing. She heard the injured man trying to ask if his wife was okay, and reassured him she was.

Jake eyes flicked back to hers. 'Can you ask him if his chest hurts?'

By the time the emergency services reached them they were able to tell them, thanks to a combination of Jake's expertise and her translations, that they thought the man had a broken rib and suspected punctured lung.

The police quizzed them briefly about what they'd seen

and Anna confirmed what the woman had told her: that her husband had been avoiding a dog who'd run into the road. Then they were free to go.

'Jesus.' Will shook his head as they all walked back to the bar. 'That's not something I want to see again.'

'Me neither.' Sara's voice trembled and Anna gave her a brief hug, feeling equally as shaky.

Sara and Will began to talk and, aware Jake was behind her, Anna slowed her pace, letting them go on ahead. Jake was quiet, his face pale, and for the first time he looked as shaken as the rest of them. 'Are you okay?'

He gave her a wan smile. 'Yeah, sorry. It's been a while. Guess I'm rusty.'

'You were incredible.' He'd played down his part, telling the police he'd helped get the driver and passenger out of the car, but Anna knew it was way more than that. He'd risked his life to save theirs.

He stared back at her, eyes now an inky blue, and she thought he was about to say something, but then his phone started to play 'The Fool on the Hill' and he cursed. 'Shit. It's Nigel.' He glanced at his watch and huffed out a breath before pressing answer. 'Yep, I know I'm late. I'm on my way.'

Anna briefly heard Nigel's voice on the other end before Jake cut him off. 'I'm not in the mood to hear the man moan.' He nodded up to Will and Sara. 'You shouldn't be alone right now. Head back to the bar with them. I'll catch you later.'

He started to run off but then stopped abruptly and turned back, shocking the heck out of her when he planted a quick kiss on her lips. 'You had the presence of mind to get Sara to call the ambulance, you calmed the wife, you translated the garbled Italian, and did it all without freaking out.' His eyes skimmed her face, his expression so sincere her heart gave a jolt. '*You* were incredible.'

With a wave to Sara and Will, and a request for them to watch over her, he jogged off, leaving Anna shaken by more than the accident she'd just seen. This was a whole new side of Jake. The ex-fireman who might have been hot-headed enough to run towards danger yet was cool-headed enough to rescue the couple in trouble. Protective enough to make sure Sara and Will looked after her. And thoughtful enough to praise her for what, compared to him, had been so very little.

Will wrapped one arm around Sara and one around her. 'Come on, you two. I think there's three stiff drinks with our names on them.'

'Good idea.' Sara angled her head towards Anna. 'We toast your Jake. He's a hero.'

'Yes.' Emotion clogged her throat. 'He is.'

Chapter Eighteen

As he climbed up the stairs to their flat, Jake finally allowed himself to think about the accident earlier. He'd shoved it out of his mind while providing taxi duties for Nigel, whom he'd deposited back in the sitting room with his entourage. Oh, and opened his very first bottle of champagne for the man, because apparently a) Nigel was incapable and b) they hadn't had enough of the stuff already. Thank God they were going home tomorrow.

But now the memories were starting to resurface.

The adrenalin rush, the moments of fear. The relief when he'd seen the ambulance and fire crew heading towards him.

The feeling of being *someone* again.

He pushed open the door, aware his hand was shaking.

He'd done this for a living once, but it seemed a lifetime ago now. Judging by his reaction, it was a good job he wasn't still doing it. He'd be a frigging liability.

Disgusted with himself, he walked through to the kitchen and headed to the fridge.

'Hey.'

He jerked round at the sound of Anna's voice. She was sitting on the sofa facing the window that looked out over the now jet-black lake. 'I thought you'd gone to bed.'

She gave him a weary smile. 'I wanted to wait up for you.'

He couldn't help but laugh. 'Taking this fake relationship a bit seriously, aren't you?'

Hurt flashed across her face and her eyes darted away from his.

Too late he remembered he wasn't the only one who'd had a shaky time. 'I'm in need of a drink.' Beer wasn't going to cut it, but it was that or open the fancy bottle of red Anna kept buying. 'Do you want one?'

She waved a hand, indicating the coffee table, and for the first time he noticed the bottle of whisky and two glasses. 'Will recommended it. Said it would put hairs on my chest but it would also help me sleep.'

Automatically, his eyes went to her breasts, and his crappy mood eased for the first time that evening. 'Be a shame to cover them with hair.'

'How would you know?'

Okay, he'd just dropped himself in it. Might as well own up to it like a man. 'You swim every morning at seven.' He settled onto the sofa next to her and unscrewed the bottle.

'I wear a swimsuit.'

'Yeah, but when it's wet it doesn't take much effort to imagine them naked.' After pouring two measures he figured were enough to dull the horror of the mangled car wreck and aid sleep, he pushed hers over to her. And found her staring at him like he'd grown horns. 'What?'

'You've imagined how my breasts look naked?'

He rested his back against the sofa and crossed his legs. 'Nah.' He waited for her to take a sip of her drink. 'I've imagined all of you naked.' She spluttered, then coughed, and being the mean git he was, it made him smile. 'That's what guys do – imagine women they fancy naked.'

She spluttered again. 'You *fancy* me?'

He levelled her a look. 'You know I do.'

'I... no.' She shook her head, hair tumbling over her shoulders. 'The kisses were for show.'

'Doesn't mean I didn't enjoy them.'

Her eyes held his and he felt more than just a tightening in his groin. He felt it in his chest. Shit, this woman was turning him inside out.

Needing the distraction, he took a swig of his whisky, savouring the burn as it slipped down his throat. Crazy day. Bellagio with Anna, the call with the Harpers, flouncing off to the bar because yet again he'd allowed his insecurities to mess with his head. The accident when he'd flipped between terror that he'd fail and a brief moment of joy when he'd felt like himself again.

'You look shattered.'

He blinked his eyes open and all he could see was her. The concern etched across her face, the soft moss-green of her gaze. 'You look gorgeous.'

Her eyelids lowered briefly. When she raised them again, her expression was teasing. 'Jake Tucker, are you *flirting* with me?'

'Depends.' He searched her face, trying to get a read on what she was thinking. And giving himself time to wonder what the hell he was doing. Hadn't he played with enough fire tonight? 'Do you want me to?'

Her teeth dug into her bottom lip and he felt another tightening of his groin. 'I don't know.'

Disappointment crashed through him and he shifted away.

Yeah, what did he expect, a *yes*? But then he felt a hand on his and when he looked back at her, her expression was as confused as he felt.

'I just mean, I don't know if it's a good idea to blur the lines between what's fake and what's real.'

'Probably not.' Christ, he wanted to though – to flirt, sure, but to do a whole lot of other things to her, with her. Things he imagined might horrify the saintly Anna.

She nodded and this time she was the one to move away, wriggling back so she was sitting at the end of the sofa, knees bent in front of her in what looked like a defensive gesture. His eyes drifted down to her naked feet, to the bright-red toenails, and he imagined them around his hips, heels digging into his back. Dragging in a ragged breath, he lurched for the whisky bottle.

Anna cleared her throat. 'I stayed up because I wanted to talk to you about earlier. I think you misinterpreted some of the things I said before the call with Penny and Henry.'

He took a moment to steady himself, to breathe, to expel his mind of all thoughts of sex. 'You mean before I flounced off?'

He was rewarded with a small smile. 'Exactly. It occurred to me that you might have taken things I said the wrong way. I appreciated that you stuck up for me in the call like you did, something I'd have found very hard to do myself. And that stuff I said about wanting to control situations – it wasn't a dig at you; it was me explaining how we're different. I actually admire the way you take life as it comes. It must be so freeing to be like that, not to worry all the time like I do.'

She *admired* something about him? He filed it away in his brain so he could bring it out when he felt that damn chip weighing down his shoulder again. For now though, he wanted to focus on her because for once he sensed she might open up a little, if he asked the right questions. 'Have you always been a worrier?'

———————

Regret washed through Anna. Why had she stopped him flirting with her? Maybe tomorrow she'd be happy about her decision, but right now flirting with Jake seemed the perfect way to put the shock of the evening behind her.

It was also way better than talking about herself and the bits of her she didn't like.

'I didn't start out life worried about anything. What kid does?' She took another sip of her whisky, liking the way it helped to smooth edges that still felt sharp, despite the twenty-year gap. 'But then Mum left.'

'And suddenly you realised life could turn to shit in the blink of an eye.' He gave her a wry smile and she knew he didn't just sympathise. He understood.

'You'd know all about that, with your dad.' *And prison*, she thought. He'd had far worse things happen to him, yet he'd managed to remain so chilled, so laid-back.

He shifted so his left arm rested along the back of the sofa, the action pulling his T-shirt tighter across the ridges of his chest. 'Yeah, but at least I knew my dad didn't leave me out of choice.'

She looked away, terrified he'd see how much his statement affected her. She should be over this but she could feel the old wounds open up again, bringing her back to that scared girl who wondered what she'd done. Why her mum had stopped loving her and then, later, if she'd ever loved her at all.

Jake cursed softly. 'Sorry. When they dished out attributes they gave me the looks but not the tact.'

She choked out a laugh, wiping at the traitorous tears with her sleeve. 'It's fine. Dad reassured me she left because she fell out of love with him, not me, but somehow I could never quite believe it. I mean, if she had loved me, wasn't I worth more than an annual birthday card?'

'Sod her. She's the one who lost out.' His eyes settled on hers, boldly blue and unwavering. 'She missed out seeing her girl grow up into a woman strong enough to pick herself up when shit hits the fan, stubborn enough to go after what she wants, and smart enough to make it happen.'

Her heart stuttered. 'I like the sound of the woman you're describing.'

'Yeah, you should.' He smirked. 'When she's not arguing with me, making me lists or giving me orders, so do I.'

Laughter bubbled in her chest and as it burst out, she felt lighter somehow. As if a weight had just been pulled from her shoulders. 'Admit it. You like my lists.'

'Said no man, ever.'

But he'd just admitted he liked *her*. A warm, fuzzy feeling filled her chest and it felt like they'd really turned a corner. That at last they were coming to understand each other a bit. 'You're not who I thought you were.'

'I'm even better looking?'

She shook her head at him. 'Such an obsession with looks, yet they only get you so far. I meant, you're nicer than I thought.'

'Nicer?' He winced. 'Not sure I'm a fan of that word.'

'It's a compliment. Take it.'

He gave her his trademark smirk. 'Yes ma'am.'

A companionable silence fell over them as they both sipped their drinks. 'It was interesting watching you rescue that couple earlier,' she said. 'It was the first time I've seen the firefighter in you.'

He glanced away. 'Ex-firefighter.'

'I'm sorry,' she said softly, feeling his pain. 'I can't imagine someone telling me I can't be a chef anymore.'

He nodded, gaze dropping to his glass, making it clear he didn't want to talk about it.

'You saved their lives, you know.'

'Maybe.' He looked back at her then, expression tight. 'I couldn't speak to them. When I was trying to help them out of the car, they didn't understand me and I didn't understand them. It was heading south, fast.'

Silence fell again, only this time it was taut, filled with unspoken images of what might have happened.

'I can teach you Italian. If you want me to.'

'Yeah, not sure that's going to work.' He swirled the remaining whisky round in his glass. 'I've been listening to podcasts.'

'And?'

Finally a small smile. 'It's pretty painful.'

She eyed him over the top of her glass. 'Will it be more or less painful if I taught you?'

His smile turned crooked. 'Maybe we'll find out.'

The phone she'd left on the coffee table began to buzz and she glanced down at it. 'Dad with a not very subtle reminder that he wants to come and visit.'

'I've had that too from Mum and my pain-in-the-arse sisters.' He tapped a finger against the back of the sofa as if in thought. 'Once we've got rid of Nigel we should get them all over before the Harpers come and it starts to get busy. Otherwise we'll be looking at the end of the year before we see them.'

He was right, though realistically that only gave them the next few weeks. 'Ask your family first. There's more of you.' Never had the small size of her family unit felt so glaringly obvious.

'It's a frigging castle, Anna. Space isn't a problem. Your dad can come at the same time.' He paused, looking straight at her. 'Unless you don't think he'd want to.'

'Why wouldn't he?'

Another smirk. 'Living next door to the Tuckers is one thing. Going on holiday with us...'

Her back straightened. 'He's not a snob.'

'Didn't say he was. Just that my lot can be loud when they get together, especially Emma and the kids. Your dad might prefer a quieter time.'

Her posture relaxed again. Seemed he wasn't the only one guilty of taking things the wrong way. 'I don't think he'd mind. You ask yours; I'll ask Dad. If they overlap, we'll manage.' The whisky was working but she found she wasn't ready for bed yet. 'Emma's your eldest sister, yes? I don't remember seeing much of her.'

'Probably because she shacked up with a guy when she was eighteen.' His expression turned fond. 'You think I'm headstrong, wait till you meet her. I told her Barry was a bad choice but she wouldn't believe me. A year after their youngest was born, he buggered off. Claimed he was too young to settle down.'

'So how old are her kids?'

'Ava's ten, going on twenty. Olly's eight.' If anything, his features turned even softer. 'Pair of them are a right handful but beneath the backchat they're good kids.'

'I've a feeling your mum would have said the same thing of you.'

'Doubt it.' His gaze rested on her. 'I've never been good.'

It wasn't just the way he said it, his voice all low and gravelly. It was the accompanying smoulder, the way his eyes narrowed and darkened with blatant promise. It sent a responding sizzle down her spine, unfurling in a burst of heat between her legs. He *was* dangerous, she realised belatedly, only his danger was pure sex. As he sat there, all muscle and cocky, unabashed sex-appeal, she knew that one touch, one more scorching look, and she'd forget why it wasn't sensible to have a fling with this guy who was so different to her. Especially when she was still raw from her last disastrous relationship.

Feeling unbalanced and hugely, embarrassingly aroused, she threw back the rest of her whisky. And nearly choked on it. 'Right, I'm off to bed.'

So great was the sexual tension pinging between them, even the word *bed* sounded loaded.

Those damned lips of his curled knowingly. 'Sweet dreams.' The eyebrow with the scar twitched upwards. 'And if you can't dream sweet, dream dirty.'

Oh God. She lurched off the sofa, her legs unsteady, and fled to the safety of her room where she flopped onto the bed and stared up at the ceiling. When she shut her eyes, the only images she could picture were of Jake, his powerful body rippling, his tattoo flexing, as he thrust into her.

Dirty dreams it was then.

Chapter Nineteen

I t was May, and the weather was warming up. Thank God, so was the lake. As Jake powered up and down parallel to the shore, he realised he was going to have to forgo his daily ogle at Anna in her swimsuit this morning. Even he didn't have the balls to do that while her dad was here.

Since the man's arrival two days ago, Jake had pretty much kept out of their way. It was one thing knowing the woman he now lusted over – and how the hell had that happened? – had a dad who was a cop, it was another looking the man in the eye.

Hauling himself out of the lake, he grabbed his towel, threw it round his neck, and walked the now familiar path back to the castle. He'd been here five weeks and already it felt like he was living a different life. Here, he was a castle manager. Hell, for the last week, a few locals had even called him a hero. He was also part of a couple – a guy lucky enough, worthy enough, to have caught and held the eye of a woman like Anna. Here, he felt respected, even though little of it was real.

As he rounded the corner, the pool came into view and he skidded to a halt.

Anna was there, as he'd expected. But so was her dad, sitting on one of the loungers, reading the paper and clearly enjoying the morning sun. Thankfully Anna was in the pool, her curves hidden. As long as she stayed in there, he was okay. He'd nod a greeting, and hurry on by.

'Jake.' Her dad raised his hand and waved.

'Chief Super.'

'I told you, call me Patrick. I'm retired now.' He nodded towards the castle and then the lake. 'Here, I'm merely Anna's father, taking a few days' holiday in beautiful surroundings.'

All true, but to Jake the man would always be a cop first. 'Well, I hope you're enjoying your stay.' He felt his skin itch and wished he'd put on a shirt or some jeans. Anything so he wasn't standing nearly naked in front of the man who always made him feel like a delinquent. *Probably because you were one.*

He was about to hotfoot it away when Anna called over to him. As he watched her lever herself out of the pool, water dripping down her long, shapely legs, costume clinging to every single inch of her skin, his tongue got stuck in his throat. *Don't look at her breasts.*

Too late. His eyes had a will of their own and no way were they not going to focus in on the sight they'd been happily enjoying for the last five weeks.

She must have been aware of the direction of his gaze because she hastily grabbed a towel and wrapped it round her.

And when his eyes finally made their way up to hers, she gave him a knowing look.

'Dad wants to see Bellagio and Varenna after breakfast. We wondered if you wanted to come with us?'

Oh yeah, that sounded like a great idea. A whole morning making polite conversation with the Chief Super and keeping his gaze focused away from Anna. 'Thanks but…' *I'd rather watch paint dry, then gouge my eyes out with a rusty nail.* 'I've got some stuff to do.'

'Aren't you the one who keeps telling me to chill?'

He glanced over at her dad, who was watching him with that intense cop gaze, the one where they tried to work out where you sat on the evil scale. 'My version of chill and yours are very different.' And his didn't involve traipsing round with the Chief Super.

Thank God his family were arriving tonight.

As he strode back to the castle, he became aware of a flip-flopping sound behind him. 'Jake, wait.'

He turned, then belatedly remembered why that wasn't a good idea when his eyes shot down to her cleavage. He could almost feel the glare of her dad's angry stare.

She cleared her throat and he looked up guiltily, giving her a wry smile. 'If you don't want me looking, wear something less… clingy.'

She rolled her eyes. 'So you expect me to swim in what, exactly? A wet suit?'

'It would help,' he muttered, though it would still outline her spectacular curves. In an effort to shake off the image, he strode off again, eyes focused ahead.

'Why are you being so off with me?' She almost had to run to keep up with him. 'I've barely seen you these last few days. I thought you didn't mind Dad coming before your family get here.'

'I don't.'

She huffed out a breath. 'Well, why are you so grouchy?'

Christ. He pushed open the castle door and stepped aside to let her past. 'I'm not grouchy,' he said, grouchily. 'I just don't want to spend the day with you and your dad.' A flash of hurt crossed her face and he sighed. 'Let me rephrase. I don't want to spend the day with your dad.'

Confusion clouded the green of her eyes. 'Tell me this isn't about the times you used to get in trouble. That was years ago.'

He drew in a deep breath, the feelings he'd had earlier about being someone again now feeling ridiculously naïve. 'You seem to have forgotten the part where I went to prison only two years ago.'

'Jesus, Jake. My dad is a kind, loving, decent guy who's always supported you, even when you were being a jerk.' Her eyes sparked angrily at him. 'Even when you ended up in prison. So have the decency to be civil to him.'

For a second, he just stared at her. Cheeks flushed, hair a wet, bedraggled tangle, goosebumps on her arms, chest heaving with emotion. She looked magnificent.

'Jake?'

His mind felt muddled. He wanted – hell, he *needed* – to go back to disliking her. It was way less dangerous than this mess of want, of respect and affection. Of wishing he didn't have a past in which he'd seen way too much of her father than he should have done. 'I can get the boat out. Take you there by water. If you think he'd like that.'

Her shoulders relaxed and a smile split her face, causing further confusing sensations. 'I knew you'd see it my way. Thanks – we'll be ready in half an hour.'

And that was how he found himself sitting next to the Chief Super – next to *Patrick* – as he steered the gleaming wood-panelled motorboat across the calm green water of the lake towards the picturesque village of Varenna. Anna was sitting at the front but for some reason her dad had sat himself down at the back, with Jake. Silence stretched so far it was tauter than a drumskin, but Jake couldn't think of anything to say. At least nothing that wouldn't land him in trouble. He didn't think *I fancy your daughter* would go down too well and he'd already tried all the polite shit about weather.

'You and Anna are still talking, I see.' Finally, her dad broke the quiet, his comment delivered in a bland tone that gave no clues as to what the man was thinking.

'You expected us not to be?'

'Thought you'd be at loggerheads by now.' He was sure the Chief Super's lips twitched. 'She likes to… organise.'

Okay, he was going to go out on a limb here. Either he'd end up in the lake, or maybe, just maybe, he'd have shared a surprising moment of bonding. 'I've had to ban her from making me more than one list a day.'

'Wise. Never had the guts myself.'

It wasn't the sun, or the reflection of the lake. There was a frigging twinkle in her dad's eye. 'I'm not sure it's guts. More self-preservation.'

The Chief Super nodded and silence fell again, only this time Jake felt more at home with it. Maybe the man really didn't look at him and see his rap sheet.

'She's not had it easy.' The Chief— no, *Patrick*, glanced his way. Figuring he wanted to get a point across, Jake kept quiet. 'I've tried to compensate for the lack of her mother, but I've not always got it right. Anna felt hurt and betrayed when she left.' He paused, clearly picking his words. 'For a long time she struggled with relationships, wanting to be loved, getting her heart broken. Then Miles came along.'

And she was left hurt and betrayed – *abandoned* – all over again.

At the unspoken message, a powerful, protective feeling balled in Jake's chest. Fucking Miles. 'She's strong. She's getting over that already.'

Again, her father nodded. 'She is. And she will. But right now, she's still vulnerable.'

The implication was clear. So much for not being judged. 'You think I'm that guy?' His voice was tight with the anger he couldn't hide. 'The one who takes advantage of women when they're vulnerable?'

The Chief Super skewered Jake with his stare. Raising his chin, Jake stared back. He'd done a lot of things wrong in his life, but he'd never hurt a woman. Upset a few, maybe, when he'd wanted a relationship to end before they had, but he'd never pretended to be something he wasn't. And he sure as hell hadn't cheated.

'Actually, I don't.'

'Don't what?' Anna, clearly sensing friction, joined them at the back of the boat. 'What have you been discussing?'

Jake decided that as the Chief Super had just given him a few uncomfortable moments, he'd return the favour. 'Your dad was warning me off you.'

Anna's expression looked the picture of horror. 'What the hell, Dad? Please tell me Jake's kidding. You know we're only *pretending* to be in a relationship.'

Her father looked unabashed. 'Pretend or not, you're still my daughter.' He rose to his feet. 'I think I'll sit at the front.' He glanced at Anna with a small smile loaded with love. 'Let my daughter cool down a bit.'

'You can't blame the man for looking out for you,' Jake murmured as her dad walked out of earshot.

'I can blame him for embarrassing me. God, as if you need warning off me.'

Jake caught her eye, feeling that pulsing connection again. The one that didn't seem to want to go away, now his body had decided it wanted her. 'Maybe I do.' Before she could ask any questions, he called out to Patrick. 'See that cluster of pink, orange, and yellow houses? That's where we're headed.'

Chapter Twenty

Anna watched, horrified, as Jake dive-bombed into the swimming pool, creating monster waves and drenching both her and his sisters who were trying to relax and take in some sun. Jake's mum and her dad were taking a tour of the grounds. The Tuckers had arrived late yesterday and other than a quick hello, this was the first real time Anna had spent with them, having decided to go out for a meal with her dad last night to give Jake and his family time to catch up.

'You dickhead.' Emma leapt up, waggling her finger at him, which only made the grin on Jake's face widen. And set his niece and nephew off into another fit of giggles.

'Language, Mum.' Olly was like a mini Jake, all blond hair, glinting blue eyes, and cheeky-as-heck smile.

'Sisters are allowed to call their brother a dickhead when he acts like one.'

'Yay.' Ava splashed her brother. 'Olly is a dickhead.'

As the pair of them hurled insults at each other, egged on by Jake, Emma groaned and sat back down. 'I don't know who's the biggest kid in that pool.'

'Definitely Jake.' Daisy snorted with laughter as she watched Jake lift Ava in the air and throw her back into the pool, creating even more splash.

Anna winced as Ava spluttered to the surface. Was she enjoying this? But a moment later, having done the same to Olly, Ava was clinging to Jake, begging him to throw her again. 'They seem to be enjoying themselves.'

Emma flicked her a look. Anna was still feeling her way round Jake's eldest sister. Where Daisy was easy-going and friendly, Emma was harder to get to know. And very forthright with her views. 'You sound surprised.'

'Not really.' She glanced back at the pool, savouring the sight of Jake's naked torso as it glistened in the afternoon sun. Her fingers itched – actually itched – to slide down his chest, over those hard pecs, and trace the outline of his lion tattoo. Reluctantly, she dragged her eyes away. 'It's just I've never seen this side of him.'

Emma raised an eyebrow. 'You mean without his clothes?'

Daisy snorted again. 'Em, don't! You'll make Anna blush.'

Not for the first time around a Tucker, Anna thanked God for her olive skin. Was it obvious she was ogling him? 'I meant fun uncle.'

Emma reached for the G&T she'd requested because *I'm on holiday and surrounded by other people who can sort the kids out.* 'He's more than an uncle to them. Their dad buggered off years ago. Jake hunted him down and made sure he keeps in touch for the kids' sake, but frankly Jake's their father in everything but name.' Her gaze rested on Anna. 'Before he came out here he used to see them every week. Only time he missed was when he was in prison.'

She wasn't sure if Emma was testing her reaction to the

reminder he'd been in prison, or just stating a fact. 'That must have been a hard time for all of you.'

'It was. The kids were devastated, especially as Jake wouldn't let us visit. He was scared they'd view him differently if they saw him inside a prison with guards watching over him. Not their uncle anymore but a criminal.'

He wouldn't talk about it, and she was starting to understand why. It wasn't just his niece and nephew he feared would see him differently.

'What about you?' At the blunt question, Anna turned to find Jake's older sister giving her a quizzical look. 'It must be weird working out here with the man who ended up in prison for punching your ex.'

'Honestly, since we arrived here I've not really thought about it. We've just got on with things.' It wasn't answering Emma's question and they both knew it. Fact was, if she'd believed Jake was fundamentally a bad person she'd never have considered asking him to fake a partnership. He was a hothead though, quick to temper. 'Violence is wrong, but so is hurting someone by other means.' She looked Emma in the eye. 'Miles isn't blameless; I'm sure he wound Jake up. Certainly Miles had no qualms about hurting me.'

'Jake was defending me. That's why he did what he did.' Daisy's quiet interruption made Anna glance over with a start. 'Miles deserved what he got.' Her eyes remained downcast. 'I just wish Jake hadn't suffered delivering it.'

'Miles is a git all right.' Ice cubes clinked as Emma took a sip of her drink. 'If he ever tries to contact you again, Anna, don't tell Jake. Please.' She glanced towards her brother, who was now doing handstands under the water, his muscular legs sticking up at an amusingly ungraceful angle.

'Why not?'

'He'll want to protect you – he can't help himself. And Miles is a conniving bastard.' Emma's face hardened. 'He'll try and goad Jake just so he can cause more trouble. Jake can't do any more time inside. It would destroy him.'

Anna was starting to appreciate the full implications for someone who'd done time. How easy for a man like Miles to create more trouble for Jake, now he had a record.

'Jake has no need to protect me.' Just as she had with her father, Anna spelled it out for Jake's sisters. 'This is a pretend relationship, nothing more.'

'Sure it is.' Emma smirked, the expression uncannily like Jake's. 'That's why the pair of you keep giving each other sly looks when you think the other isn't looking.'

'I'm not. We're not…' Was he really looking at her as often as she was him? 'Maybe we've had to act like a couple so much out here that it's become a habit.'

'What's a habit?'

Jake hauled himself out of the pool, bringing most of it with him by the look of the water running off him. Oh, to be those molecules, clinging to his skin, gliding down the ridges and bumps of his abs, past the vee and into the bright-turquoise board shorts that clung to his muscular thighs.

'Something a nun wears,' Emma deadpanned, sliding Anna another of her *I've caught you ogling* glances 'We were saying how you two seem to be getting on a lot better over here than you did back home.' She gave her brother a wicked smile. 'You used to call her Saint Anna.'

'No point trying to stir things, Em. She knows.'

'Does she also know you used to sit in the back garden and sling stones at her bedroom window at night in the hope she'd open the curtains wearing a skimpy nightie?'

'You didn't.' But to Anna's delight, Jake, he of the cock-sure swagger, blushed.

'Christ, thanks, sis. For the record, I was thirteen and not in control of my hormones.'

Emma winked at him. 'Some things never change, huh?'

The afternoon sped by and soon they were all sitting round the huge oak dining table, eating Anna's lasagne. In between throwing her extravagant compliments about the food, Jake's family bantered back and forth, occasionally squabbling, always laughing.

Jake hadn't been kidding. They were loud.

Suddenly she became aware of her dad, who was sitting to her right, watching her.

'You missed out on this,' he said sadly. 'A big family.'

Emotion clogged her throat and she put her hand over his. 'Maybe, but I got you, so I count myself incredibly lucky.'

The kids played up when it was time to go to bed but Jake hitched Ava onto his shoulders, tucked Olly under his arm, and ferried them off, laughing and giggling.

When he came back down she felt the heat of his gaze every time he looked at her.

She didn't know what was happening, only that she wasn't alone in feeling it.

Finally, everyone headed off to bed.

'You seemed to get on okay with my sisters,' he remarked as they walked across the flagstones of the huge hallway towards their apartment. 'What were you talking about?' He flashed her a cocky grin. 'Me?'

She decided his ego needed denting a little. 'Miles, actually.'

He halted, tension tightening his jaw. 'Have you heard from him?'

Too late, she remembered Emma's warning. 'Only a text to ask if it's true that I'm here in Italy with you. I replied that we were working together. This feels weird,' she continued before Jake could ask anything else. 'Your family and Dad heading off in a different direction to us.'

He slid her a look. 'We're a happy couple, remember?'

'We're a fake couple. Who said we were happy?'

He reached the top of their stairs and pushed the door open for her. As she brushed past him, her nerve endings went into full alert. Damn her body for making this so difficult.

A touch on her shoulder and she turned to find him right there, trapping her with the intense blue heat of his gaze. 'I'd make sure my woman was happy.'

The low gravel to his voice made her shiver. She had no doubt about his ability to do exactly that, at least sexually.

He trailed a finger gently down her cheek. 'Want to know something funny?'

She swallowed, her body a mess of hormones, his touch causing arousal to coil in her belly. 'Yes.'

'When we first arrived here, I had to pretend to want to touch you. Now, with our family around us, I've spent the evening pretending I don't.' His grin was lopsided, a lethal combination of sexy and sweet. 'It's screwing with my brain.'

Her breath hitched. He'd hinted before, but this was the first time he'd admitted it directly. 'I...' She had to clear her throat and start again. 'I think I know the feeling.'

'Yeah?' He angled his head, a small smile playing around a mouth now only inches from hers. 'I want to kiss you. Not for an audience, not because I have to, but because I *want* to.'

Oh God. Dangerous, so dangerous, yet part of her was

humming, thrilled at his words. 'I thought we decided this was a bad idea.'

Amusement mingled with the heat in his eyes, making them burn brighter than ever. 'You think knowing something is a bad idea has ever put me off?'

A bubble of laughter escaped her. 'Probably not.' She forced herself to draw in a breath, to ignore her screaming hormones and think rationally. 'But it does stop me.'

The heat dimmed and he took a step back. 'Fair enough.' His expression closed up. 'Guess I'll see you around tomorrow. Night.'

She wanted to believe she'd dented his ego, but there was something about the stiff set of his shoulders as he walked away that made her call his name.

He turned, eyes hooded.

Damn, this was hard. Yet he was no longer the annoying, too-full-of-himself ex-neighbour she'd travelled out with. She'd seen other sides to him: doting uncle, heroic firefighter. A man who'd stood up for her, who'd helped her when her confidence had been at a low ebb. 'It's not that I don't want to. Kiss you, I mean.' She scrambled to find the right words. 'But we're here to do a job and I... I need us to be successful at it more than I need anything else.'

His gaze held hers, sharp and far too observant. 'Do you realise how stupid that sounds? That you won't kiss me because you're afraid it will interfere with your job even though that job actually needs us to kiss, to be a couple?'

He had her there. But if he knew the truth, that she was afraid to kiss him...

He shifted, leaning his shoulder against the wall, body language sending out a clear *this conversation isn't fazing me at all* message. 'Do you want to know what I think?'

She hoped he couldn't hear the pounding of her heart. 'I'm sure you'll tell me whether I want to know or not.'

'I think you're scared you'll enjoy it a little too much.' His eyes skimmed deliberately down her body until they came to rest again on her face. 'Scared once I've kissed you away from watching eyes, you'll want me to do more things to you in the privacy of our flat. Things you're afraid of wanting.'

Because she hated that he understood her so well, she jutted out her chin. 'I suggest you save your cockiness for those bored, rich housewives. It doesn't do anything for me.' He flinched, head snapping back as if she'd slapped him. Immediately, Anna knew she'd gone too far. 'Sorry.'

'For speaking the truth?' He gave her a tight, forced smile. 'It's only what I'd expect from Saint Anna.'

He closed the door of his room with a hard thump and Anna sagged against the wall of the hallway. He'd poked a raw nerve and she'd reacted in kind, not just poking, but jabbing hard. *Once you've been inside, you're either a magnet for bored, rich housewives, or to be avoided at all costs. I don't mind being a dirty fantasy but I won't be a dirty secret.* Oh yes, she could be really proud of herself.

Wearily, she opened the door to her room.

Chapter Twenty-One

The following morning Jake waited until he heard the door of their flat shut before he climbed out of bed. He couldn't avoid Anna all day, but he could at least make sure he got his head together before he had to see her.

For once though, the calming routine of his daily swim in the lake didn't do the trick. As he headed downstairs to find his family, both the rejection and the way she'd rejected him still felt raw. She'd hit right where it hurt, her cutting words arrowing straight to the heart of his biggest fear. That he wasn't good enough for more than a cheap thrill. He'd never be wanted for who he was, warts and all.

Maybe he'd misread all the signs, thought she liked him when she was just playing her part and trying to get on with him. Whatever, now he knew. Saint Anna might fancy him, but he wasn't good enough for her.

'Wow, someone's got out of bed the wrong way.' Crossing the reception hall, he looked up to find Daisy watching him, concern on her face. 'Everything okay?'

He slapped on a smile. 'Sure, Poppy. I'm just hungry.'

She gave him the expected eyeroll at the nickname. 'Anna's got all the breakfast stuff out in the dining room. Everything you could want. It's like some sort of posh hotel.' Okay, so he'd skip breakfast then. He'd hoover up the leftovers later when no one was around. 'Mum's in there with the kids. Emma's still in bed. She told us all she's on holiday and it's our duty to look after her monsters.'

'I guess she deserves a break.'

Daisy gaped at him. 'You're such a pushover. Come with me to help Mum and see if you're still saying that in an hour's time.'

And now he had no choice but to join them.

He carefully avoided looking at Anna when he stepped inside the large wood-panelled dining room, dominated by a huge stone fireplace. Fleetingly he wondered what it would be like to eat there at Christmas with a roaring fire. Then realised he'd never find out. If the Harpers spent Christmas here, he'd be helping to serve it, not eat it. If they didn't, if it was just him and Anna... would they even be talking by then?

'Uncle Jake, sit next to me.'

Ava pointed to the seat next to her – the one opposite Anna and her dad. His heart sank.

As if she could read his mind – and maybe she could, because he'd never had a poker face – Anna immediately rose to her feet. 'Can I get anyone anything else?'

His mum flapped her hand. 'You sit down, love. There's loads left still and if Jake wants anything else he's big enough and daft enough to sort himself out.'

'Certainly daft enough.' Daisy smirked at him.

Banter was what they did, but this morning the throwaway comment felt like salt being rubbed into his open wound. Daft enough to hit a guy and end up in prison. Daft enough to think

Anna liked him. Daft enough to believe he was worth more than a dirty fling.

Thankfully, his mum was talking again, pushing a bowl towards him. 'Here, Anna made amazing scrambled eggs.' She hesitated. 'What am I thinking? Anna's not had any yet.' She passed the bowl across the table towards Anna. 'Here, take some before Jake devours the lot.'

'She doesn't like the stuff. She prefers her eggs poached.' Jake said the words without thinking. It was only when he saw the gleam in his mum's eyes that he realised he'd set himself up for a line of questioning he wasn't prepared for.

'Interesting.' His mum looked between him and Anna.

Shit. She was adding up two and two and coming to a figure that was so far off base, it was laughable.

Anna clearly felt it, too, because she cleared her throat. 'Jake remembers that from the cards I made.' Now the entire table had gone quiet, everyone staring at her. 'I thought it was important we knew as much as we could about each other before we went for the interview, so we went through things like birthdays, favourite movies, likes and dislikes.'

'When's Anna's birthday and what's her favourite film?'

Distracted by Daisy's combative tone, he shot back. '20th August. *Notting Hill*.' Realising he'd just dug himself another huge hole, he tried for distraction. 'Has to be one of the sappiest films ever made.'

Sadly, his mum was razor-sharp. 'Are you the same Jake who never remembers my birthday and still brings me chocolates even though I prefer fudge?'

'Who bought me a lovely pink handbag for Christmas even though I've never liked pink?' Daisy added, gleefully taking the metaphorical spade and digging his hole even deeper.

Truth was, he didn't take notice of the small stuff. Except, apparently, when it came to Anna. 'At least you got a ruddy handbag,' he muttered. Choosing that had been hard enough, never mind the bloody colour. Who knew women needed so many styles, in so many colours, just to carry keys and a purse?

Thankfully Olly chose that moment to knock his juice over. 'Oh shit.'

'Watch your language, young man,' his mum remonstrated. 'We don't swear, especially not round the dinner table.

'Uncle Jake swears all the time. He says shit and bloody and f—'

'Fudge,' Jake interrupted. 'The stuff your grandma apparently likes more than chocolate, which is just weird.' Grateful to his nephew, he swung the little fella onto his shoulders. 'Come on, Mr Clumsy, let's hunt down a cloth from the kitchen.'

Olly squealed. 'It's so high up here I can touch the ceiling.' Then, pulling at Jake's hair, he bent down and said in a loud whisper. 'Uncle Jakey, do you fancy Anna? Is that why you 'member her birthday?'

Christ. As Jake strode out as fast as he could, his ears burning with embarrassment, he heard his mum and sister hoot with laughter.

As he'd known she would, his mum caught up with him when everything was cleared away and Anna and her dad had, thankfully, disappeared off in her dad's rental car to visit some gardens in Villa Melzi. Not on his list of top one hundred – make that one thousand – things to do in the area.

Taking his arm, his mum led them out onto the patio and

indicated for him to sit next to her on the huge wicker corner sofa. 'So, you and Anna.'

'Are not happening.' She looked put out and God, he loved his mum, would do anything to make her happy, but he couldn't do this. 'I know you like her. I know since you came out here you've been watching the pair of us and imagining, I don't know, what colour hat you'd wear to the wedding, how your grandkids would look, her dark hair, our blue eyes.' He shook his head, wondering what the hell his brain thought it was doing. 'But you need to stop.'

'You don't like her?'

He groaned, rubbing a hand down his face. 'Fuck, Mum.' Suddenly he felt a pinch on his arm, just as he had when he'd sworn in front of her as a surly teenager. 'Ouch.'

'No wonder Olly is swearing. That boy idolises you, so set him a proper example.'

Jake slammed his eyes shut, emotion churning through him. 'He needs to find a better role model.'

'Rubbish.' A pair of hands gripped his and when he opened his eyes he saw his mum's face lined with worry. 'His uncle is the most fiercely loyal, kind, generous, loving man I've ever met.'

'His uncle went to prison,' Jake retorted flatly. 'That's not an example you want to give any kid.'

Her hands moved to his face, cupping them gently, and when he looked into her eyes, he saw nothing but blind love. 'Just because a rich man with a clever lawyer got the courts to sentence you, doesn't make you a bad person.'

He knew he wasn't, but it didn't change things. 'It doesn't make me a suitable match for Anna, either, so stop hoping for something that is never going to happen.'

She smiled. 'Can I hope for fudge instead of chocolates?'

Damn, he loved her. Wrapping his arms around her, he gave her a fierce hug. 'You get fudge *and* chocolates.'

'Good.' She gave him a fond look before rising to her feet. 'Now that's settled, let's go and check out these gardens Patrick wanted to go to.'

Jake groaned. 'Do we have to? I'd rather slam my balls in a car door.'

She gave him the mum look. 'Don't be crude. And in answer to your question, yes, we have to, because I want to take in all the sights before I go home.' She patted her hair. 'And because you're not the only one with your eye on a member of the Roberts family.'

Halfway to his feet, Jake slumped back onto the sofa again, his mouth gaping. 'The Chief Super? Seriously?'

'And why not?'

There was a hint of defensiveness about her tone, a flash of vulnerability in her eyes. 'Absolutely no reason why not.' He stood and kissed her cheek. 'You've been single way too long. Any man would be lucky to have you.' He just wished it wasn't Anna's dad. Reason seven thousand and twenty why he should stamp out this crush he'd developed on her.

'And I could say the same for you, dear son. Any woman would be lucky to have you.'

He could almost believe it. When he loved, he loved fiercely, totally. He could make any woman happy. Even a woman like Anna.

But she had to want him to first.

Villa Melzi was stunning. The house sat elegant and proud on the edge of the lake surrounded by gardens bursting with colours, azaleas and rhododendrons in full bloom. Paths wound around a Japanese lake and along the shore, statues peeped out between the bushes. It was impossibly romantic. The sort of place Anna thought she'd love to wander, holding her lover's hand. Unbidden, an image of Jake came into view. It was laughable and not just because he didn't have a romantic bone in his body.

'You're very quiet,' her dad remarked, giving her a careful study.

He wouldn't pry, she knew that. Then again, he'd never had to. His searching look was enough to make even hardened criminals confess everything they were thinking.

'Just drinking the place in.'

He made a humming noise, settling his hands into his pockets. 'So you've not been thinking about what that little chap said at breakfast this morning.'

Gah! It wasn't fair that he knew her so well. 'Okay, yes, I've been thinking about that.'

'Anything you want to tell your old dad?'

'There's nothing to tell.' *Except that when he kissed me, I melted. And now he wants to kiss me again, for real. And if I wasn't so terrified of being a crushing disappointment to a guy I've got to live with for the next year, and of getting hurt all over again, I might jump at the chance.* 'Besides, you don't really want to hear about your daughter's sex life, do you?'

He gave her a small smile. 'The details, no, but I do want to hear if she's happy, if she's sad, worried. Whether she's enjoying life here or whether she wants to come home.' He took hold of her hand. 'I want to know how she's feeling.'

Anna swallowed, clinging to the hand that now held hers. 'I don't want to come home. Jake and I, we've started to get on a lot better, and I like living here. The owners are coming in two weeks and in an odd way I'm looking forward to their visit. I had a bit of a meltdown before the first guests, but Jake really helped me through it and now, well, I want to show Penny and Henry what I'm capable of.'

He nodded, eyes filled with pride. 'Good. And Jake?'

'What would you say if I told you I liked him?'

'I'd say I wasn't surprised. He's a likable fellow.' His gaze darted away and for once he looked uncomfortable. 'And I imagine he's quite attractive to some women.'

Bored, rich housewives. Shame rolled through her as she remembered her tart words. 'If you mean that some women go for bad-boy ex-cons, then you're doing him a disservice. There's so much more to Jake than that.' She exhaled sharply, feeling angry on his behalf. 'Did I tell you he rescued a couple from a car crash moments before it burst into flames? That while we were all trying to process what we'd heard, Jake just rushed out, straight towards the danger.'

A smile cracked her dad's face. 'Actually, I was talking about his height. And the... er, muscles.'

'Oh.' Anna felt heat creep up her neck.

'So you like him then. This tall, brave man with the big—'

'Muscles,' she interjected. Then, catching the glint in her dad's eye, she burst out laughing. When the laughter died, she sighed, leaning into him. 'In answer to your question, yes, I like Jake. But I'm still very raw from Miles, and we've just reached the stage where we're not fighting all the time. It's better if we focus on working together.'

'Sounds sensible.' He bent and kissed the top of her head. 'But it may not prove as easy as that. Not when you're living under the same roof as all that height and those...'

'Muscles?' she filled in with a smile.

'Exactly.' He glanced down at his own arms. 'Reminds me. I must get to the gym.'

'Oh yes?' She turned to him, taking in his dear, familiar face. Still a handsome man. 'Anything *you* want to tell *me*?' When a flush bloomed on his cheeks, she knew something she'd suspected for a long time. 'Sheila?'

His eyes narrowed. 'How did you know?'

'You're not the only one capable of playing detective, you know.'

That stern face, the one that had intimidated so many people, softened. 'Well then, what a pair we make. Both unsure how to move forwards.'

'You should definitely go for it. Sheila's lovely.'

'Yes, she is. I've always known that, but since retiring, let's just say I have more time to appreciate her. To think about what could be.'

They wandered in silence for a while, but as they made their way to the shore of the lake, she stiffened and her heart picked up. Following the direction of her gaze, her dad murmured, 'Ahhhh…'

'There you are.' Sheila beamed as she walked towards them, but Jake avoided Anna's gaze. 'I told Jake I wanted to see why Patrick had insisted on coming here.' She sighed, glancing around her at the beauty of the setting. 'And now I can.'

It wasn't fair that Jake looked so good, Anna thought. Jeans moulded over solid thighs, T-shirt taut against the hard planes of his chest, dirty-blond hair waving in the breeze, he looked like a ruddy rock star.

Her dad indicated behind him. 'Let me show you the Japanese lake, Sheila. You know this is the perfect time to visit. The azaleas are in full bloom…'

The pair of them wandered out of earshot and an uncomfortable silence descended.

Anna glanced at Jake. 'I've seen the lake but do you want to go?'

He gave her a bland look. 'What do you think?'

'I think you might prefer it to being stuck with me.'

He snorted, raking a hand through his hair and giving her a flash of tattoo. It caused a slow sizzle in her belly. 'You underestimate how little interest I have in botanical gardens.'

'Or overestimate how angry you are with me right now.'

'I'm not angry.'

She felt the full power of his blue gaze. Not angry, she thought. Hurt. 'I'm really sorry about what I said yesterday.' It wasn't enough, not if they were going to get back to how they were before last night. 'You were right. I am afraid of you kissing me, and because I hate being like that, I lashed out.' She forced her eyes to meet his. 'You're worth more than any woman's dirty fantasy and I should never have made you feel otherwise.'

For a second, he held her gaze, his expression still tight, his guard still well and truly up. Then he shifted his gaze to the lake. 'Why are you so afraid?'

I'm afraid it won't be good for you. How could she admit that to someone like Jake? A man who had been a sex god even at sixteen, if the rumours and screams she'd heard coming from his then girlfriend were to be believed.

'Is this about Miles? That crap he mouthed off when you dumped his arse for being unfaithful?' His perceptive gaze ran over her face. Just when she feared he'd seen more than she wanted him to, his expression turned unsure. 'Or are you afraid of getting involved with a guy like me?'

'Like you?' He lifted his shoulders, but if he was trying to feign casual indifference, he was failing. His body was too tense. 'You might think you're a bad boy, an ex-con, whatever you want to call yourself, but that's not the man I've lived with these last two months.' She forced his eyes to meet hers. 'It's not the man I see with his sisters, with his nephew and niece. With his mum.' She risked giving his side a gentle prod with her elbow. 'That man's a total pussycat.'

Surprise shot across his face and then he started to laugh. 'Yeah, I don't know whether I'd prefer to be the big bad ex-con right now.'

For a moment there was quiet. Just the stillness of the lake and a fluttery feeling in her chest that both thrilled and terrified her. 'In answer to your question, this *is* about Miles. What he said, but also what he did.' She swallowed, aware that no matter how tough this was to say, it was important she said it. 'I feel bruised from it still. I know I shouldn't let it get to me and I hate that it has, but… it seems better all round if you and I stay friends.'

'Friends.' He nodded. 'Except when we're pretending to be lovers.'

'Yes.'

A small smile curled his mouth. 'Seems doable.'

'I think so.' She wondered who was kidding who. 'So, your mum and my dad.'

He winced. 'You've seen it too, huh?'

'Yep. Do you want to talk about it?'

His face paled. 'No, God, no.'

'More painful than going round botanical gardens?'

'Infinitely.'

She bit back a laugh. 'Okay then. Knowing Dad, he'll want to take his time, give your mum the full benefit of his…' She paused deliberately, just for the fun of seeing Jake blanch. 'His horticultural wisdom.' As relief washed across his face she had to fight not to giggle. Bad-boy Jake, panicked at the thought of his mum having a sex life again. 'So we've got time to kill. How about we head for the bar, grab a drink, and I see how much Italian you've picked up from the last lesson.'

'Christ,' he muttered, shoving a hand into the pocket of his jeans and involuntarily drawing her eye to his crotch. *Eyes up! Friends don't eye up each other's anatomy.* 'Just when I thought the day couldn't get any worse.'

'Hey, don't be so glum. If you're a good student I'll buy you an ice-cream.'

He glowered at her, but when they set off towards the exit, the tension between them had disappeared, though the prickles of awareness remained.

Chapter Twenty-Two

The following two weeks flew by. Their families went back home, the women all swapping numbers, which left Jake worried about what, exactly, his sisters would be messaging Anna. After they'd gone, the place felt quiet and unnervingly intimate. As his being nominated for sainthood was highly unlikely, he decided the only way to avoid getting down on his knees and begging Anna for sex was to keep his distance. He'd even begun taking his swim in the evening rather than the morning so he wouldn't be tempted to hang around the pool afterwards, gawking at her like a horny adolescent.

He had focused his energies instead into getting everything ready for the arrival of their employers. Boat polished, check. Grass mown, hedges trimmed, check. Fountain finally fixed. Hot tub good to go – he could learn from some of his mistakes, at least.

He also spent several hours a day toiling through the online Italian course Anna had found for him. He'd never be able to speak it like she could – where she gave the words a sexy lilt, he mangled them – but he figured that if he kept this up, he'd be able to have a conversation in Italian by the time he was due to head home. The irony wasn't lost on him.

With their new guests happily chatting on the terrace – Penny, Henry, and two of their friends who appeared equally loaded – Jake went to seek out Anna in the kitchen. She'd not had a noticeable wobble this time, but he wanted to make sure she was as calm as she seemed.

Liar. You want to get close enough to touch her… inhale her.

He swatted the devil on his shoulder and strode into the kitchen.

The instant he saw her, his heart slammed into his chest. Hair tied back but with a loose tendril curling round her face, a white apron sitting neatly over curves that didn't want to be contained by it, she was humming, her face alive. Happy.

'Hey.' She glanced up briefly from squirting some white stuff onto a tray. 'Guests all okay?'

'For now.' He walked round the island, watching, fascinated. 'What are you making?'

'Individual honeyed peach and pistachio pavlovas.'

He couldn't remember what the hell a pavlova was, so he went for a safe reply. 'Nice.'

'*Nice*?' She gave him that haughty look he used to hate, and now found went straight to his groin. 'They're going to be gorgeous.'

'And you accuse me of being cocky.'

'It's your fault. You gave me my confidence back.'

The air between them hummed as their gazes tangled. 'I could give it back to you in other areas, too. If you'd let me.'

Heat crept across the olive skin of her cheeks. 'You're really going to go there?'

He cursed his insensitivity. 'Sorry. That was crass.'

'Just because I don't want to jump straight into bed with another man, with you, doesn't mean I'm somehow... defective.'

She turned away, clearly upset, and he dragged a hand through his hair, frustrated with himself. 'I didn't mean... Fuck.' Exhaling sharply, he strode up to her and placed a hand tentatively on her arm to get her to face him. She recoiled, and he dropped it to his side, disgusted with himself for being so careless with her. 'I'm sorry. You have to know I don't think you're in any way defective. I was being cocky, speaking without thinking.' Her eyes swam with emotion: fear, hurt, embarrassment, and a whole bunch of other things he wasn't clever enough to work out. 'It's just... that bruising you mentioned, it pisses me off he gets to do that to you. I want to help heal it. Show you how gorgeous you are.'

Silence. She picked up the bag thing she'd been using and began to make another swirl. Just as he thought he'd totally screwed things up, she looked up at him. 'Gorgeous, huh?'

Relief rushed through him. 'Well, yeah. When you're not nagging.'

Her lips twitched. 'I don't nag. I point out what needs to be done.'

'And then point it out again. And again.' Uncertain if he'd done enough to put them back on an even footing, he searched her face for clues, but came up empty. 'Are we good? Or do you want to, I don't know, slap my face? Put toenails in my bed?'

Her eyes widened and finally he saw the smile that was beginning to become the best part of his day. 'I'm not sure what sort of evil brain comes up with that as a way of getting back at someone.'

'That'll be Emma. She did it to me once. Worst night's sleep

I've ever had.' Keen to change the subject, he looked around the kitchen. 'Anything I can do to help? I've got a beginner's badge in chopping, and an advanced in washing-up.'

The tension he'd created eased and they worked together, her telling him what to do, him making a hash of it; her sighing, giving him a mock glare before fixing it, or starting again, depending on how much he'd cocked up.

He laughed out loud when she threw her hands up in despair after he'd shaken some spice into a bowl without measuring it first. 'God, Jake. I said one teaspoon. Not a shake and a hope.'

'Hey, the chefs I watch on TV don't weigh stuff out; they go by gut instinct.'

'Number one, you're not a chef. Number two, it's safer and more reliable to measure.'

'So says the woman who always goes by the rules.' Damn. Working with her was more fun than he'd thought.

'There you are.' Penny appeared at the door, startling them both. 'I've just been speaking to Marco and Rosa and I've invited them for dinner with us. I hope that won't be a problem?'

Jake thought of all the prep work Anna had done. Four marinating chicken breasts, four filled crab shells, four leek and feta cheese soufflés.

'Of course not.' Anna's smile was big and bright. And because he knew her, Jake could also see it was hiding a mild panic.

'And will you join us later?' Penny glanced at him. 'Rosa tells me you got her dancing the other evening.'

'If I remember, it was the other way around.'

'Maybe, but she also said her hips hadn't shifted like that in years.' She gave him a small smile. 'Perhaps we'll get a demonstration.'

Okay, so he didn't mind dancing with Rosa, she was a laugh, but there was something in Penny's look that made him think it was all part of a plan to suss him out. Make sure the scruffy tattooed guy was really up to mixing with their friends. 'If she's game, I'm game.'

After she'd gone, Jake turned to Anna who looked frozen on the spot. 'No problem, huh?'

She inhaled a deep breath. 'I'll have to change the crab course to salmon and make more soufflés. Defrost more chicken breasts and make sure Rosa and Marco get those because they won't have been marinating for long enough.' She raised her arms and shooed him. 'I need to focus.'

A few weeks ago, he'd have felt dismissed. Now he knew her enough to know she needed to take control of the situation, and having him in her space was going to hinder, not help. 'Okay, I'll get out of your way.' But he paused before turning, watching as she started to drag ingredients out of the fridge in quick, efficient movements, her teeth nibbling the bottom of her lip.

Arousal flooded through him, but along with the tightening in his groin came one in his chest. He couldn't explain it, only knew that he was starting to feel something more than lust for this woman who was both annoying and funny, prickly and sweet, strong yet at times disarmingly vulnerable. She must have sensed he was watching because she looked up. 'What?'

He strode over to her, clasped her face in his hands, and planted a tender kiss on her forehead. 'You've got this, Anna Roberts.'

Then he darted out before he could question his motives.

Exhausted, Anna slumped back against the sofa. Around her there was chatter, Rosa's heavily accented English, Penny's cultured tones, and Henry's dry laugh. The occasional comments from their guests, Sue and Richard, who seemed quiet but polite. Certainly a lot easier than Nigel and his entourage.

As if they were on some sort of Jake magnet setting, her eyes darted to the doorway just as the man himself wandered into the room. He'd insisted on clearing up by himself – *if you don't look, you won't care that I'm disobeying all your dishwasher stacking rules.*

Her heart fluttered as his gaze collided with hers, their conversation from earlier bouncing around her head. She'd felt so humiliated. What woman wants the man she fancies to think she's bad at sex? Even now, the memory made her shudder. And yet she knew the man who'd gone on to plant such a sweet kiss to her forehead hadn't meant to hurt her. He'd just been clumsy with his words. God help her though, now she couldn't get his cocky statement out of her head. Could he give her back her confidence, make her feel sexy again?

Or would she be left even more humiliated, their working relationship untenable?

He levered his big body down next to hers and, in a gesture that looked utterly authentic, wound his arm round her and drew her against his side.

'We thought we'd take the boat to Como tomorrow,' Henry said to Jake before turning to her. 'The plan is to have a light lunch on board and then take a ride up the funicular railway to Brunate.'

'No problem.' Anna mentally sized up what was in the fridge. 'I can do some sesame chicken with a tomato and grilled halloumi salad, and maybe some rainbow wraps and pinwheel sandwiches to go with it?'

'That sounds fine.' Penny gave her that smooth smile that Anna still couldn't work out. Was she reserving judgement, or had she already judged and found her wanting? 'Perhaps you'd like to join us? Obviously, Jake will be needed to take us in the boat. It seems a shame for you to miss out on the trip.'

'Um… yes.' She had to work hard to focus on Penny as Jake had begun to smooth his hand up and down her right arm. 'That would be lovely. Thank you.'

The conversation flowed around them again, and Jake continued the slow, sensual glide of his hand, relaxing muscles she hadn't realised were tense. It was easy to think he was only doing it for show, but now there was the added thrill that she knew he wanted her. Maybe just so he could stick two fingers up at Miles. Prove he was better than him. Whatever the reason, surrounded by the warm press of his body, the fresh, masculine tang of whatever it was he showered in, it was hard to remember why she'd put a barrier between them.

'Shall I put on some music?' Henry asked, rising to his feet. 'Anyone fancy a dance?'

Rosa immediately looked over to Jake and gave him a saucy grin. 'What do you think? We show them how to do it?'

Jake surprised her by shaking his head. '*Mia bella Rosa, scusa mi.*'

His accent wasn't perfect, but what he lacked in authenticity he made up for in sexiness because wow, when he turned on the charm, his husky voice was made for Italian.

Rosa clearly thought so too, because she giggled like a teenager. 'Another night?'

'For sure, but tonight'—he looked down at Anna, his eyes a vivid blue—'tonight, my girl is tired. I think it's time I took her to bed.'

His words, loaded with double meaning, sent Anna's pulse into overdrive and as he helped her to her feet and placed a warm hand on the small of her back, arousal pooled between her legs.

Holy cow, what is he doing to me? How could he waken so many hormones with just a look, a simple touch?

When they were out of earshot, he let out a deep, relieved-sounding breath.

'You sound like I feel.' She watched as he dragged a hand through his hair in a weary gesture. 'Are you okay?'

'I am now.' As they climbed the stairs together she was acutely aware of him. 'Didn't realise making polite conversation was in the job spec. I'm shite at it. Gives me the heebie-jeebies.'

It was hard to believe; he'd looked so at ease as he'd held her. 'I wondered why you were running a hand down my arm. Now I see it was to distract yourself.'

They reached the top of the stairs and he leaned against the wall, right hand circling her waist. 'No.' His eyes darted to hers and he pulled her a little closer. 'That was me, wanting to touch you.'

Her heart clattered against her ribs and her breath came out in a rush. 'Oh.'

His lips formed a sensuous curve, amusement mixing with the heat in his eyes. 'Yeah, oh.' Ignoring or oblivious to the conflict raging inside her, he pushed open the door and motioned for her to go inside. It left them in the same position they'd been in a few weeks ago, standing outside their respective bedrooms, tension cracking the air between them.

'So.' His gaze ran over her face and then down, resting briefly on her cleavage, making her hyperconscious of the low cut of her top, the way her nipples stood to attention, her breasts tingling under his scrutiny. He raised his eyes to hers. 'I guess this is where we say goodnight.'

'Yes.' But damn it, suddenly she didn't want him to go. Not without sampling at least some of the promise in his eyes. 'Did you mean what you said earlier?' she blurted.

The eyebrow with the scar quirked upwards. 'Which part?'

'About helping me get over Miles?'

His eyes flared hot. 'Absolutely.'

'And...' She twisted her hands, embarrassment rubbing up against a desperate need to move forward. To be the woman Jake thought she was, not this insecure shadow of herself. 'Do you really think you can make me feel gorgeous?'

He took a step towards her and rested his hands on the wall either side of her face, boxing her in. 'You *are* gorgeous.' He dipped his head, planted an all too brief kiss on her lips. 'I can make you feel a million dollars.'

Her heart was racing so hard she felt dizzy. 'Only a million?'

His mouth curved. 'I like to under-promise and over-deliver.'

Laughter huffed out of her but then the reality of what she was contemplating began to sink in. 'I want this. God, right now I really, really want this, but is it real or are we just getting confused over playing our parts? You and I would never be contemplating this under normal circumstances.'

His body stilled, lids lowering a fraction over his eyes so she couldn't read what he was thinking. But then he shifted, pressing his hips against her. 'Feels real enough to me.'

Heat flooded her, making her giddy with desire, yet in a

corner of her mind alarm bells rang, warning her this was too fast. That jumping into bed with Jake Tucker wasn't the answer. 'I'm scared,' she whispered, even as she pushed back against him, desperate to feel more of his heat, of the hard ridge of his erection.

'Nothing to be scared about.' He sucked at her bottom lip, sending lust coiling through her. 'We can go slow.' A kiss, equally as soft as before. Just a press of his mouth against hers. 'Work up to the whips and handcuffs.' He must have seen her panic because he let out a low chuckle. 'Chill. I don't need props.' Another kiss, this one more searching, his tongue tracing her lips and then easing them apart, causing a wave of arousal to roll through her. 'Just my tongue, my hands.' As if to emphasise the point, he cupped her breast. 'And your dynamite body.'

Want pulsed through her and she felt herself tremble. Just before her knees buckled, he picked her up, effortlessly securing her in his arms as he had all those weeks ago when they'd first arrived. Then, she'd felt stiff, awkward. Now she felt drunk with desire, aching with arousal. Yet edged with a sliver of alarm. 'Where are we going?'

'To the living room.' As if he could read her panic, he smiled. 'We're going to neck on the sofa for a while.'

Chapter Twenty-Three

A swim in the lake hadn't cut it. A cold shower and the use of his hand still hadn't cut it. As Jake fiddled about with the coffee machine, his eyes strayed over to the sofa where he'd made out with Anna last night and he ached.

He could still remember the way she'd writhed beneath him, the hot panting in his ear as they'd kissed, as he'd pushed his hand beneath her bra. The husky moan as he'd thrust against her. The strangled cry as, unbelievably, she'd come apart in his arms. They'd both been fully clothed, yet it had felt more arousing, more erotic, than any naked make-out session he'd ever had.

'Morning.'

He jumped at the sound of her voice. One look at her tangled hair, her just-woken-up sleepy expression, and the throb between his legs intensified. Shit, this was not good. There were another ten months still to get through. 'Coffee?'

'Thanks.' He'd been afraid she wouldn't be able to meet his eyes, but she looked over at him and gave him a tentative smile. 'This is weird, isn't it?'

'Me making you coffee?'

She rolled her eyes. 'Well, yes. But also, you know. Trying not to think about what happened last night. On the sofa.' A bubble of embarrassed laughter escaped her. 'I can't believe I did that.'

We'd never be doing this under normal circumstances. Yeah, he'd bet she couldn't believe she'd been tangling tongues with the ex-con from next door. He couldn't believe it either. As he focused on pressing the right buttons on the coffee machine – a step up from the instant crap he was used to – he feigned a casual air. 'Reckon you'll want to do it again sometime?' Inside, he was coiled tight. He wanted to think it was only his ego on tenterhooks, but it was likely he was kidding himself. If she said no, he was going to be hurt, no question.

She nibbled that lush bottom lip, which didn't help the ache between his legs one little bit. 'Maybe.'

Not exactly the answer he was looking for. Yet when he handed her the mug, her eyes caught his and what he saw there was enough to bring out his cocky side. 'I bet I can persuade you.'

She sipped at the coffee, watching him from over the rim of the mug. Sadly, whatever she was about to say was interrupted by the buzz of her phone on the worktop. They both glanced down at it, and when he saw who it was, he blinked. Then read it again, anger burning through him.

'You're still talking to that fucker?'

She snatched the phone up. 'It's my business, not yours.'

She had a point, but still, he couldn't believe, after what the git had done to her, she hadn't deleted him from her contacts. 'Are you going to tell him I had my tongue down your throat last night?' The moment he said it, he knew it was wrong. Not just crude, not just insensitive. It demeaned what had happened between them.

But inside he was raging that a man who'd hurt her, who'd knocked her confidence, was still phoning her. That she was answering him. And mixed with all that was a twisted feeling he recognised from when he'd seen that damn photo of his ex in Barbados with her new man: jealousy.

All warmth drained from her expression. 'Why would I tell him when already I regret it?'

With that she turned and marched off to her room. He just about made out her greeting – *Hello Miles* – before the door of her bedroom slammed closed.

Cursing, he stalked over to the window, but the sight of the lake and the mountains beyond did nothing to lift his mood.

This was number seven thousand and twenty-one on the list of reasons why he shouldn't have bloody kissed her last night. Now they had to spend the day together, pretending to love each other, when all she probably wanted to do was knee him in the balls.

His anger deflating, his temper cooling, he let out a deep, agonised sigh. Would he ever learn to think before he spoke?

He wanted to knock on her door and apologise, but he had no clue how long the call to Miles would last. Or whether she'd still want to knee his balls afterwards. As he didn't want to spend the whole day in agony, he figured it best to get out of the way and let her cool down before seeing him.

Scribbling out a note he stuck it under her door.

Sorry. Gone to get the boat ready.
Jake the Jerk

He had no idea how well or otherwise his apology had

gone down because by the time he caught up with her, they were on the boat, surrounded by Penny, Henry, and their two guests. He gave her a quick glance as she stowed the cool box and tried a smile. He received a forced one back. He could only hope their employers weren't watching too intensely.

'Anything else needed from the kitchen?' *Say yes, then we can go together.*

But she either ignored his silent plea, or didn't see it because she was avoiding looking at him. 'We're good, thank you.'

So prim. And if *he* noticed it... yep, that was Penny, glancing between the two of them, a world of questions in her eyes.

And wow, just his luck, Penny decided to seat herself away from the group who'd settled at the back and join him at the front. Anna, who'd yet to sit, looked momentarily panicked: sit with the guests and make polite conversation, or sit with him and pretend to like him in front of Penny.

She must have decided it would be rude to intrude on the others as she put that too bright smile on her face again and slid into the cream leather seat on the other side of Penny.

'We're lucky with the weather today,' she said, eyes still avoiding his as he eased the boat away from the jetty.

'You'll discover this place is blessed with good weather most days.'

An uneasy silence followed and Penny looked again between the pair of them and Jake knew she was trying to work them out. 'Can't wait. We love a bit of sun, don't we, babe?' The endearment felt stilted on his tongue. When he'd first casually tossed it out, he'd done it to needle her, knowing damn well she'd hate it. Now it felt as glaringly false as their relationship.

Anna gave him a stiff smile. 'We certainly do. One of the many things we have in common.' She looked like she was about to say something else, probably to change the subject, but Penny spoke again.

'You know, you two intrigue me. Looking at you both, it actually seems as if you have nothing at all in common.'

Jake's hands clenched on the wheel and it took all his focus, all his bullshitting skills to force the rest of his body to relax and his face to smile. 'You aren't the first person to say that. Even I can't understand what she's doing with me.' A fact he'd conveniently forgotten when he'd been kissing the life out of her last night. He increased the speed a little, then shot Anna a loaded look. 'What can I say? I'm a lucky bastard.'

She was so angry with Jake. Before Miles's call she'd been about to tell him she wouldn't take his bet – he'd be able to persuade her into kissing him again, no question. But then he'd made it all seem like some sort of game just to get back at Miles.

Not for the first time in her life, she'd felt humiliated. She didn't have time to nurse her bruised ego though, because Penny was staring at her and she knew she was totally mucking this up. 'I'm the lucky one.'

And last night that was exactly how she'd felt. Lucky to be the woman in his arms, the one he'd made feel beautiful. Special.

All because he was a far better actor than she was? Or had he at least meant some of it?

She caught Jake's eyes and was surprised to find him lowering his gaze, giving his head a small shake. It was like he was saying she'd gone too far, that Penny wouldn't believe her statement.

'How did you meet?' Penny asked.

Oh God, did they discuss that? She remembered his nonsense about being attracted to her curvy arse, that they'd been going out for two years...

'We were neighbours.' Jake's reply cut through her panic and she remembered him telling her to stick to the truth as much as possible. 'When I was thirteen I used to throw stones at her window at night, trying to get her to open her curtains just so I could see her.'

So he'd see me in my skimpy nightie. She remembered Emma's words.

'When I was fourteen I'd smoke in front of her, trying to act like the big man. She just thought I was a jerk.' He slid her a look. 'By the age of sixteen I'd given up hope. In fact, for many years I used to antagonise her deliberately, trying to prove I didn't fancy her.'

Anna stared back at him, confused. Was he cleverly mixing the truth with fiction, or had he really been attracted to her back then?

'It worked,' she interrupted. 'I never knew he liked me.' She caught his eye again and held it for a moment. 'I thought he considered me too anal, too boring.'

Penny was clearly fascinated now. 'So what happened? How did you finally get together?'

'She asked me to pretend to be her boyfriend for this wedding she was going to.' Anna tried not to let her shock show – there was keeping it close to the truth and then there was playing it dangerously – but Jake kept talking in that low, easy voice of his. 'Turns out she'd told them she'd be bringing her boyfriend, but the boyfriend was a dumb bastard and let her down. Everyone she knew going was coupled up and she didn't want to go as a sad single, so she asked me.' He shot her another look out of eyes that were as blue as the sky behind him. 'It might have started out fake, but it turned real pretty quick.'

He'd bragged about how good he was at bullshitting, yet there was something about the way he held her gaze that made her heart skip a beat.

The conversation moved on, Penny talking about how she met Henry, and Anna finally started to breathe easy. Jake moored up in Como and Anna served out the lunch. Then the party left to go up the funicular railway. She tried to get out of going by protesting they needed to clear up, but when Penny realised she and Jake hadn't been on it before, she insisted they went with them.

It meant once again she felt the warmth of Jake's hand on her lower back, the touch of his fingers on her waist as they stood together in the small carriage. At one point, when they were all admiring the spectacular view from the top, he pressed a kiss on her forehead.

It made her wonder if he'd be this attentive, this sweetly affectionate, in a real relationship.

The moment they found themselves separated from the group, he turned her to face him, eyes studying her face. 'Are we okay?'

'You mean have I forgiven you for butting into my business this morning? Or have I forgotten that you basically admitted your prime motivation for kissing me last night was to wind Miles up?'

His forehead wrinkled, his eyes widening. 'You have got to be kidding me. I didn't even know you were still in contact with the bastard.' He drew in a ragged breath and took a step back. Then quickly scanned around them, his jaw tightening. 'Shit. Penny's already suspicious. We can't have another row here.'

He was right, so she reached for his hand and tried to ignore the way her pulse raced as his fingers curled around hers. 'I'm not in contact with Miles, not in the way you mean,' she told him as they walked to the next viewpoint. 'Before today I'd only heard from him once, that time I told you about, when he messaged to ask if it was true I was here with you. I only replied because I was worried he might cause trouble for us if I ignored him.'

She felt his grip tighten on her hand. 'Am I allowed to ask why he phoned you this morning?'

'He was apologising, both for having the affair and the things he said afterwards.' He'd sounded genuine enough, but Anna didn't know how much of it was real regret, and how much was because he was finding it difficult to find another chef to replace her. 'He admitted he's spoilt, used to having his own way, so he didn't take well to being dumped.'

Jake gave her an incredulous look. 'He expected you to just roll over and forgive him?'

'Apparently.' This *was* Jake's business, she realised suddenly. If Miles did as he'd promised, Jake would be forced to see the man who'd put him in prison. Releasing her hand from his, she threaded it through his arm instead. 'He said he plans to visit me here and apologise in person.'

Jake swore. 'You're really going to let him?'

'I can't see how I can stop him. I told him he couldn't stay in the castle, but he said no problem, he'd book into a hotel.' She paused, the frustration, the feeling of being powerless, burning a bitter trail in her gut. 'This isn't about him wanting me. It's about him needing a chef. And if I want a job in the restaurant business when I go back, I need to keep on the right side of him,' she added quietly. 'I thought you'd understand that.'

'There are other towns.'

'And if I want to be near Dad?'

He let out a heavy breath. 'Okay, I get it. But when we started out on this shindig, you said him knowing you were with me was a bonus. You wanted to upset him. Now it looks like you want to make nice again, despite what the git did to you.'

She was reminded of Emma's words, about how protective Jake was. 'I don't want to see Miles but if he wants to get on a plane and come over, I will listen to what he has to say. Even if what I really want to do is slam the door in his face.'

They walked silently for a few moments, arm in arm, and perhaps to anyone watching they looked like a happy, contented couple.

'Fuck it.' Jake halted abruptly, swinging them round so she was facing him. 'I know I overreacted this morning, and I'm sorry for that, but this bastard hurt you. I don't want him to have the chance to do it again.'

Not everything about them was fake, she realised then. The concern he had for her was genuine. With a rush of pure affection, she rose up onto her toes and kissed him softly. 'Thank you for caring.'

He blinked, then let out a deep breath, his body losing some its tension. 'Was that a real kiss?'

She smiled and did it again. 'Yes, Jake Tucker. That was a real thank-you kiss.'

'Just thank you?'

The air between them hummed and she knew what he was asking. 'For now.'

God, that sexy look of his was hot enough to strip off paint. All her nerve endings came alive again beneath it, her skin pricking, desperate for his touch. But Miles was still between them, and she knew he sensed it too because he glanced away and heaved in a deep breath. 'Let's go and find the others.'

He held out his hand and she took it. The same warmth pulsed through her at his touch, but this time it also felt natural. Right. 'I never thanked you for earlier, on the boat. When Penny was asking all those questions, I kind of froze. Thank God you were right about your ability to bullshit.'

He glanced down at her, eyes hooded. 'Who said it was all bullshit?'

Chapter Twenty-Four

Their guests had finally gone and as Jake bounded up the steps to the castle, having just come back from dropping them at the airport, he breathed easy for the first time in a week.

It was a similar feeling to when he'd stepped outside the gates of the prison after six shitty months.

Freedom.

'Honey, I'm home!' he yelled, striding through the great hall towards the kitchen where he was bound to find Anna.

Only she wasn't there. Feeling a tug of disappointment, he pulled out his phone and sent her a message because the castle was too bloody big to go wandering round till he found her.

Guests returned to airport. We need to celebrate. Where are you?

A few minutes later he got a reply.

Laundry room. Drowning in sheets.

He circled back towards the kitchen but then took a right, finding her hunkered down by the tumble dryer, dragging a duvet cover out of the drum. He grabbed it, taking it out of her hands, and, because he knew her well enough by now, folded it up before placing it on the neat pile with the other clean bedding.

'Leave the rest for tomorrow. There's a pint and a glass of that fancy red stuff you drink with our names on it over at the bar.'

She huffed out a breath, causing the strands of dark hair that framed her face to flutter. 'You go; I want to finish up here.'

'One day I'm going to rid you of that nasty habit.'

She tilted her chin, a sure sign she was ready to argue. 'Wanting to get my jobs done isn't a nasty habit. It's conscientious. Responsible.'

Not for the first time in the last week he wondered what she'd do if he pushed her against the wall, lifted her so she had to wrap her legs around him, and kissed the living daylights out of her. Would she shove him away? Or would she forget everything – the jobs, Miles, her carefully thought-out reasons for not wanting to get involved with him – and melt into his arms? Beg him to put out this fire that weeks of simmering sexual chemistry had created?

She's not ready.

Reluctantly, he stepped back. 'Well, as I'm neither conscientious nor responsible, I'm heading over there now.' He caught her eye. 'Will you join me?'

'Yes, when I've—'

'Finished. I get it.' He flashed her a smile. 'But don't be too long or I'll come and drag you away.'

· · ·

The bar was busy and as it was a while before he managed to catch Will's eye, Jake figured he'd get Anna her glass of Barolo.

'Being lord of the castle is getting to you, I see,' Will remarked as he poured. 'Now the man orders the most expensive red on the menu.'

'My woman has expensive tastes.' The possessive word tripped easily off his tongue. Too easily. If this felt real now, what was it going to be like by the end of the year?

For the first time since admitting he didn't just fancy Anna but liked her too, he realised he could be in trouble.

'Whoa, that's some scary thinking you're doing over there.' Jake shook himself out of his scary introspection to find Will looking quizzically at him. 'Anything you want to tell me?'

'Trust me, you don't want to know.'

Will flicked him a grin. 'Hey, I'm a barman. It's my job to listen.' He pulled an exaggerated thinking pose. 'Let me guess. It's woman trouble.'

'Think again.'

'Are you sure about that?' Jake became aware of the press of soft flesh behind him, but the woman didn't smell right. The scent was too sweet, too cloying. He turned to find Phoebe who nodded to the full glass of wine in front of him. 'It looks like Anna's stood you up again.'

'She'll be here.' Mentally, he crossed his fingers.

Phoebe ran her eyes deliberately up and down him. 'If you were my man, I wouldn't let you out of my sight.' She reached onto her toes and whispered into his ear. 'I'd be there whenever you wanted me.'

And now he smelt it on his right. Anna's perfume – some expensive citrus Jo Malone fragrance. How did he know? Because he'd never remembered anything at school, yet somehow he could recall every little nugget of info Anna had written on those daft cards.

'Is that my wine?'

She must have seen Phoebe and made up some crap in her head because she refused to look at him. So he picked the glass up, held it out to her and then, very deliberately, kissed her on the mouth. 'Here's to a few weeks of peace and quiet.'

Sara, whom Jake hadn't seen until now, obviously overheard him because she slid into the space Phoebe had left on his other side and wiggled her eyebrows suggestively. 'Ooh, have you two got some alone time?'

As if she'd only just twigged that it would be the two of them again for a while, Anna froze, then took a large gulp of her wine. 'It would appear so.'

He'd heard more enthusiasm in people waiting to have root canal treatment. 'Don't mind Anna. She's trying to pretend she can't wait to rip my clothes off and have sex with me in every room.'

While Sara laughed, Anna gave him a saccharine smile. 'Only in the rooms I haven't cleaned yet.'

Thankfully, Sara started chatting to them then about Penny and Henry. Jake zoned out, letting her and Anna talk, the image he'd created now scorching through his mind. Suddenly he didn't want to be here; he wanted to be back at the castle, no worrying about guests and no distractions. Just him, Anna, and a big empty castle.

From the way Will was looking at Sara, he figured he wasn't the only man here bursting to get a woman alone.

'Sara,' he interrupted. Both women stared at him. 'Will here has something he wants to chat to you about.' He watched as Will's eyes rounded and his face took on a startled expression. 'Come on, mate. The time for readjustment is over. Now it's time for action.' *For both of us*, he thought privately before turning to Anna. 'Drink up, babe. Let's go home.'

She looked like she wanted to disagree, to put off being alone with him, but Sara and Will were staring at each other like a couple in one of the romance movies his sisters loved to watch, so she nodded and downed the rest of her glass.

Anna felt queasy, and it wasn't from the wine she'd knocked back. As Jake wrapped his arm around her and led her out of the bar, her stomach churned.

'Phoebe—'

'Came on to me.' He cut her a look as they crossed over the road. 'I told you before, I don't cheat.'

'Even on your fake partner?'

He let out a strangled sounding noise. 'Yeah, even then.'

'But you like her.'

He snapped his head round. 'Why do you say that?'

She remembered back to Rosa's party and felt a hot spike of jealousy. 'Jesus, Jake, you had a hard-on for her when you were dancing with me.'

He came to an abrupt halt and glared at her, hands on his hips, all that tall, powerful body vibrating, as if he'd put it on a tight leash. 'I didn't get hard for her. I got hard for you.'

'Oh.' And now she felt less queasy and more... hot. Like the knots in her stomach had turned into liquid heat and settled between her legs. 'But you hated me back then.'

'I never hated you.' He crossed his arms over his chest, biceps bulging against the sleeve of his T-shirt. 'You think I'd have come out here if I had? I didn't understand you, didn't get on with you, but I always thought you were drop-dead gorgeous.'

As if he'd not just totally upended her, he grabbed hold of her hand and started to walk again. A man on a mission. And with a bubble of excitement, she started to realise that mission might be her.

They walked the rest of the way in a tense humming silence that had nothing to do with anger and everything to do with the sparks pinging between them. She'd never felt so sexually alive as she did in that moment, as they almost ran towards the place he'd just called home.

As soon as they were through the door he took hold of her shoulders and pushed her against the wall. Eyes that were the most brilliant blue she'd ever seen trapped her in their gaze.

'All that crap going round in your head about Phoebe, about maybe there being something wrong with you, some fault that was the reason Miles went off with another woman...' He inhaled, T-shirt drawing taut across his chest. 'That shit stops right now. He's the defective one.' His eyes searched hers, seeing way too much. 'The man is used to getting his own way, doing whatever he wants. He's lost all sight of how to keep hold of something special.'

It was hard to breathe, never mind take in everything he was saying, but it seemed he hadn't finished.

'While we're clearing the air, those words Miles threw at you that made you feel less about yourself? You can forget them, too. It's not the first time he's spouted bullshit because a beautiful woman has dumped his arse.'

'Daisy?' she whispered, her voice still trapped.

'Yeah, Daisy.' Jake shifted, resting his forehead against hers, surrounding her in hard muscle and fresh male scent. 'What that git has said, it's been given way too much importance.

Forget him. He's not here. I am.' His left hand cupped her face, and he used his right to smooth a thumb gently across her cheek. 'And I want you like you wouldn't believe. I wake up wanting you, go to bed wanting you.' His hips pressed into her, proving his point in the most visceral way. 'I fucking ache with wanting you.' His mouth touched hers, a light caress, a seductive slide of his tongue. 'And in case you think this is just about sex, I also happen to think you're the most bloody amazing woman I've ever met.'

Her breath hitched, her heart thundering. But he hadn't finished.

'Are you good with that? Or do you need more convincing?'

'I… Jesus, Jake, you've got my head spinning.'

'You need a helping hand up those stairs?'

She tried to calm her breathing, to steady herself from the onslaught of over six foot of heady sex-appeal. 'No, I think I can manage.'

He gave her a wolfish grin. 'Then I've not done my job properly.' Ducking his head, he found her mouth with his, and this time there was no easy seduction. This was full throttle, pure one hundred per cent sex in a kiss. When he finally drew back, her limbs felt heavy, her legs as though with one touch she'd keel over.

Eyes that burned with desire snared hers and he gave her a knowing smile. 'How about now?'

'Now, I could use some help.'

Before she knew it, she had been lifted in the air and draped over his shoulder. As she yelped, he let out a low chuckle and began to walk, leaving her head dangling against his back. 'Put me down!' She banged her fists against the tight round curve of his bum. 'You might have a first-class arse but I don't want my face bouncing off it.' Another burst of soft laughter. But still he marched on, climbing the stairs, gripping her legs firmly as she continued to curse him. 'Didn't anyone ever tell you a fireman's lift is not seductive?'

Finally, they reached the top stair and he halted, sliding her slowly down his body until her feet touched the floor. Then he smiled into her eyes. 'Chill.' With a quick flick of his wrist he pushed the door open. 'The seduction starts when we get inside.'

Oh God, she wasn't ready. That was her first thought as stepped across the threshold, feeling the heat of his body tight behind her.

But then his hand pressed into her lower back, and down, smoothing over her bum, and all she could think was she'd never been so ready.

This man, with his come-to-bed eyes, his sexy drawl, and a body that screamed sex, wanted her. That was reason enough to stop dithering, to stop worrying about the repercussions, and just go with it.

But he was more than just sex on legs. All those things he'd said to her...

As they reached the door to her bedroom, she turned to face him. 'Thank you. For what you said downstairs. I want to add to what I said before. You're not just nice. You're kind. Really, really kind.'

'It's not kind. It's me telling you the truth.'

He was there, in front of her. A vibrant, potent male. Pushing all caution aside, she did what she'd wanted to do ever since she'd seen him walk back from his swim in the lake that first week. She ran her hand down his chest, feeling the ridges of muscle, the coiled power. She imagined taking off the

T-shirt and letting all that hot, hard flesh slide against hers. 'God, you're also stupidly sexy. Like, *so* sexy, it's insane.'

He groaned, pressing his hips against hers.

'If you don't want me following you into your room…' His hands grasped her waist. 'Don't want me stripping you naked and feasting on your body…' He leaned closer, his mouth inches from hers. 'If you don't want me sliding into the slick heat of you when you're aroused and wanting….' His gaze locked with hers, his eyes a storm of blue and grey. 'Then you need to go to your room and lock the door.'

She swallowed, her insides liquefying, her blood on fire. 'After all that, you think there's actually a chance I'll lock you out?'

His smile almost blinded her. 'With you I can never be sure. I figured you might want to make a list of pros and cons. You know, pro equals *loads of orgasms*. Con equals *have to admit to Jake he's as good as he says he is*.'

'Oh my God, you did not just say that.' She started to laugh, but he silenced her with a kiss. Then lifted her into his arms and pushed her bedroom door open.

Chapter Twenty-Five

H e was ready, oh so ready. Maybe too ready, he thought, as he placed Anna on the bed and drank in the sight of her: olive skin bearing a flush of arousal, eyes a glittering jade, hair a riot of brown silk across her bed; breasts he'd fantasised about, rising and falling with every ragged breath she took; nipples so prominent they threatened to pierce through her top.

The ache between his legs turned into a pulsing, almost painful throb.

He had to get a grip, or he'd never be able to deliver on all the stuff he'd bragged about.

Yet as he slid onto the bed next to her, as he cupped her breast and felt the firm fullness fit perfectly into his hand, he looked into her eyes and saw her vulnerability. Oh, she wasn't going to show it. She was going to pretend she believed everything he'd said, but he was starting to understand this woman.

So he ignored his raging need to take, to bury himself

inside her, and smoothed his hand down her top, lifting it at the hem. 'Can I?'

She nodded, biting into her lip. 'As long as you take off yours.'

Yeah, not a problem. With one swift movement he shrugged off his T-shirt, feeling a moment of pure male satisfaction as he watched her gaze skim over his chest. He was about to remove hers, when she put out a hand. 'Wait.' Sitting up, she trailed her fingers across the lion on his left pec, causing a bolt of arousal to zip through him. Raising her eyes to meet his, she smiled. 'It's beautiful.'

Unconsciously, he flexed his pecs, groaning when she licked her lips in response. 'You're killing me here. Can we get back to the part where I take off your shirt?'

'In a minute.' She pushed at him, causing him to fall back onto the bed. Then she bent to study the tattoo further, her hair tickling across his abs.

'Saints alive.' His erection pressed hard against the zip of his jeans. When she planted a light kiss on his chest, he nearly detonated. Rearing up, he grabbed at the hem of her shirt and pushed it up, over her head. 'Holy shit, Anna.' It was his turn to run lustful eyes over her chest.

Her eyes found his. 'So when you said you liked my big tits...'

'I wasn't kidding.' He traced the top of her lacy bra with his fingers, finding the deep valley of her cleavage. With a quick flick of his wrist, he undid the centre bra fastening, and his heart jumped as her gorgeous breasts fell into his hands. 'You know I'll never look at your owner the same way again,' he told them, cupping them, squeezing them, smoothing his hands over the soft flesh. 'To think I used to call her Saint

Anna.' He glanced up at her and smirked. 'I'm definitely up for worshipping at their altar.'

'I'm not sure, technically, that you worship saints…'

She yelped as he pushed her back onto the mattress and covered her mouth with his. It started off as a way to silence her, but then his tongue found its way into her sweet depths, his body slid over hers, and everything became more urgent. Greedy hands raced to her jeans, undoing the button, sliding down the zipper. As his mouth trailed over her breasts, sucking, licking, he pushed her jeans off, quickly followed by the scrap of lace that came between him and heaven. Then, to the sound of her moans, he took his fill first with his fingers and then with his mouth until she came undone, her heavy panting filling the air.

As she lay boneless, he tugged off the rest of his clothes. When he focused back on her, he found her watching him and his heart leapt at the admiration on her face. 'You keep looking at me like that, you're going make me big-headed.'

She smiled, all soft and satisfied. 'You already are.'

And yeah, he couldn't deny, when it came to sex he was a cocky bastard. But when it came to wondering things like would this gorgeous woman regret getting up close and dirty with him tomorrow morning? When it came to that, he was a mess of doubts.

But sod it, now was not the time for that shit.

Reaching for his discarded jeans he grabbed the condom from his wallet – thank you, God, it was still there – and settled back onto the bed next to her, running his hands down her curves, watching as her nipples puckered. 'Are you ready for me?'

And what he was really asking was, are you sure about this? Do you really want to do this *with me*?

His heart stilled a moment as she nibbled her bottom lip. Then her eyes found his and she smiled right into them.

It was all the encouragement he needed and he shifted over her, thrust into her in one lusty movement, watching as her eyes widened, feeling the connection, how hard he was. For her. For a few moments he rocked gently, letting her heat engulf him, taking the time to enjoy how bloody amazing she felt, wrapped around him. But then instinct took over and he began to shift, to thrust, his mind emptying of everything but this moment.

It was as she gasped, as her mouth opened and she cried out his name, that he fell over the edge after her.

Anna couldn't move. She didn't even want to because though Jake was one heavy guy, that muscled weight felt incredible. Cocooned as she was beneath him, she felt at peace, safe.

And blissfully satisfied.

Above her, the man mountain grunted. 'You've slayed me.'

She slid a hand down the hard, toned length of his left arm, feeling the bunch of his bicep as he levered himself up. 'Okay, I'll say it.'

He peered down at her, hair sticking up messily, eyes soft. 'I'm as good as I think I am?'

She couldn't stop touching him. Never had a man's body fascinated her so much. Or satisfied her so completely. 'I guess it depends on how good that is.'

With a harumphing sound he rolled onto his back, pulling her up against him, shifting so her head slotted neatly onto his chest. 'You do know that wasn't just me, don't you?' He angled his head, making sure he caught her eye. 'I mean, I'd like to take all the glory, but you are one hell of a sexy woman, Anna Roberts.'

He let out a contented sigh and she felt a warm swell of pride. She'd done that to him. And yet... she remembered what he'd said, back in the hallway. Every word designed to give her back the woman she'd once been, before Miles. 'And you are one special man, Jake Tucker.'

Surprise settled across his features, but then he snorted. 'That's the post-orgasm glow talking. Wait till I'm driving you nuts again tomorrow.'

She had no doubt he would be. She also had no doubt she would still think what she was thinking now. He had to know he could have seduced her weeks ago with very little effort, yet he'd taken the time to build up her confidence. To make sure she was ready.

She idly trailed her fingers over his chest, her eyes drawn to his tattoo. 'Why a lion?'

'You think it's got some deep meaning?'

He looked amused, but she had a sense he was giving her the *I'm just a dumb ex-con* fob-off. It annoyed her because he was anything but stupid – he could read people, read situations, far better than most people she knew, certainly better than her. And he was way more complicated than he let on. 'Yes, I think it does.'

He stilled, studying her, then gave her a small smile. 'Might have guessed you'd call me out.' Turning his head he stared back up at the ceiling. 'The lion is fiercely protective of its family. So was Dad. The tattoo is for him, and to remind me of what's important.'

Her heart opened just that little bit more for him and she had to take a breath, a moment to remind herself what this was. A fake relationship that had blossomed into an unlikely friendship, with the added bonus of a night of the best sex of her life. 'He'd be proud of the way you take care of your mum and your sisters. Your niece and nephew.' She pressed a kiss against the lion's nose. 'Emma said you're more of a father to them than their own dad is.'

'Not hard, considering he didn't hang around to give it a proper try.'

Irritation pricked and she rose up on her elbows. 'Don't do that,' she told him quietly. 'Don't belittle what you do. Those kids aren't questioning why their dad left them, or what they did wrong, because they've got you in their life to take his place. They've got you to provide the stuff only dads can. They dote on you.'

She realised she'd said too much when he hauled her closer to his side and kissed the top of her head. 'You were a kid too, Anna. You didn't do anything wrong.' On one level she knew it, but she hadn't been enough for Miles, either. 'Do you ever think of going to see your mum?'

His question brought her up sharp. 'No.'

'Why not? She's Italian, so presumably she's somewhere in Italy. And presumably your dad knows where?'

'I've never asked him.' Her stomach knotted just thinking about it. 'She hurt us both. After a while it became easier, less painful, not to talk about her. And that's how I want to keep it.'

'But now you're in the same country, with plenty of time to kill between guests.'

His hand slid to her arm and he began to smooth his palm up and down, just like he had the other night. It was distracting, as was the reawakening of the butterflies in her stomach.

'She's had years to come and see me if she wanted to.' The old hurts began to resurface, though his touch helped to smooth the jagged edges. 'She didn't bother so no, I have no interest in going to see her.' No interest in going where she wasn't wanted.

'I'd want to know why the hell she abandoned me.' Jake's expression turned fierce and Anna knew his anger wasn't directed at her, but was on her behalf. 'I'd want to show her what a huge mistake she made. Let her see what she's missed out on.'

It was so easy to imagine him doing that. Challenging her mum just as he had Nigel. 'That's because you're fearless. You're not scared of the fallout.' What if she found out for certain her mum had never loved her, that she'd not even liked her? What if her dad was the only one who'd ever be able to love her? 'You confront the issue head-on.'

'Confrontation isn't always a good idea.' His arms tightened around her and she knew he was thinking about how he'd ended up in prison. 'But I'm here to help if you want to go down that route. Get closure, or whatever the hell it is shrinks seem to think is important.'

It sounded so easy, and the thought of having him by her side when she confronted the woman who'd walked out on her did make her wonder if maybe she could put herself through that. But it would mean raking up old hurts, finding answers to questions she was terrified of asking. And upsetting her dad. 'Thank you. Can I think about it?'

She felt his smile against her hair. 'I'd expect nothing else.'

For a few moments they lay in silence, but then his hand reached for her breast, toying with it, feeling the weight. 'I've not had enough of touching you yet.'

You will. She pushed the unhelpful thought away and shifted to face him. 'What is this?'

He frowned, clearly confused. 'Foreplay?'

'I mean you and me. What are we doing?'

He gave her that slow, sexy smile. 'Enjoying ourselves.'

Okay, she could do this. Live in the moment, not worry about where it was going. Except... 'I think we should have rules.'

He huffed out a laugh. 'You know I don't follow them.' Suddenly he shifted and she felt the hard pulsing presence of him against her thigh. 'Look, we're here, and we have to pretend to be lovers for the rest of the contract anyway. What's the harm in making that a reality?'

His words made sense. Or maybe she just wanted them to, because God, now she'd sampled sex with him, how could she not do it again? She wasn't ready for another relationship; might never be ready for one. Jake wouldn't want anything serious. When she put it like that, it made perfect sense. 'A fling that comes with its own deadline.'

'Exactly.' He ground his erection against her, but then stilled. 'Shit.'

'What's wrong?'

'I don't have any more condoms.'

The disgust in his voice made her laugh. 'You mean to tell me Jake Tucker didn't pack a stack of condoms?'

He groaned, his hips moving restlessly against her. 'When I packed, I was in a pretend relationship. I wasn't expecting sex.'

'And now?'

He grinned down at her. 'Tomorrow I'm buying a truckload of them, but meanwhile...' He began to land a trail of kisses across her cleavage and then down, down, over her stomach, edging ever lower. 'We'll find other ways to entertain ourselves.'

Chapter Twenty-Six

The next month flew by and before Jake knew it, they were well into July, the lake beautifully still – and thankfully far kinder to his balls – during his morning swim. In between two sets of guests – quiet people, friends of Penny and Henry – Jake cleaned the pool, did endless chopping back of hedges, weeded, and painted the outside of the pool house. He also jet washed the patio. It wasn't fighting fires; there was no adrenalin rush, no challenge, yet there was a certain satisfaction in sitting on the wicker sofa with a beer in the setting sun and seeing the fruit of his labours.

For the first time in years he felt content, though he didn't think it had much to do with the sight of the perfect stripes of his newly mown grass. Far more likely it was down to the regular sex he was having. Not average regular sex either, but the best sex of his life and with a woman who, he'd been delighted to discover, had an appetite as strong as his own.

It had to be that giving him the warm fuzzies. If he thought it was anything to do with the woman he was having the regular, spectacular sex with, he wouldn't be able to sleep at night.

'Reckon you've finished for the day, do you?'

Anna slid in beside him and automatically he put his arm around her shoulders. There was nobody watching them now, no pretence needed, yet he couldn't stop touching her, *enjoying* her. And when she snuggled into his side... yeah, he couldn't deny the rush of satisfaction, of pleasure. Damn it, there was that feeling of contentment again.

'What I reckon,' he replied, 'is that anything I've not done today, I can do tomorrow.' He tried not to worry about the weird feeling he got in his chest when she smiled at him.

'Sara said they're coming over around seven.'

It was their turn to host. When they hadn't been entertaining their employers' guests, Anna and Jake had seen a fair bit of Rosa, Marco, Sara and, yes, Will, who'd finally grown a pair of balls and asked Sara out. If anyone had told him six months ago he'd be sleeping with Saint Anna and hosting frigging dinner parties, Jake would have asked them what they'd been smoking. Glancing at his watch, he did a quick calculation. 'That gives us about an hour to shower, change and...' He nuzzled her neck, breathing her in, feeling every part of his body tighten.

'And?'

He loved the way her voice turned breathy when she was aroused. It made him feel like a frigging giant. In one fluid motion, he lifted her up and over his shoulder. 'And we need to get moving if we're going to fit in everything I have planned for you.'

• • •

When their guests knocked on the door, Anna was still naked and he was working out if he had time for round two.

'Oh my God, they're early.' She leapt out of bed, flashing all those incredible curves.

He smirked, lying back a moment to appreciate the view. 'I think you'll find we're late.'

'We can't be. I'm never late.' She glanced over at the bedside clock and shrieked. 'This is your fault, Tucker. You and your'—she waved her hand at him—'magical body parts. They're too distracting.'

Laughter rumbled through him. 'Never been told I've got a magic dick before. I like it.'

'Well, you need to cover it up and let our guests in.' He watched, mesmerised, as she picked some lacy numbers out of the top drawer. 'I've planned for drinks out by the pool for a change. The tealights are on the kitchen island ready to take out. Oh, and I made a pitcher of margarita. It's in the fridge. Use the cocktail glasses and slice a few limes—'

He silenced her with a kiss. 'You think I need telling how to make a drink?'

She stilled, her chin raised. 'I wasn't implying that.'

A few months ago, he'd have argued that was exactly what she'd been doing. Now he settled for raising an eyebrow.

A few months ago, she'd have argued back. Now she huffed and looked sheepish. 'You're right. I was being anal. It's just... I want it to be nice.'

And there it was, the reason she was meticulous in her planning, the reason she insisted on the small details. She took pride in what she did. 'These aren't guests; they're our friends.' He kissed her again, this time with more finesse, driving himself a little crazy for a second before he reluctantly drew back. 'Take your time. I've got this.'

He dressed in two minutes flat and raced down the stairs, throwing the door open. They all did the double-kiss-on-the-cheek thing that was another piece of etiquette Jake was starting to learn.

'I'm to send you guys off to the pool,' he told them before they marched inside. 'Anna's got this idea we should have drinks there, and don't think you get a choice on what to have either, because she's made margaritas. I'm to bring it out in the fancy-arse glasses along with the fancy-arse tealights.'

Will sniggered. 'Not hard to work out who's the boss in your relationship. Didn't think you'd roll over. Figured you as more of a rebel.'

He was. So why was he now being such a walkover where Anna was concerned? *Because you're hooked, mate.*

The thought made him pause. His palms begin to sweat. Was he deluding himself that they could keep having sex and not end up in a complicated mess involving hurt feelings and an impossible situation? Pretending to love each other when they didn't like each other was one thing. Pretending to love each other when there were bruised feelings, raw hurt, or worse… That had disaster written all over it.

But he was no softie. If he could survive prison, survive losing his job, being outcast by his mates, he could survive falling a little for Anna. And Anna was way too smart to want more than a short-term hook-up with the likes of him.

He brought the jug of margarita and the tealights out to the pool where the others were waiting. He'd had half a mind to grab the wrong glasses, just to prove he was still Jake Tucker, rebel at heart. Then he'd pictured the disappointment on Anna's face because she wanted everything to be *nice* for their friends, and found he couldn't do it.

Instead, he'd shoved a few bottles of beer onto the tray in a token effort.

As he was pouring the drinks, Will tapped him on the chest. 'I see somebody got dressed in a hurry.'

Jake looked down. In his haste to dress he'd put his T-shirt on inside out. 'I was working hard getting everything ready for you guys.'

Will snorted. 'I'm sure you were working *hard*.'

Sara dug Will in the ribs and told him not to be rude, Marco roared with laughter, and Rosa gave him a big wink. 'If you make love like you dance, your Anna is *molto* lucky lady.'

His Anna...

He tried not to get too tangled up with how that sounded. 'You and me, Rosa, we too have something special.' He bent and whispered, deliberately loud, in her ear. 'But we keep it quiet – don't want Marco or Anna getting jealous.'

Rosa hooted with delighted laughter and when Marco clapped him on the back, chortling, Jake felt a weird warmth flood his chest. Maybe it was just because they thought he was with Anna, but having spent the last few years being shunned, it felt pretty good to feel accepted, judged on face value, even if it was only temporary. And even if it was based on a lie.

'What am I going to be jealous about?'

He swung round to find Anna walking up behind him. And suddenly his heart was in his throat. Wearing a floaty green dress that emphasised her cleavage, her eyes sparkling and picking up the green, she looked vibrant, sexy. Glowing.

It was only when those full, soft lips curved into a smile that he realised he was gawping. 'Nothing,' he told her, voice hoarse. 'You know I only have eyes for you.' And unlike the first time he'd said it in front of Nigel, this time it didn't feel like a lie.

Anna's heart skipped a beat at the appreciation in Jake's expression. The words were said for effect, but there was something honest about the way he looked at her, not hiding that he liked what he saw. Whoever was lucky enough to capture his heart would feel like the most beautiful woman in the world. Certainly, this last month he'd made her feel special, desirable, wanted.

And never more so than now, when he walked towards her in his trademark loose-limbed swagger and planted a soft kiss on her mouth. 'You look fucking gorgeous.'

The husky tones, the heat in his eyes… Her knees began to tremble. This man with his cocksure smile, scruffy stubble, and flashy lion tattoo made her heart beat so fast it left her breathless.

'You two are like a pair of newlyweds,' Will observed dryly.

Jake smiled, but his eyes remained on her. 'It's the castle, the lake. I'm not going to lie, I feel closer to this gorgeous woman than I've ever done.'

Oh God. She felt the flutter of butterfly wings in her chest.

Sara clapped her hands. 'I told you this place was romantic.'

'Maybe you get married now?' Rosa looked animated, like she was already planning a wedding. 'Jake, you should propose.'

Anna stilled, some of the joy receding. Suddenly she wanted to tell their friends the truth, that what they saw was powerful sexual chemistry, not love.

'I would.' Jake looked as if he was seriously considering the question. 'But if she's as smart as I think she is, she'd turn me down, so I'm not going to risk it.'

Rosa clucked. 'You are strong man, sexy man. Sara, she says you help two people from burning car.' She turned to Anna. 'You would say yes to this man?'

The word *yes* hovered on her lips and it terrified her that it didn't feel like she was acting.

'Ah, Rosa, you don't know me like Anna does,' Jake interrupted, bending to pick up the pitcher of margarita so she couldn't see his face. 'Now then, who's for another drink?'

It was all pretend, all nonsense, but it felt as if he was somehow sending her a message. One that clearly said they would never work as a couple. She suspected he was right, yet it still hurt to hear him say it.

'Well, you're definitely smart, that's for sure.' Will came to stand by her as Jake went over to fill Marco's glass. 'You've clearly managed to tame him.'

The notion that she'd want to do that, to change Jake, settled uneasily on her. 'What do you mean?'

'Look at the guy. He's hardly the dinner-party-with-tealights sort yet here he is, doing just that.'

'Maybe he's not as easy to read as you think.'

'Maybe.' Will's gaze jumped to Sara, who was giggling over something Jake had said to her. 'Or maybe love changes a guy. Makes him reassess his priorities.'

At that moment Jake glanced over at them. The look he gave her sent a sizzle to the pit of her stomach. It wasn't love; that wasn't what they were about. Still, to be the recipient of that admiring gaze was special enough.

Their guests lingered long after the meal was over. Rosa got her dance with Jake, then Anna found herself in his arms, just as she had when they'd first arrived. Then, she'd felt awkward, embarrassed at how stiff she was, how unattractive she felt. Now, she melted against him, her body automatically fitting to his, her movements unconsciously sexy.

He groaned as she slid her hands down his arms, as she shifted her hips to press against his. 'Stop doing that; you're giving me a hard-on.'

Delighted, she rotated her hips again. 'You mean this?'

He hissed, his hands going to her waist, stilling her. Then he bent to whisper in her ear. 'You've got five minutes to help me kick them out or I'm taking you round the back of the pool house.'

Lust scorched through her. She'd never felt like this before, so easily aroused, so acutely aware of every touch, every glance. Nor had she ever had sex like this before: spontaneous, passionate, tender, athletic, creative.

Her face must have signalled her feelings because Sara took one look at her, winked, and immediately picked up her shawl. 'It's getting late. Time we went home.' She walked over to Will and took his hand. From the way Will looked down at her, Anna was certain he was glad to be whisking her away, too.

Jake stood behind her, hands around her waist, chin resting on her head, as they watched their friends walk back down the drive. The moment they were out of view, she felt his hands on the zip of her dress. Before she had time to react, he'd slid the zip down, letting it pool at her feet. Goosebumps raced across her skin as he turned and lifted her up. 'Ever been skinny dipping?'

The question took her by surprise. 'Er, no?'

Suddenly she was being carried not to the pool, but down to the lake, in only her underwear. Yet far from being embarrassed, she felt liberated. 'I thought you were going to take me to bed.'

'I am.' He trailed kisses across her face as he eased her

down onto the jetty. 'But first I'm going to swim naked with you in the water of Lake Como.' More kisses, on her nose and across her cheeks. 'Under the Italian sky. Beneath the stars.' His mouth dived lower, to her cleavage and across the tops of her breasts. 'And then I'm going to make love to you here, in the grounds of the castle, with the lights of Bellagio in the background.'

Who *was* this man? She'd always seen him as a little dangerous. A man who could be gruff, hard, menacing. Now he looked dangerously romantic. A man who could dazzle, bewitch. Who could creep into her heart with very little effort.

Was she afraid? With her track record of being dumped, abandoned, betrayed by those she cared about, she'd be a fool not to be. Could she stop? Absolutely not. Day by day he was showing her how to let go. How to embrace life, to live it rather than try to control it. Under his watchful gaze she felt herself unwinding, becoming more confident, and she liked the person who was emerging. If continuing this journey meant she had to make herself vulnerable again, it was a risk she needed to take.

So she revelled in her first naked swim, enjoying the sensuous slide of water across her skin, and then the even more sensuous slide of his body against hers. And when he'd left her gasping, crying out his name, he bundled her into his arms and carried her back to their apartment where, after a hot shower, they climbed into her bed.

She pressed a kiss to his chest. 'Thank you.'

'For?'

'My first naked swim.'

She felt his smile against her hair. 'Glad to relieve you of your skinny-dipping virginity.'

Feeding off the strength coiled in his body, in the arms that wrapped protectively around her, she made a decision, one she'd been wrestling with the last week, ever since she'd spoken to her dad. 'Mum lives about two hours' drive from here.' She swallowed and felt her heart begin to race as she rose up to look at him. 'Will you come with me to see her?'

He stared down at her, his eyes searching hers. 'You really want to do this?'

'I think so.' That was weak, and she didn't want to be weak. She wanted to be strong. Fearless, like he was. 'I *do* want to do this. I spoke to Dad and he's okay with it.' She smiled as she recalled their conversation. 'By the way, I heard your mum in the background, which I think has a lot to do with how calm he was about the idea.'

Jake winced. 'Can we not talk about that?'

'You mean the fact that your mum and my dad might be having sex?'

His face paled. 'Stop! I don't want to think about it.'

'Your mum's allowed a sex life, you know.'

'Yeah. But with your dad?' He shuddered. 'Okay, changing the subject, when do you want to go?'

'I don't know. Maybe in a couple of weeks?'

'Are you sure you can afford to skive off for the day? According to your schedule we have all the Harpers here at some point next month.'

She pushed at him. 'Yes. Clearly you're a bad influence.'

'Clearly.'

There was just something about the way he said it. 'You do realise that was a joke? That you're actually good for me. Last time Nigel came I was a basket case. You've taught me to relax. To have confidence in my ability to get the job done.' She swallowed. 'I would never have had the guts to face Mum again if it wasn't for you.'

His eyelids lowered over his eyes and she couldn't read what he was thinking. 'It's not about guts. It's about doing what's right for you.'

'I know.' She trailed her fingers over his tattoo, the lion, fierce and proud, just like the man. 'I'm not going to lie, seeing her again, finding out the answers to questions I've spent most of my life wondering... it terrifies me. But carrying on like I have been doing, never knowing, that's a frightening prospect, too. Maybe once I've seen her I can put it all behind me. Face my future without the baggage of my past.'

He drew her up his body and kissed her mouth. 'You do realise taking a guy to meet your mother is step one of being in a relationship?'

She knew she was in trouble when the alarm bells were drowned out by the steady thump of her heart.

Chapter Twenty-Seven

For all her outward bravado when they'd set off this morning, Jake knew Anna was a bundle of nerves as he pulled off the autostrada.

'There's nothing to be scared about.'

She stiffened her shoulders. 'I'm not scared.'

'That brave face you insist on wearing? It doesn't wash with me. You're shitting bricks.'

'Am not.'

He smirked. 'Are we really going to do this? Because I may be hot-tempered and rash but when it comes to having the last word I have endless patience.'

'Fine.' Her shoulders sagged. 'I might be... shitting *a* brick.'

He laughed out loud. 'Say it again.'

'What?'

'You know what. Come on, I like hearing you say rude words.' He waggled his eyebrows. 'Turns me on.'

'Everything seems to turn you on.'

'Only when you do it.'

She eyed him suspiciously, then burst out laughing. 'God, you're incorrigible.'

'I would be if I knew what it meant.'

'So bad you can't be reformed.'

'Sounds about right.'

Silence filled the car and Jake cursed himself for being an overly sensitive prick. He'd been trying to lighten the mood, to distract her, and now he'd plunged them both into dark thoughts.

'Like you told Rosa, I know you,' she said quietly. 'And you're a good person.'

The words, from a woman he liked and respected, helped soothe his jagged feelings. What she thought of him mattered more than he wanted to admit. 'Thank you.' He turned down the tree-lined road, pulling to a stop in front of a row of terracotta-coloured terraced houses which the sat nav informed him was his destination. 'I also know you, Anna Roberts, and whatever your mum says to you today she doesn't get to hurt you, okay? Unless it's good stuff, her views aren't important.'

And though her face looked tenser than it had over the last few weeks, her eyes smiled at him. 'Noted.'

'Want me to come in with you?'

She glanced at the end house, her expression clearly torn. 'Maybe just to meet her? Make sure I don't chicken out at the last minute.'

They walked together towards the house with the green shutters and used the brass knocker to knock on the dark wood door. A moment later it was opened by an attractive, dark-haired woman who gave them both a careful study with big brown eyes. He didn't need to be a genius to work out what the woman saw: Anna, elegant in a floaty patterned dress, hair in a neat ponytail; the man she was with unshaven, T-shirt faded, jeans not just faded but ripped. Usually he couldn't give a shit what people thought, but part of him – the part living in a pretend world where he was meeting his girlfriend's mother for the first time – wished he'd taken a bit more care over his appearance. Because the thought annoyed him, he gave her a curt nod and held out his hand. 'Jake Tucker. Anna's friend.' He knew the woman spoke fluent English so he didn't bother trying out his ropey Italian.

'Carina.' She gave his hand a lukewarm shake. 'Just a friend, or…?' She looked at her daughter.

Anna stared back at her. 'Does it matter?'

'Well, no, I suppose not.' Again her eyes flicked to Jake. 'I just imagined you with someone different.'

'Unbelievable.' It was only when they both stared at him that Jake realised he'd said it out loud. But sod it, this *was* frigging unbelievable. 'You've not seen your daughter for twenty years,' he said, trying to keep a tight leash on his temper, 'and those are the first words you're saying to her?'

Anna gave him a warning look, one that said *I can handle this*, and he inclined his head, anger burning through him on her behalf.

'You're right.' Carina turned to her daughter. 'Anna, it is good to see you. I was surprised to get your call.'

'I'm living in Italy for a while. I thought I would make the effort as you clearly haven't.'

Carina gave Anna a tight-lipped smile. 'I suppose I deserved that.' She opened the door wider. 'I think you should come inside. Better than, what do you English say, doing laundry in public?'

'Washing dirty laundry in public, yes.'

Carina eyed Jake. 'Is he coming too?'

He badly wanted to say yes, but he knew it was born of a selfish desire to protect the woman he was becoming dangerously attached to. Fact was, Anna didn't need him. 'I'll wait in the car.' But he couldn't just leave it there. 'I know your daughter, and she won't tell you any of this, so I'm going to.' Leaning against the doorframe, he looked down at the woman who'd had such a huge impact on Anna's life without even knowing it. 'The girl you abandoned didn't mope or feel sorry for herself. She knuckled down, took on the responsibility of running the home you left, and grew into one hell of a strong, smart, determined woman. Most people in her situation would have become bitter, cold, wary of people, but not Anna. She's warm and big-hearted.' He gave Carina a final warning look. 'She has people who care a hell of a lot for her, including me, so if she leaves here upset, I'll be knocking on your door.'

The older woman pursed her lips. 'I'm her mother. I won't hurt her.'

He couldn't believe the naivety of the statement. Did she really not know how much hurt she'd already inflicted? But when he turned to Anna to see how she felt, he found her staring at him, eyes bright with some sort of emotion he couldn't identify – anything from embarrassment at his veiled threat, to frustration that he was holding her up, to anger at the way he was interfering.

And okay, now he realised he'd acted like some overzealous minder when all she'd wanted was quiet support. With a nod to them both, he strode back down the drive, trying to keep his gait easy, light, when inside everything felt weighted and tense.

Back in the car he looked at his messages. As usual there was banter going on in the family chat. As usual, they were poking him for information about his relationship with Anna.

EMMA: Cooee, you still alive bro?

Three hours later:

EMMA: Take it from Jake's silence he's now bonking Anna.
MUM: I didn't bring my daughters up to be crude.
DAISY: [rolling-eyes emoji] That was the polite version.
EMMA: I bet whatever he's doing with Anna it isn't polite.
DAISY: [laughing emoji] Now you've got me thinking about
Jake having sex [terrified emoji]

He figured it was time to butt in.

JAKE: Thank you, I'm still alive. Will phone when I get a
break in between all the sex. [aubergine emoji]

He chuckled to himself as the phone went into buzzing overload. Then he turned it off because he couldn't answer their questions. He didn't know what he was doing with Anna, only that he couldn't ever imagine being the one to say he'd had enough.

It felt surreal. Anna couldn't believe the woman sitting opposite her on the patio in a small but carefully tended garden was her mother. Not that she'd changed much – wrinkles around the eyes and lining her mouth, her hair shorter than Anna remembered it. She looked like her memory of her, but faded somehow, like a photograph left out too long in the sun.

She was the reason Anna was so rigid, so determined to try

and manage every situation because as a child she'd not been able to manage a crucial, pivotal part of her life – the loss of her mother.

'Why did you leave me?' The question flew out of her mouth before Anna had time to question how she was going to broach the subject.

Carina – she no longer felt like a mother, so Anna couldn't think of her that way – drew in a sharp breath, then folded her hands in her lap. 'What has your father told you?'

'It's you I'm asking.'

'Fair enough.' She paused a moment, then looked back at Anna. 'Your father and I, we met when he visited here. He came to eat at my restaurant every night and I fell in love with the quiet man holidaying by himself. It is why I left Italy to live with him, why I married him, and why I had a child with him.' She paused again, running a finger over the arm of the chair. 'But living in a different country is tough. I got a job, I tried to make new friends, but my husband worked long hours and I became lonely.'

'You had me.' Anna hated how her voice trembled.

'Yes, I had you. But you were a child.' The way Carina said it, so dismissively, sent anger humming through her. 'I yearned for my life back in Italy. My family, my restaurant. Then Luca got in touch with me. He was my first love. Too wild for me, my family said, but he was easy to fall for. When he left me, it broke my heart.' When she met Anna's gaze, Carina jutted out her chin in a gesture Anna recognised in herself. 'Luca told me he wanted me back, and I began to wonder what my life could be like with a man who excited me, who made me feel special. So I left my life in England to join him.'

Anna felt the anger rise. Anger for her father, who'd been so casually discarded, and anger for herself, who apparently hadn't warranted any further consideration. 'And was he worth it, this Luca? Worth losing your daughter for?'

Carina gave her a sad smile. 'He stayed with me for six years. Then he got bored and went off with another woman.'

Silence echoed round the garden, except for the occasional chirp of birds and the sound of a car driving past. Anna tried to process what she'd heard, but there was only one thing that stuck out. 'You left Dad. Why did you also have to leave me? You could have phoned me, written to me. I could have come out to stay in the holidays.' She cursed as she felt her voice start to wobble. 'Did you ever love me at all?'

Carina glanced away for a moment before finally meeting her eyes. 'It may be hard to believe but yes, I did love you. Luca did not want a step-daughter though.' She wrung her hands together. 'And I did not want to risk losing him a second time.'

'And yet you did.'

Carina nodded. 'I did. By the time he was gone, you were sixteen. You had no need of a mother anymore.'

'You're wrong. I was at that awful age when I didn't know what my hormones were telling me. I fell in love too quickly, desperate to feel wanted, and had my heart broken easily. I began to question if I was attractive enough, special enough to ever hold a boy's attention for long. You could have helped me through it, reassured me, but instead, by abandoning me, you fed my insecurities. Dad tried to help but he could never make up for the fact that my own mother didn't feel I was worth just a tiny bit of her time, a small sliver of her love.'

'I'm sorry.'

'So am I.' Anna rose jerkily to her feet. 'I think I've heard enough. Thank you for seeing me.'

Anna walked quickly to the door. All she wanted to do in that moment was escape.

'If you ever want to talk again,' Carina said as she pulled open the door, 'you know where to find me.'

Anna stared back at her, trying to work out what she felt. Then realised what the empty feeling in the pit of her stomach was saying. She felt nothing. No love, no attachment. Not even any anger. 'No, I won't be visiting you again. I've managed without you for the last twenty years; I can manage without you for the next twenty.' She took a step away, then pulled up short. That was too final, too cold. Too much like her mother had done to her. 'But if you decide you actually want to have a relationship with your daughter, feel free to come and find me. I promise not to slam the door in your face.'

Carina's lips tightened. 'I'm not sure you can say the same for that man of yours. I think he'd like to do just that.'

Anna's heart flipped. *Her man*. He wasn't, yet in the last few months he'd stood up for her, been angry for her, and yes, cared for her, more than any man she'd ever known besides her father. And she loved and adored her father, but Jake wouldn't have let the mother of his child just walk away like her father had. He'd have hounded her, demanded she make her child feel loved. Just as he had with his niece and nephew.

'He's very protective.'

'I can see that.' Carina hesitated, then looked back at her. 'But he's also wild, like my Luca. Be careful with your heart.'

As a teenager she'd yearned for some motherly advice. Now it rubbed her the wrong way. 'You know nothing about my relationship with Jake.'

'I know you are more than friends. And I know he is very different to you.'

Anna gave her a cool smile. 'I am not you, and he is not Luca.'

With that she strode away. She was not going to let the woman prick the happy bubble she and Jake were inhabiting.

When she reached the car, she flung the door open and settled into the passenger seat with a thump.

'Okay?'

'Surprisingly, yes.'

'Good.' He paused, eyes looking straight ahead rather than at her. 'Sorry about earlier.'

'What? When you said I was strong and smart? Or big-hearted? Or when you said you cared for me? Because if you didn't mean it—'

'I did. But the part where I threatened to knock on her door if she upset you?' He winced, finally glancing her way. 'That said *creepy bastard*.'

'No, it said you were looking out for me so don't you dare apologise.' She wrapped her arms around his neck and placed a big, sloppy kiss on his cheek. 'If I looked shocked, it was only because nobody's ever stuck up for me like that before. I'm grateful.'

His features relaxed and his eyes took on a mischievous glint. 'How grateful?'

She laughed. 'You'll find out when we get back.'

'Warp speed it is then.'

The drive back was a blur, the evening spent in her bed, getting out only to put a pizza in the oven. It hadn't even been one she'd made herself. She was changing, she realised as she lay on the bed with him, satiated, relaxed, cocooned against his side.

'So.' He smoothed his hand down her arm. 'Do you want to talk about what happened with your mum?'

If this was just sex, just a fling, why had she opened up to him more than she ever had to anyone else? 'You were right to encourage me to see her.' She paused, trying to work out how she felt. 'Dad always told me her leaving wasn't my fault, but it was hard to believe that. Hard to think there wasn't something wrong with me.'

'Christ, Anna. There's nothing wrong with you. You're bloody incredible.'

Warmth settled through her. 'Thank you. Seeing her today, I realised she left because she was selfish. She chose a man over her daughter.'

'What happened to the man?'

'He left her.'

Jake snorted. 'I reckon she got what she deserved then.'

'Exactly. And the woman had the cheek to give me advice.' Her fingers trailed over the hard ridges of his stomach. 'She warned me off you. Apparently, we're too different.'

His arms momentarily tightened around her, but then she felt his body relax, his muscles unclench. 'She's got a point. Not sure we'd be a match on any computer dating site.' He tapped a finger against her nose, the gesture surprisingly affectionate. 'Or any crazy algorithm you probably use in your head.'

She couldn't deny she'd gone there, yet the more she got to know Jake, the more time she spent with him, the less their supposed differences seemed to matter. 'I don't care. I'm enjoying myself. I can't remember ever feeling so happy.'

'That's because you're having the best sex of your life.'

She let out an incredulous breath. 'I don't know whether to be amused or appalled at your arrogance.'

There was a hum of silence, and then his eyes trapped hers, their gaze dark and intense. 'It's not just sex though, is it?' he said quietly. 'At least, it isn't for me.'

Emotion settled in the back of her throat. 'Not for me, either.'

He trapped her hand in his, placing it on his chest, then let out a long, slow breath. 'Shit.'

It was so unexpected, she huffed out a laugh. 'Probably, but why do you say that?'

'By your own admission you're still bruised from what Miles did. You need someone to be careful with you and let's be honest here, I ended up in prison because I'm the opposite of careful. I'm fucking terrified I'll do something stupid and end up hurting you.'

Tears pricked the back of her eyes. 'You want to end this.'

'Christ no.' His chest rose and he heaved out a sigh. 'I'm warning you in advance, I'm highly likely to cock this up so if you want out—'

'I don't.' She reached up to kiss him. 'I like the person I am when I'm with you. I don't want it to stop.'

Chapter Twenty-Eight

Jake hauled Nigel and Clarissa's luggage up the stairs and into their suite in the west wing. He'd have to check with Anna, but he was certain this stay was only for a week, yet from the weight, size, and number of cases, it could be a frigging year.

A week would be more than enough to test his patience. And if the car journey was anything to go by, Jake would end up with frostbite long before then, his reception had been so cold.

Once he'd done his porter duty, he strolled to the kitchen to find the woman who didn't just organise his life – she was *becoming* his life. The jaunt in his step, the bounce of his heart. The smile he flashed more easily now than he had before he'd come out here...

As he'd said to her a month ago, the night after Anna had seen her mother. *Shit.*

He'd not been kidding. He was terrified of hurting her. He was equally terrified of getting hurt, though. He was a rebound, no question. A guy she'd never have hooked up with if they'd not been forced together and she'd not been so lacking in confidence.

As for him, even when she'd been annoying the hell out of him, he'd found her hot. Now he'd got to know her, to like her and enjoy her, it wasn't much of a stretch to find himself falling for her.

If he was sensible, he'd put an end to it. But sensible was something he'd never managed.

He frowned when he found her staring down at her phone, looking upset.

'What's up?'

She looked over with a start, her hand moving over her heart. 'God, you made me jump.' Then she sighed. 'What's up is that Miles has decided he's flying over tomorrow. Apparently he has a proposition for me.'

That green mist people spoke of – or maybe it was a green monster, and a red mist? Whatever, he'd never truly felt jealousy until now. His stomach clenched as hard as his jaw. 'What sort of proposition?'

'No.' She shoved the phone onto the island and stepped round it to take his hand. 'Whatever you're thinking, stop. He's talking about me coming back to work in the restaurant. Saying he'll make it hard for me to refuse.'

'Okay.' He relaxed slightly. 'But the thought of you working for him, being around that git...' He clenched and unclenched his fists.

'I can't imagine me doing that either, but we've spoken about this. When our contract ends, I'll still need a job. I don't want to work for him, but equally if this is an opportunity to run a restaurant, do things my way and still be near Dad...?' She bent her head, seeming to wrestle with her thoughts. 'I can't afford to tell him to go to hell. Not until I've heard him out.'

It made sense, but he hated the idea. Hated even more that what he thought had no relevance. This was Anna planning ahead, being sensible.

'Jake?'

He shook himself. 'Yeah, sorry, you're right to think about what happens after here.' So why did the idea of her going back, living her life without him, make him feel like his chest was being torn open? 'I should probably do the same.' Except he didn't have a clue what he'd do. The thought of going back to his old life, to only seeing Anna if he called in on his mum when she happened to be visiting Anna's dad or if he ate in her restaurant, which he'd struggle to afford because hey, he would be back doing casual crap again... it left him feeling cold, empty.

Don't think ahead. Live for now.

He pushed the morose thoughts out of his head. 'Meanwhile, our favourite guest is sitting by the pool demanding two Aperol spritz cocktails, whatever the hell they are. He and Clarissa have packed more stuff than we did, but I'm assuming they're not here for the rest of the year.'

'We were told a week. Penny and Henry are due in a few days and they might stay a bit longer.'

'*We* were told?'

She gave him that look. The one that said he exasperated her. 'You're on the email.'

'Is that the same email account I never look at because it's full of junk messages from dodgy women looking for even dodgier hook-ups?'

'It's a good job you've got me then.'

'It is.' But as he watched her making the cocktails – a slug of Prosecco, a glug of nuclear-looking bright-orange Aperol, topped off with sparkling water – he wasn't thinking about her organisational skills. He was wondering what it would be like to really have her, rather than just borrow her for a while.

Jake returned to the pool with the drinks, Anna behind him carrying a plate of salmon and caviar blinis. A simple nod of thanks would have been great. A nod of dismissal would have worked, but oh no, Nigel now decided he wanted to talk.

'When was this pool last cleaned?'

Don't make things any more difficult. Bite your tongue. 'I cleaned it yesterday, especially for your arrival.' *Arsehole.*

Nigel made a big show of staring at the crystal-blue impeccably bloody clean water. 'And how much experience did you have cleaning pools before you worked here?'

Sod all. 'Enough.'

'Remind me again, what did you do before you conned my parents into employing you?'

Jake forced himself not to react. The man was being a dick; he didn't know anything. 'We didn't con your parents into anything. They interviewed us, they employed us. If you want to know what experience we have, ask them.'

Nigel cast a look at Clarissa, who was reclining next to him on a lounger, her model body stretched out, all long legs and bony arse. 'Clarissa and I talked about the pair of you after our last visit. There's something off about you both. I believe you're hiding something and I'm going to find out what it is.'

'You are, huh? Well, knock yourself out. Good luck searching for something that doesn't exist.'

He felt Anna's hand grip his. 'We're happy to wait on you,' she said quietly, 'to help you in any way, but we're not here to be insulted. Please refrain from personal remarks.'

Jake had to force himself not to laugh as Nigel's face took on the look of someone sucking a very tart lemon.

As they walked away, Jake threw his arm around Anna and hugged her close. 'Smart remark. Wish I'd thought of it.'

'I'm not sure it was smart. I think I just wound him up.' Worry settled over her face. 'I think he's on to us.'

Jake waited until they were inside the castle before turning to face her. 'Are we sharing a bed tonight?'

She blinked. 'I hope so.'

And Christ, he didn't want to think how much those words yanked on his heart. 'No need for hope. You want to share a bed with me, you get it, any time.'

Her answering smile was a thing of beauty. 'Thank you, but how is that relevant?'

He felt his heart opening, welcoming her in even further. Trying to stop this was futile. He'd just have to enjoy the ride and hope like hell he didn't screw up. Getting hurt he could deal with. Hurting her? He'd rather end up in prison again. 'Nigel can look all he likes,' he told her, feathering a kiss across those inviting lips. 'We're not hiding anything. We *are* a couple.'

Over the next few days Anna felt she was being watched like a hawk. Whenever she turned, she sensed Nigel's eyes on her. For all Jake's confidence, she worried. It wasn't so much that Nigel would find something out – Jake was right, she realised with a flutter of excitement, they were a couple, even though that came with an expiry date. It was more that Miles was now staying in a hotel in Bellagio. Logically she knew he didn't know the terms of their contract, the fact they'd pretended to be a couple to get the job, but it didn't stop her fretting. Miles had one heck of a track record in making trouble for Jake.

'I don't like you seeing that git alone.' Jake's face hardened, as it always did when they talked about Miles. They were standing in their kitchen, him toying with the car key, ready to pick up Penny and Henry, her finishing her coffee and getting mentally prepared to meet her ex at Will's bar.

'I'm hardly alone. You insisted we meet at the bar so Will could watch out for me. And even if you weren't on chauffeur duty, you know nothing good would come of you and Miles being in the same room together.'

'He would know not to mess with you.'

Part of her liked his concern. The other part was insulted. 'I'm more than capable of dealing with him.'

His bright-blue eyes softened and he ran a finger down her face. 'I know. I just...' He exhaled a long breath. 'I hate what he did to you. What he did to Daisy. It stresses me out to think of him hurting you again.'

God, this man. She'd never had someone look out for her so fiercely. 'He won't. He can't. Not while I know you've got my back.'

'Always.' He bent to kiss her, his body pressing her against the counter. 'I will always be here for you, Anna Roberts. Always have your back.'

And somehow she believed him. Whatever happened between them, she now knew who he was. Cocky, yes, and hot-headed, but also fiercely loyal and utterly dependable. A giant of a man, a rock to those he cared for. And unbelievably, he'd decided she was one of those people.

Once she'd waved him off and made sure Nigel and Clarissa had no need of her for the next couple of hours, Anna headed down the tree-lined drive for the short walk to the bar. Her stomach churned, nerves making her palms clammy. She could deal with Miles, no question, but it didn't mean she didn't wish Jake was by her side as she pushed open the door.

The bar was quiet and Will, drying glasses at the bar, immediately looked up and smiled. 'It's my favourite chef.'

'How many chefs do you know?'

He grinned. 'Irrelevant – you're still the favourite.' He glanced behind her. 'Jake gone to the airport?'

'Yep. Is my delightful ex here?' Will and Sara both knew the history between her and Miles.

'Waiting for you in the garden. He's drinking coffee. Obviously decided to stay level-headed. Can I get one for you?'

'Better not, I've just had one. Don't want to be too wired. I'll take a sparkling water, thanks.'

As Will handed her the glass, he leaned forward and whispered. 'If you see me wiping down the same table twice, I've not lost a few more marbles. Jake told me to keep an eye out.'

'Of course he did.' She rolled her eyes, but couldn't deny that some of her nerves eased.

As soon as she stepped outside, Miles stood up. Anna took a moment to study the man she'd once shared a house with. The classic combination of tall, dark, and handsome – it was easy to see why she'd been attracted to him. Brown hair carefully styled so it fell over his forehead. Sharp cheekbones, square jaw. He wore his clothes well, expensive labels designed to accentuate his tall, trim figure. Elegant. Charming, too, she remembered as he gave her a wary smile.

'Hello Anna. I'm not sure whether we should shake hands, or kiss, or...' His shoulders gave an awkward shrug.

'Hello is fine.' She slid the glass of water onto the table and sat down opposite him.

'How is life in the castle?'

'Good, thank you.'

He appeared uncomfortable, which gave her a measure of satisfaction.

'And you and Jake? Is he proving reliable? Trustworthy?'

The comment made her laugh. 'You're a fine one to talk about trust, but actually yes, he's proving to be both of those things. And a lot more.' Miles's eyebrow shot up but before he could ask any questions, Anna got down to business. 'What did you want to talk to me about?'

He crossed one leg over the other, flicking at a piece of dust that had settled on the neatly pressed cotton chinos. 'Are we really so estranged I don't get to find out how you are?'

Much as she wanted to be cold, aloof, it wasn't her. 'You hurt me, Miles. It's hard for me to see past that.'

He turned away, jaw clenching. 'I made a stupid mistake. I was scared we were getting in too deep, so I think on one level I was trying to prove to myself I was still me. The guy who could have any woman I wanted.'

'Pretty arrogant, don't you think?'

He shrugged. 'Maybe. It was also true. Women come on to me; they always have. Tilly was no different. But this time I lost something important to me, and I regret that.'

She thought perhaps he did regret it. She also thought he'd never really cared for her, not like she'd cared for him. Yet the fact she was now able to look at him so dispassionately meant her dad had been right. A large part of Miles's appeal had been that he'd come along when she'd felt lonely, her friends all paired off. 'We would never have worked. Not in the long term.'

'Well, unless you come to your senses, we'll never know, will we?' He paused and took a careful sip of his coffee before looking back at her. 'The family have bought a new restaurant. I'm running it and I'd like you to run the one you used to work in.'

'Why? I seem to remember you slating my skills in the kitchen.'

'You know I didn't mean that. I can trust you to do a good job.' He glanced away, appeared to take in a breath, then faced her again. 'If you must know, the new chef we hired has been disappointing. The regulars are complaining the food doesn't taste as good as it used to and that the menu is uninspiring. They want you back.'

You bastard. How could he so blithely say that after crushing her confidence so callously a few months ago? Yet as she looked back at him, she realised she actually owed him a big thank-you. If he hadn't cheated on her, hadn't been so nasty, she wouldn't be here in Lake Como. Wouldn't have got to know Jake.

'Well, well, if it isn't the chef, having a tryst.'

Anna's heart let out a giant thump at the sound of Nigel's voice. Nerves jangling, she turned to find him walking onto the terrace, a wide smirk across his face. Clarissa followed a few steps behind, as she usually did.

'Nigel.' Anna swallowed, trying to calm her racing heart. 'This is Miles. I used to work for him.'

'Really?' Nigel's gaze swivelled to Miles, and she knew what he saw: expensive clothes, clean-cut good looks. 'And what, I wonder, is your old boss doing in Lake Como?'

'Actually, I'm trying to persuade her to come back and work for me.' Miles stuck his hand out for Nigel to shake. 'Miles Rutherford. And you are?'

'Nigel Harper. Anna works for my parents.' Nigel narrowed his eyes. Anna didn't think he was quite as foolish as Jake thought. 'Where, I wonder, does lover boy fit into the equation?'

'Lover boy?' Miles's jaw muscle started to jump and Anna's heart banged up against her ribs. This had looming disaster written all over it.

Abruptly, she jumped to her feet. 'Jake will be coming back from picking your parents up. I need to get back.' She stared pointedly at Miles. 'Walk with me and we can continue our conversation.'

Clearly put out, Miles rose slowly, his eyes full of questions, but thankfully he started to follow her out.

She thought she'd escaped, until Nigel spoke again.

'Miles, would you like to see the castle where your former employee now works?' Nigel looked between them again, his gaze suspicious, calculating. 'I'm sure my parents would love to meet you.'

Anna's heart thumped. 'I don't think—'

'Thank you.' Miles interrupted smoothly. 'I'd like that.'

'Come on Saturday around 6pm,' Nigel offered. 'We can show you around before dinner.'

As they walked out of the bar, Anna's stomach felt leaden, her perfect bubble at the castle with Jake deflating before her eyes.

Chapter Twenty-Nine

O nce he'd picked Penny and Henry up from the airport and left them sitting on the patio with the fancy collection of mini sandwiches and cakes Anna had left out in the kitchen, Jake went in search of her. When he failed to find her in the apartment, his heart leapt into overdrive.

She wasn't back from seeing Miles yet.

There was a high chance she'd set off late – she'd had a lot of prep to do for their employers' arrival. Still, he felt his skin itch and his stomach knot, acid burning a hole in the lining.

Damn it, he couldn't just sit around, waiting for her. He wasn't made that way.

With a promise to her – and himself – to keep it together, he strode off down the drive. He could not afford a row with Miles. Scratch that, *they* couldn't afford for him to do anything stupid.

They. The single word helped to calm his racing heart.

When he reached the road he caught sight of her opposite, the bright-red dress first catching his eye, though it was the vital beauty of the woman wearing it that drew him in. His heart came to a screeching halt when he saw her worried face. And it nosedived when he noticed who she was talking to.

Rutherford was everything Jake wasn't. Debonair in his chinos and pink collared shirt, expensive sunglasses masked his eyes, adding an air of elegance to the handsome, clean-shaven face. Yet for all his money and good looks, the guy was stupid. No other explanation for why he'd slept with someone else when he'd had Anna to go home to.

They both froze when they saw him coming.

'Well, if it isn't the ex-con.' Miles's gaze drifted down over Jake's faded jeans and plain white T-shirt.

To men like Miles, clothes were important, part of the image they wanted to convey: *I can afford quality, therefore I'm rich; I dress well, therefore I'm trustworthy.* To Jake, clothes had become a fuck-off gesture since he'd come out of prison. His – admittedly pathetic – attempt to regain control of his life after having it snatched away for six months. *I'll dress how I like. Nobody tells me what to do.* Except his life had never felt more out of control. Until he'd come out here with Anna.

'If it isn't the bastard who hurts women,' he countered coldly.

Miles flinched. *One–nil.* 'I've never physically harmed anyone. Unlike you.'

'Please, stop it, both of you,' Anna interrupted them, her eyes pleading with Jake. It shamed him enough to swallow the barbed retort forming on his tongue. 'Jake and I need to head back,' she told her ex. 'Our guests are waiting. We'll see you Saturday.'

Saturday? What the hell?

As Jake struggled to get his head round the concept that he'd have to see his nemesis again, Miles smiled. 'Ah yes. I have an invitation to the castle courtesy of the son of your employers. Nigel, I think he said.' The git's smile widened. 'I'm really looking forward to it.'

Jake looked wildly at Anna.

Immediately, her hand wrapped round his, the grip firm, steady. 'Miles and I bumped into Nigel at the bar.'

He didn't know how she managed to keep her voice so calm when he felt like he wanted to scream.

But then Miles's gaze flew to where their hands were entwined and Jake began to relax. This wasn't him versus Miles. This was him *and Anna.*

Anna tilted her chin in the defiant way he now bloody loved. 'You should be aware, I'm with Jake now.'

Miles's eyes bulged, his face turning red. 'You're sleeping with this scum?'

The insult pinged off Jake. The guy could insult him all he liked. Anna had just publicly called them an item, a couple. He felt frigging invincible.

'I'm sleeping with a good man,' she countered. 'A sexy, decent, loving man.'

The words caused his chest to puff out even further.

Miles scoffed. 'He's a violent ex-con. You're totally deluded.'

Okay, that insult wasn't as easy to ignore. Jake widened his stance, aware of his fingers tightening around Anna's. In all probability she *was* deluded.

'Perhaps I am,' Anna replied quietly. 'Then again, I thought you were a decent, loving man and it turns out you were a liar and a cheat. People aren't always what they first seem.'

'Jesus.' Miles raked a hand through his carefully styled hair. 'I can't believe you're comparing what I did to what this man has done. He punched me, for God's sake. Hard enough that the courts decided it was common assault. That he was sent to *prison* over it.'

Jake felt the anger rise, hot and nasty. 'You know why I hit you.'

Miles gave him a sardonic smile, pushing Jake's anger dial up even further. 'Because you're coarse? Rough? Uncivilised? Barbaric?'

The anger boiled, banging on the lid he'd tried to hammer down on it. He wrenched his hand away from Anna, curling it into a fist. *Doesn't matter what he's saying about you,* he reminded himself, taking in a breath, then another. 'I've never sunk to your level. Never cheated on a woman. Never badmouthed one.'

He felt Anna's hand close around his fist, her touch gentle. 'This conversation is over. We'll see you Saturday.' She raised her chin at Miles. 'If you do anything to cause problems for us, you will definitely not see me working in your restaurant.'

Jake took comfort from the fact that Miles had to watch him wrap his arm around Anna as they walked away. 'I have a bad feeling about this.'

'I know.' She leaned into his side, and he felt her warmth, her scent, cool his anger. 'But I don't think he's going to cause problems. He came all the way out here to talk to me. I think he wants to make peace.'

'You *think*? Surely you can see he's finally realising what he threw away? That he wants you back, not just in his restaurant, but in his life?' *In his bed.* Jake felt his stomach clench. The thought of Rutherford with his arms round Anna, his lips kissing the mouth that Jake would never be done kissing...

'He only wants me back in his restaurant.' Anna frowned up at him, her expression curious. 'Are you *jealous*?'

To admit it would mean he would also have to admit he

was getting way deeper into this fling than he was supposed to be. But he couldn't lie, not to her. 'Do I hate the thought of you with the man I can't stand? Of course.' Was that disappointment? He couldn't be sure, but he brushed a thumb down her cheek, and let her see what he felt. 'I hate the thought of you with anyone else but me.'

His admission gained him a flash of her wide, beautiful smile. And he was floored when she reached to press a tender kiss on his mouth. 'I hate the thought of you with anyone else, too.'

His whole body seemed to sigh, his muscles to relax. Suddenly he realised how much he needed this woman. She kept him calm. Gave him reason to hope. Since she'd come into his life he'd started to believe he could be someone again. If she left... *when* she left... He couldn't bear to think about how dark his life would become.

———————

Seeing Miles again had unsettled her, but as she strolled back to the castle with Jake, Anna was proud of how she'd handled him. She was stronger than she had been when she'd arrived here. God help her, she was also falling in love.

Seeing Jake with Miles again, hearing the latter's insults, seeing Jake win the battle to control his temper, her heart had swelled, feeling full and heavy in her chest. She now had a new appreciation for what Jake had been through. And for how much of the blame Miles should have taken for what had happened.

'Whose car is that?'

She was shaken from her thoughts by Jake's question. 'I

don't know. Did Penny say anything about friends coming round?'

'Not to me.'

As they got closer, they heard voices drift over from the pool terrace.

'There you are.' Penny waved over at them. 'Please come and join us. There's a couple I'd love you to meet. In fact, I think you already know them.'

Anna glanced at Jake and saw the same worry reflected on his face. Who could it possibly be? Someone from their past, someone who knew the lie they'd been living?

'We're not living a lie, not now.' Reading her mind, Jake gave her a quick, fierce look. 'Anyone who sees me with you is going to know I'm bloody crazy about you.'

Her full heart began to beat erratically, but she didn't have a chance to reply because the couple who'd been sitting with their back to them now stood and turned round.

And she could see they had nothing to fear.

'*Mamma mia*, it is you!'

A moment later she was being hugged by the woman from the car accident a few months ago, and Jake's hand almost shaken off by the man he'd pulled from the wreckage. In a flood of excited Italian, the couple explained they'd wanted to thank them but the police had admitted they'd not taken their names or contact details.

'We owe you our lives,' the man – whom she now knew to be Gino – said solemnly to Jake.

Jake looked at Anna questioningly, his Italian not yet good enough to understand. She translated and Jake frowned, shaking his head. Then he pointed to each of them. 'You, you, you.' He shrugged. 'Anyone would do the same. I was just first there.'

Anna didn't need to protest. Penny did it for her. 'That's not what I hear. Marcia said she was jammed into the seat, frozen with shock, unable to open the door because it had buckled. Gino was badly hurt and she knew he couldn't help. She was terrified the car was going to catch fire with them in it. But then she looked out of the window and saw you running towards them. You didn't hesitate, didn't question what you should do. Even when you'd got her out and she smelt the petrol, you rushed back to help Gino. These are not the actions of most people.'

Anna wasn't sure how much Marcia or Gino could understand but they both looked at Jake, nodding their heads, eyes flooded with emotion. It caught at Anna, swelling her heart so much it felt like it might burst. Yet instead of standing proud, Jake looked uncomfortable. Embarrassed almost. He could handle being insulted, but it seemed he couldn't handle being praised.

So she touched his cheek, smiled into his eyes, and spoke the truth. 'That's why I'm crazy about this man.'

Surprise flashed across his face, but then his mouth curved and they shared a smile that felt deliciously intimate, despite their onlookers.

It made her wonder if they really did have a shot at a relationship. If the things she was feeling, he was feeling too. If they had something that could last beyond the contract.

Later they were asked to join Penny and Henry on the terrace. It was one of those beautiful balmy evenings, the air warm and still, the sky alive with twinkling stars. One of those evenings full of promise, when everything felt possible.

'Henry and I have been talking,' Penny began once they'd

settled on the sofa opposite. As usual it was Penny doing the talking, Henry watching quietly, carefully. 'We know we said a year on the contract, but if we found the right couple, we always planned on extending it.' She paused, looking at them both. 'If we were to do that, would you consider staying on here?'

She felt Jake's big body shift. Then his hand clasped hers, holding it on his thigh. Beneath his jeans the muscle felt hard yet relaxed, while her pulse was hammering a million miles an hour. She glanced sideways at him and her stomach somersaulted at the smile he gave her. She was so gone on this man, so utterly hooked it was impossible to protect her heart.

'I'll leave that up to Anna. Where she goes, I follow.'

Oh God. It all felt too much. The prospect of a future, dangled in front of her. A job she was growing to love, living in a part of the world she was growing to love. And all with a man she wasn't just growing to love, but whom she was terrified she'd actually fallen in love with.

'I think,' she said slowly, carefully, hand wrapped tight around Jake's, 'if you were to give us that opportunity, we'd very seriously consider it.'

That evening, as they lay together in her bed, his arms around her, Anna felt a looming sense of panic. Her dream job, within her grasp. Only it was better than that. A dream job, in a dream location, with a man she loved by her side.

Her heart began to race. Too perfect.

'Hey.' Clearly feeling the tension in her, Jake rolled over to face her. 'What's wrong?'

'Nothing. Absolutely nothing.' And that was what was so

ridiculous. It was stupid to be fearful of life going so well, yet wasn't it even more stupid to think life was this easy? Hadn't she once had a joyful childhood, only to have her mum walk out on her? Hadn't she once thought of a rosy future with Miles? And hadn't that all blown up in her face? 'This is going to sound so daft, but I'm scared.'

He nodded, his expression pensive. 'Not daft. I get it. You wanted a short-term rebound fling. Now the goalposts might be shifting.'

She'd wanted that once. Now she wanted so much more and it terrified her. 'I'm not scared of spending more time with you,' she countered. 'I'm scared of this bubbling hope. Scared of the dream coming true.'

'Christ, Anna, don't ever be scared to hope, to dream.' He looked appalled. 'Hope is what drives us forwards, what keeps us going through the tough stuff.'

She had a sense he was speaking from experience. 'Is that what helped when you were inside?'

He rolled onto his back, eyes staring at the ceiling. 'Prison was… degrading, dehumanising. I learned to take one day at a time, to cross it off towards the goal of getting out. It was after, when I was out, that was the hardest to deal with. The reality of being an ex-con.' His face hardened, his gaze stubbornly still not facing her. 'All I clung to was the hope that things would get better.' Finally he turned his head to look at her. 'Then I bumped into Saint Anna from next door, and my life turned around.'

Tears burned her eyes and she reached to kiss him. 'It turned around for me, too.'

Chapter Thirty

To say he was tense was putting it mildly. The evening he'd dreaded had arrived, and Miles was already downstairs, charming the pants off Henry and Penny. Jake could hear their laughter float up from the pool terrace as he stood in the flat, staring out at them from the open window.

And now, great joy, Nigel was walking to join them, Clarissa beside him, wobbling around on her heels across the gravel path.

This was the same Nigel who suspected they were hiding something and was determined to find out what it was so he could take them down.

In Miles, Nigel now had a new best friend who could, if Nigel asked the right questions, give him all the ammunition he needed.

A pair of arms threaded round his waist.

'Chill. It's going to be fine.'

He grunted, moving so he could see her. 'That's my line.'

'Well, you need to remember it.'

Anna looked radiant in a multi-coloured sundress, her hair

loose. God help him, he was so gone on this woman the thought of signing a contract to work and live with her beyond this year – hell, to make this permanent – didn't faze him one little bit.

Yet judging from their talk last night, it scared the hell out of her. He couldn't blame her. It might be her dream job, but no way was he her dream companion.

Still, he had her now. His arms tightened around her, his body fitting perfectly against her curves. Bending, he kissed and nibbled at the lips that looked so inviting. 'How long till we have to go down and show our faces?'

'Five minutes?' Her voice sounded breathless, and her body wasn't moving away. It was pushing close, rubbing seductively against his.

'I can do a lot in five minutes.' His tongue plundered, his hips moving restlessly against her core.

'Show me.'

Within seconds he had her skirt up by her thighs, her underwear on the floor, his trousers and boxers pushed down enough so he could thrust into her.

'God, what are you doing to me?' She wrapped her legs around him as he pinned her against the wall. 'I should be down there, sorting out the canapés.' Her breath came out in short pants and her eyes were glazing over.

'You want me to stop?'

Her hands grasped his buttocks. 'Don't you bloody dare.'

He raced them both to completion, savouring her heat, the sounds she made, the look of wonder on her face when she came. Maybe in years to come she'd remember the guy who'd loosened her up and taught her how to enjoy life more.

As he slid out of her, he smiled at the picture she made, hair now wild around her face, her face flushed.

'What?'

He flicked strands of shiny brown hair back behind her ear. 'Your hair needs... attention.' And yes, he was struggling not to laugh.

'It does, huh?' Her eyes narrowed. 'Well, you're not looking so tidy yourself.'

'I imagine not.' Again his lips twitched. 'Difference is, I'm happy to look like I've just had hot sex against the wall.'

She swore and marched off to the bathroom. Just as she opened the door, she glanced over her shoulder and grinned. 'At least I got you to relax.'

He chuckled as he zipped himself back up. *Stuff Nigel, stuff Miles.* They were going to have trouble wiping the smile off his face.

As the evening wore on though, Jake's smile wore thin. He didn't mind being at their beck and call; *bring me another drink, a towel, some more ice.* Hell, he was paid to do all of that. He could also put up with Nigel making him feel like he was a bit of dirt he'd found under his shoe. Prison had given him a pretty high insult threshold. Seeing Miles lay on the charm though, watching the snake interact with another reptile?

That was proving hard to stomach.

Anna had taken Penny and Henry on a tour of her new herb garden – yes, the woman hadn't just painstakingly planted and nourished a load of weed-like things she could easily buy in a supermarket, she'd actually taken pride in it.

Since their departure, Clarissa had buggered off back to her room, complaining of a headache. Jake suspected she'd gone to sit on her bed and watch some reality TV programme while stuffing her face with low-calorie popcorn. Given a choice of that or talking to Nigel and Miles, he'd probably do the same.

Sadly, as with much of his life these last few years, he had no choice. Instead, he stood on the pool terrace with Slimy and Slimier as they talked, drank, and picked at the canapés Anna had laid out, feeling like a third wheel. He was just about to manufacture an excuse to go inside – bring more wine out of the cellar, fill up the ice bucket, hell, check the drains in the downstairs bathroom, whatever it took – when Nigel clicked his fingers. Yep, the guy really was a twat.

'Get the boat ready, Jake. I'm going to take Miles for a spin before dinner.'

Make that a *stupid* twat. 'I'd strongly advise against that. Motorboats and alcohol don't mix well.' *And you can't even manage to avoid crashing onto a sandbank after one cocktail.*

Nigel's face flushed. 'Your job is to do as I ask.'

'My *job* is to take care of the castle and contents. I'll take you if you want to go out on the lake.' And that would really add a special shine to an already glorious evening, being stuck in a boat with two men who hated his guts.

Thankfully, that didn't appeal to Nigel. Unfortunately, he decided on an even worse way to spend the time: engage him in conversation.

'While we're on the subject of jobs…' Nigel grinned in that creepy way he had that reminded Jake of a Bond baddie. 'Why don't we talk about why you gave up being a firefighter?' He twirled his glass in his hand. 'Mother tells me you rescued her dear friends from a car wreck a few months ago. So heroic, yet you gave it up to be at the beck and call of someone like me.'

'I don't need to tell you diddly squat.'

Maybe he should have been more deferential. Maybe he should have lied, given some spiel about losing his confidence, because Nigel looked almost pleased with his answer. 'Of course you don't, though that rather begs the question, what are you trying to hide?' He flicked a glance at Miles. 'Perhaps you know, being the girlfriend's former employer.'

Miles regarded Jake in the cold calculating way that always got Jake's back up. 'I don't know, but I could have a pretty good guess.'

Jake went hot and cold, his gut knotting so much he thought he might be sick. 'Guesses are useless,' he bluffed. 'For example, I could guess why Nigel is so keen for his parents to sell the castle to a certain hotel chain but it doesn't make it true.'

Pawn to rook five, or whatever the hell chess moves were called. Shame he'd never had the patience for the bloody game.

'Neat try.' Nigel stared down at the patio for a moment before looking back at him through narrowed eyes. 'The thing is, though they may not know the full details, my parents do know I want them to sell this place. I've not lied to them. Can you say the same?'

Jake swallowed. What was that, checkmate? Then again, Nigel didn't know which part was the lie. 'I didn't lie about my career record. Your parents asked why I left, I said I'd rather not say. They were happy to accept that answer. End of story.'

'Except it isn't, is it?' Nigel continued to watch him, making the hair on the back of Jake's neck stand on end. Then his gaze swivelled to Miles who was taking an undisguised interest, a hint of a smirk twisting his lips. 'I sense a history between you both. Something beyond Jake being Anna's partner.'

Miles's lip curled. 'I used to date Anna. And Jake's sister.'

Jake's body went rigid. Had Miles blabbed to Nigel before

coming here tonight? Or had Nigel sussed that if he prodded and poked enough he'd find something out?

'Interesting.' Nigel took a slow, calculated sip of his gin and tonic. 'How did it end with the sister?'

Fuck. Jake only had to look at the glint in Nigel's eye to know the bastard knew exactly what he was doing.

Miles glanced at him, and Jake knew he was thinking of Anna's warning not to cause them problems. 'I decided Daisy wasn't for me.'

Okay, so it turned out Miles really did want Anna back. The thought didn't help Jake's current state of adrenalin-fuelled dread.

'Well, if Daisy is anything like her brother'—Nigel cast his gaze up and down Jake, mouth curling in distaste—'I can't really say I'm surprised. Bet she's a bit of a slut.'

His sister's name coming out of Nigel's mouth and the offensive slur made anger rage in his gut, writhing and snapping. He knew he was being deliberately baited – even he'd realised it now – just as he knew he could not afford to cock this up and let his shit deprive Anna of everything she wanted to do. Still, his hands curled into fists and his legs propelled him to stand in front of Nigel. Only a couple of pounding, pulsing inches separating them. 'You leave my sister out of this.'

'Or what?' Nigel glanced around him before settling his stare back on Jake. 'Look at you, all pumped up. Are you about to hit me, like you did this poor chap? Maybe hard enough to send you hurtling back to prison?'

Dimly, Jake heard a gasp. When he dragged his gaze from Nigel's triumphant one, he saw Penny, Henry, and Anna standing behind him, clearly making an immaculately timed return from their walk.

Penny looked horrified, Henry like he wanted to do some hitting of his own. And Anna… His heart plummeted, a lead block in his chest. She looked devastated. Like everything she'd been dreaming of last night had been ripped from under her.

'Is this true?' Henry, gripping his wife's hand, stepped forward. 'Were you sent to prison for assaulting Miles?'

Jake stepped away from Nigel and took a deep breath. Then another. He needed to find a way of answering that showed Anna didn't know.

But then Anna was replying for him, blowing any chance of him putting her in the clear. 'It was several years ago.' Despite the pale face, the hands he could see shaking as she clasped them, her chin was up and her back straight. She looked poised, in control, while he was a mess. 'He did his time, and his rehabilitation. The conviction is spent so we weren't required to declare it for the job interview.'

We. His chest crumpled at the word. Damn it, she was making this sound like she'd been part of the decision, that they were in this mess together. 'Anna suggested declaring it but I told her I didn't want to, so if you want to take issue, take it out on me.' He dragged a hand through his hair, fighting for the right words. 'This job was, *is*, her dream. I didn't want something I'd done several years ago getting in the way of it.' He looked them both in the eye. 'If you'd known, would you have given us the contract?'

They glanced at each other, then Penny shook her head. 'It would have weighed heavily against you. We would have had to consider the risk. Just as we need to now.'

As if he was some sort of monster. A danger to them and their guests. 'Then I was right not to declare it. What happened between me and Miles is our business. It has no impact on this job.' It didn't help the awful burning guilt, the shame. No matter how he looked at it, he was responsible for this shitstorm. No way were Penny and Henry going to extend the contract now. Worse, it sounded like they'd be instructing their lawyers to find a way out of the current one.

He glanced at Anna, saw the tears welling in her eyes, the desolation she was trying to hide, and knew she was thinking the same.

'Look, if you're considering terminating the contract, you need to keep Anna on.' If it sounded like he was desperate, it was because he was. 'She's blameless in this, plus her organisation, her skills in the kitchen, can't easily be replaced. I can be.'

Unable to stay there any longer and watch what his past actions had done to Anna's dream, he made some crap excuse about needing to check the wine cellar.

As if that was the most important thing he needed to do right now.

Not console the woman he'd fallen in love with.

Not get down on his knees and beg her to forgive him.

Chapter Thirty-One

Anna watched miserably as Jake made his way back to the castle. No cocky strut tonight. Instead, his feet dragged and his shoulders slumped, bowed by a weight of emotions she could only guess at.

It angered her that Penny and Henry now looked at him differently. Couldn't they see this was the same guy they'd heaped praise on yesterday for heroically saving their friend's life? That this changed *nothing*?

Nigel wore a sickly triumphant expression, as if he'd orchestrated the whole thing and it had ended exactly as he'd planned. As for Miles, he had the look of a man who knew he shouldn't gloat, but really couldn't help himself.

'I think it might be best if I leave.' Miles gave all three Harpers one of his oh-so-charming smiles. 'Thank you for your kind hospitality.' Then he turned to her. 'Anna, please bear in mind what I said yesterday. I hope to hear from you.'

'I'll get Jake to run you back to your hotel,' Nigel offered. Then gave a dramatic wince. 'Then again, considering what he did to you, being stuck in a confined space with him might not be such a wise idea.'

Anna seethed with anger. As if Jake would harm Miles for no reason.

'Thanks, but it's a pleasant evening for a walk.' Miles looked like he was about to leave, then paused. 'Just so Anna can be sure it didn't come from me, can you tell us how you found out about Jake's prison sentence?'

'Easy.' *God, Nigel looked smug.* Nastily, horribly smug. 'When I saw the pair of you together in the bar yesterday something niggled. It looked like more than boss and employee, so I did a bit of internet trawling, thinking you were having a secret affair.'

'What business is it of yours if we were?' Anna asked, incensed at his interfering.

'You work for my parents, representing them when they're not here. I didn't want anything to tarnish their reputation.' It was such a lame excuse, yet the man clearly didn't realise how ridiculous he sounded because he carried on with his puffed-up self-importance. 'I'm still not convinced you aren't, but imagine my surprise when I found local press reports about a certain Miles Rutherford being punched, and one Jake Tucker later charged with common assault.' He glanced pointedly at Penny and Henry. 'If that doesn't convince my dear parents that employing you was a terrible idea, nothing will.'

Miles nodded his head and disappeared off down the drive. For a few seconds, there was the sound of the gravel being crunched underfoot. Then there was silence.

'I think,' Henry said slowly, his eyes on his son, 'it would be a good idea if you were to go and check on your fiancée.'

He was clearly unhappy about being dismissed, but Nigel

loped off, hands in his pockets, no doubt satisfied with his evening's work.

When he was out of earshot, Henry pointed to the chairs, his expression sombre. 'My son believes we don't know about the side deal he's got with the hotel chain if we sell, but we're not as foolish as he likes to think we are.' He levelled a gaze at her. 'I suppose that's why we feel so disappointed. We thought we were good judges of character but now I'm wondering if we've been duped by the pair of you. Is there anything you have to say?'

Duped. Guilt squirmed and wriggled in her belly. That was a pretty accurate description of what she'd done to this couple. 'I know you have questions about Jake's prison sentence. All I can tell you is he was sent down for six months. He won't tell me why he hit Miles. I only know he was protecting his sister. And that Jake would never, ever, hurt anyone without just cause.'

'We would feel better about this if you'd declared it at the interview.' Henry sighed. 'I guess that's why he stopped being a firefighter?'

'Yes. He wanted to rejoin after his sentence had been spent, but his old boss had retired and the new guy didn't want to take him on.'

Penny regarded her. 'Jake seemed to suggest it was his decision not to tell us. Perhaps he should have listened to you.'

Shame gripped her. They thought they'd been hoodwinked by Jake, but in reality she was the one who'd let them down. 'The truth is, I was the one who set out to deceive you, not Jake. Sure, he didn't want to tell you about the conviction but that was his legal right. How are people who've served time meant to get on with their lives if they have to declare their record every time they apply for a job, even when it's not relevant?' She exhaled, feeling the weight of their deception. 'But we did dupe you when we set out, and that was entirely on me.'

She told them the truth about how she'd dated Miles, why they'd split up – yes, she thought it wouldn't hurt for them to realise the type of guy Miles was beneath his charm and polish. Then she admitted asking Jake to pretend to be her partner.

'So you're not a couple?' Penny looked utterly confused.

'We weren't when we applied for the job, no. But then later, we... um, we did get together.' God, that sounded terrible. Like some drunken one-night fling.

'So you are a couple now?'

She desperately wanted to say yes, but suddenly she didn't know. What they had was so new, two people forced to live and work together, all against the hugely romantic backdrop of a castle by a lake. Was it inevitable they'd drift together? Take them away from here and dump them back home, would Jake still be interested in her? 'I hope so.'

Penny sighed and glanced at her husband. 'We need to have a think about how this affects our plans for the future, but for now we expect you both to stay on and fulfil the contract unless you hear otherwise.'

'Yes, of course.' Feeling shaky, Anna rose to her feet. 'I'll go and get the dinner ready.'

Jake was nowhere to be seen for the rest of the evening which both annoyed and worried her. She could manage by herself, no question, but she'd got used to him hanging around in the kitchen with her, helping clear plates, filling the dishwasher. Washing the pans. And it was hardly convincing Penny and Henry that, despite the initial lie, their castle management team was a real partnership.

By the time she walked back upstairs to the flat, she was exhausted, physically and emotionally.

She called out his name but when she received no reply worry began to worm through her.

When he still wasn't back after she'd showered and got ready for bed, she picked up her mobile and messaged him.

Where r u? x

Not knowing what to do with herself, she poured a glass of wine and sat on the sofa with her Kindle, reminding herself he was a grown man and it was only eleven o'clock.

Still, when the door opened ten minutes later, relief rushed through her and she jumped to her feet to greet him.

'Where have you been? I've been worried.'

His lip curled. 'You sound like my mum.'

She narrowed her eyes in suspicion. 'You've been drinking.'

'Yep, definitely my mum.'

Okay, so now she was annoyed. 'You thought that was fair, swanning off to the bar when we had guests to take care of?'

He started to laugh, but there was no humour to it. 'Fair? Nothing's bloody fair in life, you know that. Was it fair on you that Miles turned out to be a wanker? Fair on Penny and Henry that we applied for this job? Fair that my shitty past has come back to hurt you?' Before she could say anything, he marched to the fridge and flung the door open. 'Is it fair that there's no more fucking beer left?'

'You've had enough,' she muttered under her breath. She'd been hoping for a conversation, an arm around her shoulders. For him to tell her it didn't matter what happened with the contract because they'd still be together. What they had was real.

317

'Funny, Will said I'd had enough too, but Phoebe kept filling my glass.'

'I bet she did.' Jealousy mixed with the anger and upset, causing a volatile cocktail of emotions. One wrong word and she was likely to explode. 'I told Penny and Henry the truth about us.'

His eyebrows flew up. 'And what *truth* is that?'

'You know what I mean. About us lying about being a couple when we applied for the job.'

'So we're a lie now, are we?' He reached for the bottle of wine and poured far too much into a glass then took a huge swallow. 'Last time I checked, we'd agreed we were a couple.' He took another swig. 'Then again, that was before I cocked up again.'

'You didn't—'

He waved her away. 'I let the bastard bait me. How dumb was that? I played right into his grubby little hands.'

Suddenly his face crumpled, and Jake thumped the glass onto the counter with such force it shattered, sending shards of glass flying.

Swearing, he bent to pick up the pieces, cutting his hand in the process.

'Leave it.' She gave him a push. 'I'll clear this up. You need to wash the cut and then sleep off what you've drunk.'

He nodded and in that moment she saw the real Jake, the one she'd come to love. The man who, behind the drunken mask, was wracked with guilt, believing all this was his fault. She wanted to wrap her arms around him, comfort him as much as she wanted to be comforted, but he was drunk and emotional, and she was tired and emotional. Not a good combination.

Instead she went in search of the dustpan and brush.

When she'd cleared up, she dragged out her phone and, figuring the hour's time difference made it just about acceptable, pressed call on the only man she knew who might be able to make everything feel less bleak.

'Hey, Dad.'

Then she burst into tears.

Chapter Thirty-Two

He'd probably experienced times in his life when he'd felt worse: after his dad died; hearing the judge tell him he was going to prison; that first night in prison. Still, this morning rated right up there with them.

First, there was the fact that every time he moved his head, his brain – or what was left of it – crashed into his skull and then bobbed around for a while, creating a pounding sensation right behind his eyes, a churning in his stomach, and beads of sweat on his brow.

Then there was the fact he had bloodstains on his sheets from the cut on his hand, but every time he reached to tug them off the bed, his brain did more crashing.

Add into the mix the dim but annoyingly persistent memories of how he'd behaved last night, and that his heart felt like one of those scrap cars in a junkyard that had been squashed into a cube between the jaws of a crusher. Yeah, facing Anna this morning was going to be a real picnic on a summer day.

'Do you want help with that?'

He turned too quickly and his head threatened to detonate, forcing him to slump onto the floor and hold it between his hands.

'Headache?' Her voice softened with sympathy he didn't deserve.

'No. I just fancied sitting on the floor.'

'Right.' She moved to leave, of course she did, because why hang around when he was being such a prick?

'Wait.' Taking a deep breath, he slowly raised his head to look at her. And shit, she was gorgeous, no question, but this morning she had dark circles under her eyes and a tension to her expression that he knew he'd helped put there.

Somewhere a giant ladle dipped into a steaming vat of guilt and dumped the contents all over his head.

'Sorry. Last night I was—'

'A shit?'

He huffed out a laugh, then regretted it as more brain bouncing occurred. 'I was going to say drunk, but that turned me into a shit so no argument from me.'

'I'd say by disappearing off to the bar and leaving me to handle the Harpers, including Nigel, alone, you were a shit before you got drunk.'

He felt the weight of another ladle of guilt over his shoulders. 'Can't disagree with that.'

She crouched on the floor opposite him, legs drawn up, arms wrapped around her knees. 'Why did you abandon me?'

His chest tightened further, making breathing diabolically difficult. He'd failed this woman so many times yesterday it was a wonder she was still talking to him. 'Because I'm a coward.'

She gave a dismissive shake of her head. 'That's rubbish. Part of what I admire about you is the way you stand up to people.'

'And that's what I should have done.' He jammed a hand through his hair, trying to steady himself. 'I'm not proud of having a record, but I'm not ashamed of what I did, either.' He didn't know what that made him. Only that it was important she saw him for who he was. 'If I had my time again I'd still hit Miles if it meant he left Daisy alone. Except I'd make sure he had a soft landing so he didn't harm his pretty face.'

'So why did you end up in the bar?' She bit into her lip. 'Did you go to see Phoebe?'

His head jerked up so hard he saw stars. As nausea rolled around in his stomach, he swore.

Anna immediately jumped to her feet. 'Let me get you some painkillers.'

And so he sat, like a useless lump, as the woman he'd been a prick to danced attendance on him, bringing him painkillers and a glass of water before quickly and efficiently stripping his bed.

When he thought he had the nausea under some sort of control he sought her out, finding her sitting on the sofa, coffee in hand, staring out of the window.

'I went to the bar because I was ashamed I'd let Nigel sucker me into the argument. Calling Daisy a slut… he did it deliberately, knowing it was guaranteed to wind me up. Guaranteed to end with me in his face so he could do the whole *let's show my parents what a dangerous loose cannon this man really is* thing.'

But heading to the bar had turned out to be another shit decision. Seemed he was full of them. While he was there, word had started to spread. Nigel had told someone who'd told someone else. As the evening had gone on, he'd started to see people looking at him differently. Giving him a wider and wider berth. At one point he'd caught Sara whispering to Will. They'd both glanced over at him, their expressions shocked. He'd not waited to talk to them. What could he have said, anyway? *Yeah, it's true, I'm an ex-con who's been living a lie.*

Instead, he'd downed his – fifth? eighth? – whisky, then fled the place as fast as his drunken body could carry him.

Tentatively, he walked towards the sink and refilled his glass with water.

'Nigel was looking for dirt on us and he found it,' she answered quietly. 'He would have told his parents anyway.'

'Yeah, well, I'm sorry my dirt has ruined this gig for you.'

'It was my idea to involve you. My idea to lie to them.'

He smiled grimly. 'I think unwittingly hiring an ex-con trumps hiring a couple who weren't really a couple, don't you?' He sipped at the water, but even that was making him sick. 'What did they say to you yesterday? Do they want to march us off the premises?'

'No. They were actually pretty decent. Said they needed time to think about things but we should continue to work here as usual.'

'Except it isn't as usual, is it?'

Her posture stiffened. 'What do you mean?'

Christ. 'Come on, don't be naïve. The whole village knows about my record now. Do you really think when we see the likes of Sara, Marco, Rosa, and Will, everything will be *as usual*?' He let out a bitter laugh. 'You should have been there last night. People were starting to whisper already.'

Anna looked at him in disbelief. 'Who cares what *people* say? It won't matter to our friends.'

'Yeah, maybe. But it matters to *me*.'

Before she could give him any more confused looks, before he was forced to watch her expression turn to pity, he turned and headed out. No way could he explain how free he'd felt since he'd come out here. Starting fresh, nobody knowing his past, being accepted by the locals. He'd been able to stand by Anna's side, pretending to be her partner – for a few amazing weeks actually being her partner – and not feel like everyone was wondering what the hell she was doing with him.

Now it had all blown up in his face.

With a muttered curse he snagged a towel from the bathroom and let himself out. A swim in the lake would either help his head or kill him off. At least if it was the latter, he wouldn't have to face the reality of the end of his pretend life.

Anna didn't see much of Jake for the rest of the day. He didn't disappear like he had before. He worked on the estate, but he kept outside, only coming in when it was time to take Nigel and Clarissa to the airport.

She had an inkling of how well that trip had gone from the way his muscle jumped in his jaw when he walked into the flat later that evening.

'How was it?'

He shrugged those big shoulders. 'About what you'd expect. A few snide comments. Nothing original. Nigel made a big play of keeping hold of his laptop rather than letting me put it in the boot. I pointed out that I went to prison for punching, not pinching.' Jake's usually chilled movements were jerky with tension as he reached for a glass in the overhead cupboard. 'Told him his face was in more danger than his frigging PC.'

'At least he's gone home now. And Penny and Henry leave tomorrow so then we'll have the place to ourselves again.' When he didn't look at her, she felt a trickle of fear. All day she'd tried to tell herself that last night was only a hiccup. He'd slept in his own room not hers because he'd been drunk. And yes, he'd said it couldn't be life as usual now, but it didn't mean *they* couldn't carry on as usual.

'I've made you chilli.' She smiled, hoping her fear wasn't showing. 'Thought it might cheer you up.'

'You think chilli is going to help make everything right?'

Tears welled at his sarcastic tone. 'No. I think time will make you realise you're making far too big a deal out of this. The fact Penny and Henry didn't immediately dismiss us shows they're not going to do anything knee-jerk. In time they'll realise we're bloody good at our jobs and they'll want to keep us on.'

He nodded and she could see the strain on his face. 'For your sake, I hope you're right. If I've screwed up your dream job...' His hand balled into a fist and he closed his eyes.

'Forget about that.' Couldn't he see that wasn't what was cutting her up? 'What about *us*?'

He stared back at her, and now his face didn't just look strained, it looked tortured. With a sharp exhale, he pushed the glass back onto the worktop and walked over to her, sitting next to her on the sofa. Not the close next-to-her that said they were still lovers, but the distant next-to-her – the one that said they were over even before he uttered the words. 'There is no *us*, Anna.'

Stung, heart tearing, she snapped back at him. 'Pretty sure I've not been sleeping in my own bed these last two months.'

The smile he shot her was so horribly sad, she wanted to shake him. 'Two months, huh?'

'Give or take.'

'We had two months together.' He shook his head, as if he couldn't believe it.

'We can have longer,' she whispered, her voice wobbling.

His shoulders slumped and he leaned forward, elbows on his knees. 'What would be the point? We pretended, and it was one hell of a ride, but the pretence is over.' His voice cracked and he swore.

'I don't understand. We were only pretending in the beginning.'

'Come on, would you have dated me back home? Slept with me?'

'Would you have slept with *me*?'

Finally, she saw a glimmer of the old Jake. 'If you'd stopped tossing insults at me for a moment and asked nicely? Absolutely.' His eyes held hers, bold and blue and turbulent. For a split second, when he cupped her face and his expression turned from wryly amused to intimate, possessive, she thought they were okay. But then he heaved out a sigh and rose to his feet. 'I feel like shit. Thanks for the chilli but I'm going to take a raincheck. Right now, all I can stomach is my bed.'

As she watched him lumber out of the room, she wanted to be angry with him. Once again she'd been kicked in the teeth by someone she cared for. Yet Jake looked like he was hurting as much as she was.

Maybe she was making too much of what had just been convenient sex between two people forced to live and work in close quarters. In a castle. On Lake Como.

Maybe, like he said, it had just been one hell of a ride.

Maybe her heart wasn't breaking, it just *felt* like it.

One thing she did know was that she needed to get away for a few days. Get back to reality and clear her head.

So for the second time in two days, she picked up the phone to her dad.

Chapter Thirty-Three

The journey to the airport was uncomfortably quiet. Anna hadn't wanted him to drive her, but Jake had insisted. No way was he giving some smooth Italian taxi driver the opportunity to flirt with her for a couple of hours.

'You can drop me off in Como. I can get the express train.'

He thought of smooth Italian train commuters. 'I'm taking you to the flaming airport.'

'Fine.'

He really knew how to make a sucky journey suck some more. They'd been like this for the last two days. It seemed telling her it was time to stop pretending hadn't just meant no sex, it had meant no conversation. No warmth. No friendship. No *them*. To think he'd had all that for two months. The time had flown. But now it was over.

The realisation was agonising, but necessary, he reminded himself. No point tarnishing her reputation for the sake of a fling that was about to be over anyway. By stopping things now, she was protected. Thanks to the rumour mill, people would know their relationship was a pact, an agreement to get a job, nothing more. As his colleague rather than his lover, she'd be spared the judging sneers, the whispering that he'd been on the receiving end of on his last foray into the village. Christ, he'd never forget the look on Rosa's face when she'd spotted him in the post office. She'd shaken her head, her disappointment so clear he'd turned around and walked out, not ready to talk to her.

Just as he wasn't ready to talk to Will, who'd messaged three times, asking to meet up. He'd head to the bar tomorrow. Even facing the wall of whispering disapproval might be better than spending the night alone in the blasted castle.

Wanting to get out of his crappy head, he tried for conversation. 'Got anything planned when you get home?'

'Yes, actually. I'm having a meal with Dad and your mum. Apparently they've been spending a lot of time together these last few weeks.'

His hands twitched on the steering wheel. 'They're really dating?'

'If you'd phoned your mum, you'd know.'

Ouch. Guilt wriggled through him as he realised he'd not called in weeks. Too happy, too besotted with his life, then too fucking miserable to want to talk to anyone.

She sighed softly. 'For what it's worth, Dad sounded happy. He's always liked your mum, but he said it wasn't until they were out here together and spent time with each other that he realised how much.'

The words sounded hauntingly familiar. She must have been aware of it, too, because she pinched her lips shut and turned away from him to stare out of the passenger window.

For a few minutes they were back to silence.

'I'm also seeing Miles.'

His hands gripped the wheel so tightly his knuckles turned white. 'You're really going to work for him?'

'I don't know. I've asked to see the contract. Part of me expects him not to have one, but if he does, and it includes everything he promised?' She shrugged. 'I may be grateful for the job.'

Because the job she really wanted, the dream job she'd been *scared to hope for* probably wasn't going to happen now. Because of him.

And yep, now they were back to silence again. A heavy, awkward silence filled with misery and broken dreams.

'Don't park,' she said finally as he pulled the car to a halt outside the terminal building. 'Just drop me off outside.'

She was right. Parking, walking with her right up to the barrier... it was only going to pile on the misery.

He jumped out and dragged her small case out of the boot, setting it on the ground before grabbing the small wrapped box he'd placed next to it.

He wanted to haul her into his arms and never let her go. Kiss her until she said stuff the flight, she'd go back with him. But that wasn't reality and he was knee-deep in crappy reality now.

'This is stupid.' She stared up at him with those soulful green eyes. 'Why can't we carry on as before?'

Because I can't do a fling anymore. Because I've fallen in love with you. Because when Penny and Henry boot us out it will break my fucking heart.

'Trust me, this way is best.' *It protects us both*, he thought grimly.

She looked away and he knew he'd hurt her, again. But it was only her pride, he consoled himself.

'Well, enjoy the peace and quiet without me.' Her smile was

achingly tremulous. 'I've left a list of things that need doing while I'm away.'

His chest constricted. 'Of course you have.'

'Right then.' She picked up her case, but before he knew it, he'd put his hand over hers and put it down again.

She looked up at him, eyes swimming with emotion, and God help him, he felt like his heart was being ripped out of his chest. 'Be good.'

Another small smile. 'I'm a saint, remember?'

And he was the sinner.

Because he couldn't leave without touching her in some way, he bent and kissed her cheek, inhaling her scent until he thought it might seep into his marrow. 'Take care of yourself.'

The words were hard to squeeze through his throat. It wasn't so much that she was leaving. It was that when she came back, it wouldn't be to him. It would only be to the job.

'And you.'

She bent to pick up her case again.

Again he stopped her, his heart a wild thump in his chest. But when she looked questioningly at him, he didn't know what to say.

Don't leave me. I love you.

Christ. His body shook with the suppressed feelings, with the weight of what he'd done; of how he'd fallen in love when he wasn't supposed to.

Suddenly he remembered the box in his hand. Speaking of way too good... what had he been thinking? She deserved something better. Embarrassed, he had half a mind to stuff it in his pocket.

'What's that?'

Crap. 'It's nothing. Just something stupid.'

'Something stupid covered in magazine paper?'

He pushed it into her hand. 'Yeah. Happy birthday for tomorrow.' Again, he looked down at the hastily wrapped gift. 'Sorry, I forgot to buy wrapping paper so I had to improvise.'

She bit into her lip, her eyes wide. 'You bought me a birthday present?'

'Don't get excited. It's just something—'

'Stupid,' she filled in, but she handled it like it was important. Precious.

'It's not going to explode.' When she frowned, he added, 'I mean, it won't cause any problems on the X-ray machine.'

Amusement flickered across her face. 'Good to know.' Then her whole expression softened. 'I can't believe you remembered.'

'I remember lots of stuff about you.' He gave her a crooked smile. 'I had a good teacher. And cards. Lots of bloody cards.'

She laughed, but it sounded strangled, as if someone was pressing on her throat. 'I should go.' She waved the box at him. 'And thank you. It was sweet of you.'

He screwed up his face. 'I'm not sweet.'

This time she was the one who reached up to kiss him. A brush of those soft lips against his. 'Actually, you are.'

And then she was walking away from him, trailing her case behind her, ponytail swaying along with her hips. The ache in his chest intensified and Jake had to drag his eyes away before he did something really stupid, like cry.

Five months after she'd lain in her childhood bedroom, nursing a bruised heart and scared for her jobless, homeless future, Anna was back. So much had happened in the intervening months, yet alarmingly it also felt as if nothing had changed. It was likely she'd lose both her new job and place to live at any moment. And though her heart was no longer bruised, it felt *broken*.

A sob wrenched from her and she stared at the now opened gift – she'd never cheated before, never unwrapped a present before her birthday. How could a man give her such a thoughtful gift, and not want to be with her anymore? How could he look at her with such yearning, as he had at the airport, yet say they were over? That they'd only been pretending?

How could she feel this cut up, this devastated, if it was only convenient sex?

None of it made sense.

Her phone began to vibrate and when Anna looked at the caller ID, she winced. That was the fifth call she'd had from Sara. If she ignored her again, she was going to lose a friend. Taking a deep a breath, she pressed answer.

'At last, my friend answers. Are you okay? I've been worried; Mum and Dad are worried. Will is worried. We all want to talk to you and Jake but you both avoid us.'

Sara sounded not just anxious, but cross. 'I'm sorry. It's been a crazy few days. Forgive us.'

A deep sigh echoed on down the phone. 'Of course I forgive. But please, you talk to me, tell me what is happening. The gossip stalk says Jake is a criminal who beat up someone so bad he was sent to prison. People are worried for you; they say you and him are not really together, that he forced you to pretend to be his wife so he could live out here in the castle.'

Oh God. Anna lay back against the pillows, trying to curb her anger. 'First, it's a grapevine, not a gossip stalk.'

'Bah. Your English phrases are ridiculous.'

'Not as ridiculous as people thinking Jake enjoys beating up men and forcing women to live with him.'

For a moment there was silence. When Sara spoke again, her voice sounded hurt. 'I did not think these things.'

Tears welled and Anna wiped furiously at them. 'Sorry. It's just, the man you laughed with, the one you watched risk his life to save a couple he didn't even know? Jake is still that man. He did hit someone, but he had his reasons. Plenty of men get into fights and don't end up in prison. Jake was unlucky.'

'So you really are together? He didn't force you to pretend to be his partner?'

Anna squeezed her eyes shut. 'I was the one who asked him to pretend to be my partner. It's a long story, one for an evening on the terrace when I get back, but while we started off pretending, we… grew close.'

Sara giggled. 'You mean you are sleeping with him.'

The pain in her chest was so real, Anna put a hand over her heart, trying to soothe it. 'I was.'

Sara could clearly hear the tremor in her voice. 'Oh Anna. You have broken up?'

'I think so.' She swallowed, hunting round in her bedside drawer for a tissue. 'Ever since Penny and Henry found out he was in prison, Jake has acted differently. First he got drunk, then he said we needed to stop pretending. But it wasn't pretence, not by the end.' Aware she was rambling, she sucked in a big, shaky breath. 'And now he's given me this daft present for my birthday. Only it's not daft, it's lovely.' She reached for the copper measuring spoons, neatly nestled in the box, and her heart somersaulted. 'Maybe I'm deluding myself, but this ache in my chest, it feels real. We felt real.'

'Of course you did. You two were good together. We could see that.' Sara's voice lowered. 'Maybe he's just a bit, how do you say, embarrassed? Not happy the town is talking about him? Mum was in the post office yesterday. She was upset to hear people saying bad things about him. She said Jake came in, but when he saw her, he turned and walked out. It made her more upset.'

Anna thought of all he'd told her about life back home. The way his friends had disappeared, his fire station refusing to give him his job back. How difficult it had been to get work. He'd wanted a fresh start, away from judging eyes yet once again he was the centre of gossip. *Do you really think everything will be as usual?* He knew, from bitter experience, that it wouldn't be.

'He's worried that you, our friends, will see him differently. See *us* differently.'

Sara made a dismissive noise. 'We don't listen to gossip. We trust our instincts. Jake is a good man. You make a good couple. I hope you will both come to dinner with us again when you get back.'

'Thank you.' She felt a lump of emotion rise in her throat. 'That means a lot.'

A moment later, her dad called up to her. 'Sheila's here.'

Nerves buzzed in her stomach. Sheila had been like a mum to her, but now she was also the mother of the guy she'd been sleeping with. Would that change things, make it awkward?

But the moment she stepped into the front room, Sheila rushed over to her and wrapped her in her arms. 'Tell me what's going on,' she pleaded. 'Jake phoned, but the signal was terrible. Either that or he sounded terrible.' She scrutinised Anna's face and sighed. 'Oh dear. It was the second, wasn't it?'

How to start? 'I don't even know what you know.' She looked to her dad, wondering if he'd said anything but he gave a small shake of his head.

'I know everything came out in the open about his record, about you pretending to be a couple to get the job. Beyond that...' Sheila sighed. 'Jake is useless when it comes to talking about his feelings. All I know is what I saw with my own eyes.' She put a hand on either side of Anna's face. 'I know my son was falling for you, and you for him. Now tell me what went wrong between you both and I'll tell you how to fix it.'

Anna felt tears prick her eyes. 'I don't think it's that simple.'

Chapter Thirty-Four

When Anna had repeated the tale of the last few days, she looked over at Sheila and at her dad, who'd gone to sit next to Jake's mum.

No, not just next to her. Close to her, Anna realised with a tug on her heart as she saw her dad's hand clasp Sheila's and bring it to rest on his thigh. God, she was thrilled for him. It was so lovely to see him happy, yet to her shame she also felt a nasty twinge of jealousy, too. She wanted that closeness with Jake. He'd held her hand and she'd leaned in to him, but would they ever do that again?

'The last time I saw Jake drunk was that night he came back after the fire station told him they wouldn't take him back.' Sheila shook her head, clearly upset. 'My poor boy.'

It was so odd to hear Jake – big, tough, sexy Jake – referred to as a boy. Anna nearly smiled. 'Obviously he's frustrated, and angry that it has all come out and people are gossiping about him. I can totally understand that.' Anna looked back at Sheila. 'But there's no reason why it should affect *us*. Sara thinks he's pushed me away because he's embarrassed, but that's not the man I know. Jake doesn't hide away, scared to face people. He confronts issues head on.' Tears stung her eyes as she faced her worst fear. 'Maybe he just got caught up in the pretence and once that was over, he realised he wasn't falling for me after all.'

'I don't believe that for a moment. Nor do I believe Jake is angry that people are gossiping about *him*. I believe he's angry that you've been dragged into what he sees as his mess.' Sheila swallowed, clearly struggling to keep her emotions in check. 'If I know my son, he sees you as part of his family now. It means he will do anything he can to protect you. Even if it means protecting you from himself.'

Anna felt like she'd been sucker punched. 'But that's ridiculous.'

'It doesn't mean he sees you as weak. It's just how his dad brought him up.' Sheila gave Anna a considered look. 'Did he tell you how his dad died?'

'I think it was a heart attack, wasn't it?'

'Yes. He was shooting basketball hoops with Jake when he suddenly collapsed.' She smiled sadly. 'Seeing his dad die in front of him, being powerless to help, had a profound effect on Jake. At first he went off the rails, trying to deal with his grief, and with his anger that his dad had been snatched so cruelly from him. It's why we moved from the estate. I was scared he'd get himself into serious trouble with the gang he was running around with. Sadly, moving didn't help much and he still ended up getting in trouble with the police. But something your dad said to him finally sunk in and he pulled himself together.'

Her dad shook his head. 'I only asked him what he thought his dad would say if he could see what he was doing.'

'It did the trick.' Sheila looked at Anna's dad tenderly. 'After that Jake became determined to make his dad proud. That's when he decided to become a firefighter. He also took on the mantle of man of the house, taking care of his sisters, his mum, just like his dad would have done. I think all he's doing by pushing you away is making sure you're not tainted by his past.'

Maybe. Or maybe he was saying he couldn't see a future for them. They weren't exactly compatible, after all.

'Do you think Penny and Henry will keep you both on?' her dad asked, concern etched on his face as it had been ever since he'd picked her up at the airport.

'I don't know.' Anna smiled at him, determined to lift the mood. 'Worried I'll soon be back home, cramping your style?'

He glanced at Sheila and gave an embarrassed laugh. 'I'm not sure there's much style to cramp.'

Sheila looked down at their clutched hands and gave Anna an awkward smile. 'Are we being insensitive? Is this okay with you?'

'Oh Sheila.' Anna jumped off the chair and crouched in front of the woman who'd been such a friend to her over the years. 'Look at Dad's face.'

Her dad frowned. 'What about my face?'

She patted his cheek. 'I know he's concerned for me, but that light in his eyes? That smile hovering just below the surface? That's happiness.' She placed her hand over theirs. 'And I'm made up for you both.'

'Do you think Jake is?'

'I think Jake loves his mum. If you're happy, he's happy.'

Her dad harumphed. 'He'll be even happier when he sees sense and stops pushing my girl away.'

Anna smiled fondly at him but in her heart she wondered if

that was true. If perhaps Jake would be happier without the woman he didn't used to like, the woman he'd been thrown together with. Maybe he'd be happier with someone like Phoebe.

———————————

The next two days went by slowly. She saw Miles and read through the contract he'd put together. She didn't sign it though. Instead, she took it away with her, promising him she'd think about it, then tore it up and put it in the bin.

No matter what Penny and Henry decided, she would move forwards, not backwards.

She spent time with her dad and Sheila but all the time she missed Jake with an ache that no amount of hugs from her dad, or shopping trips with Sheila, could soothe.

If this was pretend, God help her if she ever really fell in love.

Stop kidding yourself. You already have.

Finally, Anna zipped up the small case and lugged it downstairs.

Her dad jumped up from his position on the sofa where he was reading his newspaper – some things hadn't changed.

'All packed?'

'Yep.' She went up to him and gave him a fierce hug. 'Take care of yourself and that gorgeous lady next door. I meant what I said; it's bloody lovely to see you so happy.'

He kissed her on the forehead. 'I want to see you happy, too.'

'I am happy.' Her voice wobbled. 'At least, I was, and I will be again.' Her dad's expression was one of such pride, such love, that Anna felt her eyes well. Thankfully the moment was broken by a knock on the door. 'That'll be Daisy.'

When Anna had bumped into Jake's sister yesterday, Daisy had offered to run her to the airport. *Save the oldies getting the car out*, was how she'd phrased it.

Sheila came to see her off and Anna definitely felt the sting of tears as she turned to wave and saw her dad wrap his arm around Sheila's shoulders.

'They're cute together, aren't they?' Daisy grinned. 'Makes me wonder why they took so long.'

'Dad was so focused on his career. I think he only really started to notice who was living next door when he stopped work.'

Daisy smirked. 'And how long have you and my brother been noticing each other?'

Anna wanted to laugh, but the mention of Jake felt too raw. 'We didn't like each other when we lived here.'

Daisy must have heard the catch in her voice because the smile slipped from her face. 'And now you do, huh?'

'I like your brother an awful lot, yes.'

'And you don't know how he feels?' Daisy paused as she negotiated a roundabout. 'He's pretty simple, my brother. Straightforward. If he likes you, it should be obvious.'

Anna thought of the way he'd helped her build back her confidence, the things he'd said to her late at night, the copper measuring spoons nestled in her handbag. 'He likes me now.' *Just not enough.*

'Of course he does. He's just being Jake.'

Daisy didn't say anything else until she pulled to a stop outside the terminal. 'Mum told me Jake was being funny with you and you didn't know why.' She took her hands off the steering wheel and twisted them in her lap. 'I'm not saying I do, but I think you're dead good for him and I'm worried you might think he's not worth fighting for so I want to tell you why he hit Miles.'

'You don't have to. I know Jake well enough to realise he had good reason.'

'Maybe. But it's important you know who he really is, and not who people like Miles would like you to believe.' She inhaled a deep breath and stared straight out of the windscreen at the travellers dragging their cases across the road. 'Only Jake knows this. Even Mum doesn't know the whole story because I'm ashamed, and even though it happened years ago, and even though he ended up going to prison over it, he's still never betrayed my secret.'

If Daisy was determined to make her fall in love with Jake even deeper, it was working, Anna thought with an ache.

'I was a barmaid in the same pub I work in now when Miles came in and flirted with me. I was flattered. I mean, I was seventeen and he was dishy, older, and rich. I slept with him a couple of times but it was soon obvious I was just easy sex for him so I ended it.' She bit into her lip. 'He wasn't happy. His ego got a battering so he started slagging me off. When Jake got to hear he was livid and he squared up to Miles, telling him to stop badmouthing me.' She stopped, her chest heaving with the emotion of reliving it all. 'It might have ended there. I wish it had.'

Daisy wiped at her eyes and Anna felt a wave of compassion. 'Please, you don't have to do this.'

'I want to. It's important you know Jake's not just some wild tearaway who likes using his fists.' She swallowed, her gaze shifting to her lap. 'I found out I was pregnant,' she continued in a whisper. 'I was terrified. Jake was home when I did the test and he heard me crying so I told him.' Her lips quivered as she smiled. 'He was angry, but also strong, you know? Like he kept all his anger to himself and stayed really calm when he went through the options, even when I said I wanted to keep the baby.' Tears ran down her face. 'I knew Miles and me weren't going to be a couple, but I thought he had the right to know, to be involved if that's what he wanted.' She drew in a shuddery breath. 'Oh bollocks, have you got a tissue?'

Anna scraped around in her handbag for one and handed it over. 'I have an awful feeling I know where this is headed.'

'Yeah. I told Miles and he... dismissed me, you know? Said he didn't even believe it was his. That if it was, I must have deliberately got myself pregnant so I could trap him.' Her voice trembled and she wiped at her eyes. 'Jake overheard and dragged Miles outside. I followed them out.' She blew her nose on the tissue. 'Jake threatened Miles. Told him if he heard him saying anything like that again, he'd punch him. Miles said he could say what he liked, it was a free country, and I was clearly a money-grabbing slut. That's when Jake lost it. Sure, it's wrong to hit him, but it was wrong of Miles to do what he did, too, and he came out of it all blame-free. How's that fair?'

'It isn't.' It made Anna feel sick that she'd slept with Miles, that she'd moved in with him. That she'd fancied herself in love with him. 'What happened to the baby?'

Her face crumpled. 'I lost it. I was only about eight weeks, too early to show. Jake wanted me to tell Mum but I couldn't; I knew she'd be so disappointed in me. So he made me go to a counsellor to talk it through. It helped, and Jake doing what he did definitely shut Miles up and stopped him spreading nasty rumours. But he ended up in prison and losing the job he loved.' Tears streamed again, rolling down her cheeks.

'He told me once that he didn't regret it,' Anna said softly, shifting so she could hug the younger woman. 'That if he had his time again, he'd do the same.'

'Yeah, because he's stubborn and rash but he's also the best guy I know.' Daisy heaved out a sigh. 'I'm not sure if any of that's convinced you it's worth putting up with the bullshit that comes with him, but I wanted to fight his corner like he's fought mine.'

Anna didn't know what to say. It wasn't her who needed convincing that she and Jake should be together. 'Thank you for the lift. And for trusting me. I promise I won't say anything.'

'Maybe it's time I told Mum anyway. She's so loved up with your dad I think she'll be cool about it all now.'

'I think,' Anna said softly, 'that your mum is very special and you're lucky to have her.'

'I am.' Daisy grinned. 'And maybe if things carry on this way, we'll soon be sisters.'

'I'd love that.'

As Anna walked into the terminal, she tried to be happy that she might always have a link with Jake, even if it was just through his family.

And when she walked through customs in Milan and saw Jake waiting for her, his bright-blue eyes searching the crowds, she tried not to hope that he was there because he wanted to pick her up, because he couldn't wait to see her. Not because he felt he had to.

Their eyes connected and for a second everything stood still. Slowly he slipped a hand into the pocket of his jeans. Even more slowly he gave that devastating crooked smile.

Her heart leapt in her chest and she knew then what she'd suspected for a while.

This wasn't pretence, or a fling, or sex with a convenient expiry date. Not from her side.

She'd gone and fallen in love.

Chapter Thirty-Five

J ake's heart was going to explode, it was beating so fast. Christ, it was good to see her. She looked frigging amazing. Tired, maybe, but still dazzling – that hair, those mesmerising eyes. The smile that twisted his insides.

'Hey.'

The need to wrap her in his arms was almost overwhelming. 'Hey yourself.'

There was an awkward pause and he knew she was waiting for him to take the lead. If he gave in to temptation, if he bent to kiss her, she'd kiss him back, no question. For a second he bent, desperate to taste her. But then what? Could he sleep with her and *pretend* it was only sex? Then go to the bar and pretend they were only work colleagues?

At the last minute he swerved, avoiding her mouth and instead bending to pick up her case.

Disappointment flashed across her face and his insides twisted. He was hurting her, he knew that. It didn't matter that he was doing it for the right reasons, that she'd thank him in the long run.

'So, do you want the good news or the bad news?' he asked as they walked to the carpark, trying for a levity he didn't feel.

'Bad news.'

'Penny phoned. She and Henry want to talk to us.'

Anna's face paled but she gave a sharp, efficient nod of her head. 'It might not be bad news. They might want us to stay on anyway.'

'And you want to?'

'Of course. Don't you?'

He did – fuck, he did. But he also didn't because living with her and not *being* with her – that was going to be sheer bloody agony. 'Hard to beat working in a castle on a lake.' Her face flooded with fresh disappointment and he knew he'd ballsed up again. Was it really so hard to be friends with her? Wasn't that the only way they could make this work if – big if – they were asked to stay on? 'Sorry, that came out wrong. I was trying to be cool.'

'Well, you succeeded. You were so cool, you were cold.'

Damn it to hell. He cursed as he threw her case into the boot. By ending things now he might be doing the right thing, but he was going about it in a really crappy way.

'What's the good news?' she asked as he shifted the car into gear. Her expression looked about as tight as his chest felt.

'They're not flying over. Apparently they still want to see us though, so we've got a Zoom call with them tomorrow morning.'

'We have the castle to ourselves for a while then. It hardly feels like good news right now.'

He deserved the slight, but boy, did it hurt.

The journey was quiet and Jake could only see a whole evening of stilted conversation or worse, one where each sat on their own bed, avoiding the other. And he only had himself to blame. If he'd just shut up, kept things as they were, they could be spending the evening in bed, together.

But this is right for the long term, he reminded himself.

'I think we should go to the bar,' she announced as he pushed opened the door to their apartment.

He almost fell over his feet. 'What?'

'We hardly want to be stuck here with just each other for company, do we?' It was only what he'd been thinking, but the way she said it, as if she didn't want to be alone with him, felt like a punch to the gut. 'Besides, Sara messaged to say she was going to be there and I'd like to catch up with her.'

'Fine. You go.'

She gave him a dry look. 'Since when did you turn down an opportunity to go to the bar?'

'Since the room goes quiet when I step inside.'

Her expression softened. 'Is it really that bad?'

'You think I care what reaction *I* get?'

Her eyes searched his and she sighed. 'Okay, you're worried about me. That's sweet but unnecessary. Just let me freshen up and then we'll head over.'

He could see she was determined to go so he nodded. 'I'll wait outside.' He figured they both needed the space.

Five minutes later they set off down the drive, his hand itching to clasp hers as he'd done on so many occasions. At first it had been to pretend a closeness they didn't have, then because he'd wanted to feel that closeness. Now he was in the worst of both worlds: pretending he didn't want to hold her hand.

Christ, it was a mess. He was a mess.

When he pushed open the door to the bar, heads turned. Some stopped talking to stare, but it was fewer than last night. He gave them all his cockiest smile.

Will looked up, and as he waved them over Jake burned with gratitude. These last few days had shown him that Will *was* his friend. And just as Anna had predicted, the guy didn't give two hoots about what had happened with Miles. As an aside, he also thought Miles was a sleazy bastard. Proof Will had good instincts.

'Welcome back, Anna.' Will gave her a wide smile. 'Jake's been a right moody bugger without you.'

Anna glanced sideways at him, then back to Will, her expression confused. 'Thanks, but you know Jake and I aren't actually a couple?'

Will waved a hand at her. 'I know you weren't when you first came here, even though you pretended to be. Then you were. And now...' He smirked. 'I know if I took your hand, like this.' Jake's blood pressure started to rise as Will enveloped Anna's hand in his. 'And if I leaned across the bar to kiss you, like this.' He shifted his body, reaching across the bar, his mouth far too flaming close to Anna's. Jake saw red.

'Stop that,' he growled – yeah, he actually growled like a frigging big cat.

Will burst out laughing and shifted back. 'I rest my case. Now then, what can I get you guys to drink?'

Anna was utterly confused by the mixed messages Jake was giving her: one minute cool, the next looking daggers at Will for getting too close. One thing that had been cleared up, though, was why he'd not wanted to come with her to the bar. She couldn't believe the dirty looks some people were giving him. It made her blood boil.

He'd been trying to protect her, just like his family had said.

They'd known, because they'd had to handle the same reception back home, too. At the time she'd only given the gossip about Jake going to prison a sparing interest. She remembered feeling sorry for his mum, mainly. Now she wished she'd intervened.

'Anna?'

Sara's voice cut through her thoughts and she shook herself. 'Sorry, I was miles away.'

'I was just saying that Mum and Dad are coming over.' She screwed up her face. 'But you look like you have more important things you are thinking about.'

'No, I'd love to see Marco and Rosa.' She looked around her at the packed bar, then over to Jake who was nursing his beer, clearly waiting for Will to finish serving. Before, when they'd come here, Jake had chatted with the other bar-goers. Nothing in depth – he was still learning the language – but between their broken English and his basic Italian, they would smile, laugh.

Now he was left isolated. It broke her heart.

She downed the half-glass of wine she was holding in one long gulp. 'I need another drink.'

Sara raised an eyebrow. 'Okay.'

'Thirsty?' Anna turned to find Phoebe smirking at her. The same Phoebe who'd no doubt heard that Jake was single. 'Can I get you ladies anything?'

'Another glass of red, please.' She needed it even more now, Anna thought grimly before looking over at Sara, who shook her head.

'One red coming up.' Phoebe swivelled away and marched over to the bar, hips swaying. She stopped for a moment at the bar and said something to Jake which, damn it, made him smile.

Sara looked bemused. 'Why are you drinking wine like water?'

'Dutch courage. You'll see.'

A moment later, Phoebe returned with a full glass. 'It's true what they're saying then?' she asked as she handed it over. 'You and Jake were only pretending to be a couple so you could work at the castle?'

It hurt Anna to admit it. 'It's true, yes.'

A smile burst across her face. 'I knew there was something odd about you two. At Rosa's party you were kind of distant. It was like you'd rowed or something, but then I saw you together here, too, and you were all, I don't know, stiff, formal. It didn't look right. I mean, how could you be with a hot guy like Jake and not put your hands all over him?' She giggled. 'I'd be touching him all the time, making sure everyone knew he was mine.'

Anna just bet she would. The thought of her hands on Jake... She swallowed another gulp of wine.

'He's a free agent.' The words had to be forced out of her. 'I guess there's nothing to stop you now.'

Phoebe glanced over at Jake and sighed. 'I offered ages ago, after Rosa's party, but he turned me down.'

Shock rocketed through her system but then she wondered why she was so shocked. It had been clear all along that Phoebe fancied Jake. Yet at Rosa's party he'd not even liked Anna. Funny how her fake boyfriend with the bad reputation had remained loyal, whereas a month earlier her real boyfriend, the respected restaurant owner, had not.

As Phoebe walked away, Anna turned to Sara. 'I'm sorry if what I'm about to do embarrasses you. I'll understand if you don't talk to me afterwards.'

Then she strode up to the bar and motioned to Will. 'Can

you get everyone's attention please? I'd like to talk to the room.' Nerves buzzed in her belly and Will looked at her like she'd gone mad. 'Just do it, please. Before I lose my nerve.'

'What the hell, Anna?' Jake stared at her, his face lined with worry. 'Are you okay?'

Such a typical Jake response, fretting for her, not for what she was about to say. Though her stomach felt as if a thousand bees had set up camp down there, she tried to give him a reassuring smile. 'Just doing what I should have done years ago.'

Will tapped on a glass and asked everyone for quiet.

Anna swallowed hard and spoke in Italian.

'You will have heard rumours about Jake hitting someone and going to jail, but I want to set the record straight. Yes, Jake hit a man and spent a short time in prison for it. What you don't know is that the man he hit was intent on spreading defamatory lies about Jake's seventeen-year-old sister. Lies that would have ruined her reputation and damaged her emotionally.' She glanced round the room, trying to look everyone in the eye. 'Ask yourselves, what would you do to protect your family? Because that's all Jake was doing. Trying to stop someone hurting his sister.'

There were murmurs of agreement, nods of various heads. She risked a look at Jake who looked both frustrated and confused. Clearly, he wanted to know what she was saying but his Italian wasn't yet good enough.

Suddenly from the doorway, she heard clapping. Anna turned in surprise to find Rosa and Marco beaming at her. Sara joined in, then Will.

A lump formed in her throat as others began clapping, too.

'Will someone tell me what the blazes is going on?' Jake looked agitated. 'I heard my name, something about a sister.'

He stared at Anna, his gorgeous blue eyes pleading with her. 'The rest might as well have been in Klingon which, actually, I'd probably understand better as—'

'*Star Wars* is your favourite film series. *The Empire Strikes Back* is your number one pick.' Anna felt a wave of nostalgia deep in her chest as she remembered the car journey when they'd gone through the cards.

He blinked, emotion whirling in his eyes. 'Exactly.'

'I remember lots of stuff about you, too,' she said softly, repeating what he'd once said to her.

His eyes fluttered closed and she thought maybe, just maybe, this break-up was as hard for him as it was for her.

'Anna told everyone why you hit the sleazy bastard,' Will supplied, breaking the moment.

A second later Marco and Rosa were swarming round them and, in a gesture that broke the dam and made Anna cry, Rosa wrapped her arms around Jake and hugged him to her. 'You run away from me the other day in the post office. Why?' she demanded in that adorable way she had.

He looked shell-shocked. 'You shook your head at me. I thought—' He broke off, swallowing. 'I thought you were disappointed in me.'

She shoved at him. '*Cretino*. I was disappointed in the stupid people who stare at you. You are my dance partner, yes? We stick together.' She reached for his hands and hauled him off the bar stool. 'And we jive together!' With that, she started to wriggle her ample hips at him.

Looking dazed, Jake put his hands on her waist and began to dance with her, controlling the movements in that commandingly sexy way he had and making everyone around them roar with laughter.

Their friends stayed the rest of the evening. They talked

and they laughed, just as they always had. Every so often she caught Jake staring at her and he'd give her a small smile. She figured it was his way of saying, *Okay, I admit it, you were right. Our friends don't care about what happened in the past.*

It was only when they'd waved goodbye to Sara and her family and turned into the castle driveway that Anna had a chance to talk to Jake alone. 'I hope you don't mind what I did,' she said. 'I'd just had enough of people judging without knowing the full facts.'

'The full facts.' He peered at her. 'Has Daisy spoken to you?'

'Yes.' She leaned into him. 'I thought it was about time someone protected you, like you seem so intent on protecting others. Including me.'

'I protect the people I care about,' he replied gruffly. 'I told you that.'

'You did.' She stared back at him, at those achingly beautiful eyes and that small, crooked smile, and felt the woosh of her heart as it filled. 'And so do I.'

He sucked in a breath, averting his eyes to hide from her whatever demons he was wrestling with. Yet when he drew his arm around her and hugged her tight, when he kissed her oh so tenderly on the forehead, she could believe this man cared very deeply for her. Far more deeply than he let on.

Chapter Thirty-Six

When Jake slowly came awake the following morning, he instinctively turned to look at the pillow next to him, just as he had for the last few days. And just like the last few days, his heart plummeted when he realised he was alone. Every fibre, every cell of his being longed to be in the bed across the hallway.

What a titanic struggle it had been last night, walking to his own room. He'd begun to question what the hell he was doing. Anna had not only stood up for him, she'd put her faith in him in the most public of ways. He'd had Sara translate for him afterwards so he knew what she'd said but also he'd heard what she didn't say. *I trust you. You're a good guy.*

It was humbling.

It shrieked loud and clear that this amazing woman wasn't concerned about what being connected to him would do to her reputation. She was strong enough not to care about gossip. Probably he should have seen that because she was the one who'd asked him to join her here in the first place. Sure she'd been desperate, but she'd known exactly who he was and what he'd done, and she hadn't cared.

But… she only wanted a fling from him. One *with its own deadline*, was how she'd put it. And that fling was about to come to an end, so there was zero point resurrecting it.

But… what if Penny and Henry wanted them to stay on? The thought dangled, like a big, fat, juicy carrot… No, bollocks to that, a juicy steak.

But… wouldn't that mean she was only shacking up with him because he came with the job – her dream job – and not because she really wanted him?

Christ, he was making himself crazy.

A knock on his door drew him out of his head. 'Yeah?' Her gorgeous face appeared in the crack as she opened it a few inches. 'You've seen me naked,' he pointed out, sitting up in the bed. 'Seems a bit daft shying away now.'

The door was flung open. 'I wasn't shying away. I was giving you the distance you apparently want.'

'It's not what I *want*…' He trailed off. With everything going on in his head right now he did not need this. 'How can I help?' Her gaze slipped to his chest, and he felt his groin tighten at the way she looked at him. He was seriously deranged. How else to explain why he was putting them through this torture. 'Stop ogling my chest.'

She huffed. 'This isn't ogling. It's reminding myself what you look like so I can do a proper comparison with the next man I see naked.'

Jesus Christ. Jealousy ripped through him and he fisted the sheets. 'Don't.'

Her gaze drifted back up to his and she sighed. 'I just wanted to check what time we're talking to Penny and Henry.'

Jake picked up his phone and winced. 'An hour.'

'Thanks.'

That was all he got. She shut the door again and he was left with his exploding brain and tight, angsty, aroused body.

Grabbing his trunks he headed for the lake, figuring it might be the last time he could. When he trudged back half an hour later, Anna was stepping out of the pool. Water ran across her smooth olive skin; the red costume clung to her curves and he wanted so desperately to get on his knees and beg her to look at him as not just a fling, but as a partner. A man she could build a life with even if their contract ended today.

What's stopping you then?

How shaming to realise it was his own lack of self-worth. He'd always been cocky, confident. Always gone after what and who he wanted. Prison hadn't just taken away his freedom, it had taken away his pride, his self-esteem. His belief that he could make someone as smart, as gorgeous, as vital as Anna happy.

She must have been aware of his eyes on her because she glanced over at him. Goosebumps chased across his skin as their gazes collided, and heat scorched his blood as her eyes travelled from his, down his body, and back up to his face. But then she averted her gaze, her focus on the towel, on drying herself, no longer on him.

With a heavy heart, he headed for the shower.

Two minutes before they were due to Zoom, Jake wandered into the living room. He found her dressed in a classy grey silk top and designer jeans, her freshly washed and blow-dried hair loose around her shoulders.

'You look beautiful.'

She stared back at him and he was shocked to see something that looked like pain cross her expression. 'Why do you say that?'

He tried to shrug, but his shoulders felt stiff. 'Because it's true.' He nodded at the laptop in front of her. 'Are we good to go?'

'If you mean did I make sure I was here early to open up the PC and find the link, then yes.'

He smirked, but his face was so tight he probably looked like he was having a stroke. 'It's how we roll. You do all the hard work. I turn up.'

He expected a roll of her eyes but instead she gave a frustrated huff. 'Why do you do that? Why do you put yourself down? I couldn't have managed this place without you. I know it; you know it. So stop saying otherwise. It makes me so cross.'

As if to prove it, her fingers rattled against the keyboard as she typed.

He didn't know what to say but as it turned out there was no time for further chat because Henry's face loomed larger than life in front of them.

'Ah, there you are.' He frowned, his face so close they could see way more of him than they wanted. 'Not quite sure what I'm doing with all this new technology.'

'You, ah, might want to move back a bit,' Anna suggested, wincing.

'What?' Henry peered further into the screen.

'Sit back on the sofa,' Jake told him. 'Right now we can see all the way up your left nostril and it isn't your best feature.'

'Oh, right you are.' Henry shifted back a bit and Penny came into view. 'Is that better?'

'Better that we can see Penny instead of you, yes.'

Too late he realised he should be more tactful and gave Anna an apologetic look. This time she did roll her eyes.

'So, anyway.' Henry cleared his throat and suddenly the

breath left Jake's lungs. This was it. He was going to find out if he'd screwed Anna's chances of staying on in the place she loved, doing the job she loved. 'We've had a talk about things and done some poking around which, in hindsight, maybe we should have done when we first recruited you. With the sudden departure of June and Steve we were so keen to get a management team out there, it resulted in us not being as diligent as maybe we should have been—'

'Goodness, will you just tell them what we've decided,' Penny cut in, taking the words right out of Jake's mouth. 'You can see they're anxious.'

It was only then that Jake realised Anna was holding tightly onto her hands in her lap. He reached out and covered them with his, squeezing gently. Clearly startled, she slid him a look, but she didn't wriggle out of his hold.

'Yes, yes, sorry.' Henry peered again at the screen, clearly not sure where the camera was. 'All things considered, we'd like you to say on at the castle.'

Silence. Jake wasn't quite sure he'd heard them properly, but before he could ask Henry to repeat it, Anna was talking.

'Is that until the end of the contract?'

Penny let out an exasperated breath. 'What my husband is trying to say is the more we asked about the pair of you, and the more we talked it out, the more it became clear how lucky we are to have found you. It's not just that the castle has always been immaculate when we've been there, or that we adore your cooking, Anna, or that we appreciate that things Steve struggled with, like servicing the boat and making the fountain work, you've been able to rectify, Jake. It's more that we believe you are both genuinely nice people. We enjoy your company – Marco and Rosa won't stop raving about you. And we have two dear friends who wouldn't be alive without you.'

She paused and emotion crossed her face. 'So we'd like you to stay on indefinitely. An open-ended contract of employment. It doesn't matter to us whether you're together as a couple or not. Indeed, if needs be we can find other accommodation for one of you.'

It was exactly what he'd wanted and yet he wasn't excited. His heart didn't pound. He couldn't work over here and not be with Anna, he realised. And he couldn't be with her, because while she desired him, liked him, cared for him even, she didn't love him. Not like he loved her.

_____

Anna's heart was pounding. The chance to stay here. With Jake. God, she wanted that so much it hurt.

'What if only Anna can stay?' Jake's question cut into her thoughts, bursting the bubble of hope.

Penny looked taken aback and she glanced at Henry before answering. 'Well obviously we'd like to keep you both on, but if Anna chooses to stay and you want to go, we could look to see how to accommodate that.'

Anna didn't know what was going on in his head, only that she couldn't bear the thought of staying here without him. 'I'd love to stay, but I can't do it without Jake.'

Beside her, he exhaled sharply. 'You can easily find someone to replace me.'

God, was he really this dense? Or was this his way of wriggling out of a situation he no longer wanted to be in? 'I could find contractors to do your work, yes, but I couldn't replace you.' Her throat tightened, her heart pounding so hard she was certain he could hear it. 'It's impossible to replace someone you've fallen in love with.'

'Jesus.'

She turned to find him staring at her with wide blue eyes and a stunned expression.

On the screen, Henry coughed. 'Perhaps we should leave you to think about this and get back to us.'

'Thank you.' Hands shaking, she clicked the mouse to end the call.

'Are you crazy?' Jake's face was a picture of wild shock and tightly suppressed hope.

'Apparently I am. I'm crazy about you.'

He looked at her as if he didn't believe her. 'But this is your dream job. You can do it without me.'

'The job was never the dream. The dream has always been finding someone I love that I want to spend the rest of my life with. You're my dream.' She continued to stare at him, not holding back anything she felt, certain her eyes were no longer round but two giant hearts beating for him.

'Fuck, you really mean this?' He shook his head, then started to laugh, his big shoulders heaving up and down. The more he laughed, the angrier she became.

'Seriously, I pour my heart out and you laugh at me?' Humiliated, *devastated*, she jumped up. She'd been stupid to think he felt the same way. What did they say, a triumph of hope over experience?

Suddenly a pair of hands snapped onto her arms, pulling her back down.

'Sorry.' Blue eyes blazed into hers. 'I'm laughing because I'm a nut job and I can't believe this is happening. And because I'm so in love with you I couldn't stand the thought of staying here only as your fling, or your colleague – something I didn't have the guts to tell you because I didn't think you could ever feel the same way about me.' His gaze was full of such tenderness, such adoration, she felt tears prick. 'You seriously love me?' She nodded, her throat so tight the words couldn't come out. 'You want to make this work, you and me, living in Italy permanently?'

'Yes.' It sounded way too weak for such an important answer so she coughed and tried again. 'If you want that too, then yes.'

'*If* I want that?' He shook his head and, to her utter amazement, she saw his eyes well. It looked like both of them were in danger of crying.

But just as she thought he might kiss her, he turned to the computer. 'How do you get Penny and Henry back?'

'You want to call them back now?' She tried not to sound put out. 'You don't even want to kiss me first?'

He bent to kiss her, demanding, passionate, but way too brief. 'Get them back. Please.'

His voice sounded strained and Anna felt a prick of worry. It was a humming moment before their employers appeared on the screen again.

'This new contract...' Jake dived straight into the conversation. 'Can we change it so you need us to be a married couple?'

They looked bewildered. 'Well, actually, as we said,' Henry began, 'you don't have to even be together.'

'Just say yes.' There was a fierce intensity to Jake's expression that sent her heart hurtling into her mouth. 'Please.'

A slow, understanding smile crossed Penny's face. 'We can change it so you have to be married, yes.'

'Thanks, we'll get back to you.'

He ended the call and turned back to her. 'So, what do you say now? You still want to do this, even if you have to marry me?'

Suddenly she realised what he was doing. He was raising the stakes, expecting her to duck out. 'I still want to do this.'

Jake looked thunderstruck. 'Holy shit, you just agreed to marry me.'

His astonishment was so obvious it made her laugh. 'So I did.' But then she clasped his face. 'But I would marry you anyway, job or no job.'

'Okay, okay.' He inhaled a deep breath. 'Scrub that from your memory bank. Lake Como, castle, I can do way better than that as a proposal.'

'You don't get it, do you? I don't need better than that. I want you, I want us, exactly as we are. Mismatched and bound to drive each other mad.' And now she felt her own insecurities come through. 'I am going to do that, you know. I'm not quite the same person Miles cheated on, or the ex-neighbour you didn't like; you've knocked off some of my sharp edges, but fundamentally I'm still practical. Sensible. A planner, an organiser, a list maker…'

Finally, she got the kiss she'd been after. At first soft, tender, and then deeper, his tongue tangling with hers, driving her mad for a few minutes before he slowly drew back. 'I don't love you despite your practicality and obsessive planning, I love you *because* of it. You're the organised to my chaotic, the sensible to my crazy.' He kissed her softly on the end of her nose. 'The calm to my impetuous. You're strong when I'm weak, smart when I'm stupid. Brave when I'm a coward. And I bloody love every part of you.'

That was it – tears broke free and ran down her face. Never had anyone looked at her like he was looking at her now. 'Even the weird parts?'

He huffed out a laugh. 'Especially the weird parts.' Then he stood and hauled her into his arms. 'And the parts that are hidden behind way too many clothes right now.'

He waggled his eyebrows and gawped down her cleavage, making her giggle.

But before she lost her mind to him... 'We need to call Penny and Henry back.'

'Nope. First, we need to seal the deal, so to speak.' He gave her another blindingly hot kiss then pulled her to her feet and started to march them towards the bedrooms. 'If there's any doubt in your mind, that means I plan for us to have sex. Lots and lots of sex.' He smirked. 'Looks like I'm a bit of a planner myself now.'

'It's not just the planning,' she reminded him, her heart full to burst. 'You have to follow it through.'

He barked out a laugh. A moment later he threw her onto the bed and executed his plan in the most satisfying way.

Epilogue

Jake rubbed at the collar of his shirt. Yes, he was wearing a frigging collar *and* a tie. But apparently that was what love did to a man. Made him put a suit on.

A lot had happened in the last year.

'Hey, looking very dapper, Mr Tucker.' Will slapped him on the back. 'What's the occasion?'

'Very funny.'

'You know she's not expecting you to wear a suit, don't you? She said, and I quote: *I don't care what he turns up wearing, as long as he turns up.*'

'As if I wouldn't.' He looked around him: chairs set up in rows facing the lake; a castle as a backdrop; strategically placed pots brimming with flowers. 'I do live here.'

Will laughed. 'And we both know that's not the reason you're currently sweating in a suit.'

'I'm not sweating.' It was May, the weather a pleasant twenty degrees, the sun glinting off the lake and making the whole setting like one of those photos in the glossy magazines of a fancy celebrity wedding. It was almost unreal.

'Holy crap, my brother's in a suit!'

'Double holy crap, he's had a shave!'

The arrival of his sisters blew the celebrity wedding fantasy out of the window.

'Guess he looks kind of okay though.' Emma gave him a thorough once-over, making his collar feel even tighter.

'Anna will probably think he's hot,' Daisy supplied with a grin.

He grinned back. 'Thank you, Sweet Pea.'

She huffed and went to straighten his tie. 'Mum's on her way. She's just faffing around with her hat.'

'Christ, she's really wearing one?'

'Yep, we couldn't talk her out of it. Told her you were getting married in a back garden not a church but she insisted.'

'What did I insist?'

And there was his mum. She wore a blue patterned dress which looked good on her, and a wonky blue hat complete with a few straggly feathers, which frankly didn't.

'You insisted on wearing that weird hat,' Emma remarked dryly.

'It's the first time I've been mother of the groom.' She looked pointedly at her daughters. 'Of course I'm going to wear a hat.'

Then she turned to him and fiddled with his tie. What was it about his family and ties? 'Hey.' He put his hands over hers and gently removed them. 'Daisy's just done that.'

'Sorry.' She bit her lip and then drew in a shaky breath. 'I just… I never thought I'd see this day.' She looked up at him with glistening eyes. 'My son, getting married.'

Emotion clogged his throat as he stared down at her. Daft hat aside, she looked like she'd always looked to him and he felt a big, warm surge of gratitude. Of love. She'd had to put up with so much from him over the years yet she'd always stuck by him, always put her arm around him and made sure he knew he was loved. Something Anna had never had. Bending to kiss his mum's cheek, he smiled. 'Ignore my sisters. You look great, Mum.'

Her smile wobbled. 'So do you.' She brushed non-existent specks off the lapels of his jacket. 'Very handsome.'

Daisy and Emma burst out laughing.

He gave them a withering glare but didn't have the chance to indulge in any more verbal sparring because Rosa came up to him and gave him a noisy kiss. '*Buongiorno, bello mio!*'

'*Buongiorno mia bella.*' The woman cracked him up. She was like his second mum, only with wildly inappropriate, but totally harmless, flirting.

'You put the form in, yes?'

The rest of his family looked confused at the odd question, but Jake held Rosa's hands and smiled. 'I have an interview next week.'

'It will, how do you say in English, be a walk of cake?'

See, she cracked him up. 'I doubt it will be a cakewalk or a piece of cake but keep your fingers crossed for me.' Once this amazing woman had found out he used to be a firefighter, she'd marched down to the local fire and rescue service detachment and demanded he be considered as a part-time volunteer. Of course there were hoops to go through, and his Italian had to be better, but having that as an aim, something to shoot for... As Anna had wryly informed him, he'd got his swagger back.

Suddenly the strains of Matt Monro sounded through the portable speakers and the hairs on the back of his neck stood up.

Showtime.

'That music is minging.' His nephew put his fingers in his ears. 'Sounds like some old dude.'

'Blame Anna, not me.' She'd chosen it. Apparently, it was the soundtrack from *The Italian Job*. Yeah, she had a weird sense of humour, his soon-to-be wife.

Wife.

Before he could panic, Will wrapped an arm round him. 'Come on, you're with me, at the front.'

Jake sucked in a deep breath. He was fine. Cool, collected.

'You've got the rings? Please tell me you've got the frigging rings.'

'Relax, man, I've got the rings.' Will patted his pocket. 'Said you wouldn't regret asking me to be best man.' He looked over his shoulder and whistled. 'And we all thought you looked pretty in your suit.'

Jake almost gave himself whiplash, he turned round so quickly. And his heart burst out of his chest at the sight that greeted him.

'Saints alive.' His jaw was on the floor as he stared at the woman who was about to not only become his wife, but take his name.

On the arm of her dad, Anna made her way slowly towards him, a huge smile on her face. Dressed not in white but in her beloved crimson, she looked beyond stunning. Vibrant, elegant, but sexy as hell. If it was possible to fall in love with her any deeper, he would have done.

As it was, all he could do was watch in awe, in wonder, as this incredible woman made her way towards *him*.

When they drew up alongside him, Patrick caught his eye and gave him that steely cop stare. 'Look after my girl.'

Jake swallowed. 'Always.'

Patrick took Anna's hand and, in a symbolic gesture that

caused the backs of Jake's eyes to burn with tears, he placed it in Jake's. And smiled.

'So, what do you think of his suit?'

Anna stared over at where her husband – the word sent the butterflies in her chest flapping again – was chatting to her dad. The pair of them got on so well now, their relationship having shifted ever since Jake had insisted on asking her dad's permission to marry her. It was like he'd needed the reassurance that her dad accepted him.

'I think,' she said in reply to Sara's question, 'my husband looks sexy in anything he wears, but he looks even sexier in nothing.'

Sara gigged. 'Sadly I'll have to take your word for that.'

'Don't give me that. You only have eyes for Will.'

'I suppose.' But the dreamy expression on her face told Anna exactly where her heart lay.

At that moment Jake's bright-blue gaze found hers and he gave her a devastating smile.

'*Cazzo*, look at him.' Sara shook her head. 'The guy doesn't let you out of his sight.'

It was true. The difference between Jake as her fake lover and her real lover had been so obvious that their friends couldn't believe they'd not realised their relationship had been all pretence in the beginning. Real-lover Jake took every opportunity he could to touch her, to run his hands down her arm, her back, to whisper something sexy, sometimes downright dirty, in that lazy, husky voice that sent shivers skating down her spine.

He also looked at her like he was now, as if he wanted to devour her, and worship her, at the same time.

Sara began to fan herself. 'You two are scorching the air. You need to start your honeymoon before we all go up in flames.'

And they would, tomorrow. In the castle, because when Penny and Henry had said they wanted to give them a honeymoon as a wedding gift, Jake and Anna had told them they didn't need to go anywhere – they were in their favourite place in the world already.

As if aware she was thinking of them, Penny caught her eye. After giving Henry a nudge, the pair of them began to walk towards her.

Sara drifted away as Anna was enveloped in a warm hug – another relationship that had shifted over the last year.

'Thank you so much for coming,' Anna smiled back. 'And for letting us use your home as our wedding venue.'

'Nonsense. It is your home, too.' Penny waved over to Jake, indicating for him to join them.

A moment later he slid his arm around her waist. 'Hey, wife.' Would she ever not feel her heart beat that little bit faster, her blood feel that little bit thicker, when Jake smiled into her eyes as he was doing now?

Penny cleared her throat, then glanced at them both. 'We have something we'd like to give you both. Don't we, Henry?'

'Ah, yes.' He patted the pockets of his jacket and frowned.

Penny sighed. 'You put it in the inside pocket, dear.'

'Oops.' He chuckled, then dug around in his jacket, finally bringing out an envelope. 'Here you go. It's all in there.'

Anna took it and glanced at Jake who shrugged. 'What's in there?'

Penny gave her husband a frustrated look. 'Tell them, Henry.'

'Oh, yes, well.' He slid his hands into his pockets. 'The thing is, when we shuffle off this mortal coil, which of course we don't plan on doing anytime soon, but we are old, you know. At least I am – Penny of course still looks as young as when I met her.'

Penny kissed her husband's cheek then turned to face them. 'What Henry's trying to say is the envelope contains a copy of our revised will. When we die, the castle will go to you and Jake.'

'Sorry?' Anna was sure she hadn't heard that correctly.

'We love our son dearly, and he will inherit everything else we own, but he clearly doesn't love this place. Not like we do.' She paused and smiled at them both. 'And not like you both do.'

'My wife is right, as always.' Henry gazed fondly at her. 'You are the fourth couple to choose to marry here, and if the other three are anything to go by, you will have a long and happy marriage.'

'I...' Anna couldn't speak. And when she glanced up at Jake, she knew he was having the same trouble.

'Frigging hell.' Jake inhaled a shuddering breath. 'Do you guys need to get assessed or something? You know, to check you're not out of your minds?'

Henry chuckled and Penny joined in, far more comfortable with Jake's sense of humour than she used to be. 'I can assure you we're both in our right minds. Of course, we plan on hanging around for a very long time, but we were thinking, in order to prepare for when you do inherit, you might want to think about opening some of the castle up as a restaurant...'

Anna listened as Penny began to talk about the ideas she'd had. Ideas that left Anna feeling dazed.

As if he sensed it was all too much, once Penny and Henry had left, Jake took her hand and led her down to the jetty where they'd sat on that very first evening. There he loosened his tie and shrugged off his jacket, then pulled her gently down to sit next to him.

With a sigh of pure contentment, she leaned into him. 'When we sat here on that first night, I wanted to push you in.'

He let out a crack of laughter. 'I know. I was ready to drag you in with me.'

'Wow, so mean.' She smiled back at him. 'We've come a long way.'

'Sure have. Ex-con to future castle owner.'

She dug him in the ribs. 'I meant you and me. Our relationship.'

He grinned, flinging an arm around her. 'I know.'

Resting her head on his shoulder, she stared out at the beautiful lake. 'So what happens now?'

'We go back to our guests. And have two weeks of honeymoon sex.'

The thought sent a delicious shiver through her. 'And that differs from normal sex how?'

He winked. 'There's even more of it.'

'Okay, I can go with that. And then what?'

'And then'—he smiled straight into her eyes—'we carry on living the dream.'

Acknowledgments

As the writer, I get my name on the front cover, but the truth is it takes a lot of people to get a book published. Without them, Jake and Anna's story might never have made it into your hands.

So a huge thank to all at One More Chapter involved in *The Italian Job*. And yes, that includes you, Charlotte Ledger. Not just the inspiration behind the story but an inspiration to write for. It's thanks to Charlotte that Jake and Anna escaped to a castle on Lake Como. I originally had them working in a stately home in Dorset. Much as I love that area of the country, I fear it might not have been exciting enough to persuade either Jake or Anna to put up with each other for a year. After Charlotte gently suggested a more glamorous venue, I had no hesitation in packing my hero and heroine off to the shores of Lake Como. It was a place I visited a few years ago and fell in love with. Possibly because I imagined George Clooney round every corner...

I also want to send a big thank you to Laura McCallen for her guidance when I was putting together the outline for the story. I find it so helpful to get that fleshed out at the start so I know that I'm going in approximately the right direction when I start to write. And though I may veer off course now and again, Charlotte and the other fabulous editors at OMC are there to tug me back again! And what about that cover? Isn't it gorgeous? I'm indebted to Lucy Bennett for giving *The Italian Job* such an eye-catching look.

I'm not just lucky in my publisher. I'm lucky to have a gang of really supportive friends and family who still, after all these years, ask me when the next book is coming! That includes my Mum and Dad 2 (Anne and Keith), cousins Shelley, Karley, Kath, Kirsty and Hayley, my sis-in-law Jayne, friends Charlotte, Laura, Sonia, Jane, Carol, Tara and Priti (who I hope I've converted to romcoms now). And not to forget my biggest fan – yes, that's you Mum! Thank you everyone, your continued enthusiasm means a great deal to me.

I'm not sure where any of us writers would be without the amazing bloggers who are kind enough to read, review and shout about our books, so thank you all. A special hug to Rachel Gilbey and Anne Williams who were there at the start of my journey, and are still cheering me on nineteen books later. You are superstars.

Finally, a message to you, dear reader. Like Jake at the start of this story, my Italian is non-existent, but grazie and buona lettura - according to Google Translate that should be Italian for thank you and happy reading. I sincerely hope you enjoy this trip to Italy as much as I enjoyed writing it.

ONE MORE CHAPTER

YOUR NUMBER ONE STOP

FOR PAGETURNING BOOKS

The author and One More Chapter would like to thank everyone who contributed to the publication of this story...

Analytics
Emma Harvey
Connor Hayes
Maria Osa

Audio
Charlotte Brown

Contracts
Olivia Bignold-Jordan
Florence Shepherd

Design
Lucy Bennett
Fiona Greenway
Holly Macdonald
Liane Payne
Dean Russell
Caroline Young

Digital Sales
Hannah Lismore
Fliss Porter
Georgina Ugen
Kelly Webster

Editorial
Charlotte Ledger
Laura McCallen
Bethan Morgan
Jennie Rothwell
Tony Russell
Kimberley Young

Harper360
Emily Gerbner
Jean Marie Kelly
Juliette Pasquini
emma sullivan

HarperCollins Canada
Peter Borcsok

International Sales
Hannah Avery
Alice Gomer
Phillipa Walker

Marketing & Publicity
Emma Petfield
Sara Roberts
Helena Towers

Operations
Melissa Okusanya
Hannah Stamp

Production
Denis Manson
Simon Moore
Sophie Waeland

Rights
Lana Beckwith
Samuel Birkett
Agnes Rigou
Zoe Shine
Aisling Smyth

The HarperCollins Distribution Team

The HarperCollins Finance & Royalties Team

The HarperCollins Legal Team

The HarperCollins Technology Team

Trade Marketing
Ben Hurd

UK Sales
Yazmeen Akhtar
Laura Carpenter
Isabel Coburn
Jay Cochrane
Sarah Munro
Gemma Rayner
Erin White
Leah Woods

And every other essential link in the chain from delivery drivers to booksellers to librarians and beyond!